KW-262-994

Angels on the Point of a Pin

By the same author

NON-FICTION

Souza
Alfred Wallis
Braque
Josef Herman
Elisabeth Frink
The Pilgrimage to Santiago

Angels on the Point of a Pin

Edwin Mullins

SECKER & WARBURG
LONDON

First published in England 1979 by
Martin Secker & Warburg Limited
54 Poland Street, London W1V 3DF

SBN: 436 29511 3

Printed and bound in Great Britain by
Cox & Wyman Ltd, London, Fakenham and Reading

"I must tell her what I think of it and what I have decided to do," he would say to himself. "But what shall I tell her? And what have I decided to do?"

Anna Karenina.

Part One

February 1 to February 14

Day One

Gareth Penrhyn, film-maker, married seventeen years, three children. Aged forty-two, a time of life when events cast a shorter shadow and there is less urge to hunt for orchids in the shade; when I am growing a little surprised at being here at all, in good health, able to laugh, think, work, make love, and my children spill like ragwort on the world. I have not attempted suicide, entered the church, gone macrobiotic, taken up golf, joined the National Front, even suffered a total crack-up – though Christ knows why not. But I have walked a precipice too long and am losing my head for heights: the end could be very nasty.

Yesterday, January 31, Jennifer announced she was going to leave me. She has asked for a month before going.

Am I a masochist to have accepted such terms?

No, just passive. To be active would be to assume I knew precisely what I wanted. My ability for radical action is limited to closing my eyes and taking a desperate leap, yelling like a samurai in the hope that the cacophony may drown my own protests. And for once I am not going to do that. She can bloody well go over the top first. I shall stick around, hurt pride or not. I love her. Only Jennifer can release me from needing her, if she has the nerve. I don't.

How did it end up this way? Have I always known it would, wished it would? Was it written in my Book of the Dead? I have a month to find out, and shock is an urgent incentive to try.

Today is the 1st of February, and February is going to be a long month. Day One.

*   *   *

In the mind there is a landscape we constantly retread, seeking to discover the way we have come. And that route is not a narrative: the route of human experience never is. It is more like a half-finished painting over which the eye wanders, starting roughly in the middle and then following contours that wind out of view to the left and right, constantly distracted, constantly refreshed: now and again the eye returns to the starting-point like a retriever to dump a forgotten bundle of memories at our feet. Was this, I wonder, the meaning of Cézanne's search for the ever-changing secret of his mountain; that somewhere within those elusive screens of rock and field skulked the fugitive he was, and only by refusing to call off the search could he be sure he existed at all, since in most other respects he did not? A shoddy old man in a bowler-hat.

Searches are obsessive; one is already into injury-time. My own search, since I am a film-maker, will be a film-show in those dawn moments when the imagination runs naked before the pain begins. They are in a sense offcuts from films I shall never actually make, should make, maybe should be prevented on pain of death from ever making. They are my own documentary, fancified I suppose in the interests of truthfulness, yet as truthful as the process of distillation and recall can ever be. They are films which memory makes for me; and if they are fantasies then maybe life at the highest temperature always is fantasy, merely perceived as reality because the participants were once flesh and blood.

They are films about women, even about love; and I begin with Lal, eight years ago, because she was the last of my beautiful gorgons. After Lal everything changed: there is only one more film after her and I shall leave it till last. It is of such a different complexion that I shall not show it until I have gone back through all the others I made before, retracing the path of experience until I arrive at the moment when – as it seems to me – somebody thrust a life-script into my hands with the command "Live it!" But what did it say? That is what I need to discover.

* * *

(*Landes,* July, year 34.) She is leaning against the rock of the forest, her body modelled by evening shadows. Sunlight stirred by birch-leaves dabs her shoulders. A river of black hair is parted by naked breasts. Strong fingers wear gipsy rings, and are splayed out to support the weight of her hips on the rock. Her green dress is at her feet in the bracken. She steps out of it, one foot then the other. Red-painted toenails.

She is gazing at me gazing at her. A squirrel scutters along a high branch and dislodges a pine-cone. A bee hovers in a beam of dust. Silence. Lal is naked in the summer.

Love-making distances me, lifts me into a slow orbit above the night where, later, we gaze from an attic room at the fireflies in the garden. Lal grips her shoulders and shivers. I admire her body as she moves from the open window to the wash-basin and reaches for the tap. Her breasts feel rubbery and my hands make her shiver again. Her nipples sharpen. I stroke the water down over her belly. We make love on the bed, exploring each other's response in slow-motion. I am raised above her on my palms, her head turning from side to side on the pillow. I rest on her in silence, sweat cooling on me, her arms limp, lips open. There is a breeze from the window. I can feel her muscles relax and tauten round me. I grow again and her throat gives out a soft gurgle. There is enough light to see a smile on her face.

Lal has drawn me out of myself. I am only my prick, and it stands for me. I respond sightless in her, as though I am conducting a blind orchestra by means of signals I scarcely understand. No discords. No interference. Let me stay awhile. Play.

And laugh. I open my eyes. It is impossible to imagine anywhere I would rather be.

In the restaurant we touch fingers, drink chilled wine. Say nothing. Her eyes are hooded, nipples dark through the white cheesecloth blouse. My eyes peel her. Lal gives a shudder, runs a hand on my thigh. At neighbouring tables husbands blink little gimlets at her and guzzle grey fish. Lal refills her glass again, then mine. The heat has brought out tiny beads of sweat between her breasts. There is only one button fastened.

She is drunk. I am drunk. We have got to get out of this room. I size up a straight line to the door past the gimlets and the fishbones. I steer Lal and cough importantly. Hum a little tune. The button looks strained. At the last lamp on the terrace beyond the tables she runs into the garden and the fireflies, shaking off her blouse. A slim back in the quarter-light. Now I can't see her in the garden, but I can hear the belt of her jeans scrape on the concrete by the pool. A laugh. A splash. She is facing me by the edge of the pool, shaking wet hair. I strip off my clothes and dive into the tepid water. She is still laughing as we clamber out and run towards the children's pool. She lies back in the shallow water.

—Come with me, darling. Stay in me. Love me.

The hotel has dissolved: the silent waiters, the guzzling couples, the trays of coffee, the Citroëns, fireflies, cicadas, forest, stars, night, tomorrow, Lal, me. Anaesthesia. Ritual exorcism. The gorgeous impersonality of fucking. Cunt, prick, water. Hard and soft elements; consuming, consumed. Lal, lovely Lal, of course I do not love you, but you have drawn me out of myself into you, opened up my body and wrenched the sex from it. Sloughed skin, dry, deboned.

Now let me sleep.

* * *

I know when I turn my head she will have tears in her eyes. Eyes staring wide at the ceiling, body tense. It is that tension which tells me she is awake. Jennifer hates me most of all at this hour of the morning.

A white nightdress wraps her from head to foot. There are Victorian paintings of novices being led to their chastisement which put me in mind of her. Fear of sex has multiplied over the years: bad sex, like bad cooking, gets worse. Now we are two coffins laid side by side on the marriage-bed. She neuters me.

Knowing I am awake she makes an awkward stiff movement with her hand on the sheet, as if she thought I was going to hit her. I try to smile gently, but I don't feel gentle. I think I do want to hit her. I also want to weep, but my eyes are neutered too. Another awkward movement and without a glance she has slipped from the room and locked the door of the bathroom behind her. Another day of marriage has begun.

I am relieved that she may soon end it. But I am also afraid.

* * *

Jennifer and I never made love because we wanted to. But we did get married because we wanted to: we walked freely to jail. We loved one another. I had got me a wife till death do us part.

Once the prison doors had clanged it felt as if the battle might be over. Time for the wounds to heal. Time to get on with the business of living. On the plane to Italy I was horribly ill from the wedding party, assisted no doubt by Uncle Freud, and Jennifer read Kafka. That was our wedding night, courtesy British European Airways. I didn't fuck her in the loo, nor imagine myself as a barbarian riding down on the citadel with my amazing lance. It was not an hour for heroes. Nor for tenderness. There was not much whispering and cherishing. Our eyes on one another did not seem to be saying, "How lucky we are: we have found what we wanted." We both perhaps recognised that we had found what we deserved.

In Rome we slept and made love in the afternoon. A Roman honeymoon was a sunny jail. Or parole. Then we talked and walked and forgot to make love. We got on so well. We began to lay the foundations of a beautiful friendship. I loved her. We took a cottage in the Lipari Islands with a secret garden within high walls and a hibiscus in flames of blossom. She never undressed – I never undressed her – in the sun. I admired her dress. We used to walk hand in hand, and our eyes shared the same secrets in the world we walked. We were two flowers opened to the sun, growing side by side. We did not want children; there was too much to enjoy around us, too much to share.

I loved you. I knew I would never leave you. And I was wrong.

* * *

Downstairs the children will be munching Shreddies and squabbling over *Beano*. In five minutes Jennifer will have swept them into the car and off to school. The house will be still: the big house on the river which we bought creaking with sitting tenants who went white and died one by one upstairs, and we gathered up the newspapers and sardine-tins and moved in, until one day the whole house was ours at last and Jennifer started to have conscience pangs and threatened to fill it up again with more homeless and more newspapers and sardine-tins. We had children instead and I built walls of Purbeck stone to break up the long rectangle of garden and grow sapphire lithospermum and morning glories which the children dashed out to count each morning before breakfast in the summer.

The house is silent now. I clear the breakfast things and pour myself a cup of luke-warm tea. A light frost on the lawn ends in a diagonal stroke where the sun is creeping up from the river. I throw open the french windows and feel the winter air tauten my skin. A fleet of barges passes the end of the garden. A dog is leaping from one barge to another and yapping at the water. They pass – *Annie, Louise, Mary Lou, Dunkirk, Vigilance.* Strong women and strong sentiments for frail men. The gulls turn on the wind, piloting the river home.

The empty garden under my feet. Witch-hazel by the river wall beginning to lose its lustre. Tiny winter irises jammed blue in a pocket of sunlight. A rusting swing. The weathered greenhouse where I grow seedlings in quantity, forgetting each spring that I have no acres to plant them. The white tom shakes its paw primly in the wet grass and curls its back round my legs. I realise that I am readjusting to being here alone. My home, my security, my memories. Soon it will only be me and the cat. I'd like to keep the cat. I wish the others would all go – now! Gone already! I could walk back from the garden into a house empty of all detritus of the past seventeen years. No toys, books, bed, mail, clutter. Nothing. No love-marks anywhere. Just bare boards. The cat and me. How could I be lonely once there was nothing left to make me lonely?

Suddenly I am exhilarated. I'll make some coffee. Phone Wardour Street. The boss is not coming in today. David, press on with editing that VD yuk for the United Nations. Get Janet to put the skids under the lab-people: we need a rough-cut of the Swiss tourist film soonest. Start laying the commentary if you have time. Book a studio for next week and tell the distributors. Oh, tell Scofield too; he may want to see it, and they'll be more impressed if you can get him to be there. So make sure it's not rehearsal time for his play coming on. Call me if there are any problems.

Oh, lucky man, my wife is leaving me for a lover.

I can't imagine them making it so well. How ridiculous, but I do want her to be happy. More than anything. Set me free, too. No more guilt. Of course I won't lose the children. Dads are important to them. I'll have them half the year, whenever they want. Their rooms will be waiting for them. Deirdre, you'll understand. At twelve, you understand already: those glances across the silence at meal-times. Seth, I love you the most vulnerably, you must never die. You will be puzzled, a little frightened, distressed. But you will be doubly loved and your skin will toughen. Little Ennis, for you it's all too early to matter: another stir in the muddied pool you gaze in ("Mummy, are you Daddy's mummy? Grandpa's asleep because he's dead and tomorrow he'll wake up and when I go to sleep I'll be dead. Daddy will be back soon"). Daddy will always be back soon. Always. I feel a pain, but I am free. Darlings, your daddy is a real man and to prove it he's alone. Look, no hands! The sun is on the river and in my house and in my head. I'm alive. I'm free. Oh, lucky man!

My own smile in the tall mirror by the window: perhaps I should film it just to prove I can smile this morning. Alas, says Camus, after a certain age every man is responsible for his face. Why "Alas"? Alas if he were not. Painters, I suppose, regard their faces more closely than most, surveying the landscape of time. I think of Picasso's face: burning, intense, the face of a sensitive pugilist. Or Braque, whom I filmed in his last years: what a windfall of a face, dropped from that thicket of white hair like a fruit dried out in the sun. Van Gogh created his own face in the mirror and painted it to last, knowing the real one would not. Monet buried his within a beard cultivated like the garden he hid in.

This morning I saw Lal's face in my mind, and there was nothing there. Eight years ago I thought I loved her in a way. Whatever does that mean? I loved Jennifer, too. I loved Lal because I loved Jennifer, too. The more I loved Lal the more I knew I would never stop loving Jennifer. Lal was love's ultimate expendable work of art. She danced on the point of my prick; and one day when she asked for a cast of my *membrum virile* (like the lady called Reilly who valued her husband so highly) to travel with her in her suitcase (she was a highly successful model then) I could as well have given her the real thing with a note round its neck saying, "Keep this, I get along better without it."

Lal never wanted daily life, she wanted lollipops, and so did I. Or sometimes soap-opera, depending on the mood. A day without lollipops and she'd scream suicide, fill herself with anti-depressant pills, or pot, and cry and cry. And get herself fucked by anyone with an hour to spend. The last time I saw her was in her tiny house in Clapham. She was slumped on a wooden chair by the window in the kitchen like a Millet peasant, all resignation, her hands over her face, baby-food on the dress from the second-hand stall in the market. The child was with her husband somewhere. The man Lal was living with – a bored beautiful boy – was sitting opposite her with a glaze over his eyes, holding out thin hands to her, helpless. She said nothing. I placed the salmon-trout I had brought as a birthday present in the fridge and left.

Next morning she rang me in Wardour Street and told me how happy she was. Dick and she were going away. (With my salmon-trout?) Morocco. She'd sing and he'd play the guitar. Wasn't it fantastic? She wrote a few times. Then nothing. I wonder if she's dead.

Day Two

(***Diyarbakir, Turkey***, October, year 33.) Breakfast on my hotel balcony to the sound of donkey bells. Turtle doves and small hawks flit over the police headquarters. Yesterday's rain has turned the summer dust to glue in the streets. There is thunder in the mountains to the west where we are going today, and every variety of cloud formation to confuse us. Olcayto the guide has gone off to haggle over the price of a hire-car for the next leg of the journey – one hundred miles to Eski Kâhta on dirt roads, if we can find any road at all. From there it will be mules.

While I am waiting I wander round the town. Stacked melons larger than pumpkins. Bread in broad hand-patterned discs. Girls in lurid velvet carrying cans on their heads. Boys with shaven scalps and snotty noses. Grey donkeys with bells. The smell of coffee and sewage. Flies, hornets, aubergines. Shoeshine boys, cripples, crones. A Turkish tin-roofed settlement which has shrivelled within its Roman walls.

The crew is stirring by the time I return. Jim is leaning on his camera tripod with that air of magisterial boredom endemic among well-travelled cameramen. Mike, his assistant, is loading up a huge red Chevrolet Olcayto has extracted from somewhere. Kevin the sound-recordist is a well-practised eccentric: this morning he is a Gauloises advertisement – beret, shorts, grey goatee beard, red neck-scarf, missing teeth.

—Mornin', he says with a Marty Feldman grin. Mornin'. Got some good thunder for you, young Gareth. It looks as though you may be needing it.

And he taps the tape-recorder slung from his shoulder. We pack into the Chevrolet. We are going to film the giants of Nemrud Dagh. Turkey – my last assignment for the BBC. After this I am setting up my own company. It feels like the end of school. The Chevrolet moves off, taking a run at the pot-holes.

Anatolia is rubbed brick-dry by a summer of sun and wind: the skin of an aged country scarred in patterns of fields and dried rivers. This abandoned cocoon of mankind. Not much sign of rain here. We gaze out of the window at the stubble-coloured plain. Straggling sheep and strings of camels. Cows looking mournful among boulders. Fields of cotton and tobacco by the roadside. The crew are lolling with eyes closed. They have been here a hundred times before – in Mexico, Mali, Gobi, Nularbor. How the bored sleep. We climb into the hills, trailing a skein of dust.

Noon. Eski Kâhta at last. We are damp and squashed. Numbed. Olcayto and I play football with a crowd of village children. I am clobbered by the altitude. Aziz, the *muhtar*, appears. Olcayto knows him. There is reassurance in his smile of gold teeth. Yes, he will fix the mules for 6 a.m. tomorrow, and come with us. A little rain tonight, he says, and tomorrow should be fine.

Supper with Aziz at dusk: soup, eggs, yoghourt, flat bread, sweet tea, laid on a round brass tray at our feet. I am a cumbersome Western animal who bends the wrong way. My mattress on the earth-floor feels like jumbled drain-pipes, but no matter. The evening rain brings hope, and I sleep well.

The early morning is cloudless, as Aziz predicted: the air clear as water. We load the mules and depart. A spectacular scenery of rivers and rocks: soil is spread thin over the bones of this landscape. My mule is docile but with an affection for precipices. I am powerless to tug her from this mulish brinkmanship. *Yurū! Yurū!* I have learnt the command to kick her with. She shakes her ears.

Jim is silent behind me. I suspect he is truly animated among his roses. Mike is taming the wilderness with Cockney jokes.

Kevin is laughing to himself through a rustic pipe and singing "The train I ride is twenty-one coaches long". Soon the silence of the mountain closes in: there is only the click of kicked stones. Scattered autumn crocuses by the track – mauve splashes in the dust. Above us raw hillsides and the sun.

At last we are climbing out of the ravine. Anatolia is unfolding, falling away towards Syria, unrolling towards the white Taurus Mountains. We are under a mile from Nemrud Dagh now – and there it is, a bald pate thrust high above the plateau. We clamber stiffly from our mules and hump the gear up the last shale into the wind. The heart pounds in the thin air. We have made it. Nemrud Dagh!

Is this the most unreal place on earth? A guardian lion holds an entire landscape in its jaws. The head of Hercules, lopped by an earthquake, rests higher than a man. Apollo and Zeus, similarly decapitated, loll above us around the bare terraces. Our cameras worry them like summer flies. And here is King Antiochus of Commagene, on the scale of the rest of them and carved to resemble the young Alexander the Great, surveying the preposterous burial-place where he determined he would never be forgotten. King Antiochus – buried on the pinnacle of his kingdom, a mouse within the mountain he lies in, belittled by the very fantasies he conceived to ennoble. Oh King Gulliver of Commagene, puny amid the monstrous vassals paying court to your dreams, like your nurse Glumdalclitch who gave suck with "her monstrous breast, which I cannot tell what to compare with. It stood prominent six feet, and could not be less than sixteen in circumference. The nipple was about half the bigness of my head, and the hue both of that and the dug so varified with spots, pimples and freckles, that nothing could appear more nauseous."

It is late afternoon already. I take what was once the ceremonial road to the empty North Terrace, its relief carvings toppled on their faces like giant playing-cards. Then to the chill and sunless East Terrace. A line of hunched torsos is backed against the tumulus where Antiochus is buried. Dismembered beasts lie scattered: an eagle's wing, a lion's mane, a foot, a claw. Ice has formed in the crevices of the stone. Six months will pass now before it will melt.

Clouds wrap the mountain. It is bitterly cold. The monsters are gaping into a mist. Commagene has already vanished down there in the valley. Aziz calls that we must hurry. We pack the cameras and scramble down among loose rocks. The mules slip and slide into the shelter of the ravine. A full moon lights the gorges black and white. The clip of mules' feet on boulders, echoing in the night. We pitch camp by a stream where we wash and drink and eat hot lentils and fresh fruit to the hiss of a kerosene lamp.

As the fire dies my eyes chart the contours of the night. I lie back in my rug staring up into Gulliver's enormous heaven in this cleavage of the mountains of his kingdom, thinking of his Maids of Honour who would strip him "naked from top to toe" and lay him "at full length on their bosom; wherewith I was much disgusted" – says Gulliver. "The handsomest among these Maids of Honour, a pleasant frolicsome girl of sixteen, would sometimes set me astride upon one of her nipples, with many other tricks, wherein the reader will excuse me for not being over particular. But I was so much displeased, that I entreated Glumdalclitch to contrive some excuse for not seeing that young lady any more."

Gulliver, you lie! Here in Commagene they acknowledged such aberrations more freely, and Antiochus built a holy mountain to prove it, landscaping his realm with the whopping flesh of his dreams.

Eski Kâhta again. I pay off the muleteers while Mike unloads the camera gear. Jim is stirred from his worldweariness by the predations of a flea army which struck in the night. Kevin puffs his pipe and recalls the leeches in Borneo, enough to make the statues of Nemrud Dagh look like pygmies, he says.

—Don't be so soft, Jim. Just a few fleas. Let 'em run around.

—I suppose you recorded their mating-call, Kevin?

Jim is feeling decidedly sour. He goes on scratching.

The mules clop up the street. Stiffly we walk into Aziz's house. Olcayto has gone to cast an eye over the Chevrolet. We leave tomorrow. Nemrud Dagh and its giants are in the can behind us.

The door is a faded carpet nailed to the wooden beam above the entrance. We remove our shoes and step inside. The room is warm, dark at first. Deep-red rugs cover the earth-floor. Woven bolsters are laid round the walls where we slept two nights ago, and shall again tonight, before the drive back to Diyarbakir and the next leg of the journey northwards towards Lake Van.

I lower my pack and stop still. The room is not empty. I'll say it's not.

—Hi, she says!

Oh, Glumdalclitch, what have you done now? The mountain has moved. We shall all be engulfed. Nausea, Nausicaa, on what shore have I been washed up? Antiochus, she has come to pay homage to you, your Maid of Honour; only you, King Gulliver, could have dreamed up this heap of flesh.

—Hi, she says! I'm from Nebraska. Heard you were here.

She is horrible. My God she is horrible. Are you here to give suck to all Commagene with your nipple half the bigness of my head? Will you set me astride it, along with many other tricks wherein the reader will excuse me for not being over particular? Antiochus, she is part of your landscape, this mighty pilgrim from Nebraska. Take her for your holy mountain. Her breasts will irrigate your kingdom, her clitoris will fly your standard, her belly will breed you a master-race. In her burial-mound you will be truly immortal. But let me try first, since we have chanced to meet.

Maid of Honour, put me down. I have climbed Nemrud Dagh.

—Gareth, Gareth, what a fucker you are!

* * *

—Gareth, what a stupid fucker you are! Now we'll have to pay the studio fee twice. Just because you were too bloody idle to come in yesterday. You make me feel a right tit.

—Nothing wrong with the left one either, darling.

—Enough from you, David. Can you give me a lift home?

Janet has a long fur-coat wrapped about her, chin tucked into it.

—We'll leave Gareth to sort out the cock-up he's made.

—Goodnight, sweetheart. Goodnight, David.

—See you tomorrow, Gareth. Don't work too late.

Six o'clock. I am alone in the office. In my office. Fourth floor, Wardour Street. Penrhyn Productions it says on the door. Three rooms, that's all. Why don't you expand, treble the output, stop turning away work, Gareth? Because I like making films – all of them, VD, army recruitment, Swiss tourism, Antarctica, desert irrigation, the lot. The bloody lot. Fifty-two films in nine years. The most gifted hack in the business, Eric says. Except that he's too well-mannered to call me a hack. I pay Eric £10,000 to stay with me. The only indispensable person in my life. He is the paperweight of Penrhyn Productions. He uses two secretaries and an office like the chairman of the bank. He plays golf and lives at Gerrards Cross. I never ask his advice. I like that. He leaves sharp at 5.30 every evening. I like that too. He bores the pants off me. He gives me the confidence to go on being lazy. Creative, I call it. He respects that, and I like that too.

Then there's David. He's twenty-eight: a terrific guy. Filthy-tempered. Marvellous editor. I plucked him from the BBC two years ago. He co-directs with me sometimes on big jobs; that's why he came here. The BBC would have kept him editing all his life for some piddling union reason. David has an eye for the things I miss. When we were shooting the VD film in the Far East he kept going when I just wanted to throw up. We lost two cameramen on that job. They just quit. One of them had been through Vietnam. The other ended up crying, said he'd never be able to fuck again. After that David came back here and began to edit the whole thing down as if he were trout-fishing on the Windrush. Then went home and I imagine fucked his wife. Janet wishes it were her. Maybe he does. Not in the office anyway: Eric wouldn't approve. Eric fucks on Friday nights. He told me so a little sober at the Christmas party. David less sober said that means you've had it off 546 times, old mate – I did better than that on my honeymoon.

The office is empty. I look at the awards round the wall. In such bad taste it might have been a compliment to have been spared them. Eric puts them up there. One of his secretaries dusts them on Monday mornings. He insists it impresses clients. It impresses Eric. It impresses me. I won them.

I love my office. I love everyone who works in it. I like it when their families come in. I like the sensation of a small machine in order. I like it when it's touch-and-go – we could go out of business if we don't pull this one off – like last week when Lord Waldron rang up to talk about a series on the Arabs. Eric, who could get another job tomorrow (I couldn't), kept taking me aside all morning with little suggestions how to impress him. I don't need to bloody impress him.

No, of course I don't know how we're going to do them. Not yet.

Waldron's the moneybags. Or, rather, he's got a hand on the Saudi moneybags. So he came in. Of course he had to come here, Eric. No good taking him out to the Savile when everything I'll need is here. Anyway he came – puffed up four flights of stairs.

Janet gave him a mug of coffee. Great girl, Janet. – Sugar, she said? And stirred it for him. D'you smoke?

I sat on a stool while he talked. He was unsure of himself because he hadn't a clue what he wanted, and talked the more for that. But he scents a fat profit and believes I can create it for him. I probably can. David simply went on editing the VD film. Eric covered his embarrassment when Waldron asked about it by saying (twice) it was for the United Nations. The United Nations, you know. I persuaded Eric to do something in his own office – probably phoned his wife to tell her about Waldron. Sorry I have to go now, dear, Lord Waldron's here.

By midday it was pretty clear: a six-part series for the cassette market. Funds recouped from TV sales, the rest profit (for Waldron, and a fat slice for me). The BBC would be sure to take it. France too: they like to lick Arab arses. Germany. America so long as it's not anti-Jew. We don't need a front man, so there'll be no language problems. Just six major locations to cut costs – Morocco, Egypt, Yemen, Syria, Qatar and one other. We'll think about that. The rest bench-work. This'll be the shape.

And I pulled out a huge sheet of cartridge paper and drew a plan of the whole series. Looked pretty. I've grown skilled at this sort of thing. Gave him rough dates, rough cost. I'll direct the lot myself (that always throws City men: they feel embarrassed, as if they'd encountered the Postmaster-General serving them stamps; it tickles me). And off he went dripping thanks.

—I'll see my board on Thursday.

Ah, you see, you're not quite your own boss. Big fleas have bigger fleas. Eric stood at his door waiting to shake hands, but moneybags forgot and shook hands with Janet instead, not quite getting round to fancying her but thanking her for the most delicious coffee. She looked aware of her breasts and his title, and laughed.

So we have another big contract. It arrived this morning, along with an invitation to Wopping Grange at the weekend for Jennifer and me. That seems pretty unlikely at present. No, I shan't go. I want to be with the children. I want to cling to the children.

Yes, for Christ's sake, why shouldn't I have the custody of them? The two elder ones at least. How lucky I am after all. Jennifer's lover has a big comfortable flat – pity it's just across the river, but I guess I shan't be tempted to use field-glasses. I've got the house. I can cook well enough. The kids can go to Jennifer at weekends and when I'm away filming. I reckon she'll owe me that for walking out. Uncomplicated Comprehensive children of the Middle Classes take this sort of thing in their stride, don't they? (Seth's a sissy, Seth's a sissy, his parents aren't divorced!) As for little Ennis, I'll keep in touch. There'll always be a room for him at home. What else are *au pair* girls for but situations like this? For once I'll choose the *au pair*. It'll be like a slave-market. Think of it! Ring a few agencies. Specify age, capabilities, religion, country of origin. Interview a few. Take the Danish one with tits and a look in her eye, half my age. Jesus Christ, it's Rent-a-Cunt!

Maybe it will work out. Maybe I *can* chart my life as I chart my work: I've simply never given it a chance.

I pick up the coloured plan I roughed out for Waldron. No, I haven't the slightest doubt this will work. And if it doesn't work exactly like this, then I'll reshape it just as easily. Waldron trusts me. So does his board. I trust myself. I know my world.

Then take that confidence home with you, Gareth.

I lock up and walk out into Wardour Street. An ugly gutter where I feel at home. My real home is beautiful by the river and I do not feel at home there at all.

Already I feel the cross-fire. Shadows of self-doubt spreading between the street-lamps and the strip-clubs. I should live alone. I can't live alone. I shall have to live alone.

Perhaps I shall live a mogul's life of will and appetite: why not? I wish I were an iron mogul. I wish I could walk unarmed through the world. Instead, I am a coward armed with skill. What a pro! Gareth who's never put a foot wrong. I'm growing old.

My Jaguar slips gently along the King's Road past the lonely people. Not me. More armour. Never alone in a Jaguar: every gleam of it warms me with the companionship of success. I feel rich and protected. There goes Gareth in his new Jag. Knows where he's going.

He's going home.

* * *

Home was a two-room flat when we returned from our honeymoon in Italy. We settled down to being us. Jennifer's friends and my friends and gradually *our* friends came and were cooked for and they invited us back. We dressed up and we dressed down and at the end of each sortie we undressed and lay back on the big marriage-bed and gave ourselves marks. We exclaimed how tired we were and slept.

We visited sale-rooms and acquired furniture.

We visited art-galleries and acquired small pictures.

We read the reviews and acquired books.

We acquired friends who were writers and painters and read what the critics wrote about them.

We bought a sports car and toured the Dordogne.

We sent many Christmas cards and received even more.

We went to the theatre once a fortnight, the cinema once a week and ate out in favourite restaurants twice a week.

We lived on Jennifer's salary as an accountant, with pocket-money from my journalism. Then I chucked journalism and got accepted as a general trainee at the BBC. We bought the house on the river.

We flew our flags brightly.

* * *

The black Jag pulls into the right-hand lane in Wandsworth High Street to take the turning after the traffic-lights for the Putney Bridge Road. On my left the Spread Eagle. On my right the Ram Inn. That conjunction always makes me happy; except that the Ram Inn's now been renamed something more innocuous. Did the brewer feel concerned for his Babycham market, I wonder? The ram's still there, I notice, emblazoned on the face of the building: doesn't look as if he'd be much good at it. Perhaps that's why they demoted him. I'm reminded of Botticelli's "Venus and Mars" in the National Gallery, with Venus looking randy and Mars lying exhausted by his efforts, while fat little cupids finger his lance to taunt him. Mars are marvellous indeed! Even the God of War couldn't manage multiple orgasms.

Jennifer will be giving the kids supper right now.

I need a drink.

Nobody knows me here. I like that. Neither the angels nor the demons I spend my life with, forever transforming the one into the other as though alchemy were the proof of a divine power in me. I have been thinking of my flesh mountain from Nebraska, my Maid of Honour. In what spirit did we make love in that dry river-bed of Gulliver's Country? Is nausea so far away from eroticism? I remember her right breast blotting out the moon as she floated over me like a hungry Zeppelin. What a fucker you are, Gareth.

I test my growing older by the people I am no longer frightened of, no longer love, no longer need.

The Jag pulls up. A successful man is coming home from the office.

Jennifer is leaving me at the end of this month. Maybe it's about time.

Day Three

(*Paris*, Winter, year 31.) I'm looking again at this photograph lying on my work-table by the window. It perfectly identifies her for me. It's a 19th-century photograph which I came across in a junk-shop yesterday near the hotel, and it portrays a naked girl nailed to the Cross, or pretending to be, with a frayed rope dangling from her waist as a *cache-sexe*.

Certainly the colleen would have looked more exciting in this pose than the girl in the photograph. She would have required a more elegant Cross, less stumpy, to accommodate those long legs of hers, and that lithe body which seems to go on and on as if an extra section were inserted between hips and ribs. The girl in the photo is altogether too Renoiresque. I know they liked them that way in *La Belle Epoque*: on the other hand when did you last see a fat Christ? Unquestionably the colleen would have been far better suited to the part, especially since she also lived it.

Only an Irish-Catholic girl could have enjoyed such a delicious confusion of pleasure as she has toyed with this past week. The Sisters of the Sacred Heart with whom she is living at Vincennes must have been through similar flushes on the road to celibacy, I imagine, or they would never have accepted her absences so sagely or offered their bosoms to her tears. They were such sweet nuns, she said from the bathroom one morning as she scourged herself before the mirror on the rough hotel towel. So very sweet and kind. Her voice suggested they had all earned their virginity the hard way, so to speak, and what a wonderful way it must be: she too must drink at the spring of the holy martyrs before becoming a worthy bride of Christ. Holy Mary, mother of Our Lord, will you take this sullied creature in my bathroom to be your daughter-in-law?

I met the colleen in Paul Frost's bookshop set back from the river near the rue St-Sévérin on the Left Bank: the Carousel it was called then. Paul has known every Englishman in Paris who likes the smell of books and girls since the late 1940s. His wispy beard acts as an antenna for drifting souls. As for me, I found myself at the Carousel back in the early 50s, in much the way everyone sooner or later found themselves there, dropping in out of the street on an aimless day and allowing the place to cloak them in an anonymous fraternity for an evening or a lost afternoon. Like everybody else I go there to browse and forget and wonder whom I may meet.

There are not too many religious books in Paul's stock – at least not the conventional religions. But you may be sure that it was he who had guided the colleen, as soon as he had summed her up, towards some suitable shelf of mysteries; and it was here that I became aware one blustery winter afternoon of a crouching girl dressed in grey whose auburn hair brushed the unswept floor while she reached for some slender volume on the lives of Irish saints at the bottom of a small bookcase in the corner. I paused. She was grasping a book in both hands as she straightened up beside me – my own height almost – and turned as if determined to share her find with a stranger.

—I didn't expect to find McCafferty on Visions here, she said in a soft brogue that was full of wonder.

I nodded. She lowered her eyes in order to raise them again. She was very lovely.

—I have exciting visions, I said solemnly. And she lowered her eyes again, which made me look at the way her hair glistened against the austere tweed buttoned high under the chin. She must have brushed it admiringly before she ventured out in search of McCafferty. I had a feeling she admired quite a lot of herself before wrapping it neatly up in grey. After a short silence she went on.

—I'm staying at a convent here. I'm going to be a novice next year. I've never been to Paris before.

We were drinking coffee in La Bûcherie nearby. I was looking at her. A nun. An embryo nun. Then what the hell are you doing sitting on this bar-stool next to me, green eyes beaming out vibrations like this? She lifted a grey skirt a few inches and curled one long leg over the other, and went on talking. I lit a cigarette to absorb some of the shakes.

She talked about Paris and her nuns and the visions of the saints for the best part of an hour, my eyes roaming over her and those wide green eyes of hers fixed on me, slender fingers occasionally tracing the rim of her coffee-cup.

Had I ever wanted a girl so much in my thirty-one years? Maybe she was the Virgin Mary's personal agent sent to test me, in which case she needn't have wasted her time. What was she doing to me, this package of purity cloistered in grey?

Yes, damn it, I did respect her wretched faith and her nougat-coloured visions of sainthood and her Mary Poppins search for Holy Bliss; so much so that I wished she could have wrapped it all up now and locked it away under her wimple for ever and stopped plaguing me with a thirst worthy of the desert fathers.

She wanted to go to the Sainte-Chapelle, she said. I couldn't take any more of this crap so I asked her out that evening, told her (orders are orders whether from up there or down here) to call at my hotel room around eight. It was pure cheek. But the eyes merely looked a little larger and greener, and her forefinger went on tracing the rim of the coffee-cup; and she said:

—All right, tell me where you are?

Then her hands swept her auburn hair back over her shoulders with a slight tilt of the head and she left, smoothing her skirt and clasping McCafferty on Visions to her breast. It was five thirty. I went back to the hotel, told the porter I was expecting a lady around eight, took the lift to the top floor and gazed out over the cold roofs of the Latin Quarter in the dusk. I poured myself a large Scotch and Perrier, then another, and began to laugh. I don't believe it: I simply don't believe it. So now what? Alternatives?

One: spread out as many holy postcards as possible of the School of Fontainebleu on which I am currently working for a film

Two: have a couple more Scotches, fall asleep and let her arrival take me by surprise.

Three: be in the bath with the door open humming a cheerful tune.

Four: depart at seven forty-five leaving a note on the door, "Back in five minutes: the bed is comfortable."

Enough! This morning there is only the photograph lying on my work-table by the window. She is with her Sisters of the Sacred Heart, lying in her little cell no doubt and looking up with love and understanding at a wooden figure of the Crucifixion suspended above her on the wall, just as she described it to me while she lay here that first evening, green eyes floating happily in tears, left hand covering her breast, right hand grasping the miracle of the saints which had come to her so sweetly in a vision on the fourth floor of the Hotel St-Sévérin.

As for me, I have had my fill of standing in for Jesus Christ Superstud.

* * *

Why do I stick around here drinking? Why did I actually hurry home from the office this evening, saying No to a pint with David, which was unkind of me since he'd been scissoring away at that yukky VD material all day and needed a hand on his shoulder? Instead, I said No and came back here. I even think of it as home. My home. Though, God knows, it's more like stepping into a minefield. I feel the danger of Jennifer throughout the house. After a while I try not to say anything at all for fear of another mine going Powwwhhh in my face. Wipe the blood off, pick out the shrapnel, take a step backwards and begin again. Pour myself a whisky.

—Gareth, if you're not doing anything you could give Ennis a bath.

Jennifer's voice from the kitchen. Not "could you?" but "you could": quite different message. I seem to have turned off the telly almost before she spoke. Reflex action. Jennifer doesn't like telly. Doesn't like me either.

—I can't do everything! (Her voice again.)

—OK. Where is he? (No answer. Pause.) Do you happen to know where he is?

I am by the kitchen door now, glass in hand. She looks awful.

Jennifer turns down the gas. Bony hand. She crosses the room and reaches for an apron on the hook. She misses it first time; gives it an irritated flick. I make way for her to go out into the hall.

—Oh I'll do it, she says. My irritation is rising.

—Don't be silly, I'll do it. I'm happy to do it. I only asked if you happened to know where he was. (She is halfway upstairs by now. I shout after her.)

—Jesus Christ, I could have looked for him just as easily. Just thought you might know.

No answer. End of conversation. How many hundreds of thousands of times have we been here before, fuck it? A sip of whisky. I notice the glass is empty. There is the sound of bath-water upstairs, and of Jennifer's voice being incredibly gentle with Ennis who doesn't want to leave his toy train. I'd better have another Scotch.

I switch on the telly again. Close the door first. Highlights of the Fourth Test at Adelaide. A sip of whisky. Sweet uneasy nirvana. Brave rearguard action by England. The crowd is giving Boycott the bird. Throwing beer-cans. Eric says the Aussies pee in them first. Bloody animals, he says. Lillee bowls at the kidneys. Bloody barbarians, the lot of them.

Why do I stick around here drinking? I'm miserable, but I'm home. I'm getting drunk. I always get drunk at home. Jennifer never touches it. She never touches me either for that matter. Almost never. She finds that as yukky as I find David's VD film.

Yet here is where I have ripened and decayed. I love the ordinary familiar streets and the park by the river where I take the children on winter afternoons: push-chair, Wellingtons, gloves on the end of elastic, puddles on the asphalt. Our children we wanted. My homeland. My peace of mind. I would have papered over everything for this.

—But you were never here. Jennifer is back at the stove while Ennis is in the bath. You were always off filming whenever it suited you. Of course I resented you coming back radiant. There was nothing for me; only presents from abroad.

—You never welcomed me.

That used to hurt more than you'll ever know.

—I always wanted to come back to you.

—With the smell of happiness on you. Always from somewhere

else. Someone else. I used to wonder how you could bring back so much. I was grateful, and I hated you for it. You must have given them all so much. I got it second-hand. It belonged to them.

—I wanted it for you.

—Oh, fuck off.

—Believe me.

—Hand-outs, Gareth.

—It's not how I wanted it to be.

My voice sounds resigned. Jennifer goes on cooking. Stewing her resentment.

—All right, don't believe me.

I retreat into self-pity. I pour another whisky. I want to be here. She's awful. She deserves more than this. So do I. I'll go and read to Seth. My pictures on the staircase wall. This one she gave to me. She must have tried to love me then. I can't imagine trying to divide up all this dependable clutter. Emotional detritus. It hurts. How it hurts!

—Yes, Seth, I'll be with you in a minute. Find the book you want. (Will I be too drunk to read it?)

—Daddy, these Roman soldiers are going to attack that castle, and these are the enemy, you can see their long knives: and this man is going to kill that soldier, but this soldier's going to get him first. And that's the king there. He's Tarzan.

Sounds of my walking discothèque, Deirdre, drift from the bathroom. "I was born . . . with a smile on my face. I was born . . . with a need to embrace." Bless her. Bless her. Daddy's home. Daddy's gone a-hunting and Daddy's home again.

* * *

Yes, we flew our flags brightly. Defiantly, some would say. If we tried hard enough it must work out all right: wasn't that what we'd been taught? Life is a worthy struggle or it's not life. Maybe everybody else had the same problems we did, and they just didn't let on.

That wasn't, admittedly, the look they wore on their faces: the radiance of fulfilment that made me want to scream. I used to turn my head away and hope Jennifer hadn't noticed. We'd talk about something safe.

And I worked. My God, I worked.

The BBC likes people who dig themselves in and keep a straight bat. If I had any real talent then I kept it to myself, and they liked that too. This young fellow can be relied upon. We used to have an annual assessment by our superior officers of our efforts over the past year. They'd nod and pass pompous remarks and I would nod back and be humbly confident, and they liked that too. They weren't letting any Trojan Horse in with Gareth Penrhyn. Oh no, I was officer material. They nodded and made me an assistant producer in General Features. They nodded when I made my first long film. Under-budget naturally. The Director-General rang up my boss in the department and said he was nodding too. Then another film and another. God, I worked. They started giving me special assignments, travelling to South America to follow some twit canoeing down the Amazon (which was easy) and chatting up a war hero who'd completed the twelfth volume of his self-indulgence (which was hell). I even did an In-Depth interview with Miss World who giggled into her cleavage and identified with Anna Karenina, or was it Anna and the King of Siam? She wasn't quite sure. I'd prepared a portfolio of questions and solemnly put them to her in her swimming-pool (that was my idea: the viewers liked it). It was a terrible film; it caused Jennifer some mild jealousy, got an audience rating of six millions, and won me a few sneers and promotion. I became the youngest producer in the BBC. I didn't make Miss World, but I'd made it.

I'd made it and I'd tied a knot in my prick. Put a tourniquet on my dreams. I wanted to be a good boy. What did I do, wank in the loo? Not even that. I clung to my work and I clung to my marriage: twin institutions I had set up to govern my life. Gareth Employment Inc. and Gareth Domestic Bondage Ltd.

Both were a reliable source of worry. Work worried me in case I should make a mistake. Marriage worried me because the wounds were so raw and the strain of believing in tomorrow was so punishing. There was a sharp gleam of winter about our lives, and the years began to pass and it grew colder.

Jennifer took to undressing in a locked bathroom.

I worked late and came to bed tired.

We bustled out of sleep into breakfast to get the day going about its business.

We cried, which broke the tension and made us feel close.

We discussed psychotherapy. I determined it was she who

should go, and she went. I waited for results and none came, except that it gave us more to talk about.

I waited for tomorrow and none came.

* * *

The house is silent now. The children are asleep. Jennifer has gone to bed. I shall slip into bed when she is sleeping. Perhaps I should make up a bed in my workroom but I have refused to do that. It is our bed, my bed. She must move out of it if she wishes. I don't want to torture her. I don't want to make love to her. I don't want to leave her.

My marriage is a diseased limb that is decayed almost beyond pain and I am waiting for it to wither away. Then maybe I'll be maimed but I'll be free.

And if the disease has spread then I'll not survive.

—I'm sorry for you.

Jennifer meant that. She believes I am incapable of loving, incapable of living except by destroying the love offered me.

I am rich in love to give and love I have taken. They ferment together. I am that searching and brave thing, an ordinary man. I have a heart, a mind, a sense of loneliness, a sense of joy, a sense of fragility, a sense of compromise. I eat, I play, I fight, I fuck. I am ordinary. I want to come to terms, and I don't dare.

We have driven ourselves out of the common lot.

I want to trust myself again.

I want to laugh.

I want to say "I am".

The house is silent. Midnight already. Wind scourges the windows. A few lights on the river are distorted by the rain. My children are asleep. Such anchorage. If I had been a Medici I should have had children by every woman I've loved. A polyglot race of squabbling spoilt heirs – all marquises and mistresses. Children like Green Shield stamps. All except the colleen who lay across my big brass bed like a randy octopus thrashing her pale limbs in an ecstasy of dying. Her children would have been still-born. The Sisters of the Sacred Heart would have carried them to a scented grave under the cypresses. She knew how to die and wished for it with a passion that has no heirs. She deserves a beautiful reliquary of holy sperm.

Day Four

(*Chelsea,* Autumn, year 30.) I bisect them, sleeping. The bed-cover is decorated with flowers. A shadow of dawn between the curtains. A few coughs on the pavement outside. I shiver and pull a blanket to my shoulders. They are sleeping, Beryl and Kate, her niece. Forty and twenty: I bisect them. Today is my thirtieth birthday. Such mathematics of lust.

Beryl's legs and arms are accessories stretched out beside me. If I were an Ottoman Sultan my confectioner royal would make me Turkish Delight in slabs like Beryl. A firm fatty jelly wrinkling with age and heavily powdered, smelling sweet. A shape to knead, grow fat on, roll on.

She is asleep, sweating and powdered like a *Pierrot.* Beryl who danced on the table through the empty wine-bottles after the party was over, peeling off the shawls and the widow's weeds of her loneliness and holding out her breasts like buffalo cheeses towards her niece in a challenge of blubber and peroxide hair. Kate who joined in with the amorality of a girl inquisitive for power. Beryl who was firing from the hip with her hands and singing "Annie get your Gun".

—I can make anyone . . . Anyone. I can make anyone better than you; directed at Kate who with such a laugh fed her aunt a wine-bottle and began to unbutton her jacket.

—Go on, auntie. You first. Show me how you do it.

And as Beryl danced naked and pulpy on the table, laughing, yodelling, screwing herself with Chablis, hurling her tits and ankles to the music on the gramophone, I peeled off my clothing to join her.

Beryl was holding a full bottle in one hand, swigging it and brandishing it while she clicked the fingers of the other hand, rings glinting in the candle-light, feet pounding the table, knees snaking, belly concertina'd above a mat of dark hair. A rivulet of wine splashed down her neck and shoulder. Canals of sweat split from the folds above her hips. Wondrous cow. Beryl is a torso made of Turkish Delight.

—I can make anyone better than you. Come on! Show me!

Kate had unbuttoned to the waist. The imprint of a bikini-top formed wing shapes where her breasts met. Her thumbs were thrust into her jeans, fingers hesitating over the popper, eyes moving rapidly, frightened, excited, between her aunt gyrating in all that flesh and me on the far side of the table. The room dark. Glasses, bottles, ashtrays etched out of the shadows. Two figures in the candle-light. Beryl's hair was loose over her face, shoulders shuddering, a finger thrust between white thighs. Head thrown back.

—Come on! Show me! Here!

Wine was splashed over her belly, smeared by the arm writhing. A gold ring twisting in a mat of moist hair.

—Here!

Kate raised one hand inside her jacket and closed her eyes, mouth open, face tense, shoulders bunched forward. Her breasts pressed together as she breathed.

—*Olé!* Beryl was clapping, snapping her fingers, spiralling, stroking herself, hips quivering. Come, matador!

Kate was leaning against the wall in the half-dark. As I gazed at her I folded my arms round the huge white buttocks on the table. Armfuls of it. Pubic hair dampened my chest. My fingers ran down between her cheeks. Beryl tumbled from the table and I staggered with her to the door of the bedroom, laughing, prick pointing the way like something I didn't own, one arm supporting tyres of midriff, the other grasping Kate's hand as I passed. Beryl collapsed on the floral bed. I let go Kate's hand. I knelt over a giggling heap of Beryl lathered in wine and sweat.

—I can make anyone . . .

I knelt above her holding the arches of her knees, my hands on her wet thighs. Her bleached hair lay over her mouth. Her breasts lolled on her forearms. Small hands spread.

Kate's face was expressionless where she stood. Dark hair over shoulders and jacket open. Perspiration spread over her belly. She held her hands over the front of her jeans. Her fingers moved, slid open the zip, pulled the jeans and a strip of white pants below her knees. She lifted one leg free and rested the foot on the edge of the bed. Then she raised both hands from her thighs and pulled the jacket from her shoulders. Kate was naked by the bed, hands an inch or so above the counterpane, her breasts deep over the rib-cage, pressed within her arms. Beryl turned and turned her white head, let out little whimpers far away. Kate leant over and slipped one hand between her aunt and me, drew me towards her, into her, and with the other hand gently fed one breast to her aunt's open mouth. I came within Kate in a tide of thirst.

My thirtieth year in the shadow of dawn. My thirtieth year to heaven:

My birthday began with the water-
Birds and the birds of the winged trees flying my name
Above the farms and the white horses
And I arose
In rainy autumn
And walked abroad in a shower of all my days.

* * *

Morning again. I feel disturbed and sullied by my own dreams. Grey light over the river. The wind is boxing the bare trees. The ducks will be huddled under the river-wall.

The only erotic recall is masturbation. It was Colette who said that a good masturbation is better than a bungled coitus. But then isn't a good fuck the best masturbation there is? Is it possible to lie with a girl you want without unfurling before the mind a life's canvas of love and lust? Love is compound, not singular. The scars and excrescences of the mind are bared each time we undress, and each naked experience adds a few more. The longing for wholeness and single partnership is a chimera haunting our lonely days. It is hard to cope with that night prowler, the sense of the possible. We weep into the pillow instead.

No, Beryl was not my mother, neither was Kate the nymph-child with the centre-fold breasts. The experience was as I filmed it, the documentary reality was not. The difference is the elixir.

T.S. Eliot surprisingly comes into my mind. Eliot thought of that elixir as a shadow, as death rather than life. But then he is a poet of the shadows: that is where his experience most powerfully dwells:

Between the idea
And the reality
Between the motion
And the act
Falls the Shadow.

The shadow was to Eliot a moment of dangerous awareness, something wonderful and fearful, an experience which drew him closer to, and in closer need of, God.

Between the potency
And the existence
Between the essence
And the descent
Falls the Shadow
For Thine is the Kingdom.

I have never understood what this had to do with God: what fascinates me is that Eliot should have located that shadow, that moment of fearful perception, of longing, as the moment of dawn. It is the hour of the waking dream, the hour when lost chances are found again, when the condemned man is set free, when the path he has taken and the path he might have taken are the same; the hour of love:

Waking alone
At the hour when we are
Trembling with tenderness
Lips that would kiss
Form prayers to broken stone.

For Eliot, fantasy is a form of prayer, perhaps the only form of prayer any longer valid. And he makes me think of my colleen in Paris, who with her visceral perception of spiritual matters could only approach God, be worthy of God, love God, through the experience of human orgasm.

Kate was also a novitiate of a kind. That it was her own aunt who supplied the vicarious preparation is a nicety I savour, at once a mark of family respect and a bid for power in which her breasts, by their capacity and their fecundity, were the crucial instruments.

As for Beryl, Mother Superior who could make anyone better than anyone, here was a mock challenge to her own declining powers – oh, she could still pray but very soon God wouldn't be listening any more – and it was a ritual initiation to the novice. This is my beloved niece in whom I am well pleased.

I feel sickened. I wonder if I shall go mad.

* * *

I am picking up some film stock this morning around ten. Janet usually does it. They'll be disappointed to see me: they chat her up and she comes back to the cutting-room with a grin on her face and some jokes which Eric always turns up to hear. So I'll take Deirdre and Seth to school on the way, Deirdre to her Comprehensive up West Hill, then Seth to his Primary School in Barnes. I enjoy it. I feel in a good mood this morning. The wind has dropped. Thin February sunshine. Metallic river. Jennifer is silent and distant: I've come to accept it. I wonder when she finds time to sleep with lover-boy. If I asked her she'd explode, and quite right too. I'll shut up.

—Tarzan had a Jaguar, Daddy.

—Silly! That's an animal, Seth.

—I know, I know. He bridles and is quiet. Put down again. Deirdre looks disdainfully out of the window, clutching her satchel.

—Mr Marshall uses make-up, Daddy. He's married.

I wonder what I'm supposed to say.

—Is he married to a man or a woman?

I've said the wrong thing. She doesn't understand. I think I should have said I expect his wife likes it, and that would have satisfied her. Deirdre needs things to be right. She has no time for irregularities. We've arrived at the school entrance.

Lover-boy teaches here. He's very smug about it. I think he believes he's Mao's gift to education. He's clearing up the mess we oldies have been making for two thousand years. He's twenty-eight, fifteen years younger than Jennifer. I'm conventional enough to find that strange. Obviously it isn't a matter of just screwing or he'd find that dolly of a PE teacher more fertile. I don't imagine he likes athletics. Pillow-talk maybe. The thoughts of Mao in her ear. That must help him get up the Yangtse.

—OK. Goodbye, my darling.

I put my arms round her which I don't normally do outside school. Deirdre is pleased and embarrassed.

—See you this evening.

She becomes one of a few hundred blue uniforms and raincoats with their backs turned. My contribution to the ILEA's teenage headache.

—Where will I go to school, Daddy?

—Where would you like to go?

I don't know where Seth will go. We are edging across Putney Hill in the rush-hour, and across the Heath. Seth's Primary School is the State's proudest advertisement for privilege. Fathers buy houses to be near it. There's a school orchestra or two, they're into Kung Fu, and among the optional extras in particular favour are Sanskrit and the *viol de gamba*. Seth's friends have birthday parties compèred by Nobel prizewinners. Mothers stand back and congratulate each other for supporting socialism and tot up how much money they've saved. There's a miraculous change, I've noticed, when the kids are rising eleven; then it's off with the socialist constraints, and either Grandma's paying for St Paul's, or it's down the straight at a gallop for scholarships.

—Emma's such a gifted child. I really feel we owe it to her.

I think I would like Seth to win a scholarship, then I too could wring my hands and say, What could I do? Seth's such an exceptional child. Cynicism is my own inept privilege. I'll probably pay the fees for St Paul's like everybody else.

—Goodbye, darling. We'll read some more Tarzan this evening.

I can't imagine not having children in my life. Jennifer's children. I've never seriously wanted anyone else's: well, almost never. What a strange admission. Is it by trusting her so unquestioningly as a mother that I am distancing myself from her as anything else? At least those painful tugs of regret, those heady regenerations of hope, are stilled this time for good, aren't they?

I never imagined we should want kids. Children were love-children. How could they breathe and thrive in the smog we choked on? We might, perhaps, just win through on our own, fighting the good fight with all our might, weathered survivors of a war well lost, supporting one another like heroes to the cenotaph. A wreath to our fallen hopes. There would be some companionship in that, a tear at sundown.

Would that not be worth while?
Why on earth did we bother?

I can't pick up the film stock till ten. A twinge of sadness: if I had a marriage that was a real marriage I would stop by at the house now and have coffee with Jennifer. How good that would be. Of course it's out of the question: what is sadder to me is that in – what is it? – seventeen years would I ever have been able to do that? Jennifer would have been hoovering, or cooking, or phoning, or unblocking the sink (which she felt quite rightly I might have done): no matter what, there would have been something to ensure an anti-welcome. And I should have kept out of the way and made the coffee myself, and No of course she didn't want any, it was too early, too late, there was no time, or she had to finish this first and the cup would be still there cold when I left – with a taste of acid on my tongue.

Why do I complain? How could it have been otherwise? My presence, especially when unexpected, taunted her with what her life lacked. I hated her for her hatred and felt powerless to disperse it. I was not a man.

But I was a man, am a man: a randy, warm, soft, starving man, choking on the sour gruel of our love.

I park the car off the King's Road and sit in a coffee bar. The coffee is slopped in the saucer. Daddies' Sauce on the Formica table. A croissant that breaks like chaff. Butter in a mean sticky packet. A blonde dreams by the window, holding a fag with stained fingers.

This is the pit of winter.

Day Five

(*Colchester*, Summer, year 29.) Another hotel room. You are leaning by the window in a white blouse. Your smile acknowledges very gladly where you are. Even your hand looks amused holding the glass. The champagne bottle, half-empty, lies in its ice-bucket on the bedside table. I am talking, talking to you, happy to be here, happy to gaze at you, happy to have champagne for you, happy to want you, happy not to love you, happy to know we shall soon make tremendous love, happy to put it off while we talk and I watch you, happy to cherish you, happy to know that tomorrow I'll drive you to the station and say Good-bye, happy anticipating the sad levity of your tears. Fragile Lily, you are a box of bright toys sparkling in the aura of my vanity.

For a capsule of time we are each other's. We know the rules.

Next year I shall be thirty. Is this the way romance shall be hereafter: played by Watteau lovers with a wink and warm light hearts? Lily, my bright shepherdess, come dance with me: the world beyond this summer stage is turned to stone statues grimacing in the shade. Dance! Dance!

Erica Jong would call this a "zipless fuck"; which is really what the 18th century was on about, it seems to me, although I suppose they mightn't have put it quite like that at the royal court of France. A *fête galante* sounds more appropriate to their station: fancy-dress and a mask hiding the externals, and music orchestrating the desires so liberated. That way you never needed to know a thing about a man except the love-notes he made, or about her but the signals she sent. Life reduced to sweet vibes. A zipless fuck for courtiers with a classical education.

It was never part of my classical education, my dear Lily. Something got in the way. Freud? Wesley? Lord Byron? Queen Victoria? Or just Dad, who was a mixture of them all in his way? In any case it certainly wasn't a *fête galante* when you and I first met. Do you remember? Oh, I can enjoy the pleasure of you by the window *now* – the painterly pleasures. Our fancy-dress will be to undress, and champagne will have to do the work of the lute. But it's taken years to see it that way. To know that I shall not be punished, my prick will not fall off, I shall not bear the burdens of the desert martyrs all my days. I am free, free to savour, free to sup, free to acknowledge that when our eyes met that first time and said loud and clear, "Let's fuck," we should have run laughing and lustful from the party of wives and hostesses, boy-friends and neighbours, nice people and other menhirs, and fucked.

What a clear, ringing message it is: let's fuck, Lily, let's fuck.

You have laughing eyes I want to kiss.

You have fair hair I want to comb black against the sun.

You have lips that make witty shapes when you are close to me.

You have shown me that imagination is a dimension of love.

You have a body that welcomes and feasts.

And you have a husband I can very easily ignore as apparently you can.

I would not like you to love me. What you give me is enough.

Let it be this way, dear Lily, now the sun is setting golden on your face: come and lie with me.

* * *

Waldron is quite a different man on his home pitch. Some pitch too. I've accepted his invitation for the weekend, pleading pressure of work to cut it to twenty-four hours. I ran the Jag through the car-wash just far enough from Wopping to ensure it would dry before I arrived this afternoon. The tyres made a stately crunch on the gravel, and his lordship was there to greet me.

He is, I suppose, seventy or not far off. A remarkably ugly man. Nothing fits. His lower jaw is too large for the upper, which makes his voice sound like an elephant's at a water-hole. One ear is higher than the other. One nostril bears a beacon of a wart. One eyelid droops, though I believe that might be drink. His teeth are variously akimbo. I bet his penis is lopsided – though, just to be perverse, his balls are probably quite regular, unless he's got three like a pawnbroker's sign.

—Well, Gareth, good to see you at Wopping again.

The hand grasping mine was absurdly large for so small a man. I expected it to come off in mine like a clown's.

Waldron paused for a moment to survey his acres. A nod of the head and a little grunt registered that special relationship of an Englishman with his land: this shy, stumpy man in his tweeds, proud of his money and what he's done with it, given through long habit of bachelorhood to reserving his intimate moments for himself. Skeins of evening mist wrapped the lime-trees and blurred the empty fields. I felt warm towards Waldron.

—I'm delighted to be here.

I meant it. He turned and led the way heavily into the house, hands dangling. A Tudor mansion in Buckinghamshire, warmed by log-fires and chilled by draughts. I already knew the famous

Waldron picture collection: I once came to film it in my BBC days, which was how I got to know Waldron.

Does anyone know Waldron? Probably not. He has a reputation for being a tough bastard in the City, which I'm sure the City deserves. But he likes putting out awkward feelers of friendship which catch you by surprise – a gift of a Degas drawing once, a crate of champagne at Christmas. Always things bought. Expensive things. He's lumbered around a stockade of friendship for so long now, sniffing to get in, always taking fright like a startled warthog when he discovers a chink. England's made him and ruined him. The way he looked at Janet's tits the other morning was deceptive – comfort-seeking. I imagine he's homosexual if he can raise himself to be anything. There may have been some heavy breathing behind the gym at Eton once upon a time.

—You know these, Gareth? Of course you do.

The collection gives away little of the man. Should an art collection? Degas' portrait of his friend Duranty: a frank gaze out of a wall of books. I should have thought it might have made Waldron avert his eyes. On the wall opposite, the Degas pastel of horses in the rain. It's about the only painting of horses I don't find as boring as horses themselves. Come to think of it, I wonder if Waldron isn't a bit like Degas: a grunting squat capon of a man whose sensibilities leak out through the seams of convention. Then David's portrait of Robespierre. How the hell did Waldron fix on that one? And Kokoschka's study of Freud. Even more amazing here. I came to the conclusion that a man collects art from within a special sealed-off compartment of himself.

—This is new since you were last here, Gareth.

Waldron led me towards the dining-room and stood by the door saying nothing. A single canvas filled the end wall. The last of Braque's great *Atelier* series in which the old man filtered the most familiar objects of his studio through a grey mesh of dreams. Braque, a man aloof among people, who for his most intimate statements painted not the women he loved but his own workshop. His easel was the mirror of his thoughts, his palette took wing, his guitar was his madonna. Braque couldn't help putting me in mind of Waldron gazing out at his acres, counting his cash tenderly, walling himself up with his pictures. Soft humanity retreating behind a carapace of objects. Another mask.

—I bought it from Kate Copperfield. She's here. And Kemp of

The Times. D'you know him? You must. They're going through drawings, if you feel like joining them before dinner.

I didn't. Waldron's three thousand drawings by Van der Velde the Younger had already mopped up not a few winter evenings. Boats. Boats. Boats. The Dutch passion for getting wet and going on about it. The idea of bending over all that rigging with Kemp and Kate Copperfield made me long for the pub. Oh God, Waldron, why didn't I stay at home? I would have done if the children hadn't gone to Jennifer's parents for the weekend. Besides, Jennifer has her private life, as they say. So I came up here to my room to spend a long and permissive time unpacking. The maid offered to do it. I said No. She would do it too quickly. It was dark. I couldn't even go for a walk in the grounds.

So Kate Copperfield's here: another one-time subject of my candid camera. And what an excruciating experience that was. Kate's a fiftyish wealthy Canadian whose father made a fortune out of French letters. Young Kate was an only child and inherited the royalties, as it were. With these letters of accreditation she decided that art was the life for her, so off to the South of France where as far as she knew it was all happening, and before anyone could cry "Rape!" she was installed with Picasso. Kate knew enough Spanish to cry "*Olé!*", which seems to have been sufficient for at least a month and then Picasso kicked her out. She took fifty pictures with her and wrote a book about the maestro called *Taking the Rough with the Cube* which the BBC felt merited a serious profile of its author: enter Gareth Penrhyn, bright and eager in those days. By this time Kate's walls were hung nose to tail with studio loot from umpteen sources, even Braque, though Braque was hardly one to fall for writhing heiresses, I should have thought. So she's selling them off now, is she; or leaving them like visiting-cards, with the bill sent later? Just like Kate to collect Waldron. Moneybags. Social connections. Maybe they fuck. What a horrible thought ("Let me show you how Pablo liked it, darling"). Jesus, I'm going to need some of that famous Waldron cellar to get through this evening.

Kemp too, what's more. Well, at least he can be ignored or politely insulted. Think of being art critic of *The Times* for thirty years. Three articles a week forty-eight weeks of the year. That's four thousand three hundred and twenty published articles. At an average of, what, six hundred words, let's say? That makes two million, five hundred and ninety-two thousand words of blameless aesthetic dissertation. About forty novels' worth. Dear God, where do old critics go?

At least Kemp's a randy sod. No, not a sod: definitely not. I've noticed he prefers women with colossal chins. I didn't attach any importance to it at first, but now I believe there is something in it. A chin fetishist. It must be a "first", I do feel sure. Anyway, I never met one before. They obviously find him devastatingly attractive, these chinny women. Perhaps he's fabulous in bed. But what do you do with a chin in bed? There's clearly a lot I don't know. I wonder what he says when he's chatting them up, because whenever I'm with him – which isn't often – Kemp talks exactly like one of his reviews which invariably begin, "Significant representations of domestic life are to be observed in the recent paintings of Hubert Grosseprikke currently on view at the Kashin Gallery", or words to that effect. I wonder if he writes his reviews in bed, resting his tripewriter on the current lady's chin. If the chin wags the exhibition gets a high rating: if it drops the poor artist gets a pasting. Dear old Kemp. He must be at the Van der Veldes right now, down on his knees with Kate Copperfield. Perhaps they'll be discussing rigging. Two more adept riggers you never met.

Oh, I do love hating them both. It's quite cheered me up. People of influence. People of wealth. Why do I savage them? After all I'm modestly influential and almost wealthy. There must be a nasty sound of envy somewhere, an insecurity problem to take a look at when I've nothing better to do.

I judge an evening by whether or not a movie director I respect might choose to film it. The evenings I've most enjoyed recently are Robert Altman's: lots of mental sword-play, irony and booze. Catharsis in many colours. I had a Polanski dinner party once. The host died. There've been several terrific Fellini evenings, at least one of which Bertolucci took over after midnight. I think I'll invite Jean Renoir tonight. I'll have to ring up a hostess agency and the girls will arrive in furs and a snowstorm and a great stretched-out Delahaye *coupé*. Kate Copperfield can give me the phone-number of an agency which supplies lonely artists. And then we can all dance into the dawn under the Degas and the David, and wander off in our crumpled evening clothes into the park at first light, leaving wine-glasses in the flower-beds and a thousand assignations pinned to every tree.

Can't stretch the unpacking any longer. I think I'll go down and find a Scotch and a lonely billiard-table. By now Jennifer and lover-boy will be separated by a candle in some Mario and Franco restaurant, and soon by nothing.

* * *

One day I just walked out.

We had been married two years. We were both exhausted. What did this futile relationship have to offer any longer? Each struggle was a little harder and more desperate and the truce won more fragile. At twenty-nine Jennifer had come to look drab and brittle: every movement of her body was a kind of twitch. Long winter shadows were already licking across our lives.

We talked less, shared less, smiled less. I worked ever more intensely, the BBC's bright-eyed boy. Those twin institutions I had set up, Gareth Employment Inc. and Gareth Domestic Bondage Ltd, now functioned so efficiently that the two managing directors, Jennifer and Gareth, would soon have to be kicked upstairs, redundant. We had achieved a triumph of automation in which we ourselves had all but ceased to exist except as motors for generating pain. We were seen to be alive only by the bills we paid and the tears we shed.

So I walked out. There could never have been any question of "agreeing to part": we should have protested and wept and hurled abuse until, defenceless with exhaustion, we wrapped our arms round one another and forgave all. And indeed for the next twenty-four hours the horizon would have looked distinctly brighter, and another little cell of intuition would have died.

Jennifer might have done it herself in time. Resignation to the malice of the gods has always come more easily to her, but before long even she I feel sure would have crashed her foot into our institutional filing system and yelled, "No! No! No!" I never waited to give her the chance.

I left everything except the contents of a suitcase and a typewriter. Organised it in half an hour as Jennifer stood there in disbelief. She did once utter a half-stifled cry. I picked up the telephone and ordered a taxi. I didn't even know where to. The heavy front-door slammed. The engine was running.

—Good morning, sir. Here, let me put that in the front for you.

The park was yelling with children. A sludge of yellow leaves glistened on the pavement. Cobwebs between black iron railings.

—Where to, sir?

—Victoria!

I said goodbye to three years in a state of bewildered exhilaration.

The single word Victoria had leapt from my mouth. It was the way out. The ticket marked simply Away. Away to where? I had no idea. It didn't matter. I sat back and closed my eyes. I was twenty-seven. Life had not yet begun. By God, it would.

I stood outside the station with my suitcase and typewriter on either side of me. Now what? I stirred myself and walked inside. Looked up at the Departures board. Brighton. Hastings. Bognor Regis. Eastbourne. Lewes. Littlehampton. Croydon. Hopeless! You can't run away from a marriage to Croydon. What about Continental Departures? Yes, I'd thought to pack my passport. Paris. Rome. Zagreb. What about Zagreb? No associations. No reason to go there at all. What a marvellous idea – Zagreb. The train was leaving for Dover at 14.32. Just four hours' time. I went over to the booking office. No, first a bank. I wondered how much a single to Zagreb might be. And how much would I need to take with me?

—Yes, sir, what can I do for you?

—Zagreb!

—Pardon, sir?

—Well, hang on a minute. I think I'd better go and work it out.

Suddenly I felt awkward. My case caught in the swing-door. Oh for fuck's sake . . . Now calm down! Find the Left Luggage and relax.

I went and had a cup of coffee in the Self-Service.

Why the bloody hell Zagreb? It must be very drab there in winter. It must be very drab there in summer. Not much fun. Whom would I meet? A few large tram-conductresses. I'd feel a bit foolish coming back on the next night train.

Another cup of coffee. What about some proper breakfast?

No, if I was going to get the hell out of it I had far better go somewhere I could enjoy myself. Sun. Sea. Was it still summer enough to swim in the Mediterranean? Italy then. I spoke the language. No, not Italy. France? St Tropez. Sea-food and wine in the autumn sunshine. Boats in the harbour. Night-clubs. Disillusioned cunt peckish for more. Wasn't that what I needed? Oh, yes! What should I do: ring up the BBC and say I'm ill? I shall need to be away for a week.

Wait! Already I had put a bracket round it. A week.

Then an infinite hopelessness settled on me. The breakfast was revolting. What was I doing sitting in this shitty place on Victoria station dreaming about tits in St Tropez? Come on, get off your arse. At least find a place in London as a base for a few days. Settle things first. Get drunk. Phone a few friends. Go and talk to them. Find your feet. Then go away when you're calmer, by all means.

So I retrieved my bags from the Left Luggage, went to the nearest house agent and took a furnished room in Pimlico. Home!

That afternoon I slept and dreamt I was at home. I woke up in my grave and listened to the rain.

Day Six

(*Piedmont*, Spring, year 28.) I am bringing her here because I love this place. Will she, through some local osmosis, love me in the place I love?

I can sense her irritation as we drive. She will be a sullen trophy. Her hair is a mess this morning. Her shirt carries yesterday evening's wine-stains. Her thoughts are floating away into this beloved landscape of olives and brilliant corn. Come back! Come back! At least when I'm inside her she can't run away. For a few moments she's mine: there's no room for two in her cunt, or three or four.

Except – how do I know she isn't pretending it's someone else: some Italian stud, Mario or Stefano or Vittorio or God knows who she may be slotting into her mind like a cassette whenever I move into her? The harder and deeper I fuck her the more she may be growing randy at the prospect of how much harder and deeper Mario or Stefano or Vittorio will screw her once I'm out of the way. Because tonight will be our last night together. Tomorrow, still mushy with my semen, she'll catch the train back to Perugia where she's studying, and she'll walk from the station beneath a ceremonial canopy of pricks raised in salute. Rise, Sir Mario, and thou, Sir Stefano, and thou, trusty lecher Sir Vittorio, lend me thy staff. *Caterina, Caterina, ecco, la bella inglesa é ritornata!* Dancing in the streets. A round of discothèques. Laughter echoing under Etruscan arches. The creak of an ancient door at midnight (beware, ancient grandmother creaks too, in an iron bed above!). The shadow of an arm reaching to turn out the light. Silence in the airless night. Jesus! And all the time me here on a bare mountain pickling my loneliness in Campari to the accompaniment of a nightingale, lovesick and paranoid, at liberty to wank under the stars. Gareth, your obsessive jealousy is not a pretty sight.

So I'm in love with Catherine; frantically, foolishly and miserably in love with Catherine. And I've brought her here because I love this place. We've begun the climb up from the raw valley, the open car snaking the hair-pin bends under black ilexes.

Catherine says nothing, holding the bag of ravioli and wine, occasionally resting her head back to let the breeze ruffle her hair. Sunburn has multiplied the freckles between her breasts. I shift position to slip a hand under her blue shirt. Her breast is damp with sweat.

—Gareth, for God's sake keep your hands on the wheel.

—I want you now.

—Where the hell are we going? That's the fiftieth hair-pin bend.

I feel better now we're talking. It's almost like it was when we started out, threading through London in the pelting rain on the Dover road, necking at traffic-lights, running from the car-park into the first country pub we saw, standing on the open foredeck in a gale feeling too drunk and drenched to be sick but being sick all the same, trying to fuck in a hip-bath in Boulogne, lying in bed the whole of the next day because we had too heavy a hangover and too much lust to get up. Then Northern France. Alsace. The Black Forest. Salzburg. The Gross Glockner Pass. Venice: we'd neither of us been there.

Then what? Did we run out of invention? Run out of laughter? Anyway the curtain-raiser was over. End of fun. I grew morbid. Now I wanted to fuck her to possess her. I sensed Catherine was going back to someone she maybe wanted more than me. Suddenly, never having wanted her at all except as a companion in bed and booze I wanted her urgently in every other way I could think of. Desperately. No tits like hers. No cunt so warm. No laughter so rich. No moods so understandable. No fart so acceptable.

Stefano, Vittorio, Mario, keep your hairy hands off. By thy long grey prick and glittering eye, now wherefore stopp'st thou me? She's mine. And mine is the spider love. I'm Gareth, twenty-eight, film-maker, lover, love-maker, fucker and fornicator, dreamer and drunk, apprentice failure and fascinator, unholy and unwhole, my love the only security I hold and even that I know to be a lie. Give me your love, Catherine, that I may throw it away. Mirror, mirror on the wall, I wish I could smash your bloody face in.

The afternoon has thrown a shawl of hot dust around the hills. There is a drag of sheep-bells among the rocks. An invisible nightingale. Offerings to the wind. Catherine has said nothing here. What can she say to a man she does not love but merely accommodates, who has brought her to a place he loves so that he may love her the more? Spider love!

She is picking honeysuckle among the abandoned terraces. Crickets explode from the dried grass as she walks. The road slaloms into the heat-mist towards the coast. Up here you can see the entire world and not be seen, only by the eagles that wheel about the high peak. They are the only wildlife fleet enough to avoid the hunters. Nothing stirs between an eagle and a butterfly, until the evening when the fireflies patrol the shadows of the lane. I try to distract them with my cigarette lighter. Catherine laughs for the first time in days.

—Thank you for bringing me here, she says.

* * *

A strange feeling: for the first time I no longer identify myself with the figure on the screen. Did Gareth the twenty-eight-year-old die up there on his mountain with the honeysuckle and his ardent jealousies? Or grow up a little, maybe? Not that the capacity for jealousy died: volcanoes like that have too much fire in their belly to give up so easily.

No, what died was a kind of romance. Love as a tearful *bel canto*. That died up there. Catherine saw through it, and must have taught me to see through it. She didn't believe in me at all, which was a mean and salutary lesson. All that fervent prick-waving aroused only a shrug.

—Come off it, Gareth, put it away until we both feel randy. Stop wearing your heart on your knob.

True! Until I met Catherine I must have teetered through my days as though life were a kind of sexual egg-and-spoon race, my fresh and fragile love balanced on the tip of my cock, ready to drop with a resounding splat at the feet of any likely maiden.

So, the figure on the screen, growing younger and keener, will he turn into a figure of fun? A Gareth puppet-show? It mustn't be. I must find myself in him, or discover him in me now – the tenderfoot aching to be the honeysuckle Catherine is picking, to be the path she treads, the air she breathes; Gareth inviting his tender web to be torn.

But it is past, and from now on these films will have to be set in the past.

Meanwhile it is Sunday, February 6. More than three weeks still to run till Jennifer leaves.

* * *

In the grey light there is a grey figure by the window. She turns as if on a pedestal. Her head is lowered, her hair falls over her shoulder, her feet are bare. As the light strokes her face she raises her eyes to gaze at me and shakes her head.

The pedestal turns. My eyes blur with tears.

Now she has wavy hair. Her hands are very small, raised to the window indicating something outside. I cannot see what it is: I cannot move or respond. She wears a long dress embroidered at the wrists and ankles. Slowly she lowers her hands and stares at me. I cannot move towards her. She waits. She shakes her head. A shadow settles over her face and body. She has gone. There is only the grey light of the window. Dawn.

I am aware that my fingers are clutching the pillow. My stomach is convulsed. There is no one by the window. The morning light is empty and cruel. I want to scythe at it with a scream. Come back!

Which of you? Either of you: interchangeable lovers I have taken and rejected, who have loved me, warmed me, freed me, hoped for me, and who have turned away with a finality of sadness.

—Gareth, you don't know how to love.

Winter branches ooze rain beyond the bare window. Bleak fields are parched of light. A magpie hitches its tail and swoops on to the gravel. It hops on to the grass. Pretty thief.

—Gareth, you devour love, and you do not know how to love.

God, Wopping Grange on such a morning as this. Dreary, damp. Important people farting and stirring into life around me: Kemp of *The Times*, Kate Copperfield of the art. The social life as a barrier to serious living. Thank heaven for thick walls and a late breakfast. I can stay here a while yet, caressed by wealth. The guest-rooms are furnished with third-division heirlooms Sotheby's would itch to handle ("Property of a Gentleman").

My thoughts, dissuaded from dwelling upon all this, are phallic and trenchant. Why, after forty-two years of heaven and hell, does the Grand Old Duke of York still conduct my life, with my prick as his baton? When it is up it is up, and when it is down it is down, and when it is only halfway up ... so runs the tale of my marriage.

At least, on this bleak and lonely morning I do not feel compelled at first consciousness to switch my attention to the dilemma of how to make it with Jennifer, rigid in her tomb next to me. Lover-boy can focus his talents in that direction from now on. Maybe I do him an uncharitable injustice. Maybe at this instant his prick is steepling at the thought and touch of Jennifer, and her nipples are going "ping" in response. They never did to me. Yesterday's omelettes.

I quickly learnt to call in help. Of a pretty disreputable kind, perhaps, but in the mess I'd wandered into it was all I could manage. Of course, a show-down would have been preferable. How wise I can be about it now. How wise everyone else was at the time, except – that is – the shrinks. And the shrinks we kept in business in those early years were of two kinds. There were the happily married ones who were cynical about marriage from the start and vowed we were having a lovely battle. And there were unhappily married ones who, along with the philanderers and the pooves, viewed marriage as a state of sanctity. Neither type was prepared to interest himself in the exquisite fact that Jennifer and I had taken pains to find in one another a partner for life as physically accessible as Fort Knox.

Then there were the amateur shrinks – the Encounter Group-leaders, the Co-Counsellors, the Gestalt Theoreticians and the Primal Scream merchants – each of whom touted their particular faiths with varying degrees of brutality and screwed us up into a state of gibbering self-awareness. Before long I grew convinced that I possessed the largest private collection of self-knowledge in the Western world – beautifully documented too, with provenances, dates, measurements, the lot – but what in Christ's name was I supposed to do with it? Donate it to Oxfam?

So, abandoning the shrinks, I called in my own help in those early hours. It was like the call for morning milking-time. This was no trouble at all if there happened to be some bird I was fancying at that moment. Just close the eyes, slot her into the retina, and Bingo! It was during the off-seasons I ran into trouble. Then I really had to delve; and, oh boy, what I did find down there. At first I had trouble with my WASP conscience, but that didn't last long, not with gritted teeth next to me on the pillow and only half an hour before the day had to be got moving. I had to act fast.

A quick scene-change would take place. A swimming-pool. Among trees. Pine-needles underfoot. Scent of resin. Oleanders. Evening. Water-boatmen stirring small ripples (very un-Hockney ripples). Hummingbird hawkmoths above the lavender. A girl has sun-bleached hair (corny images are invariably the most potent). Her small breasts scarcely move as she walks towards the water. I do not know who she is. She stands in the sun for a moment. Skin is drawn taut between hip-bones. Then she dives. Her golden image is caught in motion: a scimitar in the sunlight above sharp water, weightless. Drenched strands of hair are around her face as she joins me by the side of the pool. In the curve of her back light down dries in the sun, warm to my lips. She turns her body to my tongue, eyes closed, arms stretched in the grass, nipples twin studs on ribbed flesh. She breathes deep, eyes still closed. Muscles on her thighs stand out.

The young Britt Ekland sun-nymph image, stretched across the tropic of my lust, she used to refill my deepest wells of need.

On her off-days another girl would take her place, a huge-breasted dark girl who'd lean over and spin around my prick in a maypole dance, plaiting bright ribbons in the twilight. A Cecil Sharp idyll cast by Fellini and shot by me at sundown.

Other fantasies would come and go. There were sometimes

comic heroines I was fond of, like the Chinese identical twins who made love with me – or with one another – and who rose from my bed to record their orgasms on a dart-board slate, and whom I could only tell apart because one of them chalked the score with her left hand. And there were my soft-porn inflatables: clouds of variegated nymphets and leviathans who flitted across my life like putty paying homage to my rod and who would vanish with a squeak, their job done.

Hard-porn never, or only on rare angry occasions when I loathed both Jennifer and myself in equal measure. Shit never turned me on, nor whips nor wallopings, nor slippery clothing, high heels, black belts, crucified erections, blood-bolted second comings and all the rest of the tribe. Sex and Belsen have remained far apart in my imagination. At the first hint of pain the maypole would sag and the fête was over. Sex has been fair and sweet, or dark and ravenous. Lollipop or Christmas pudding. Always an excess, it is true; always a self-indulgence. There had to be more and more and more of it until self-hypnosis set in and the prick seemed to generate an energy of its own while the mind floated in nirvana. Not that I am turned on by Indian sexual mysticism. There is nothing holy about fucking; it's not that grave and self-important. It is fucking – ideally fucking with Boucher's dumpy Irish girl, Louisa O'Murphy, cunt-downwards on her tumbled couch, little feet spread wide on velvet just as she was left seconds ago by the lover she follows with her eyes, now no doubt pursuing matters of church and state. The perfect zipless fuck, Louisa O'Murphy, gentler than any Erica Jong dreamed of, richer and more warm. Louisa died a toothless hag two hundred years ago; yet the experience of her to the painter's eye and to mine is of a fulfilment deeper than the womb.

* * *

I was separated at twenty-seven, slumped in a bed-sit in Pimlico, free and lost. I could not go back that afternoon of the rain, numbed with drink and aimlessness. I was here. I had to rebuild.

So I worked. Relieved of Gareth Domestic Bondage Ltd, Gareth Employment Inc. found no check or competition. Colour television was new, a new channel was cut to carry it, and here was bright young Gareth Penrhyn on the spot ready to steer Cleopatra's golden barge like a ship of state into the homes of all those sons of the Sixties who never had it so good.

Neither did Gareth. I strutted the corridors. I hobnobbed with bosses I despised. I patronised peers I envied. I put in a good word here and there. I made sure I received good words everywhere. I knifed a few static retainers who were slowing my progress. I talked socialism in the Club. I acquired that special air of benevolent condescension towards the outside world which is the badge of BBC producers accustomed to believe they have the exclusive contract to distribute manna from heaven. I made films about notorati who were flattered and whom I begged to dinner with friends who were impressed. I slipped into the swim at El Vino's, and gossiped enough to be rung up (rather embarrassingly) at the office where I kept the door open as a matter of principle. I was always available, always ready to help out, always ready with advice, always ostentatiously overworked, and always on the edge of my seat to collect the prizes. I did well. People said so. I said so. I even cared about my work. The licence-payers' got their money's worth, and I got promotion. It was a fair bargain.

I even got Catherine. Naturally so successful a young producer as Gareth saw to it that he got the pick of the assistants' pool. My colleagues – as I now called them – tended to acquire as assistants rinsed-out matrons in woollies, or grey-haired permanent-under-secretaries with memories of Lord Reith and Alvar Lidell.

Catherine was not exactly like that. Bob in Staff Planning tipped me the wink about her in the Club one day. He knew I was single all of a sudden and rather fancied himself as a sex-broker. When she came into my room she hung up her coat, looked at me looking at her, and tossed her hair as if about to climb into my bed, which that evening she did. And there she stayed more or less for two months, getting her hair done in between, and putting in the odd hour at the office to collect her pay which she didn't need, Daddy being a director of a chain store. She'd park her Aston Martin outside my slummy new flat in Ladbroke Grove for blacks to scrawl obscenities on it. She would drive in it naked to Daddy's country seat during the early hours of a weekend, holding my prick between gear-changes. She was the first girl I'd had since my marriage more than three years before. And she LIKED it. God be praised, it wasn't just me that was wrong. I hadn't known till then. Catherine would lean over and brush a nipple over my prick as we entered the long drive. Ten minutes later I entered her in the west wing.

And in the mornings she was with me crooked into the curve of my body, a hand asleep in my crutch, hair across my chest, breasts warm against my belly. She taught me the companionship of flesh. And I was happy in a way that I had never known.

Until, that is, I fell jealously in love with her on that journey through Italy; and even then she taught me the folly of that.

—Thank you for bringing me here.

But that was the best part of a year later, and by that time many other things had happened. I had learnt to live without Jennifer. I knew Jennifer wanted me back. And I had bought my Shangri-La.

* * *

Wopping Grange. Another country seat. Do I seem to collect them? Things have changed in fifteen years. Catherine will have breasts round her belly by now – four kids, the bulk of Daddy's inheritance and a couple of marriages later. She used to drive me home naked in an Aston Martin. Yesterday I drove to Wopping fully clothed in a Jaguar. What's the difference? Oh, a lot. I am alone. This morning, this grey morning, I woke alone in my bitterness, nobody crooked into the curve of my body, nobody to sheathe my prick as she stirred. And it doesn't help to reflect that Catherine may have tarnished more than I. Her body, any woman's body, would have warmed me this desolate morning. Jennifer is with lover-boy, the world is with his wife, and I am about to have breakfast with Kemp of *The Times* and Kate Copperfield of the art. And Lord Waldron of the moneybags who will fund my Arab films, and who told me last night (over port, naturally) that he'd be prepared to fund virtually anything I direct if I cared to break into feature films.

He believes in me, just as the BBC used to, just as they all do. Do I?

Here's my chance, the moment I've been waiting for, hoping it might never come.

Right now I only know I feel trapped. Sunday morning in Buckinghamshire with the rich and confident. I want to hold a pair of tits in my hands. I must go downstairs and say Good Morning. So this is the way the world ends, not with a bang but a simper. A pun as rotten as my mood. Dear God, I am going to be famous.

Day Seven

(*Edinburgh*, August, year 26.) Here was proof that they'd been right all along, those ad-men who had presided over my education and guided my experience of life. Nature could, and did, imitate commercial art!

Sheila had been scissored from a travel hoarding I had noticed at Edinburgh Airport, and then placed in the front seat of my car driving south. Nineteen, South African, blonde as her beaches, a sunripe surf-siren – no hyperbole was adequate: she was my goddess with the perfumes of summer about her, golden legs flowing on for ever, blouse swelling like a spinnaker straining for home. She was a golden package with a label attached on which was inscribed "For Gareth Penrhyn, with love from your dreams."

We took the byroad to Innerleithen across the Moorfoot Hills. Ricky, I said to myself, you deserve a magnum for this; and my warmest thoughts went out to the bouncy little Scotsman who had gripped my hand in thanks outside his theatre where we'd been filming the previous night.

—Gareth, he had said. Gareth my friend; do you have room in your car for a passenger if you're really off tomorrow?

—Yes, Ricky, I expect so.

Edinburgh had been balm. I was returning to the grey life. Even some TV electrician bumming a lift and charging it to expenses would have been welcome.

—Certainly I do.

—There's this girl been working for us wants to visit the Lake District. Could you possibly take her somewhere near, d'you think? She's quite beautiful, as a matter of fact.

The words "matter of fact" he had spoken with that clipped Scots lilt emphasised just ironically enough for me to glance sharply at his face. Probably his grandmother, reeking of black pudding and virtue, knowing Ricky. But he was already looking back towards the open stage-door.

—Is she just, Ricky?

—Yes, sweet girl, Sheila, he'd said as an afterthought. Very well brought up. Gareth me boy. D'you think you could pick her up at the Connaught in the morning? Just say the time and I'll make sure she's there.

—Around nine?

—Around nine. Thanks a lot.

Ricky waved goodnight and strode quickly through the stage-door where the camera crew were packing up their gear. I made my way back to the Caledonian Hotel beneath the hulk of the castle where the lights of the tattoo still blazed. Edinburgh at Festival time.

I hadn't intended driving anywhere near the Lake District, of course. But still, a short detour in the interests of even a nicely-brought-up girl might sugar the day. Why not?

As Sheila emerged through the swing-doors I had forgotten the Lake District was to be a detour. And by the time her second leg had straightened out beside me and I had reached over across her to pull the door shut, I was already launched on a journey that as far as I was concerned could take me anywhere just as long as it might never actually end.

It was hot. The sun shone across me on to Sheila's face and arms. Her blouse was no more than a broad cotton band crossed over at the back below her shoulder-blades, then tied round in front in a bow above her bare midriff. Supporting laces over the shoulders carried two smaller bows just above the collar-bone. The blouse rested loosely so that the slightest movement of her body, or jolt of the car, was recorded like a hypersensitive device by the tremor of her breasts. Edinburgh's cobblestones were a blessing, roadworks a godsend. My body was in a state of some pandemonium.

We must have talked. I was mainly aware of an empty feeling in the stomach. My eyes took in the heather and the hills. We passed Traquair, Mountbengerhope, Tushielaw, on and on over the moors with the roof down. I grew obsessed by those breasts. The experience of her body close to me and the landscape around me became fused. The hills were her torso in the sun. She lay stretched between firth and firth. The car followed her contours much of the morning.

I didn't want even to touch her yet. Let it keep. We were on a long journey. I wanted to relish it, explore, save it up, enjoy each fragment, each small conquest and discovery. I heard my own voice saying calmly that we ought to check the route, and we pulled up by the side of the road. I laid the road-map open between us and we both leant over, she to see the route, I to view her breasts.

—Nether Dalgleish: there, you see?

And I traced the mountain route with my finger. Her blouse gaped a little more. There was a hum in my head. I wondered if she could hear it. I began to feel sick.

—Then down to Craigcleuth.

It was small type, cunning bugger, and she had to lean a fraction further. No bra, that was for sure. I could glimpse where the cavern widened at the base of her breasts. I tried to blink away the perspiration. Her left hand moved to trace the yellow thread of road with her finger, and the left breast sank on to the right. Dear God, my whole body seemed to be vibrating with every hammerbeat of the heart. Couldn't she hear it now: didn't she know? The left nipple could only be a particle of an inch out of view. A centimetre perhaps.

—After that the Longtown road to Carlisle. Cathedral city. We can find a pub there for lunch maybe. Then the A6 to Penrith. There. Almost as far as Ullswater.

She nodded and smiled. Eyes soft and bland; round, blue. She settled herself back in the seat. End of vision. What next? I tried to think, tried to use the time slipping away all too fast, tried to think of barriers that would delay its progress. She was going to Windermere, she said, but sounded rather vague about it. Could I not engineer so long and delightful a day that she couldn't possibly arrive tonight? There was that pub at the head of the Kirkstone Pass: they must have rooms. Two rooms? A single room? Would that be possible? No, she was a well-brought-up girl. Ricky had said so. Her eyes said so. Innocent. Only an innocent girl would wear no bra with a strange man miles from nowhere. Quite innocent. Must be. Certainly a virgin. Only nineteen. South African too: Dutch Reformed Church and all that. So mustn't spoil anything. Meanwhile a host of pleasures. Walks by the lake. A log-fire in the mountains. Wine. I might kiss her. Soft shy lips. Afterwards anything might be possible. Soon. Or another time. Mustn't be hasty and spoil everything. Christ, she was lovely. Perfect. I wanted her so much I could afford to wait. I could afford to be sneaky-eyes but no more. Unless, of course, she made it clear. Perhaps she would. What a thought. But she must make the first sign. Definitely.

Oh those breasts! I had to catch a sight of at least one nipple. That was the immediate landmark. I'd feel better then. I'd been so close already. What would they be like, her nipples? What information did I already have? She was a big girl; not fat, but big. Full. 38″ perhaps. Maybe more. So the nipples would be large too, wouldn't they? But did blondes have dark nipples or fair? Was there any rule? Probably not: it was all to do with pigmentation. Sometimes you could tell. Red-heads have white freckled skin and pale-pink nipples, I knew that. Not attractive. Sheila didn't have that kind of skin at all. Almost dusky. So perhaps her nipples were dark. And what shape? Flat coronas with what look like stitch-marks round the edge and an acorn in the centre. Or maybe they'd be conical, corona and nipple swollen into one hillock as they show sometimes in the girlie magazines, or on tailors' dummies. Who models for tailors' dummies? And what kind of girl had those? Perhaps you had to be pregnant, or a Masai. No, surely not. Not all the nudes in girlie magazines were pregnant or Masai. Wouldn't it be marvellous if Sheila had conical nipples? And would they emboss her breasts or weigh them down? I glanced at her beside me to see if I could possibly tell. I couldn't. The flower-print confused the outline. I wasn't getting very far.

Then panic. Supposing I never got a chance. She might want to go straight to Windermere and say goodbye and thanks for the lift. A cheery wave and a nice smile, then back into her South African travel poster and that would be that. I'd never know; be haunted by not knowing for the rest of my life. End up by advertising desperately in the *Capetown Gazette.* No, that mustn't be. I must devise it somehow.

Carlisle delayed us a bit, but not enough. She drank one lager-and-lime in a timbered pub. The publican eyed her as lecherously as I felt, and his glances made me feel proud. My bit of stuff, this. In no time we were back on the road and it was still only early afternoon. Dull country, what was more. No, the Lake District itself was my only hope.

It was Beatrix Potter who came to my rescue. An unlikely saviour with her clogs and feathered friends. We took the minor road along the east side of Ullswater in the late afternoon. And there across the water with the sinking sun over to the left was Owl Island. Did she not know Squirrel Nutkin, and old Mr Brown? Of course. Her eyes lit up, and she gazed out over the water. Was this truly where he lived? Surely! Did she not remember – how could a girl with such breasts care about Squirrel Nutkin? – did she not remember the little rafts of twigs that set out in line to gather nuts from Mr Owl's island, each squirrel with its tail for a sail? Remember the pictures of the old trees overhanging the lake? There they still are. Truly.

She was amazed. Delighted. She ran over from the car and began to clamber about the giant tree-roots down on the shoreline. I walked to the top of the bank while she explored and exclaimed below. Again that marvellous valley between deep breasts, widening and closing as she peered for traces of Squirrel Nutkin. But still no nipples. Pale or dark? Spreading or conical? I was getting quite academic about it.

The stones on the foreshore were slippery and black. Already the sunlight was filtered through a comb of pine-trees towards Helvellyn. It was quiet, windless, warm. Splashes of pale orange zigzagged over the lake. We were standing with our feet in the water. She looked thrilled. The odalisque had transformed into a naiad, hair loose over her shoulders, jeans rolled above the knee, midriff smoothed by wet hands, arms semaphoring to keep balance. The only sound a ripple of water against our ankles. The lake grey, the trees above us still ablaze.

She couldn't leave now, could she? This place had discovered her, must keep her awhile.

—We should bathe, I said.

Had she heard? Soon it would be twilight. Warm and still. The lake cold and magnetic. She could not take her eyes off it.

—Wouldn't that be great, I added? I hoped my eagerness sounded nonchalant enough, as if to suggest that what, after all, could be more normal than jumping in all starkers here and now. If she was that innocent it wouldn't matter, modesty only being required for the damned. There's no one here for miles, I said, and felt I'd said enough, while my heart thumped away like a beam-engine.

If she said Yes, then this had to be the moment. I would have to see her nipples. I could hardly fail to, surely. Even if she had a swim-suit in the car she'd still have to change, and change out of it again. And would she have a towel? No, we would just strip off in happy innocence, the two of us.

Of course she might say No! But she continued to say nothing at all, watching the light turn grey and the lake soft like velvet. Then she turned and walked under the high bank, and I followed.

She unzipped her jeans. I froze. Her back to me, she slid them off, balancing carefully on one leg, then the other. Then her pants. There were roses on them. Then three deft tugs on the bows holding her blouse, and she unwound it, dropped it behind her with the flick of a hand. Without turning she picked her way over the stones. Long, long legs, buttocks, slim tapering back, sloping shoulders streaked with blonde hair. As she held out her arms for balance at the water's edge the crescent of her breasts broke the line of her back on either side.

I had only to join her and she would turn to me. Even to think of touching her now would pollute such paradise. We would share the water like an element of the spirit. She was up to her thighs as I reached the water's edge. I was glad she had her back to me after all. Everything was waiting for the right moment. It would be perfect.

And then quite casually she turned. Was there a second in which I knew what was happening before it happened? Enough, anyway, to be aware that I was rising to her like a football crowd. Help! This golden creature who had never set eyes on a man, who had displayed such trust; what treachery was I committing? And I clamped both hands over my shame and stumbled as fast as possible into the freezing lake with my eyes lowered. When the flash of panic was over we were both in the water, swimming peacefully into the silver twilight. I did not believe, to my relief, that she had noticed.

And I had seen nothing.

"Dear Gareth", Ricky's letter began. "I only wanted to write and thank you for your tremendous support at the Festival. We're all looking forward immensely to the programme tomorrow. By the way, I thought the best token of my appreciation to you would be Sheila. Lucky bastard! I had to share her with half the cast. What a fantastic fuck, isn't she? I told her I'd heard you had the biggest prick south of the border, and she said she couldn't wait. I bet you stopped at the first inn outside Edinburgh. How about those innocent-looking girls, then? Here's to South Africa. À l'attaque, mon vieux. See you soon, if you've recovered. All the best, Ricky. P.S. If you come across a pair of tits like that again, send them north, will you? I think at least you owe me that."

* * *

It still makes me angry. Who the hell taught me to respect innocence and slobber over it? Honour thy virgins and thy urges! Like a stockbroker hiding his erection under a bowler-hat. It's the sort of thing I'd expect Eric to do if he had the chance.

I'm reassured to see Eric through the half-open door this morning, the balding head bowed over receipts. Immaculate papers being fed alternately to the two plain dollies he keeps as secretaries. Janet's sarcastic about them. I adore Janet. After my dream of tits this morning I'm more than usually aware of hers. I suppose I could have them, *droit de seigneur*, but it's David she fancies and I'm too proud to interfere.

I've got a writer in mind for the Arab films. Phoned Waldron to tell him this morning, and to thank him for the weekend. Barry O'Rourke the novelist and travel-writer. Waldron thought it a marvellous idea. O'Rourke lived in Damascus for years, then in the Gulf with the British Council. He's an international name and he's known to be cynical about the Jews, which will help grease Arab palms. Not that I can bear British Arabists. They seem to me the most detestable bunch of prats ever spawned by the public school system. That series I did for the BBC about desert explorers finished them off for me. Privileged perverts, all of them, flagellating their way through the stink and heat to claim some miserable swamp for England before retiring to write purple prose in the shires.

O'Rourke's not at all like that. None the less he is "moved" by their endeavours. He admires the heroic quality in Arab life. He sees an underlying order in it. I'm buggered if I do. The Arab world is tolerable only when it's at least half Westernised, like Cairo or Algiers, sufficient to clean up some of the tat in the streets and tarnish some of the wailing bigotry of the mind.

Yes, O'Rourke will do it well enough. He's obviously running out of his own ideas, and is maybe ready for mine. These films will keep him from reflecting on his own decline for at least a year. He'll love it, I'll phone him and arrange lunch. Janet can come and poke her tits in his watery eye. She'll like that, the little bitch.

Of course I'm edgy today for other reasons. Waldron's offer of a feature film was a bombshell, much more than I realised at the time. How did he know, with his hard City wisdom, this was just the offer to taunt me most? It feels like now or never. At forty-two I've sailed safe long enough, been married long enough, made enough money, made enough women, grown bored enough and sharp enough and bitter enough to be able to strike for gold without fear. I can afford to employ a top-class number two for the Arab films to take the pressure off me; and by the time David begins to edit them I can have the big film worked out, even cast in my mind. I shall write the script myself, and direct and edit. Do or die. Unless I put that much into it I shall never do it at all.

How neat it all sounds. I feel elated, only a little scared. I'm on the move. Watch out, Gareth's coming. Polish up the Oscars.

David looks up from his reels of black spaghetti.

—If you don't get bloody moving, Gareth, and fix a studio, those United Nations pricks are going to be here for their dose of VD and we'll have nowhere to give it to them. What's up with you this morning? Too much of the old claret down at Wopping?

—Stuff it! But you're right, I must fix that studio. And Janet, sweetheart, look up Barry O'Rourke in the London phonebook, will you? If he's ex-directory, which he may be, get it from his publisher. Thurber and Thurber. And phone him.

—What shall I say?

—Just put him on to me.

—What d'you want him for?

—Invite him to lunch tomorrow. With you.

—Me? Is he as sexy as his books?

—I need you to be nice to him.

—In other words wear something see-through.

—How did you guess?

—Gareth employs you for your tits not your mind, didn't you know that by now? (David didn't raise his head from the cutting machine.) I merely get them in my face when I'm trying to edit a VD film.

Janet looks annoyed and jerks her sweater down to flatten them. Gives David a kick. David doesn't respond. He goes on turning the handle of the cutter forward and back, to get the right frame. Janet reaches for the telephone directory. I dial the number of the studio. I haven't thought about my marriage all morning. I wish I hadn't remembered it now.

I couldn't bear to go home last night. Went to a hotel. Straight from Wopping to Wandsworth would have been too much. I don't think I'm particularly jealous of lover-boy, just sad and envious of what he can get that I can't, never will be able to now. I even feel a gust of happiness for her that he can make her happy.

But he'll not have my kids. I want none of his pie-in-the-sky Trot culture smeared over them. Deirdre, Seth, Ennis – I find myself repeating their names, and there are tears in my eyes now. Sometimes I break down when I'm alone and think about being alone, think about them alone. Small creatures asleep as I go to bed. Yes, I know children are only borrowed and all too soon handed back, but I want to be part of their growing up. And in the family house. Not just in a bachelor flat where Daddy moved after Mummy left him, far from their friends, their books, their toys, the places they know, the things we've done together. I cannot smash all that or it would smash me. I might smash lover-boy if he touched that.

So I'm mean. It's our home by the river. We've made it. We may have made a muck of it, but we've made it nonetheless. And there I stay. Jennifer can leave if she chooses, but the children and she and bloody lover-boy will know that here is home. Deirdre, Seth, Ennis: come home! Do you really want to live with Mummy and that man? Figures in the wilderness.

It will be dark when I get home this evening. But I know every stone I cannot see. Flowers are still flowers in the night.

And blackest night sits in the mouth of the moon.

* * *

It was a new spring of the heart. I was obsessed by the need for my marriage to be reborn. Why? I didn't need Jennifer any longer. I had lived more or less happily alone. And yet . . . what was it? That Jennifer, I knew, wanted me back? A sense of unfinished business? Or was it plain masochism: let me live my life in darkness? I don't know.

But I did need to go back, although not in too much of a hurry.

That, too, I wanted to savour, prepare for. And the womb of those preparations was the Casa Bella.

It was March. I'd been separated six months. A friend told me about the Casa Bella. In the hills above Bordighera. It was an eagle's nest, he said, on the shoulder of a mountain with a view of the sea, even Corsica on a fine day. Was I interested? He couldn't afford it. Wished he could. Surely I could. It wasn't much. Then I could lend him the place, couldn't I?

I flew to Nice that weekend and hired a car. It was a spontaneous gesture, a risk, a waste of money and all the things I felt thrilled to overrule. The Riviera was drenched in the scent of mimosa between violent spring storms. Deep damp snow in the hills. I spotted the house from far down the valley, a white spot against an alpine sky. The road zigzagged through the slush. Tree-heather bent by the weight of snow. Brilliant blue anemones under the pines. Hoopoes darting before the car on black and white wings. Wayside trattorias with weathered sun-blinds. Terracing. Ranks of low glasshouses. Finally bare hillsides threaded by goat-tracks, stained green here and there by hidden springs.

I parked the car some distance from the house and pulled on a heavy sweater against the cold. The light was sharp; mountains hard as diamonds all around; a distant glimpse of the sea laid like a carpet of ice far down the way I had come. A track led off towards a pine-wood, emerging again under a high crag. I set off – before even calling at the house – my feet slipping on stones loosed by rivulets of melting snow. A squirrel leapt the path and showered me with ice-cold water. Strokes of sunlight crossed the path. I paused for breath with my hand on a rock. Everywhere total silence. No wind. I came out on to the hard shale under the crag and sat on a stone in the sun. Took out an apple from my pocket. Down there was the wood I'd walked, below it the white house perched on a blade of rock, and beyond the slalom of road disappearing towards the sea.

Yes! Here was where I would be reborn. Even my love for Jennifer would be reborn. This space, this peace, this banquet before me; here were ingredients to nourish the soul, and the mirror of all my hopes. Here no man could fail a second time. Here we would grow, and feast. Here we would have children. We would learn who we were. Tomorrow had become a mighty book to be absorbed.

Day Eight

(*Camden Town*, May, year 24.) It wasn't exactly a sadness which accompanied her always. She could brighten in a second with that enchanting shy laugh half choked-back. No, not sadness. It was more something absent in her mind, a vacancy, she didn't know what it was, only that she couldn't always understand what was going on. It gave her that look of being elsewhere, nowhere. At these moments the small face would soften, eyes search for some lost contact, and the diminutive body appear helplessly exposed and threatened. These were the moments when I loved her most. If she'd loved me I should have married her, certainly. But then if she'd loved me . . . what does that mean? She did in her own way: it was another lost contact her eyes searched for. It was as if even then she sensed she had left it too late to be young; that there were already shadows across the springtime.

Shadows across the room. She was by the open window seated on the white-painted table, arms clasped across raised knees. Only her toes moved to a tune I couldn't hear. Her eyes were watching her toes. Small arched feet. A taller arch of slender legs was crossed by those white arms. Knees pressed together, muscles taut. Arms brushed by down as fair as the skin. Buttocks resting on the white table. Creases, not folds, across the stomach above a light thatch of hair. The ripple of a backbone, bow-shaped and outlined against the open window, against the trees, houses, chimneys. White shoulders hunched, clouds moving behind them just perceptibly. Face almost hidden by ashen hair. Hair over the eye and cheek, over the arms, some curled there, some curtaining the thighs, some cascading to the belly falling free of the breasts. Small triangles of breasts pin-pointed. The toes still moved.

No, not a sadness. An absence. Absent from the room, from me, from herself. She simply *was*, like a portrait. Was that why I loved her? Being able sometimes to coax – a painting to life?

She raised her head. That shy tremor of a smile again. She reached for me with one hand, lowering her eyes to me. Then the other hand. I cupped her breasts. The nipples hardened against my palms. I kissed her. I loved her.

* * *

By June the Casa Bella was mine. It needed only a small loan repayable over two years. No problem with a job like mine. The word "prospects" cropped up at significant moments.

—We're happy to help people like you, the bank manager said.

—Thank you, I said.

Within a week I drove out to Italy – alone. I was exultant. I was still holding Jennifer off. Unfinished business. I was not ready yet. She didn't know about the house. That could wait too. I was also feasting off my freedom, now I knew it would soon come to an end. Catherine had gone and had left me with a taste for my pleasures raw. Raw work, raw success, raw self-confidence, raw bodies. All were new to me. And yet within the brash boy a new love ached to be born.

It would be born here among these hills. I remember that first morning, waking to the sunlight under rough blankets on a bare mattress. I stepped on to the balcony and breathed in the mountains. It must have been around six o'clock. Before the wind rose. I tried to picture what the downstairs of the house – my house! – looked like. The kitchen with the ancient range and red-tiled floor. Dark. The sitting-room dark too: small windows and massive walls to keep out the summer and winter. And the little room next to it that was already my study in my mind, with windows on two sides, one on to the lane I'd walked up that first morning in March, the other opening on to the little private garden behind low walls and lilac-trees, a garden of lavender and acacia bushes and a crumbling well. And beyond the screen of bushes glimpses of a scabby hillside sweeping out of sight into the valley.

I wanted to see that room again: I couldn't exactly picture it, and I ran out of the bedroom, down the staircase, the marble slabs cracked and loose under my bare feet. (I'd fix them. Today even.) Then I lifted the heavy wooden latch into that tiny room. It was half-dark. The window catches were damp and stiff. The french windows creaked open towards me. I pushed out the green wooden shutters and instantly a hum of early morning filled the room. Bees were criss-crossing over the lavender: a swallow-tail butterfly floated on the air among the acacias. I stepped on to the deep grass, so green there must be a spring here somewhere. The sun was on my naked body. I felt slim, in good shape. I pissed on the path, waving my prick about to spray the bushes in a gesture of ownership which made me laugh. Holding my prick made me wish I had a girl here, and I felt it rise in my hand. I looked down at such a machine, free-standing now and looking a bit ridiculous there all alone winking at the sun. I shook it from side to side and it slapped my hips left and right. I laughed again; walked round the little garden wondering what an erection looked like from that buzzard's vantage-point up there. Perhaps it was just what he'd been waiting for all spring. "*Buzzard takes BBC man's erection.*" I was just standing there minding my own business, officer, honest!

The buzzard floated away on the air currents across the valley. I was here alone because I wanted to be alone. I stepped back through the french windows. This room I would make my own – to work in, think, dream, heal. I'd go and buy some furniture for it today. I had enough money with me surely for a desk, a couple of chairs, a bookshelf, an electric fire, a table-lamp. And a rug of some sort. A cocoon. Perhaps some of it would have to wait. What did it matter? What did anything matter so long as I could retreat here, build myself anew here?

I had never wanted children until I came here. Now I did. I looked forward to them. And there was no question in my mind, they had to be Jennifer's children, and would be. Already Jennifer belonged here in my life as she had never done. The thought of bringing her here, sharing all this with her, thrilled me. We'd find space for one another, we'd begin again with lessons painfully learnt, mistakes not to be repeated. We'd even love, make love. Wouldn't we? Would not fear melt away in the peace of our lives? Would not tenderness turn our bodies together in warmth and trust and gratitude? Wasn't that enough to kindle a fire? If we could learn to laugh. If we could forget. If we could hold each other's hand. It would all come in time, wouldn't it? Yes.

That morning I went down to Bordighera and shopped in the market. I was not a tourist: this was my home. I bought two litres of red Bardolino. I bought half-a-dozen round fluted rolls and a great hunk of Parmesan cheese. I bought white peaches and huge fat misshapen tomatoes. Then I called in on the electricity office, the water board, the lawyers, the police. Did all the proper things. Now I belonged. Soon I'd even be in the local telephone book.

Then I drove back to my eagle's nest and laid out my picnic in the garden among the grasshoppers and the hawk-moths, and full of wine I lay and blinked up at the sky. My sky. My peace. My future. And I slept with an arm over my eyes and thought of nothing at all.

Back in London, still I didn't return to Jennifer. We phoned. We met. We spat. Mostly we prowled round one another out of striking range. She insisted on more time. (I was relieved.) We both had vital adjustments to make, had we not? Maybe. I went back to the flat in Ladbroke Grove and screwed Catherine, who was back from Italy with an appetite.

In some ways these were the most despicable months of my life: at least they seem so now. During the evening I parleyed and parried with Jennifer, holding out my sincerity with both hands: at night I fucked Catherine: during the day I made films about culture.

If I'd been honest with Jennifer she would have screamed and gone for good. If I'd been honest with Catherine she'd have laughed with contempt and gone too. And if I'd been honest with myself the films would have gone as well, for they too were compounded of pretences each set against the other, though the results were highly professional and therefore beyond reproach. Journalism, like art, keeps its own standards of excellence which eschews all account of motives. So long as you were seen to do it well, you got away with it and your integrity was taken for granted. Certainly I believed, swore, that Gareth Penrhyn was an honest man. And under that banner I strutted to a modest glory.

And Jennifer? I believe she loved me. Hardline shrinks implied that ours was the marriage of true masochists, and that we found our true satisfaction – even creativity – in the intervals between blood-letting. Certainly I believe Jennifer, like me, experienced a nostalgia for the awful and exquisite peace that settles on a battlefield at the end of the day. We shared a conviction that without fighting the good fight the process of days was uncomfortably simple – flat, stale and unprofitable. What, after all, was real pleasure unless hard-fought, hard-won?

* * *

So O'Rourke will do it. I feel pleased. The six Arab films will be in good hands. It was clear from our lunch that he regards working in the media as prostitution, and that nothing would give him greater pleasure. That's an endearing quality successful authors have: they make a song-and-dance about the purity of their calling, and the first moment they get a chance to corrupt it they behave like Sidcup housewives called up on the stage in a TV chat-show.

If all's well we'll go to North Africa and the Middle East on a "recce", the two of us, next month. O'Rourke will be good company, and the trip will take care of my first month after Jennifer departs. It's all working out happily.

Janet and I are walking back along Old Compton Street, having said goodbye to O'Rourke outside the Epicure. It's a cold afternoon. Dust in the eyes. A flurry of torn newspapers. Rotten fruit in the gutter. Janet's hands are deep in the pockets of her green overcoat.

—He's fun, isn't he? . . . I think he fancied me.

—Are you surprised?

—Well, you did ask me to look sexy.

—I know.

My eyes had been on that see-through blouse most of lunch; at those dark nipples presiding over the *steak au poivre*. Janet really does have the most spectacular tits, I tell myself as if I'd had no time to notice in the six months the girl's been working for me. It's just that they haven't been thrust at me quite so nakedly before. What is it they say: if a girl can hold a pencil beneath her breasts then she needs a bra? Jesus, Janet could hold a pair of roofing tiles and the builder wouldn't know where to find them. Coarse bugger, Penrhyn.

—You'd better put a bra on this afternoon or David'll do no work at all.

Lucky David, the bastard! It's for him Janet wore the see-through, not O'Rourke or me.

I feel old. Janet's twenty years younger than me. It's a long climb up to the office. The boozy slump of the afternoon. I'll plunge into work and swim through it.

Eric's waiting at the door of his room, that frightened excited look on his face which always means someone important has phoned.

—Lord Waldron phoned, Gareth.

—I'll ring him back. Get me Waldron, will you, love?

The fake Cockney familiarity covers up the fact that I cannot remember the receptionist's name.

Waldron is at his City office. I can tell he's been at one of his power lunches. NBC in America would definitely like the Arab films, he says. What would I consider a reasonable price? Something unreasonable. A hell of a lot anyway. Why the hell's he asking me? He knows what he can get. More trust. Great, now no problems about the "recce" next month, nor about an assistant director to free me for the feature-film.

What feature-film?

My feature-film, remember! There'll be no turning back now, Gareth bach.

I steal one of Eric's secretaries and dictate letters to the Arabs dressed in the most elaborate courtesies. Confirmation of this and that to Waldron. A stream of memos. Letters to banks. Letter to the UN film department inviting them to view VD. Letter to the Swiss tourist board. Letter to the Head of General Features at BBC Television. Letter to NBC in the States. Finally a jovial letter to O'Rourke, which I enjoy. I realise I like him a lot. He's many things I admire. He's a good deal older than I am for a start. He's well read; he's worldly. He's ruthless and compassionate. He laughs a lot and his laughter sounds like a dimension of his wisdom. He is not fooled, therefore I don't feel the need to fool him, an intense relief. My cynicism about his dried-up talent is really an inverted admiration, I realise. If I could achieve what he has achieved at sixty I'd be happy. Why else do I admire him? Because he's been through the fire, I think, in a way I've never quite found the courage to do. A bloody-minded optimism has sustained him, a deeply engrained conviction that in the end life couldn't really drop him in the shit. He'd come up with an answer in time: maybe that deep belly-shuddering laugh would be enough to save him. He'll be good to travel with. Maybe he'll be just the man to spark off ideas in me for the big film. My feature-film! The one that matters.

Why should it matter so much? Why did that gesture of confidence from Waldron only three days ago have such an effect? Let me try and clarify it to myself. At forty-two I've now done what I was taught to do. I've achieved all that was ever expected of me. I've made good. And yet I've failed. They would not say that I've failed back in Portmadoc, where they're all waiting to make me mayor as far as I can see; the BBC would not say it either – I'm the bright one who got away; Wardour Street would not say it – I'm a success, look at this outfit I've got. But I say it. Because my life has been devoted to the application of acquired skills, and each skill has been another coat of armour, another carapace, behind which I have learnt to shrink in safety but also in fear. Instead, I long for enterprises which will wring my soul and which in turn will mould me and bring me strength.

Oh, Gareth bach, you sound like Hamlet playing the Fool again. All the same I feel euphoric. I'd quite forgotten the little slip of a secretary sitting there smoothing her skirt with small fingers, shorthand pad on knees. Here's Janet coming over to show off. Still no bra. The girl, pencil-poised, shrivels a little within her Tudorose Angel.

—OK, Ann. Don't bother to start typing all that tonight. Tomorrow'll do. Take yourself off, love, if you want to.

—Thank you, Mr Penrhyn.

—Goodnight then.

She nods shyly and slips out of the room. Eric will be fussed that I sent the girl off a quarter of an hour early. Matter of principle. Who knows what they may expect next? David's due back from a dubbing session. Janet'll be waiting for him. That's why she's hanging around.

—Any more lunches coming up, then?

—Haven't you done enough damage to a man's libido for a while?

What an irritating girl Janet is. Nothing in her head at all. All out in front. Heavy-handed too. Unsubtle. I'm sure she smells of sweat in bed. I don't like her. Wish I'd never taken her to lunch.

—Thank you for today, Gareth.

Her face is soft. Serious for a moment. A smile in her dark eyes. It takes me by surprise. I am grateful.

—I'm glad you came.

She has only half turned to go. She pauses.

—It must be hard for you.

Now I'm confused, startled. I have never thought of Janet as a feeling person. So it's my insensitivity; type-casting again. Does she mean my marriage? Of course she must know what's happening. Or perhaps she just means it's hard for me in my job, running the show.

—Sometimes.

I am non-committal to avoid misunderstanding her. So I say it again, string it out, giving her the chance to elaborate.

—Yes, I suppose it's hard, sometimes.

There is silence between us for a moment.

—I can't imagine going home to someone I didn't love.

So she did mean that. Suddenly I am very lonely. Such a small, almost brusque sign of caring from someone I don't care about. Enough to dispel the exhilaration. I don't want Janet to walk away. I wish she'd stay and talk. What could I say that would keep her here? I need to share a little warmth with someone who knows me and means nothing to me. I don't want the afternoon to end. I don't want to walk alone down those stairs into the street. The hostile, uncaring street. I want someone, anyone, to be by my side.

David is back, fucking and damning about the incompetent dubbing-mixer. He fixes his eyes on Janet.

—Jesus, dem watermelons! Wow-ee!

Janet bridles and brushes past him. He calls after her.

—You don't need a bra you need a bloody fork-lift!

I am angry with David. And hurt. He has a wife. He has a life to go home to. A welcome. My God, how I would love a welcome. I have a large car and a house on the river which will soon be mine alone. Jennifer is leaving me. Why should I care; she has never been by my side?

How does a man begin again? By being very stubborn, very courageous, is that it? Knowing himself extremely well? That's harder. Don't we always assume we know ourselves intimately until things go wrong and then we're suddenly lost? Or perhaps it's a matter of being more honest at every step than is comfortable, and not asking where the path leads; of being honest about all the unimportant things. Perhaps a man can be pieced together out of those thousands of insignificant fragments until one unexpected day he's there on two feet in the sunlight. But where does the process begin? Now – yes! Always now, this moment, one step at a time, one thought at a time. Remember, the last compromise is the compromise of the heart.

The office is empty. I am going out into the street. I am going home.

Day Nine

(*Oxford*, June, year 23.) On Finals day they sent me a rose. It didn't help with Dante and Boccaccio but it perfumed the day with dreams. And in the dusk they flitted across the shadows to the fence opposite my window and whispered:

—How did it go?

There were six of them. Their finishing school lay behind the lighted windows facing my rooms and behind the curtains which, as they grew bolder, they took to leaving a little parted while they undressed for bed, taking it in turns to pass and re-pass across the chink of light like naked tinkerbells. Once Imogen, whose father was something grand in port and far enough away to believe his daughter might be acquiring the gloss of Oxford without any dangerous thoughts, dared to stand in full view for at least five seconds. And the giggling and demonstrations of shame that went on afterwards, the peering round the curtains to see if I'd noticed – Jesus! Had I noticed! – continued for the best part of an hour, with me thumping in my heart for it to happen again and for rather longer next time, but nothing did.

Not that Imogen was the one I fancied most. She had mousey hair, an adolescent spotty face, and deflated little breasts perking up as if to ask for more. There were two girls I really liked there, but neither of them ever stood naked by the window, alas. There was Lola, who was not Mexican nor Spanish but pure Sunbury-on-Thames with a theatrical mother several divorces back, she told me, which accounted for the name, as well as for the larger-than-life gestures, the extravagant hats, eye make-up and faint lisp. I adored Lola: occasionally she'd slip away from her corrective establishment under the pretence of posting a letter and pay me a frantic visit, hiding from the window all the while as I willed the kettle to boil faster so that she could gulp a cup of coffee before hurtling off again in a jangle of beads. I never knew whether she expected me to seduce her in that time, though the thrill and prospect of seduction would hang over our heads like a heavy scent the entire ten minutes she'd be there. She burst in once and clasped her bosom to her hands:

—Thank heaven you're here, she gasped, the hamster's got out.

The other one I specially fancied was Harriet. She was the only one who didn't giggle. When I passed them in the High Street (they were permitted to attend approved lectures on art, Shakespeare and constitutional law – why constitutional law?) Harriet was the one who didn't nudge and twitter. She kept a straight face and pretended not to see. Harriet was serious, was not interested in lost hamsters and trysts at twilight. But then Lola, on one of her breathless visits, told me it was Harriet who had dared Imogen to stand naked by the window, that Harriet would have done it herself if she hadn't thought I would be ashamed of her, that it was Harriet who moaned on her pillow at night, Harriet who regarded me as hers for ever and ever and who would scratch the eyes out of Lola if she knew Lola were at this very moment having coffee here when she'd told her all she was doing was going to the post.

What's more Harriet had sent the rose. Lola told me that, too, the day after my Finals were over. She arrived in a cascade of black hair and black shawls early in the morning to say they were breaking up tomorrow, and please would I try to meet Harriet this evening. She had an excuse and the old vixen had let her out for supper. She'd be under the lime-tree by the gate to the Meadow at eight. Please be there. Then Lola was gone. She darted back to kiss me goodbye: did she really want to be Harriet's hand-maid? I felt her breasts against me as we kissed longer than goodbye; then she broke away and was cantering down the stairs and across the lawn. It was the last I saw of her (though I did see her photograph in the papers a few years later when she married a playboy, and another of her later still when she left him for a racing driver).

So Harriet had sent the rose. The idea excited me. She was the one I had least suspected. We had scarcely exchanged a glance. But who was Harriet? What sort of girl was she? I realised I scarcely knew what she looked like. I kept looking at my watch. It was still only 7.30. I couldn't stand pacing up and down the room any longer. I walked to the river, taking a path which I knew must occupy twenty minutes at least, even if I hurried which I determined not to do. That would only leave ten more. I felt agitated, shaking. I was meeting a girl who – it seemed – loved me blindly, who had never spoken, who had been clocking my every movement for – how long? – the past two months certainly. Irresistible. Yes, I had always fancied Harriet from a distance, come to think of it; I liked the quizzical look of her face (intelligent, sharp, reflective she must be); liked the shape of her, liked the trim way she walked, liked the purple blouses she wore, like the freckles on her face and the small prominent ears. But particularly I liked that walk – she seemed to pivot as she moved. Yes, I wanted to love her. Yesterday she was just a pretty girl; today I was ready for her to be mine. We'd never spoken, only observed one another in our own time: wasn't that a perfect beginning? An Oxford idyll. Here I was, at the end of my schooling, at the door of the world. I would walk through that door with Harriet hand in hand. The summer evening seemed to bless such thoughts. Swallows dipped over the river.

It was almost time to meet her. What would I say? Hello? And in what tone of voice? And what was her voice like? I had no idea. I had heard occasional bursts of laughter across the lawn; that was all. There was the big lime-tree: no Harriet yet. Soon they'd close the Meadow. We'd climb over. I knew a place. I'd help her over. Carry her: she must be very light. The feel of her slight body in my arms. A charge shot through me.

And there she was at the end of the lane, walking slowly, close to the wall. I waited under the lime-tree as she approached without a smile, eyes down. Harriet was coming close. Hello!

I fell in love like a man on a water-chute. I was swimming in love, swimming in her eyes – deep blue, I had never noticed their colour before – swimming in her soft hoarse voice, in the feel of her hands ("nobody, not even the rain, has such small hands"), in the smell of her, the touch of her, in the stillness of her as the darkness gathered round us by the river where I kissed her lips and her tongue slipped between mine. It didn't seem in the least romanticised and rubbishy: not at all, it was true. For once all the voices were in tune; "somewhere I have never travelled", and would never, never need to travel again, because I had arrived. Harriet's long intense kisses would explore the rest of my life.

I saw her only once more. Daddy was a company director,

Mummy the Lady Something. Their Queen Anne mansion surveyed Cranborne Chase via sauntering peacocks on the long lawn. My father is a butcher in Portmadoc. Harriet's former playroom was her disco. We jived (remember jiving?) and her movements were as sleek as a whippet's. Her blouse was opened low, her breasts freckled as far as the line of her bikini. Her eyes were wide and full of wonder. Deep, deep blue. There was a tap on the window: Mummy was wagging a forefinger. It was time to go. My motorcycle spat up gravel along the drive. She never even invited me to her coming-out dance.

* * *

In September I went back to Jennifer. It had been eleven months. She was thirty. I was twenty-eight. I had gone back to jail. We were both meticulously polite: at first it was an effort to be so – the old sensation of walking in a minefield. At the same time the watchfulness with which we trod brought its quiet rewards. We paid precise attention to small things – little courtesies and little pleasures – and this surprisingly enhanced their quality: meals, saying good morning, walks by the river, discussing films, shopping, the garden. We were slowing up the pace, finding time to stop and admire the flowers by the roadside. An atmosphere of peace settled on us like a fixative. Life was slower, smaller, safer and more numb. At least I felt more numb, and sensed Jennifer did too. It was as if we had made a deliberate effort to anaesthetise powerful feelings of any kind. They might be explosive; best not to risk them. We were convalescents taking great care, holding one another gently by the elbow. Ours was the way of survivors. And between my legs hung a little thing to pee with.

Only fleetingly did dark fires flicker in my dreams, and just once they flared and brought a stab of pain. It was an evening before Christmas. A party. Jennifer couldn't come, wouldn't come, I can't remember. I would go, I said, for an hour; no more. There was a throb of rock-'n-roll. A heavy wine punch. One room with lights on low corner-tables; a room next-door with none. I was a prisoner on parole. A black girl with a black slashed dress had predatory hands which brushed my neck and hair as she danced. I drew my fingers down her bare back and kissed her like a starving man. She laughed and pressed against the bolt of my prick.

—Man, you want it bad, don't you? You're a fucker. I think I'd like you tonight.

—I can't. Not tonight.

—Whyever not, honey?

—I have to go home.

She laughed in a flash of white teeth in the darkened room.

—Is Mummy waiting then?

—A wife.

And she laughed again.

—Darling, you'd so much rather come with me.

And as if there could be any doubt she let her dress fall from her shoulders and placed my hands on her breasts.

—Tell me you don't like that.

—I want you like crazy.

—Take me for the night, then – all night! None of your "Wham bam thank-you, ma'am!"

—I can't.

—Fuck you!

And she vanished, returning her breasts to her dress. I felt about fifteen and virginal. I picked my way across a tumble of bodies on floor-cushions near the door. Two couples were making love like automata side by side – bottoms up, bottoms down. A man all alone lurched across the television, holding a wine-glass above a plate of baked-beans studded with cigarette-butts. A girl with stringy red hair was holding out her bra absent-mindedly to a man with a glass he was bringing her; his trousers were tripping him around the ankles and his pants were stretched between his knees. From behind her a pair of hands found her breasts and pulled her back into the shadow. There was a gurgle of laughter, and the man with the glass looked around perplexed. A hand reached up, singed his pubic hair with a cigarette and said "Pardon!" The silhouette of another man wobbled into a shaft of light holding his cock in one hand and a glass in the other, and farted. A girl was kneeling being sick into a waste-paper basket in the corner, tits dangling like damp sacks. A man with a small sad erection under his belly looked on. There was a desolate mist of rain in the street. I was going home.

—Nice party?

Jennifer was reading in bed. She smiled happily, maybe choosing not to notice I was drunk.

—OK. No one I knew.

—Pity.

—I'm tired.

—Come to bed then.

—I'll do that. Just do my teeth.

I did my teeth.

—Goodnight, darling!

—Night!

I was grateful for the night. An owl hooted across the square. I laughed aloud.

—What is it?

—I farted. Sorry!

—Christ!

—Goodnight!

Before Christmas we redecorated the flat and hung new pictures.

We listened to music on a new hi-fi.

We bought a new car and explored the New Forest at weekends, spending my salary well.

We re-established selected old friends who understood.

We put up Christmas decorations and I came in the door with tears in my eyes.

We began to feel safe.

And in the spring we were going to drive out to the Casa Bella. I told Jennifer about it cautiously, hoping she would not take fright. It would be waiting for us in the sun and wind within a panorama of all my hopes.

* * *

A grey blade of river in the dawn, curving towards Battersea. Over the water a block of flats is awakening like distant campfires. That is where Jennifer will soon be, curled up with the Thoughts of Mao. Meanwhile she has moved into the attic to sleep. At last! A small point scored by me. Why should it make any difference? But it does. It has made her parting a reality. She is leaving. So long as she was sharing my bed it still felt like a painful game we were playing. Now she is really moving away, moving out of my life. I feel alone here. The house is quiet. I shall not move from it. The river protects me: my moat. The children are still asleep, Deirdre within a shambles of homework, Seth in a battlefield of Lego, Ennis with the cat. They shall not move over there; that is the enemy camp. I do not need Jennifer, but I need them.

And what about them? Do they need me? Of course, as father and all that, yes! But do they need me day by day? Do they need to be here with me? Jennifer feels on principle they should be offered the choice. She is full of that kind of principle. (Another is that she would never deprive them of me. She would!) So far she has baulked at offering them any such choice, maybe out of fear of the answer. Instead she snaps about not wishing to make the children pawns in our chess-game, by which she means I already do. I do. On principle she doesn't. She does. I love them: lover-boy doesn't, I say.

—That's irrelevant!

—Not to me it's not.

—David cares for me and he's responsible.

—For what?

—He's a responsible person, that's all. He can help provide a home. He would care for the children because he cares for me.

—And what about them?

—Children need a mother.

—But what about them? Their feelings?

—For Christ's sake, Gareth, they'll get used to it.

—Get used to seeing you in bed with David?

—Oh, God! It's impossible talking to you. You're utterly unrealistic and bitter. What is it you want? To punish me some more? Haven't you had enough?

—This is their home. I'd like them to live in it, that's all.

—What d'you mean, home?

—Where they live. What we've built for them.

—Shit!

—All right, take me to court.

—You really are a shit. You always play it dirty, don't you?

—You make me hate you.

—You always have.

I chucked the dish-cloth at her.

That was last night. She swept upstairs, grabbed an armful of clothes and moved into the attic. I heard her stomping around. Yes, I was a shit. I wanted to be. I wanted to hurt her for giving up when she has every reason to give up. I wanted to hurt her for not believing I had always loved her when she has every reason not to believe me. I wanted to hurt her for not being prepared to smile and call it quits when she has every reason to believe I would take advantage of the truce to move up my armour. I wanted to hurt her for not making me desire her. I wanted to hurt her for not being happy. And for all these reasons she hates me, and I wanted to hurt her for that, too. Oh, in heaven's name where do you go from here, Gareth? Why don't I sensibly and quietly leave?

The last compromise is the compromise of the heart. I love her.

Icy wind from the river with the window open. Gull, carry my life on black wings.

Growing used to someone you've grown away from brings despair beyond strength, as splinters of past happiness scuttle in the memory.

Deirdre diving off rocks into a mountain river, and breaking the surface with laughter, Ennis shrieking excitedly on the shore. Seth found an enormous caterpillar in the heather and sat by it for ten minutes waiting for it to transform into an Emperor Moth.

—Tomorrow I'll come back, he said very seriously.

—Don't be stupid, Seth, said Deirdre, it takes a year, didn't you know?

—How d'you know the year's not up?

Jennifer on a Nile-boat in the evening, the great felucca sail rising like a drawn bow into an opal sky. Only the creak of a rudder and the sharp cry of a kingfisher.

Harriet with her feet beside me in the water, our ripples stirring the reflection of the moon.

Where did all that joy go?

Well, good morning dirty old Thames. Today I must make plans. Much to do. Coffee. Deirdre and Seth to school. A few pretty mothers to nod to. Morning in the Library of Oriental Studies. Lunch with Waldron and a director of Wessex Television, plus the chief backer for the Arab films. I think I'll try to get Archie Hill along. Janet can keep his Sufi hang-ups in check, and he works well with Matlock who's just about the best documentary cameraman in the business. I'll have to put up with his being queer.

What else? Dry-cleaning: I can drop that in on the way. Visas! God, yes! One of Eric's mice can fix those up. At least Waldron will see to all the rest of the red tape: he'll magic it into red carpets if I know him. O'Rourke should be funny on that one.

And now – shower, shave, clean clothes, breakfast with Jennifer hopefully absent, into the car and on with the day. Gareth's in gear. I'm all right today. The black birds have flown: dawn migrants. My world is waiting for me.

Day Ten

(*Cyprus,* May, year 20.) Our malice towards June camouflaged a collective virginity. It made each of us feel safer in our thin skin. At No 43 Royal Army Education Centre, Akrotiri Camp, we were ten National Servicemen, sergeant-instructors, a little scared of the brigadier, a good deal more scared of the war, and scared most of all of our pricks: nonetheless full of bonhomie, full of booze and full of school. We were here, ten virgin soldiers, because we were "edificated" (the regulars called us), and our task was to teach beribboned veterans the three Rs and a few slightly more sophisticated skills which their own education had failed to effect long ago; which is how June came into our lives.

How to describe June? She was a shade ridiculous with her little Marilyn Monroe affectations: that thin purring voice, the pert giggle with eyebrows raised, the pursing of the lips, the awareness of her own body centimetre by centimetre, the air of studied disingenuousness. All of this was rendered the more incongruous by a sergeant's uniform which bulged and flapped and fastened in unbecoming places.

June was a Christmas-tree fairy in battledress. What she could be doing in the Army I found it impossible to imagine, and maybe it was this evident absurdity which invited mockery. Not to her face, of course, we were too "edificated" for that; but behind her back we sneered with the kind of sadism special to young men used to playing tennis with nice girls and then wanking with *Health and Efficiency* in the loo. June was a spy in our house of love, and therefore disconcerting. She knew, too clearly, all that we did not know, all that might prove us to be inadequate. We joked about the size she would need, sensing that we hadn't got it; about how often she would want it, sensing that once might be all we could muster; about how she would like it best, sensing that we didn't know. And after classes were over and she'd left, the smell of her lingered about the corridors; not scent, which I don't believe she ever wore, but a body smell that was rich and hallucinogenic. The ghost of June that haunted No 43 Royal Army Education Centre in the evenings was not a stocky-looking figure in khaki battledress, livid stockings and sensible shoes; it was naked and luxuriant, and it troubled our dreams.

We arranged to meet in Niki's Bar in Byron Street, one of the few places troops were allowed in Limassol. Somehow amid this melodrama of hate there lay low an understanding between the British and Eoka that life must not be allowed to become entirely bestial. Certain sanctuaries therefore were respected: soldiers must not be in uniform, there would be no bombs thrown, journalists could meet their contacts there, soldiers their pick-ups, and in this way the subversive traffic of humanity could flourish. The Greek's knew, and we knew – yes, even we National Servicemen knew – that Makarios would win and should win; and Niki's Bar, like the bar of the Ledra Palace Hotel in Nicosia and the Spitfire Bar in Famagusta, was one of those places of assignation which ensured that the British Government's official view of the war would not corrupt us all. The regulars were different: they were mostly committed to beer and battle, and that was that. Theirs not to reason why. A terrorist was a terrorist the world over, and by such myopia and obedience the Governor and the Colonial Office safeguarded their own fantasies which were securely founded on an alloy of prejudice and ignorance. We did our tiny bit: we had to teach current affairs, and there were ways and ways of explaining to a thug corporal from the Gorbals what he was supposed to be doing here. As he usually didn't care a damn why he was here, subversion was not particularly difficult: neither was it particularly effective. Mind you, we had to be careful: one strong complaint and it would have been one-two-one-two-one-two, a court-martial and two years' jail.

Though they were murdering the Turks daily, I noticed that the Greeks still called it Turkish coffee, and a tiny cup of it on the wooden table in front of me sent up thin spirals of steam. The taste was bittersweet and I ordered another cup from Niki. He was a squat, unshaven man who seldom spoke except to shout at the vast Mrs Niki every few minutes as he swept the sawdust and the dead flies into a pile by the open door, and cast a baleful eye at anything in a trim skirt passing by. Niki was teaching me Greek twice a week. I'd been coming here for almost a year now, and today he seemed to sense I was not just dropping in as usual on a Saturday morning. He gave me his gold half-smile as he set the second cup on the table.

—So, who is today, Mr Gareth? A girl, heh?

—Maybe, Niki.

—I know, Mr Gareth. You nervous.

And he tapped his forehead, moving an empty chair opposite me a few inches and back again as if to emphasise the point.

—Greek girl?

—English girl.

—Ahhh! Very good, Mr Gareth. You all right here. But Greek girls better.

He clenched his fist and muscled his forearm.

—Much better!

And he ballooned his cheeks and spread a pair of hairy hands round enormous imaginary breasts. Maybe Mrs Niki was not so unfavoured after all.

—Melons!

Then, with a philosophical air,

—Very good!

Normally this would have been the curtain-raiser to one of Niki's more squalid tales, but not this morning. He was enjoying waiting for my girl.

Niki was right. I was nervous. Surprised too. How had this happened? I tried to recall the precise sequence of events on Thursday – two days ago. I'd finished teaching. Gone for a pee. Emerged into the corridor with my arm full of teaching notes, thinking about Cedar Valley where I'd decided I might spend the weekend. It was another of those sanctuaries, in what the Army called the Green Zone. My mind was miles away in the mountains amid the cherry harvest. Suddenly there was June right in my path on her way out of the Centre. In three seconds she would have passed me. I might have just smiled and waved goodbye as usual. I half thought I had. But no, I'd said something else: what was it? I don't remember; anyway it checked her step and there she was looking at me with black eyes and pursed lips not smiling, and that ridiculous hat, and I was saying come and spend Saturday with me in Limassol, and she was nodding and still not smiling, and her face was beautiful and young. Much younger than I'd thought: maybe twenty-three or twenty-four. Eleven o'clock at Niki's, Byron Street, d'you know it? Yes, she said. That's all she said. Yes! Softly like silk, and she was gone, and I was back in my room, sitting quite shaky on the bed still clutching my teaching notes. I kept saying to myself: What's happening to you? What the hell? What's happening? And all the time I knew what was happening to me perfectly well. I was going to have an affair. My first affair. I was going to be a lover. A real lover. Virginity goodbye. All those phantoms were going to blow away and I was about to step out of the classroom into the world.

I had never seen her out of uniform. Through the open window there was a girl in sunlight on the pavement, one hand on a leather-shoulder-bag, the other smoothing a white cotton skirt. Her legs were good, her feet small in open sandals. Her blouse was pink, tight over her breasts, hair glossy black with that becoming streak of white combed through it, and gold bracelets loose over her left wrist. As she hesitated by the open door Niki was staring at her, cloth partly raised. She came towards me. I felt proud.

—Coffee, Mr Gareth! And for you, Madame?

He paused to take a further look.

—Perhaps some very good Cyprus wine. The best for you, Mr Gareth. You a lucky man.

And he bent over me confidentially.

—Like Greek girl, he said in a stage whisper.

I thought he was going to do his big-tits routine but I underrated his delicacy. He went on admiring June as he ceremoniously pulled back the wobbly wooden chair.

It was midday, and muzzy with Niki's wine we walked through the tiny zoological garden behind the natural history museum. She talked in a light voice that was soothing and soft. Her face was soft too, and her hands. She shook her bracelets up her bare forearms and in the same movement steered a lock of hair from her eyes with her forefinger. I wanted to be with her.

She talked. She was half-Indian, from Wolverhampton. No father. Her mother had died five years ago. That was when she had joined the Army, to get away. The white streak of hair was natural: she was born with it. Do you like it, she said, turning to me? My fingers ran through her hair, and those damson eyes looked up at me. She took my hand in her cool hand. We stopped. I looked down at her eyes, her small nose, lips a little parted, the hollows of her shoulder-blades shaded by the lapel of her blouse, a thin shadow darkening between the rise of her breasts.

My arm was round her shoulder along Haggipavlou Street, where the kebab stalls smoked on the pavement and seafood restaurants sheltered under awnings tugged by the breeze. Old men in collarless shirts squatted by the roadside chewing pipes through grey stubble, hands resting on gnarled sticks. I looked at June and wanted her. We talked about Wales. I talked about my father's shop in Portmadoc, about the mountains, about the curlews on the moor, about the rocks and the sea. We gazed at the sea. I looked at her by the sea.

It was three o'clock: the air a weathered slab of heat. Thin cats stretched among fish-bones under café-tables. A dilapidated truck juddered over ruts towards the port, leaking gravel. A lone figure bent under a sack stuffed with greens shuffled past a row of Turkish shops, bombed and boarded. Beyond, the skeletons of offices, abandoned part-built, sprouted iron spikes into a haze of factory-smoke, and in the distance the forests of the Troodos Mountains lay colourless against an iron sky.

Our elbows were propped between wine glasses on a green metal table.

—Come to Katani with me.

I had never asked a girl anywhere except the Odeon. My little '39 Fiat Topolino was parked in the dust of Hellas Street. We could go now. Or swim first in the wine of the afternoon.

—I've got no swim-suit but I have got a weekend pass, she said.

I don't remember what else she said, but she looked. She looked. Dark hair over small hands under the chin. She was smiling, in the sun, in the war, in the doorway to my garden.

Six o-clock. The plain of Cyprus lay northwards under a shawl of evening. Her fingers were spread cool between mine. Chestnut trees overhung the path. She let go my hand and walked out into the sun, throwing back her head. The car was parked by a rock where a stream spouted beneath the road and spread out among cherry trees. The light shone through her blouse and a breeze rippled it against the shadow-line of her belly and the under-curve of her breasts as she turned. I wanted her: I followed her through the dust, and as I reached her she stretched up and picked a cluster of cherries overhanging the rock and held one to my lips. She wound her tongue round another, looked at me then placed one hand on my hip and slid her fingers up across my ribs. My hands smoothed her neck and she pushed her head forward to be kissed. My fingers were in her hair.

—I want you, I said.

—Where can we go in Katani? Is it really the Green Zone?

—Yes! Promise! No bombs. There's the Marangos Hotel.

—Do you always take your girls there?

She stepped back a little mockingly.

—I've never made love to anybody.

—I don't believe you.

—It's true.

She just looked at me. Then she spread her bare arms back across the bonnet of the car.

—Kiss me again.

I leant over her against the car and could feel the hard bone of her pelvis. Her hips seemed incredibly cool and liquid. She kissed for a long time, then took her weight off her hands and wound her arms round me.

—I do want you, she said under her breath.

The light was beginning to fade as I pushed open the rusted shutters of the french windows. Beyond the balcony the wooded valley lay deep with cherry and chestnut trees, studded with points of lights clustered in villages. A mule laden with a double-pannier of cherries clopped below the window. There was a peach-coloured sky over Morphou Bay to the left.

June was facing me across the room in the half-light. We said nothing, looking at one another for a few moments. I held out my arms and she came over to me by the window.

—Gareth, she said very softly when we'd kissed; is it true you've never made love?

—You know.

—Because I want you to want me. Very much. She was undoing the buttons of her blouse, slowly. Wait, she said, stepping back as I reached for her. Let me show you. She was watching me all the time with those deep dark eyes. I really want you to want me.

The fading light stroked the skin of her shoulder. Her hair fell forwards as in one movement she unzipped her skirt and stepped out of it and out of her shoes and pants. Then, steering her hair clear of her face she bent one arm behind her and hollowed her back. The other hand held the bra loose before her, watching me over her left shoulder. The right hand dropped and June was naked. Her nipples were dark on deep breasts. She looked down at her body.

I just gazed at her, numbed. She looked over to me.

—Do you like it? she said quietly, turning a little until she stood in profile. Half her body stood in deep shadow now, a grey form without substance, except for the faintest contour of a shoulder parting the curtain of black hair. But the left side of her shone in the dusk like violet glass in a band of light which broadened and narrowed down her body, alternating with pools of shadow beneath the chin, beneath her breast, within the diagonals of her hip and pelvis, and down the length of her leg.

—Yes I do. I do want you.

I was undressed by the bed. She came to me in the almost dark. Her breasts brushed over me and her body was cool and rhythmic. In the night I felt her hands caress my back as I pressed down on her and kissed her awake. I slept in the sweat of her shoulder, her leg across my thigh; and in the early morning felt her nipples harden in my hands.

—My lover, she whispered. How good you are. Kiss me.

I wanted to kiss a new morning and a new world. No more fearful tremors of withdrawal, no more lone and fetid longings. I was a man.

* * *

To think that was more than half my life ago. Was there anything ever again like that rich wartime morning in the mountains as the sun blazed on to a new man? That ecstatic feeling – it works it works! All those bits and pieces of me that had been hanging around with nothing particular to do all those years, imagine them actually doing what I'd read they did and been told they did and secretly feared they mightn't do after all; might instead do something entirely different, pee or seize up or shrink away or drop off.

It didn't matter that she became a girl in battledress once again, thrusting out her breasts and her lips in the front of map-reading classes at No 43 Royal Army Education Centre, Akrotiri Camp, to the strains from a distant room of "And the hairs of her dicky-di-do hung down to her knee". She was once more the pneumatic fantasy of rugger songs.

It didn't matter that soon afterwards by some coincidence she took a week's leave in Naples at the same time as the camp adjutant found himself attending a NATO conference there without his wife and children.

It didn't matter that one day after classes a Physical Training instructor passed round the back row – and afterwards to me – a photograph of her being screwed on the beach.

It didn't even matter that a week before I left finally to be demobilised she was killed. An Eoka bomb was lobbed through a café window in the Turkish quarter of Nicosia just outside the cathedral of St John with its twin horns and its carpets laid askew towards Mecca and the mutterings of the Koran. We'd been there that first Sunday afternoon, her body full of my semen, her hand in mind, her eyes in mine.

So she was a scrubber and she was dead. It didn't matter. I was a man.

Bloody hell! Of course it mattered. I was knifed. It only feels like nothing half my life away. June's been dead now twenty-two years, and I still see her by the window coaxing to be desired, shedding clothes like guilt for maybe the hundredth time, knowing I knew nothing about her or about anything and that for a few hours I could hold up to her an undirtied mirror of her dreams. The first time I took her body, entered her body, was the first time I had taken life in my arms and given myself to its embrace. I was a man.

Am I still? In my Jaguar, in my office, in my power and success, in the respect I have planted around me like a perfumed garden, in the self-destruction of my life? What have those twenty-two years done for me? Is this why I have to step out of my marriage, why I have to make a film (and of course it will be a film about love), why I have to risk everything just as it felt then that I was risking everything when I took June?

I do not even know if it is possible, and that is part of the risk.

I've told no one about it: Eric, David, Janet, no one at the office. I may even have to dismantle the whole show. Penrhyn Productions in voluntary liquidation. I can't run a company with my head and make a film with my guts. I'll form a new team round me simply for this one film. Can one really do it that way? But there's no other way it can be done. Ditch everything I've so cautiously built up over the years, taking with me only my instinct and skill. Waldron is the only man who knows: Waldron of all people, who's done nothing with his life except make money, and to whom I only talk money. Somewhere behind that watery eye must lie an old scratched image of what he might have been many board meetings ago, many years of loneliness ago.

A film about love. But there are hundreds of thousands of films about love: how banal it sounds. If I really want to inscribe my name on that muddy scroll then why don't I just do it, get on with it, dismantle nothing, merely get a good screenplay, adapt George Eliot or Doris Lessing or Gore Vidal or who-the-hell, and make it? Make it, pocket the praise and move on with a bigger name, a bigger car, a bigger house out of tax reach, a bigger blonde, an ever-more-perfumed garden to stroll in and an ever-lengthening entry in *Who's Who*? Why not?

Because it cannot be done that way; and I am scared.

—Morning, Eric!

—Wessex Television rang, Gareth. Could you ring back?

—Fuck them! All right!

Janet looks different. Softer. I had forgotten our few moments' conversation on Tuesday afternoon. No, I don't really desire her at all. No more talking my passage to bed. No time any more. Perhaps I'll just ask her to strip one day, straight out; do a dirty-mac routine just to get a quick rise out of those tits. Oh, forget it. Right now I need to make a film not a bird.

—Morning, Janet! David!

A film from my guts. The trouble is, it's in my guts where I'm scared. That canker of self-doubt which feels like boredom and rationalises itself with such insidious ease, tells me "Stick to your last, Gareth; stop playing fantasy games; if you had a real film in you you'd have done it ten years ago when you first had the chance; so take Janet or some other willing chick with you to the Middle East if you need to, screw the arse off her and get on with it; enjoy your little perfumed garden and thank your lucky stars you've got one at all."

I want to scream.

* * *

Jennifer looked happy. Under the pines a crust of snow still brindled the mountain on the sunless slope. Blue and white anemones smeared the grass between the weighted gorse. We found the track of a boar and a trail of dark blood where yesterday's hunters had slithered over the snow, waking us at dawn with frantic dogs and the crack of shot-guns. Two eagles wheeled over the high rock, and the wind sent a shower of icicles in our path.

Jennifer was pregnant. It would be all right from now on. It had been our New Year resolution to have a family: we felt adolescent putting it that way, but it also felt like the most binding commitment of my life. We were close. I wanted her child. To be a father was the distant shore after a long storm; and already we were within the embrace of land.

I took such care of her. Made her rest, went out early in the mornings to buy fresh bread for breakfast, made the coffee. made the bed, made love when she felt well enough, asked her if it was good, lay back and enjoyed the sky and the distant sparkling sea. The Casa Bella was my rebirth: my child and I were being reborn together and Jennifer would tend us, watch over us, feed us, keep the evil spirits at bay. Oh yes! Shine on, glorious sun. Oh yes!

Day Eleven

(*Tonfanau*, November, year 19.)

—22567849 Gunner Flack!

—Bombardier!

—Windows! I want to see your arse shine in them. 22730970 Gunner McKay!

—Sir!

—Bombadier, you cunt!

—Bombardier!

—Latrines! So sweet I want to be able to eat out of them: got it?

—Bombardier!

—22725563 Gunner Penrhyn!

—Bombardier!

—Outside area! Garden to you. And if I should see anything growing in it I'll have yer balls for breakfast. Understand?

—Bombardier!

It was the worst duty of them all. At least the latrines were more or less indoors, almost warm. But the Outside Area round Hut "C" took the horizontal wind straight off the Irish Sea. Every two minutes, right on cue, it would hoist the dust-bin lids and send them bowling and ricocheting into the pre-dawn darkness scattering sweet-papers and French letters which I had already once, twice, three times winkled from the ice and mud with my fingers. Torches were not supplied, nor gloves, nor pointed-stick, nor sack; and woe betide the spot of water on my boots at inspection time at seven. It was one of those ludicrous and impossible routines the Army was so good at inventing to tame the tigers in us. Timid tiger-cubs, most of us. Our bombardier was the god we hated, and true to custom we had a whip-round for him at the end of our training in proof of our longing to love and be loved.

It was Wales. Not my Wales, yet barely thirty miles from my Wales a little north up there beyond Barmouth and Harlech. It seemed a double irony that I should have been sent back here to my land of peace to train for war, and that I alone in this place could speak its language. Only the buzzards circling Cader Idris and the bronze bracken on the hillside told me I was home. Tonfanau, I tried to think of you as my own on those mornings knifed by wind and curses.

On Saturday evenings we swam in warm NAAFI beer, more and more and more of it until we lined the road back in each other's arms bellowing and belching, breaking for a piss in the ditch, and bearing yet more flagons of beer back to Hut "C" to swill away the night and sing of whores.

Jock was the one who knew all about whores; black ones, yellow ones, spotted ones, ancient ones, whores who were somebody's mother or sister or daughter, who sucked you in and blew you out in bubbles, who gave you such clap you turned green and had to bathe it in Jeyes' Fluid and mustard. How he had known so many – how he had even heard of so many in his eighteen years I could never understand. His tales and his songs gave me a sense of awful wonder at a life I'd missed in my safe Welsh town: the pungent, raw culture of the slums. In the late hours of Saturday night Jock held court, and the tender among us learnt about life.

It was a lurid, wanking world of pin-ups and stale underclothes. Jock had a side-kick called Pat, who was rat-faced and blotchy, with hair – or what the Army barbers left of it – that was the texture of a discarded broom. Pat was silent, dockland-Irish, from the Clyde. The rest of us suspected that Pat had done many of the things Jock was good at talking about. Pat himself didn't exactly talk: that would give a false impression. He communicated in gulps and glottal-stops. His front teeth were missing, he had warts on his hands, and white shaggy ankles; but his chief badge of rank for which we all held him in some awe was his prick which was colossal and which he and Jock talked about frequently. Jock was as proud of Pat's prick as Pat was – it was Jock's *doppelgänger* – and I used to wonder if they had ridden to war in the Glasgow stews armed with the same heroic lance. If they'd been out into Towyn for the evening Pat would come back and hang it over the basin and carefully bathe it before tucking it up in bed. No other part of Pat received so devoted a soaping.

We regarded the Jock-and-Pat double-act with mixed awe and disbelief. Certainly when I went to Towyn at weekends it seemed the least likely place in which to find the sort of provender they talked of meeting there. They were prim, Welsh-speaking girls, contemptuous of National Servicemen and deeply suspicious of my efforts to bridge the gulf by talking Welsh. Obviously I was a quisling or an English spy, and they promptly shut up or, if it was a shop, called for mother who would spread her skirts and glower as though I were a rapist.

A frequent butt of Jock and Pat's double-act was a NAAFI Valkyrie called Annie who served beer, so both of them saw a lot of her. And my God there was a lot of her: twelve stone at least, and most of it in her bust. She must have been around thirty, give or take ten years, it was impossible to tell; with a beehive of screaming magenta hair and lipstick to match, and a grotesque mole on her upper lip which sprouted black hairs like a stevedore's nostrils. Her hands were rather small and pink and perpetually moist with beer, which she would hurl across the counter Western-style amid a flak of expletives, followed by a swig of the pint she kept permanently by her and which we took turns to buy her in fear of our lives. Annie the Fanny we called her: Jock addressed her less poetically as "My Cunt". Pat rarely addressed her at all, but grabbed her by the tits whenever she leant within range. Where Annie came from and where she went at night I never knew, but by closing-time most evenings she was three-parts cut, and one Saturday near the end of our two months at Tonfanau she passed out altogether.

Jock and Pat went round the back of the bar and took hold of an arm each. There were about ten of us still in the NAAFI, most of us nearly as pissed as Annie. I was setting a course for the swing-doors when I noticed Tony, who was a clergyman's son and teased unmercifully by Jock for his accent (I was lucky to be Welsh and therefore classless). Tony was holding the half-open door but staring back, I noticed, towards the bar with saucer eyes. I placed one hand on Tony's shoulder for support and turned to look.

It was Pat. He had slung a sagging Annie across the beer-barrels at the back of the bar and was in the process of peeling her like an orange.

We all made for the bar and hung across it, our mouths agape like a Bateman cartoon. Even Jock was silent: he was standing lurching a little against the other side of the counter watching Pat with empty eyes. Pat was lurching too: a few uneasy steps back and then he would stumble forwards against the barrels again to where Annie lay slumped and out cold. And each time Pat staggered within reach he seized hold of a garment. She was down to her bra. Finally, after several tremendous excursions that came away too with a terrific twang and Annie's tits ballooned over the side of the barrel.

At this Annie seemed to come to life a little. She raised her head and laughed, a thick long beery laugh. She heaved a tit into place and extended an arm vaguely in the direction of Pat who had by this time managed to remove his own trousers and pants. He was now standing unsteadily in a voluminous khaki shirt, from the front flap of which dangled the end of a long and very limp prick.

His boots were set apart wide to steady his stance, and there he swayed, cursing his hopeless beast into action with the voice of an outraged muleteer. We watched with growing astonishment, Tony holding one hand before his mouth as if about to vomit, the rest of us gawping. Finally, with some cumbersome help from Annie who was pulling his prick like a bell-rope, Pat managed to raise it, and advanced lance in hand to bury it with accuracy amid those folds of flesh, one arm supporting his weight on the barrels. Annie's legs folded round his khaki shirt behind his back, her buttocks squelched against the barrels and her breasts plunged enthusiastically from side to side. After much groaning and sighing she let out what sounded to me like a long death-rattle. Pat worked away a while longer before collapsing on top of her with a deep roar.

And that was it. Pat lay still. There was not a sound. Tony's hand had slipped from his mouth and he continued to look extraordinarily pale. The rest of us had begun to shift uneasily and glance at each other, a good deal more sober now. Then Pat did move. He rose slowly to his feet and stood gazing supinely at the flesh he'd fucked. Annie had apparently passed out again, magenta lips parted, the magenta beehive still perfectly assembled but hanging suspended. A grin began to light up Pat's face, and he stooped down behind the barrels, showing a large area of white arse. There was the sound of beer being tapped, and Pat rose up holding a pint in his hand, his grin even broader. Then, raising one of Annie's squishy legs high in the air he directed the full pint ceremoniously into her cunt.

* * *

Jennifer's legs were arched wide, the sheet pulled on to her swollen belly. Her fingers dug into the side of the bed, tense as wires. I held them between my hands; wanted to calm them, comfort them. Her head turned and turned on the pillow. I pressed the cool flannel to her brow and she relaxed a little, resumed her breathing exercises, panting, in control again, even managed a thin smile. I'm all right, she said. There were tears on my face. Of course you're all right: how calm I sounded. The midwife was so calm too. Was everything really all right? Jennifer's body convulsed again. Push now, as hard as you can: the midwife's voice was unconcerned and reassuring. She'd seen this a thousand times before, hadn't she? Nothing to it. She was leaning forward now, a gloved hand reaching between Jennifer's thighs. It's coming now, I heard her say. Just one more good push. Jennifer was gripping my arm now, eyes tight shut. Push, Jennifer, push now, the midwife was saying. It's coming. How could there possibly be room for it? The gloved hands were holding something, twisting it – pink and slimy. Pulling it back. What was it? It might fall off. Careful! For God's sake! It was a face, tiny and crumpled, huge eyelids closed. Green mucus round the nose. And now an arm, a hand. Another twist. Another hand. Minute wet fingers curled and limp. Bottom, legs and feet all at once amid a bloated umbilical cord. The midwife was forcing open the mouth, inserting a tube, sucking the tube, turning the child over on the palm of her hand. There was a thin, catlike wail. Little fists wobbling and clenched. The wail staccato, in bursts. The midwife was binding the cord, cutting the cord. The afterbirth slithered out like offal. Jennifer was laughing, crying now, feebly holding my hand, gripping my hand. What is it? A girl! Deirdre was born. She was being bathed in the warm bowl, pink and furious. Held up by her ankles to be measured. Careful, she's not a string of onions. Nineteen and a half inches. Then weighed. Seven pounds. Our daughter.

Nothing I have ever done equals the magic of watching my first child born. It was five in the morning: a late-spring dawn. Too early to phone anyone. There were only the three of us in the house now. Three, not two any more. Jennifer and the child were sleeping. I went in to watch them: the small blob of flesh in its cot wrapped in a pink blanket. Jennifer, hair spread out across a fresh pillow, still. Three of us, not two. I walked into the garden and listened to the dawn-chorus, Looked at the soft sky turn ice-green over the river. My entire future felt committed from within me. I sat on the low wall with a cup of coffee. There was the sound of a milk-float passing the gate. A sports car cut the silence and vanished into deeper silence. The sky white now. One blackbird singing. Slow white petals from the may-tree fall.

I was born on a spring morning in London.

* * *

Who the fucking hell do I get as a script adviser?

—Eric, who the fucking hell do I get as a script adviser? As if Eric would know.

—What d'you say, Gareth? Eric pokes his head round the door.
—Who do I get as a script adviser?
Eric looks as though he feels he should know.
—I don't know.
—Eric doesn't know. Neither do I.
Eric trickles away. David looks up from the cutting bench.
—What about Archie Hill, doesn't he know? You've brought him in on the act, and he's into all this Islam stuff.
David is irked I haven't asked him to be assistant producer.
—I've asked him. D'you know who he came up with? A professor of Koranic Studies at Aberdeen University who's a convert to Islam and gave me a lecture on the phone about never laying the Koran on the floor.
—Quite right too. How would you like it?
—He'd drive me bananas.
—Good for your soul.
David goes into the wailing prayer routine he's been perfecting ever since the Arab films were mooted, raising his arms and eyes, then laying his hands on Janet's shoulders and burying his head in her breasts. She gives a shrug of irritation but stays there.
—Talking of breasts, Gareth, have you seen Eric's new secretary? There's competition for you, Janet, watch it. She'll get his knickers in a twist. Needs a bloody periscope to type.
I don't want to make the Arab films. I suppose I could hand the lot over to Archie Hill and just grandly call them a Gareth Penrhyn Production. But I need to get away, don't I? Yes, by Christ I do. To hell with a script adviser for the time being. I know what kind of films I want to make – did I say "want" after all? And by the time I've done the recce I should be able to put at least a draft script together myself. Then I can draw up a list of questions, feed them around to a few scholars and get completely contradictory answers to reassure me I was quite right to do the script myself.
Fuck the experts. Written by Gareth Penrhyn. Copyright Penrhyn Productions. Christ, is that me? No, I am not Ken Russell, nor was meant to be. Am an attendant bawd. Who the hell wants films on the Arabs anyway? The market is ready for them, Waldron says in his sickening City way. The Americans want to learn to love the Arabs so long as they can go on loving the Israelis too. So what do I do? Film a sequence of happy harmony on the West

Bank? Love Abraham. Love President Carter. Colonel Gaddafi is every mamma's Bar-Mitzvah boy.

I do need to get away. I'm rotting here and I'm rotting at home. But Jesus, the children! Why has it never occurred to me before? All this talk about I'm having the children, not you lady-lay. How can I possibly get away next month if I'm to have the children? I can't even do the recce, let alone stay in some sexy Aegean pad afterwards and plan My Great Feature-Film with Waldron on the blower every other day to find out how the Maestro is getting along. I shall be cooking baked beans and buying cat-food. Oh, my God! Innocent abroad that I am.

So what's more important, my freedom or the kids? Serious question. Both! Serious answer. Obviously then I've got to capitulate to Jennifer and let her have them, if I want any freedom at all. Whoever heard of a father bent over the Bendix being Mum and trying to live a selfish creative life? I'm just being witless and stubborn. Ridiculously short-sighted. Jennifer can have her way, after all. She might even be pleased. Do I want to please her? Yes! Not at first she won't be. She'll seize on it as another stick to beat me with.

—So what about my life?

—You wanted the children.

—I want a life too.

—I'm not stopping you.

—Yes, you are. What am I supposed to do, be grateful to let you have them when it suits you?

—When it suits both of us.

How wet and placatory I sound.

—Oh, I know your kind of fifty-fifty arrangements. Heads you win, tails I lose.

—Then for fuck's sake what do you want?

—I want to live. Live a little. Don't you see?

Screams. Crockery. Thump. Hands over the face.

—Just go away. Go away now. Stop torturing me.

—I only . . .

And so on. But in time it might work out for the best that way. Why am I so buoyant? Almost philosophical? Am I really resigned to Jennifer leaving me? Can I really see a rounded life for myself when this is all over, with my children away or with me of their own free will, and what the hell does it matter about lover-boy? He won't last anyway. She'll go a-hunting and find a crèche to put that baby-bunting in.

Yes, after all we'll sort it out for the best, and in a few years' time I'll be wondering what the fuss and pain were all about. I'll be free, and she'll be free, we'll all be free together: we'll be all right in the middle of the night, being free together.

Now I am a bachelor, I live with my son
And we work at the weaver's trade.
And every every time that I look into his eyes
He reminds me of the fair young maid.
He reminds me of the winter time,
And of the summer too,
And of the many many times that I took her in my arms
Just to save her from the foggy foggy dew.

Why are there tears in my eyes? There is snow on the ground today, on that small patch of England that I call my own. Property is theft, said Proudhon. This morning the aconites held small golden torches to replace the sun, and the river ran black between white shores. Oh, who would be alone by choice? Deirdre! Seth! Ennis! Migratory birds, don't leave too soon. My hands can feel the skull under my skin.

Day Twelve

(*Portmadoc*, July, year 17.)

Now I have a motor-bike
And up and down the roads I hike,
Never heeding hoots nor warners
Especially around the corners:
And even on the steepest hill
Providence saves me from a spill.

I was going to collect Shirley. On Friday afternoons sixth-formers at Portmadoc Grammar School – there were half a dozen of us – were let out at 3.30, which was a full quarter of an hour earlier than the fifth-formers of the Convent of St Teresa of Avila at Criccieth. It was four and a half miles along the road which ran west on to the Caernarvon peninsula under the shadow of Moel-y Gest, where as a child I had played witches with my big sister Gwen until she died without ever telling me if witches were true.

Most days I walked to school. It was only ten minutes down the High Street from Dad's shop and up the hill towards the station; but on days when I fetched Shirley I would take the BSA-250 in the mornings and mother would know not to bother about the fresh barley-bread for tea. Don't be late for your homework, Gareth, she'd call out every time, though she knew perfectly well if it was Friday that I had the entire weekend for my homework and that Friday or not we'd most likely end up at Shirley's grandfather's house at Maentwrog, and once there who knows what time I'd be back? She never minded, however much she fussed: she was pleased that her son's girl was the granddaughter – and such a pretty one at that – of the most famous man in the entire county of Gwynedd. Whatever people might say about his morals and the wives he'd worn and shed, old man Parry-Jones was fine-looking and famous like no other man in Gwynedd was famous, and look at that fancy place he'd built down by the shore there – all temples and castles and old coloured places – why, people flocked from England and even further to see it and call Grandfather Parry-Jones a great man. And rich too, by the way. Gareth goes out with his granddaughter, d'you know? Only fifteen but a lovely girl. A boy couldn't go wrong with a girl like that, now could he? And the butcher's shop sprouted turrets and campaniles before her eyes, and she was proud if I was home when the owls were about.

If I left school promptly at 3.30 and old Richards didn't keep us with his Rugby tales I could be changing gear past the Criccieth town clock at a couple of minutes to the three-quarter hour, and be waiting at the gate as Shirley came out, as always, pretending not to expect me of course, but making sure all the same that she was just in front of a group of older girls who'd watch her clamber on the pillion showing off her legs; and I'd make a spunky roar up the hill while she clung to my waist closer than necessary.

—She's a bitch, Shirley, said Owen. My sister says so. She only fancies you because you're going to a posh university.

Owen's sister had spots.

—I'm not there yet, boyo.

—You will be though. Everybody knows that. Poetry and all that stuff.

I didn't know quite what he meant by that, and neither did Owen probably. But it was true we read poetry. This was one of the reasons Shirley and I used to go down to Grandfather Parry-Jones' place after school. Once the gates were shut and the crowds gone, the romance of the place was ours. I was bewitched by Grandfather Parry-Jones. He was nearing seventy then, and in the summer evenings he used to sit out on the terrace overlooking the estuary, with his memories in his eyes, and his wide straw hat and a silver-headed stick supporting his hands. And he'd tell me how he built Maentwrog out of his dreams. Each dream for a different lady, he'd say with a chuckle: the castle on the hill for his first wife who was Welsh and died of consumption forty years ago; the Elizabethan street for a girl he met in an old inn in Warwick. Just a barmaid and the most beautiful barmaid in the world. Did she ever know? What? About this place? Yes, of course, I brought her here, he said. But he never said where she went. And then the Moorish courtyard and the Italian fishing-village and the *Schloss*? Ah, I travelled, you know; and he smoothed his grey moustaches with some satisfaction. Yes, I travelled! But I worked hard too, my boy. I've been the only architect Wales ever had. Don't forget all the castles we're proud of were built by the English. Well-built too! In Wales we know nothing of art, and since Welshmen never travel – can't afford to – I brought some art here to Wales. It's been my poetry!

It was Shirley's and my poetry too. We read Keats together by the harbour, our feet hanging in the water. She was Fanny, or Lamia, or La Belle Dame sans Merci: I was Porphyro, or Chatterton with two years to live and she would water my name with tears after I'd gone.

—Come and watch the sun go down, Gareth.

She jumped up, and taking my hand in one of hers and her shoes in the other she ran round the harbour and we clambered over the rocks to the far end of the promontory. The estuary was already green and orange, rippled grey by the breeze. We were warm with Keats, and from the wine which Grandfather Parry-Jones had opened for us with a chuckle at dinner. You can say your grandfather taught you the good things, he said.

—Gareth, do you love me?

She was my princess. Her fair hair hung in Shirley Temple curls to her shoulders: she had a small nose, laughing mouth, slim body buttoned into a dark-blue convent uniform; knees wrapped in sunburnt arms under the chin as she sat facing me, waiting for an answer.

—I love the mole by your collar-bone.

Shirley never minded being teased. Her lines of thought were always urgent, and they skipped over such obstacles.

—Do you think they made love in Keats?

—He never says so.

—He wouldn't, would he?

—I think he was innocent.

—At twenty-four?

—Why not?

—I shan't be innocent at twenty-four.

—I love you.

—Grandfather must have made love a lot.

—Probably still does.

—I hope so.

She stretched out her legs along the rock and smoothed out her skirt. I leaned over and kissed her on the mouth: then I held her hands in mine as she opened her eyes. Great blue eyes full of questions and statements.

—You don't! You only like the mole on my neck. I think Grandfather knew that wine would make me feel sexy. Do you?

—Do I what?

—Feel sexy?

—You know I do. I just want to kiss you.

—Is that all?

—No!

—I bet you don't know where the other one is.

—The other what?

—Mole.

—Let me guess. Here?

—No!

—Then here? And I placed one hand against her stomach.

—Almost! And she took my hand and raised it on to her breast. I caught my breath.

—It might be the other one.

—Don't you know?

—Of course, but you don't.

—Then I shall have to find out.

—Do you want to?

With awkward fingers I unfastened her blouse button by button, and gently pulled up her bra over her breasts. So round and white and soft.

—Oh, Shirley!

—Do you love me?

—I want all of you.

—So do I. But I'm scared.

—So am I.

—Just hold me. And down here. Let me feel you too. I've never touched a boy before.

—It's for you. I want it to be everything when it happens.

—Do you really love me, Gareth?

We walked very slowly back along the rock-path, she snuggled to my chest, my arms wrapped round her. Every few steps I raised her head to kiss her, my hands against the skin of her back. I was in love, so in love with her. For a while we stood and watched the lace-work of the trees against the water, and the tide stroking the sand. She laid her head against my back as I drove her home. A white owl ducked into the headlight and vanished again.

—Goodnight, darling!

I'd never used that word before.

—Goodnight! She spoke in a whisper, brushed my cheek with her hand and ran indoors. I stood on the gravel and gave a long, incredibly deep smile of happiness at the stars. I never knew that I had always been alone until now. Never again, I said. Never!

* * *

Each morning around six Deirdre woke us with her gurglings as she lay and batted with tiny hands the beads strung across her cot. After Jennifer had fed her she would sit playing on the bed, stretching for toys out of reach and toppling sideways very slowly with a surprised expression. I would raise her gently with my foot from under the bedclothes. I'd pile breakfast on a wooden tray and carry it into the garden by the ilex-trees, strapping Deirdre into her plastic chair where she chortled and patted her belly and watched with a wobbly head the caravan of ants dragging megaliths of bread into holes in the dust. Far down the steep terracing the olive line followed the contours of the valley; and threads of road looped out of sight and reappeared further off under bastion villages raised like stone beacons on the worn-out hills.

It was autumn in the mountains. Ever since I left Wales I have longed to live among mountains, stand among mountains where the only vertical is man, and all perspectives are made up of diagonals. I have built my workrooms in roofs to be among those same diagonals. Is it that same tremor of the nerves which Baroque painting induces? I think of Rembrandt, of Danaë raised on one elbow, diagonal, naked for her lover on a gilded couch, and starting at the sight of Zeus so that the shadows ripple obliquely across her flesh: one arm is raised at an angle towards the gleam of gold which falls at the same angle; the other arm presses a breast up into the light; the lips are tilted and open for love. She waits.

The far peak, snow-capped always, was Monte Bego. And along that high valley below the western slope early man scratched a hundred thousand messages on slate slanting like mirrors to reflect the magic of the mountain between the Black Lake and the Lake of Hell. What names! I climbed there with Jennifer, Deirdre in a papoose on my back; and we returned at dusk with a haversack of mushrooms from the pine-woods: red and green mushrooms that bled in the pan and tasted like steak. We ate them with purple Borsalino wine from Lombardy and slept out a storm that brought the tiles crashing outside the window.

In the morning the mountains were laundered fresh and the air translucent and sharp. The child slept on. I weighted the roof-tiles with stones, painted the old shutters the green of laurel, and chatted to Michele who came past with a gun under his arm and dangling two rabbits.

Jennifer looked serene, at moments radiant. She was slimmer than ever after the child, moving now at a slow pace, bare feet on the sandy path, Deirdre on her hip. Now into her thirties the skin of her face hugged the bones softly enough. She was beautiful. I had never thought this before. She took to wearing striking rings, which altered the way she moved her hands, and bright clothes which she carried with a new self-consciousness. She took my arm when we walked, placed her hand over my body when we slept, smiled when we woke.

The child between us gazed at first one then the other, registering us, responding to our voices and our touch. We bathed her in a tub on the front doorstep in the evening sun, cradled by the mountains and by our love. It seemed hard to imagine that anything could ever seriously go wrong again. What we had was forged in a fire and tempered by past loneliness.

* * *

Another weekend. What shall I do this weekend? I have planned nothing because I know I would like to be here; I would like to be quietly around the family, taking great care, and maybe even choose my moment to raise the question of the children. I would like to give Jennifer something, a small offering of generosity. I know it will be difficult: perhaps she will not be able to take it. And then – Whoops! Tempers will be out in gale force again. How good it would be just to be able to sit out the February slush over coffee in the kitchen, or light the fire and roast chestnuts, play Scrabble with Deirde, or ping-pong, or help Seth with his new glider kit.

I am beginning to sound noble and self-pitying. In a minute I shall be cherishing the supreme sacrifice I've made in not taking up O'Rourke's offer of his cottage in Norfolk. So why haven't I been bloody selfish and gone there this morning, or last night for that matter? The reason could not be more boring and reasonable: how can I possibly hope to come to an agreement with Jennifer over the children if I piss off leaving her to cope alone with them one entire filthy February weekend? It didn't take long to see it that way; but before I rang O'Rourke back to say No, I'd indulged in several alternative possibilities, each of which seemed wonderfully attractive myths at the time.

The first alternative was a myth which often comes to me when I'm enjoying being overworked and overwrought. It's been with me as long as I can remember; and in it Gareth One is a kind of spruced-up reincarnation of Wordsworth's leech-gatherer. He stands alone, posing for himself – generally on a smallish rock, looking introspective and interesting. His own nature and Mother Nature are one: they complement and need one another. Gareth One in essence communicates only with himself, and landscape is meaningful solely as an extension of himself: his mirror and his echo. O'Rourke's cottage by the bleak mud-flats provides him with the ideal solitude in which to regenerate the inner self numbed and subdued by the social nexus. Gareth One enjoys the society of others when it suits him, out of a need for personal display. He has no friends, only company he can gently dominate and reject as it suits him. He is kind because it feels good to be kind; he loves because a fly-trap needs a fly. He listens to music a great deal because music is a pure and impersonal orchestration of his own feelings without any need of an object. He gazes out of the cottage window this weekend, a glass of whisky in his hand, wrapped within a mood of renewed self-awareness and cosmic content.

The second alternative followed on swiftly when the first began to grow a little lonely. This was the myth of Gareth *domesticus redivivans* – Gareth Two. Out of the floodwaters of misfortune he has dragged himself to a small Norfolk village where a pitying local perceives his bruised goodness and offers him a cottage at a peppercorn rental. The cottage is warm and well-equipped, and the daughter of the landlord an amenable red-cheeked girl in fawn Cashmere wool. She visits rather often to ensure that the linen is aired and the visitor contented. Before long she does not go away. Soon a family arrives, and this wonderfully capable creature blossoms in maternalism and calm attentiveness, smoothing cares and troubles from his brow and surrounding him with home-bakes and happily laughing children. She inherits her father's smallholding and income, with which and on which the capable Gareth Two supplies the family with delicious organically grown vegetables and fat livestock, the envy of the neighbourhood who compliment her on her husband and him on his wife. Their good and untroubled life passes into an old age of reflection and mutual regard, and death comes kindly, without warning, to both simultaneously.

Does everything in my life contradict such a persona too? I fear so.

What about the third alternative? This was the myth of Gareth the subtle and irresistible lecher, much given to respectable hypocrisies and *droits de seigneur.* Eric's new secretary is eighteen and anxious to please in her new job. She is much in awe of lord and master who is Gareth Three. She may not have heard of him before but he is almost, Eric has confidentially implied, famous. In fact in his own world he is very famous indeed. And clearly a handsome and kind man much overworked. What then could be more flattering than an offer of weekend overtime helping to prepare for an important new series of films which will be shown the world over? Thank God she is neither a fool nor a virgin, and the implications of an affair with the boss during the first week of her first job place her top of the league-table among her chums from the Kensington secretarial college. Wait till they hear about this on Monday evening at 112a Ennismore Gardens. Naturally Mr Penrhyn has a Jaguar and a cottage in the country, and brings with him a hamper of food and wine from Fortnum and Mason. The cottage has a huge log-fire, and no one but her chums will ever know that she was sitting by it naked with a glass of brandy in her hand while Mr Penrhyn said she had the most beautiful body in the world and was making love to her in several ways her boy-friend had never shown her. Mr Penrhyn was so warm and so sexy and really cared about her, never ill-treated her; she felt like an empress and wondered if every weekend could be like this, and what she would say to Eric on Monday morning.

That one went out of the window, too; perhaps not quite so fast as the others because it contradicts a good deal less of my life than they do. Not so much a myth, more a way of life – lust is the way of life of a lonely man – though none the less a myth for that.

Power! A yearning for power! They all seem to have that in common. Power over people. I don't like it to be so. But what is the alternative to power? How can we live except by profiting from the role we play – albeit lovingly, caringly, with generosity, even with humility? Power is still the zest. Even if the power be the power to make God listen, or the power to stand alone in defiance. I detest the implications of these thoughts. Is this what I really want with my own children, power to compel them to love me, need me, respect me, miss me? Jesus, how awful! So Jennifer is fleeing that. She needs a relationship of peers, not one of dominance. Of course. I have stifled her, wrung loathing from her, clung to her, run from her when she has needed me, run to her when I have pushed her away, demanded trust which I could never offer, sworn promises which I could never keep.

Yes, but I have cared.

What does it matter any more? It's at an end, and we can only try to leave the pain behind the door we close. She can have whatever she wants. I'll make the offer and put up with the flak.

Day Thirteen

(*Caernarvon*, November, year 16.) Nothing ever used to be said. We would go because of what went on. But we never talked about it, either before or after. We just waited for the next one, and dreamed a little in between. They were just parties. Owen enjoyed arranging parties. He was a King's Scout, what's more. 8th Caernarvon Troop. He laughed about it at school of course (I could tell you about wide games, Gareth bach!); but it meant that he could borrow the Scout Hut most Fridays, down by the quay. A rambling wooden hut, it was, with a cast-iron stove over on one side presented by the minister, and an upright piano on the other, tuned for bellowing:

When you're scouting, scouting, scouting,
Keep your eyes on everything:
You must know each sound,
Every track upon the ground,
And the clear cool spring
And the bird upon the wing;
When you're scouting, scouting, scouting . . .

Owen shaved every day. Same age as me, sixteen, but he looked like a man. Brother a Rugby forward. Played for Bangor. At the university. Thick he was. Owen too. Thick and black and wonderful, the pair of them. And they knew all the girls. That's why we had parties. Owen would always bring the girls. So many of them too.

But nothing ever used to be said. You didn't talk about such things. At least not then. At least not in Wales. You talked about the things you didn't do, or which other people did, or what you hoped they did. Owen's parties were a cabalistic secret guarded with a nod by Owen's friends. And I was Owen's friend.

So it was usually Fridays. There'd be maybe twenty of us all told. Usually more girls than boys, which was strange and wonderful – like Owen. There they were, huddled a bit, fresh out of uniform from Caernarvon Secondary School most of them. Sexy as hell, too, all tits and velvet. Shandy we had, nothing stronger. Wouldn't have been right. There'd be a ring of chairs in the middle, arranged by Owen. We'd sit round on the chairs, waiting. Then Owen would lay a lemonade bottle on the floor in the centre, and spin it. There'd be this tremendous silence. We'd sit there watching it spin. Whoever the bottle finally pointed to, girl or boy, had to wink; and whoever was winked at had to come over and be kissed. A bit demure it was to begin with. Not for long. The kisses began to linger. With some girls especially.

Like Olwyn. She was a plump fourteen-year-old in red with long hair. Owen used to say she was too young – kids' stuff – and never winked at her, which didn't stop her winking at him clear enough to summon an army, and then impaling him on her tongue with her eyes squeezed tight and one hand ripping his shirt high up his back, just as she'd seen Ruth Roman do in the movies. The rest of us were amazed, not a little excited.

When we'd all snogged enough and the shandy was fizzing a little in our heads, Owen, or sometimes Luke or Kyffin, would propose Fumble. This was a game that froze me solid when I first played it, until after a while it lit up every scout party we ever had, besides doing plenty to determine what clothing the girls wore. You could tell a lot from that. First the boys would empty their pockets of pennies and place them in a pile on the floor. Then there was a share-out, two pennies per boy, and we all sat in a semi-circle. This done, Owen or Luke or Kyffin called for the first volunteer, or more often the girls themselves pushed forward the girl with the lowest-cut blouse which of course she'd put on for that purpose. The girl knelt facing the boys, her hands on the floor in front of her. There was only one rule of fair-play after Owen gave the signal to shoot. It was that no boy was allowed to stand up and actually drop the penny down her blouse. If he did he was forbidden to fumble for it. No, it had to be properly flipped in an arc. Not easy either, depending to a great extent on the cut of the blouse and the co-operation of the target. Generally speaking the girls who wanted it got it, which was not at all true of the boys who were apt to aim wildly astray with excitement the more invitingly a cleavage peeped at them – except Owen, that is, whose skill at ball-games made him immune to such nerves and ensured that he invariably lodged his penny where he could fumble the best boobs in the party.

There was one little lad called Bryn who looked about twelve and was very pretty, and shy with it. Most of the girls seemed to fancy him like crazy and would practically strip to pocket his penny, however wildly he threw it in his embarrassment. Then the lucky one would seize him, protesting feebly, and thrust his hand down her blouse, to hell with where the penny was, and squirm and squirm until there was a bulge in every pair of trousers in the room. Once the girl waiting her turn couldn't bear all this massage any longer, and leapt forward and ripped poor little Bryn's pants down to his knees. We were collectively a bit shocked at that. A fumble was one thing; this seemed like dirty stuff. The sight of Bryn's unwilling willy all white and dangling there took much of the heavy breathing out of the evening and the game soon broke up. Bryn didn't turn up any more, and I often wondered what inhibitions he had to live with ever after.

Not that we were exactly prudish; but there were rules, unwritten rules, and to break them broke the enjoyment and the thrill and the safety of our evenings. After Fumble, the girls would sometimes demand their own game. We, the boys, would stand in a line in the dark. The first volunteer would drop his trousers and pants and the girls, one after another, would feel for his thing and try to guess whose it was. The first girl to guess right had to let him undress her, and the next lad would take his turn, and so the game went on until we were all standing in the grey dark in naked couples, writhing ghosts murmuring and sighing, learning marvellous things about bra-straps and bellies, but not – really I believe so – ever making love. It was another of those unwritten rules. There we would stand palely in the almost dark, pair by pair, like embracing statues in a store-room, savouring the promise of when one day it would all be for real.

—I like you, Monica.

—I like you too, Gareth.

We were walking back through the damp winter evening under

the hulk of the castle and along the quay, my arm round her thick coat, her hair against my cheek. A few reflections smeared the black water orange and yellow. Fishing-boats lurched on the mud, studded with gulls asleep. Lights in upstairs windows. The silhouette of a man brushing his teeth. A party swaying home from the pub. Laughter. A solitary cyclist. A cat.

—I guessed better than you flipped.

—Glad you did.

—I like you.

—Like you too.

—You'd better hurry or you'll miss the last bus.

—See you next Friday, Monica, shall I?

—Expect so! I'd better go now. Mum said to be back by 10.30. Goodnight!

—Goodnight!

The bus was waiting.

—All well at home then, Gareth? Dad better, is he?

—Yes, thanks.

—Off we go, then.

Off we go home.

* * *

That feeling of life having fucked off and left me leaning on the bar. Coffee by the window. Another grey morning. The children are upstairs: I hear their thumps on the ceiling. How unaware they are. Are they? More philosophical than I am; their needs so definable – beaks open in the nest – and their expectation so much more flexible. How vulnerable and yet how tough they are: their wounds bleed and heal rapidly. At least so it would appear.

—Daddy's not going to live with us any more, Jennifer announced quietly over breakfast.

Deirdre just shrugged: I suppose she knew it was coming.

—And will you be back for tea, Ennis piped up?

Seth's little face screwed up and his eyes filled with tears.

—Oh! he said. A long sob of an Oh!

I could not feel his pain then, but I knew a knife was sliding through me. Now I feel it, twisting on numbed nerve-ends, and I know I will live with it for ever. That little cry – Oh! It will never leave me.

Now Seth is playing with his Lego, and laughing and thumping upstairs. Has the wound healed already? My face is wet. I long to go and hug him. It's all right, Seth; it's all right! Daddy's here. He will always be here. He's not going away from you. Not so as it counts.

How could I say that when I was?

—Daddy's not going to live with us any more. It was an unkind way of putting it, since she was the one who was leaving. Jennifer was scoring again. Indignantly she denied it, and knew she was.

—I think they should be with you, I had said. I had finally got it out, elbowed a path between the sewing and Radio-4 once the kids were in bed.

—I really think so.

A long pause. I was overstating it. No reaction for a while. And then . . .

—Do you just?

Another long pause.

—I see! she went on. If I'd been more composed, maybe if I'd loved her, understood her more, I would have heard the cogs of panic whirling in Jennifer's brain. Such a bone of contention, the children, and here was I letting go so suddenly. What could she say? She was buggered if she was going to be nice and say Thank-you! She's never been much good at that.

—Do you just? I see! she said again. That's good of you. So you can do what you bloody well want, I suppose.

The defences were coming up with a clang. She was getting the oil hot and ready. If she could get me angry, hurt me, she'd feel better about being ungracious. God knows, hadn't she hurt me enough? She went on sewing briskly. Silence except for Radio-4. A clever young writer on Kaleidoscope was doing his four-and-a-half minute assessment of Scott Fitzgerald, trying to pretend he hadn't learnt his epithets by heart. Verbal porridge.

—What about me, then?

—I thought you wanted them.

I shouldn't have said that.

—Wanted them? Wanted them? She was screaming at me, needle between her fingers. A fat lot you care what I want. It's what *you* want. *You!* You just want to imprison me; have them when it suits you.

I was beginning to have an urgent need to hurl the radio.

—When you're not filming. When you can't think of anything better to do. When the blonde's got the curse.

I didn't hurl the radio. The presenter's voice was tidying up: "Scott Fitzgerald: The Sodden Years, by Professor Reuben Goldblatt, is published by . . ." I dug the carving-knife half an inch into the kitchen table. Jennifer's a bitch, remember! She's leaving, not me! Remember! She asked for the children, remember! And I've said Yes!

I didn't say anything.

"On Kaleidoscope tomorrow" (that consulting-room voice still) "Menuhin on Casals, and the Kampala Festival of Light. Meanwhile, from me, it's goodnight and sod you!"

I didn't say anything. There was too much to say to say any of it, and it had all been said before so many many times in different permutations and different crescendoes of exasperation.

Instead I went to the pub in a state of misery and shaking fury. I don't even remember if I finished my drink or if I even ordered one, or many. I chain-smoked and came home. Home! That mocking word again. The light was on in her room. She'd be reading in bed. There'd be no more fights tonight. Godfathers, must it be like this? These are our children we're fighting over, our lives we're fighting for. I can't wait to get out. Will I ever get out?

This morning – still nothing. I've kept my distance. I feel better. A little voice tells me I didn't do badly last night. I said what I wanted to say and not what she goaded me to say. Dear other cheek, would that you were not so bruised.

I have a feeling things may go better from now on.

I hate her bloody guts!

Oh, Seth, that cry!

* * *

Seth almost never cried. He grew rounder and rounder, and chuckled as he grasped one big toe and contemplated it with delight. What toys the world had given him. Deirdre was suddenly a grown child next to this little pot of flesh on the carpet in the sun.

My father stirred from his depression to hail a grandson and the continuity of the family name. I pictured flags all over Portmadoc. Seth, Seth, that's not a name for a Welsh boy. Gareth, you've grown too big for us – but we're proud of you. Doing well with the BBC, you know, he is. Yes, the BBC, indeed! Fancy that!

Actually I was about to leave the BBC. Nobody had ever done that in Portmadoc before, but then nobody had ever joined it either. Nobody had ever left anything in Portmadoc, except bones.

Wonderful thing is education. Always did know where he was going, Gareth. D'you remember him and old Parry-Jones? Now there's a man who knew. Still does, even though he's eighty-five or more. Used to go and hob-nob with old Parry-Jones, did Gareth – remember! Liked him too, Parry-Jones. Always did. Knew he'd go somewhere. Whatever happened to that granddaughter of his Gareth went out with, on his motor-bike? Remember? What was her name? Shirley, that's right. Shirley! Lovely girl. Beautiful. What a figure, as they say. Gareth liked her. Didn't marry her, though, did he? She went to London: so did Gareth. Why didn't he marry her then, I wonder? Both in London. Can't understand these young people. Found someone else, I suppose. What's her name: Jennifer is it? Not a Welsh girl. From somewhere else. Fine girl all the same. Saw her last year. She was down. Tall. Not Welsh. Makes him happy. Now he's got a son. Father must be pleased. Needs something to think about now he's given up the shop. Knew about meat, mind you, Old Penrhyn. Nobody better. Always went to him for beef. Got a bit expensive. But that's life, isn't it? Mustn't complain. They tell me he's dying. Shouldn't wonder.

He'd always been Old Penrhyn. "Old" wasn't a mark of age, even a token of respect; more the acknowledgment of a barrier, as if they were saying, "There's Mr Penrhyn nobody knows". Like people drink socially, he didn't drink anti-socially. Yet that's what he wanted to do, I'm sure; drink like hell sometimes. Mind you, it wouldn't have been easy. You couldn't drink in Wales, not as a butcher. You were a public figure: people knew you. You didn't drink, except as fun. Then you drank too much. That was all right: people would say, "He's been celebrating. A man's got to celebrate." But Dad hadn't much to celebrate once I'd gone. He celebrated my departure with a glass of South African sherry, went back to his shop and my mother. She cooked. And he grew old. Retired. Sold the shop. Finally he had a grandson. That pleased him. The line was assured. The line to where?

—Come and stay, Gareth boy, he said on the phone. When you're not too busy. I know you are. But your mother would like to see you. How's Jennifer?

Jennifer was flourishing. It was never easy to be sure. She was never one to spring up and exclaim, "Oh, how happy I am with you, darling." These were times, at least, of truce; when the minefield we walked seemed to be defused. And I was grateful, content at better moments to believe that the mines might no longer be there at all.

They were: all the same it was better. I went on telling myself it was better. We told one another it was better. It *was* better. No doubt about it. What was better was the recession of fear. A small real tenderness had encroached. The children were evidence, if not of our passions, then of our capacity to care. We had children because we wanted children, and I couldn't think of a better reason for their existence in our lives. The children bolstered us, reassured us we were not the perfect marital disaster we had often suspected. It was not bliss, indeed not, but it was no longer warfare. It was a good kind of life for those who lived on the dark side of the hill.

* * *

It is late Sunday afternoon. A time for nurturing pathetic fallacies. I feel my dead father's depressions wrapped within this damp blanket of a day. All my life he had nothing to live for. All passions spent. No, not spent, rather withered on the bough, expiring of neglect. What could he have done? He made his decline appear so inevitable, such an unalterable exercise of an unjust law wrought on him by the powers at large. Who were they, those stern judges? We none of us around him ever seriously asked that question until too late. What could he have done? What, indeed?

Much, of course! This was his moment of choice, now, where I stand on this grey dying afternoon, where the choice lies between capitulation and self-assertion. More than that, between expansion or contraction of the spirit; between laughter, even, and self-pity. He must have had many such moments, when things are so bad you have to take yourself by the scruff of the neck and march in just one direction where a point of light shines. A narrow course, maybe, but a forward step with your baggage on your back. And if you can see no light? Ah, yes! Then invent it, as an atheist sometimes has to invent God. I do not believe, therefore I will believe. An act of creative humility to snap the chains of thought.

Could my father have done that, have leant that heavily on the forces of his nature? I wonder. Is my mother much to blame for putting up with it so destructively? Or my sister for dying? Or I for not caring enough? No, Old Penrhyn, we are fabric of the road we walk, and that we learn for sure before we talk. There's my jingle for the day.

The day is dying. My father is dead. I loved you, despaired of you, listened to your long count-down until – suddenly – you were a skull on the hospital pillow, jaw askew, screened. And out of the confusion of your dusk I heard you croak, "Oh hell!" I'm glad you went that way. And I turned to the window and wept.

Day Fourteen

(*Ashridge*, October, year 15.) It was for bright kids throughout the nation, even North Wales. A half-term conference on Economics.

—What's that, then, said Taff who wasn't going?

—Money, said Kyffin, who wasn't going either. They're going to teach him how to make money. That's what it's all about.

—For kids with prospects, my mum said. I was a kid with prospects, suddenly. I'd thought I was just a kid.

—Economics. Think of that. I never. Could do with that here. She wasn't given to jokes usually. Economics, d'you hear that, dad? Mind you listen, boy!

We were collected in a coach from Beaconsfield station, through woods such as I never saw, and down a long, winding drive. Elitist socialism, it was, in the days before the Comprehensives took over.

—To teach you a bit about the world, the Head had told me solemnly when he took me aside. For future leaders. It seemed there was still a world to lead, even if we had just given up an empire. Well, that was something to know.

Gareth Penrhyn, fifteen, rising sixteen, five feet eight inches, dark hair, shaved a bit, leader. Think of that!

I wasn't sure if I was quite ready to lead the world yet: even so, you couldn't help but rule it in a place like this, surely. What a mansion! Such a pile of it. Great windows, ceilings high as clouds, and a staircase that swept round and round above us. We could sit under it drinking coffee – real coffee mind you – and spot the girls' knickers as they came down to supper.

We weren't allowed up there. The boys were lodged in Nissen Huts the Army had scattered across the great park during the war. We were kept apart after eleven at night. Doors to the main house locked. Good girls inside, bad boys outside. I found a French letter on the ground the first morning.

There was this Trades Union fellow addressing us. It would be our turn soon, he said. Looking round the room I wondered whose French letter it was.

—Look at that, I whispered to Jim. Jim was sharing a room with me and came from Cardiff. Jim nodded. There was this dark-haired girl two rows up with a tight sweater like Jane Russell.

—I'll have the little blonde next to her, boyo, he whispered. We shared a confidential silence until the lecture was over and we all filed out for biscuits. The two girls were just behind us. They both smiled and my stomach stood on its head. Marie and Emmy they were called. We listened to a Member of Parliament on post-war economic recovery and a bishop on social services, and then the four of us walked in the park in the sun. I thought the sun fell on Marie and nowhere else. And in the evening I put my arm round her and kissed her. She put her tongue in my mouth. I could feel her breasts against me, and I tried to stick my arse away from her so she wouldn't notice what she was doing to me.

That night I lay on my bed in a state of wonderful confusion. So this was love? How would anyone recognise me back in Portmadoc now? Who was I?

—Hell, they want to get screwed, boyo, you wait. Jim seemed terribly calm. How were you supposed to know what a girl wanted? Jim must know; after all he was sixteen. I didn't feel like telling him Marie was the first girl I'd kissed. He'd probably had dozens in all manner of ways. Portmadoc felt very small next to Cardiff. I'd heard about Cardiff.

—Look! The room next door's spare, Gareth boy. Right? Simple then. Tomorrow night we'll stay out in the park till they've locked the doors, the four of us. Then we'll come back here. I'll move in there with Emmy. In the morning we can sneak out into the park again before anyone's up and stroll in for breakfast, casual like. No trouble at all!

A bloody genius, Jim. The great adventure was about to begin. I was excited and a bit scared. Jim made a growl and bounced his arse up and down in bed. Get up there, Long John Silver, he said. At 'er boy! Then another growl, and he turned over facing the wall with a final heave of his arse under the bedclothes. I lay awake wondering and waiting for tomorrow. Suppose, suppose, suppose . . .

My brain drummed all next day. Marie wore a green blouse with white buttons, and a wide black skirt with a belt which made her breasts and hips stand out. I noticed her legs too, and that heron-like way of walking she had. She came from Luton, she said, and I thought Luton must be the most exotic place in the world with her around.

After dark I kissed her again by the lake, only this time I didn't stick out my arse. She pushed at me all over and our tongues met and twiddled.

The two girls colluded so effortlessly in our plot that I felt almost let down, but Jim and Emmy were giggling in whispers as they ran through the darkness towards the Nissen hut, so I caught Marie's hand and we ran too. There was a side-entrance right next to our room which we'd left unlocked, and we slipped inside without anyone noticing. No turning back now. We hastened into our room and closed the door.

I waited for Jim, master-mind, to make the first move. He'd dreamed up this scheme; I assumed he'd take charge. I imagined he'd done this kind of thing dozens of times before. But what about the girls? Had they? Would they? And would all this combined experience carry one tenderfoot sweetly along? I waited, and tried not to appear nervous. I looked at Marie for clues. Then at Emmy. Then at Jim. We sat on the two beds, two and two. We held hands. We talked in low voices.

It seemed like half the night had gone until the to-ings and fro-ings ceased in the corridor outside and the place was silent. Now; it had to be now. I looked at Marie, then at Jim.

Jim got to his feet, pulled Emmy to her feet.

—Better go to bed now, he said, all matter-of-fact. Let's get you both next-door.

They followed him out of the room. What about me? Something was going wrong. What did Jim think he was doing? Was he going to have both of them?

In a few minutes, maybe four of five, Jim returned.

—That's OK then, he said removing his jacket. The bastard was chickening. He'd just left the girls and come back. Bloody wanker. All that talk and growling and bouncing about in bed. He didn't even look sheepish about it, just ordinary. He began to undress. I felt cheated, furious. I hadn't even said Goodnight. Jesus Christ, after all that. And he was just going to bed – by himself.

—I took Emmy my pyjamas, by the way. That's all he said: I took Emmy my pyjamas. He'd even bloody worked it out.

—You might take yours in too, boyo, he added. And with that he heaved himself into bed in his underclothes and rolled over away from me. And that was that.

I sat on the edge of my bed. What should I do? How the hell did I let myself in for this? How the hell? Jim was asleep already, or feigning sleep. I had to do something. I seized my pyjamas from under the pillow and tiptoed the few steps down the corridor. There was no sound. I waited a moment outside their door, listening. Nothing! Perhaps they were asleep already. No, there was a blade of light under the door. Very lightly I tapped.

A few seconds and the door opened. Just a few inches. It was Emmy. I could see nothing but her face peering round.

—Ah, it's you, she whispered. Come in. She sounded welcoming. I felt a lot better. We thought you were asleep.

I closed the door behind me. Marie was sitting on the bed by the window, still dressed. But she didn't look up.

Then I saw that Emmy was standing dressed only in Jim's pyjama-top. They came down just to the top of her legs, which were bare. She was holding the pyjamas together in front of her. They were unbuttoned. I just stood there, looking at her, her face small and smiling, her hair curling over her shoulders, the light pressure of her breasts under the pyjamas, her hands gripping the garment too large for her loosely to her waist. Long legs. Bare feet. She had a curious smile.

—I've brought Marie some pyjamas, I said, and I held them out, not to Marie, still not looking at me, but to Emmy. As she took them her pyjamas fell open showing a bush of fair hair below her belly and small pointed breasts. Her other hand made no effort to hide anything. She was still smiling. The V of her collar-bone matched the V of her hips. She was slim as a weasel. Marie looked up for the first time.

Emmy laughed and placed the pyjamas I had handed her on the bed.

—Pyjamas for you, Marie. Gareth brought them. You'd better put them on. And she laughed again.

Was Marie ill? Was that it?

—Why don't you stay and make sure they fit, Emmy said. I hadn't moved an inch, my eyes still fixed on her.

Now Marie stood up. She was still wearing her tight green blouse. She looked across at Emmy, saying nothing for a moment.

—Do you think Gareth would like that?

It was the first time she had spoken. She gave me a thin smile and removed her belt.

—I don't believe Gareth knows what I told Jim, do you, Marie?

Marie went on gazing at me now with those black eyes.

—Maybe that's what Gareth likes, said Emmy. Let's see. And she slipped out of Jim's pyjama-top and stepped towards Marie. Marie didn't move. Nor I. Emmy's small hands reached out and began to unbutton the green blouse. Button by button to the waist.

—I believe Gareth likes big breasts, don't you, Marie? I'm too small for him.

She was round behind Marie now, slipping the blouse free of her arms and unhooking her bra. Marie was still looking at me; Emmy too, over Marie's shoulder, as her hands felt round the girl's waist and began to ease the brassière up over Marie's breasts. They were quite bare, white and swollen and Emmy was lifting the white garment and letting it drop on the bed behind her.

Emmy was gently turning the dark-haired girl round by her shoulders to face her. They had both stopped looking at me; were gazing at one another. Emmy was drawing closer until her own sharp nipples were brushing Marie's, gyrating them with a movement of her shoulders. Emmy was bending forward, her tongue touching the girl's neck and down between her breasts, the tongue circling one nipple then the other until they stood out. Marie's eyes were closed. Emmy's tongue continued to move down, deep under her breasts, down over her belly, Emmy's hand unzipping the skirt and letting it fall, her face between Marie's legs, tongue buried in her hair, mouth wide. Marie was falling back on the bed, head turning on the pillow, knees arched, fingers pressing at the head of the blonde girl, mouth open.

The door closed. I walked and walked in the damp night. I stumbled across fields, skirted a beech-wood where branches dripped on me, sweat turning chill across my chest and back. I stood by a gate I don't know for how long, shivering in spasms, until the cold began to pierce me and I walked on. My feet were drenched with dew, my hair damp. I was crying. Lightly crying. Tears mixed with dew and rain. I found a summer-house in the park and sheltered among garden chairs within sight of the great house. I have no idea how long I huddled there, but I remember every so often wiping the tears from my face. And I remember the upstairs lights coming on one by one, then a blaze of lights downstairs in the dining-room. I could see figures moving in the house. Someone came out on to the terrace and vanished inside again. I could just hear the sound of the door closing.

Three figures were hurrying in the shadow of the trees approaching the house: a girl with fair hair, a dark-haired girl and a man.

They disappeared into the house.

—Glad you're back, Gareth! Your father's just having a bath. I know he'd love to hear all about it. Must have been wonderful. Old Mrs Tuke has died. A mercy really. Take your things up, then come down and tell us all.

Dad's door was half-open as I carried my bag upstairs. He came out of the adjoining bathroom as I passed but he didn't see me. He was standing there with just a towel round his neck, a white hairless figure with blue veins on spindly legs and a slack belly over a little shrivelled cock.

Old Penrhyn the butcher – my father! Why did I detest him then? I hurried to my room, locked the door and fell on to the bed with my hands clenched in fury, staring at the ceiling. Twin images were scratched on my eyes. Marie, black angel, writhing in an ecstasy of hair, pinned, engorged. And my father, scrubbed and shrivelled in his separate room.

My icons, my corrupt gods leading me by the hand.

* * *

What was that shoddy initiation: not life, surely? Those mirror-images of betrayal lie frosted on the memory. Images of betrayal breeding self-betrayal. Was it really by their grace that the path turned the way it did, led this way, to this end-game on this St Valentine's Day?

Green dawn over the river: a knife with a glint of spring. I am alone again, as then. Anguish turns in the gut: pain, like alcohol, concentrates the mind, focusing it on bewitching details.

A slide-show for St Valentine's Day.

Mother coaxing the old fool on their wedding-night, holding him up with one hand, showing him where to put it. She told me so one evening after he'd died. He wanted a son – me! – and she wanted to forget.

A train-journey as a boy: the gaze from across the carriage which said to him, "I'm seventeen and I've got no bra, you're fifty-five and you've got no erection."

Father behind the green baize table, mouth set thin over the patience-cards. Heavy fingers turning the cards like prophecies. Mother across the fire behind a Victorian romance. Walls of domesticity. She was grey by then.

How her eyes lit up when Uncle David came to help out while father was ill. Footsteps in the night. She wore earrings, I remember; the only time.

Mother sipping gin-and-water, saying she would have left him then but for the war. The chill of realising that was when my nightmares had begun. Then my sister died. I was six.

When he came back from the nursing-home his surprise, tears almost, as I threw myself into his arms: Daddy, Daddy, you're home again. My surprise, too. A lonely spark.

The dark hooded girl, nipples pressing a blue shirt, I invited to supper. His discomfort, disapproval. Mother's silence had the face of grief. Years later she told me about the Italian boy who'd taken her on the hill and she'd been told never to see him again.

The wedding photograph in the drawer I found in a leather folder, rarely opened. The Welsh are good at being photographed, good at cheating. Why did you every marry him? I asked. Because he wast there: because he needed me. That's all.

Her pain when he died. Her face choked by it. That had *not* been all, which made it worse. She loved him.

They loved each other, and they exiled the love they could not make. I half-understood that. Sometimes I was able to laugh – that the best butcher in town should be so good at meat and possess a revulsion to flesh. Perhaps my mother should have been a carcass and he'd have known how to cope.

If only my sister had lived to laugh with me.

It was hard to laugh alone. I was the exile.

And in exile this is my kingdom: Penrhyn Productions. I am here before Eric this morning, before the secretaries even. Eight thirty; an empty office. The boss is at the helm. A memo on my desk: I don't believe it! The go-ahead from the British Travel Association – at last. Please contact immediately. Well, at least they'll keep us in cash for a year, with the Arab films as well. It's almost a year since I put the idea up: six films on "The Sound of Britain". Such an obvious idea I found it hard to believe no one had done it before. No commentary, so no language problem, a huge potential sale on the Continent as well as the United States. "We're in the money, we're in the money . . ."

—Can I have some, since you're singing about it?

—You're here early, David.

—I've got to earn your salary somehow, mate. Come on, bloody Janet. She said she'd be here by eight forty-five. Probably still screwing with some black bastard.

—St Valentine's Day: what else would you have her do? And what else did the British Travel people say on Friday?

—Nothing much! They just want you expresso. They had some high-powered meeting apparently, and your mad scheme got the thumbs-up in a big way. Can't bloody think why.

—What's his name, Tattersall? I'll give him a buzz as soon as he's in. Not before ten I'd guess, for someone whose job it is to sell Britain.

—Better than VD, anyway. If I haven't got the clap after two months on this job . . .

—We're going to need a really top sound-man on this. Who do we know, David?

David likes being consulted. I know the answer. And he knows I know. He wants to direct the travel films, I'm sure of it.

—Would you like to direct?

—Serious?

—Sure!

—I would, yes!

—Even though it's a mad scheme?

—Ah well, maybe I can make something of it.

—You should be virtually finished with the clap film this week, shouldn't you, so you could be free. But I can't spare Janet, too. And I'll need a new editor here for the other work.

—All six?

—Why not?

David's really pleased. It's the best idea in Wardour Street suddenly: I can see it in his face. A smile is fighting with his scowl. What a patronising bastard I am. Of course he'll do it well; I wouldn't have asked him otherwise. And it frees me yet again. He doesn't know about the feature-film. Neither does anybody apart from Waldron. Yes, I'm going to see this Tattersall bloke, fix it all up, dump it on David. Thank God for that. Then I'll do the Arab films with O'Rourke and Archie Hill. My swan-song as a documentary film-producer. And the end of Penrhyn Productions. I'm scared, but I'll do it. The others will get jobs easily enough; no need to have a conscience about that. Those who haven't got ability have got tits.

And if I fail? Don't think about it. Mustn't think about it, or I'll be making films about VD and Billingsgate Market for the rest of my life. There's going to have to be a way forward.

—I'm going to find some breakfast, David. I'll be back in half an hour.

Nine o'clock. Soho. I walk round the corner into Old Compton Street. Buy a *Guardian*. I hate the *Guardian*. Why the fuck do I buy it? The liberal face: I am seen to care. Even in Portmadoc I bought the *Guardian*. Why don't I buy *Mayfair*, or *Boobs Galore*, or something fitting for a Monday morning breakfast?

I order croissants and coffee. Feel warm and elated. Gareth Penrhyn is going somewhere – again! There must be someone, some glorious bird all body and spirit to join me on this great adventure in this swarming, teasing world I do not know. Here's your man, lovely lady, he's having coffee and croissants in Old Compton Street right now. I need you. I'm worth it, d'you hear, wherever you are?

* * *

After my father died we went down to Wales more often. I had left the BBC and set up Penrhyn Productions with a little borrowed capital and surprising good-will from the trade. Those were the fat days for the documentary film industry: all the work, fast cars and dolly-birds anyone could handle. Oil was cheap, the pound still up, property prices still down, London was "in" and so was the pill. Cameras raked the world: not a sunset over the Cyclades but it was shot by six production companies, not a sand-dune in the Sahara but a model from Courrèges was posed upon it. Iced daiquiries tinkled from Manhattan to Machu Picchu.

I was working even harder, but now I took time off when I wished, when I could. We'd pack the children in the car at dawn and be in Portmadoc by lunchtime. Mother had a small terraced house on the edge of the town. Within a couple of years I had put up £5,000 towards the house she always wanted down near the harbour with a garden in which she planted bougainvillea and palm-trees in memory – I wondered – of the Italian boy who had once taken her on the hill and and whom she'd been told never to see again. It was a sweet romantic autumn of her days. The children loved her. We loved them, and we loved one another. We'd made it. What did it matter if I travelled with interchangeable blondes in the seat beside me, who kept identical shot-lists by day and were marginally different in bed by night? They spiced the dish, were consumed, forgotten, and they ensured that Gareth returned home content in soul and skin. Jennifer bought new dresses, said little, sometimes inquired where I was going next. I was a happy man. I told myself I was a happy man. Everyone said I was a happy man.

Each of the the compartments of my life felt secure, warm and fecund.

* * *

Monday night, Jennifer came to me with almost a smile. She had, she said, been unkind. She had felt so miserable. Miserable not for herself – that didn't matter any more – but for the children. She was glad now. Through all this misery it seemed the best thing to do, to share them between us. Perhaps we could manage it amicably after all, even if only for their sake. Did I intend to sell the house or go on living here – with whatever new girl? She couldn't resist slipping that one in.

—Of course you will. You've got everything a girl wants. I'm sure you're a wonderful lover.

That hurt. It always does. Even now. Embers of old jealousy were stirring in her and the pain was warm. She was looking at me. Was she looking for a sign? Of what? I believe she wanted me to confirm my rejection of her just one more time; perhaps she wanted me to say, Yes, there *is* this girl and she loves me as you have never been able to love me, and we're going to be very happy. That would have sealed off her pain and left her free. I knew then that lover-boy meant nothing to her save a little comfort. How sad, very sad. And how overjoyed I was. Poor little bugger! Did she really hope I would pull out one last confidence trick and say, Jennifer I still love you?

I do still love her.

The house by the river is silent. Oh, my Jennifer.

Part Two

February 15 to February 28

Day Fifteen

There they are, my gorgons. They are dangling along the wall of my cutting-room, impaled on hooks: twenty years of off-cuts filmed by the libido from the years fifteen to thirty-four.

And if I am to make a film about love, what parts will they play? Figures in a bacchanalia? A chorus line? Sirens?

Now disperse! You've sung your song; it's time for a star to step forward. It is year thirty-five and onwards.

* * *

Encounters are a kind of lie, like memories; they are fabrications, conspiracies hatched out of a yearning for change. We paint a rose on an empty pane.

Sarah, there are quiet places where I still know you. A beach where you stand in the wind, hair astray, feet parting the tide, hands salty to my face. A room where you lie enfolded by the night: Pompeian ash could not make your body here more calm. A garden where you walk under the last leaves, your breath quick, needles of frost on your fur, dark hair cocooned.

The garden is where I first met you. I was leaving. I looked up at the sound of feet on gravel. You had a child in either hand, the elder such a miniature of you it made me smile, a wraith of a girl wtih dark eyes searching. The younger girl was solemn and round-faced, dangling on your hand, unbalanced as you walked. The gate hung open behind you.

The children ran indoors. I did not know who you were, or why you were here. I looked at you.

—I'm Gareth.

—And I'm Sarah.

For a while it was as though we'd set up two tape-recorders

which conversed politely in the dusk, while our eyes enjoyed the silence.

—My father works with you sometimes, doesn't he? He told me.

—That's right. I make films. Stephen's writing some music for me. I didn't realise who you were. I remember now. Collecting the kids from school, have you?

—Just Tamara. Natasha's too young.

—Russian names!

—Yes, my mother's Russian.

—And you live in Chiswick?

—Round the corner.

—Convenient? Or isn't it?

—Sometimes.

And you laughed.

—For baby-sitting anyway. Mine have always been three hundred miles away, up in Wales.

—We're only just back from Germany. The house belongs to my mother.

—I suppose you're lucky then.

—Yes . . . I'd better go in and give them their tea. Maybe I'll see you.

—You probably will. I hope so. Stephen and I have had enough for one day. Goodbye, Sarah!

Your hair caught the light from the kitchen. You were very slim. You had the step of a dancer Finally you turned your head as though you felt you perhaps shouldn't. Good-bye, you said.

The garden was empty, the gate still open. I wanted to close it so that you should never leave.

Sarah's impression on me developed gradually like a Polaroid image in the sun. It was months before I saw her a second time, again at Stephen's house, and again she was occupied with the children. She looked up with a smile which troubled my waking and working hours. A while later I met her a third time, in Chiswick High Street. This time she was alone and we talked on the pavement between supermarkets. From then on I felt pleased to know that she was around whenever I visited Chiswick: the fact that she lived there warmed the place. A slice of my attention had begun to be reserved for her. She was a secret bloom in my garden, and I used to go to Chiswick more often than I strictly needed.

I never invited her out, not even to coffee or a drink in the pub. I'm not sure why. Most women half as attractive as Sarah I would have made a fairly obvious bid for by now. Was it a desire to respect her as some kind of superior being, to elevate her above other women, to crown her with a courtier's love? Or was it the fact that she was married – and for all I knew happily married? The thought of her clutching some gilded stockbroker in the night disturbed me, and I preferred not to think about it, preferred to keep her as a bird of passage encountered always on the wing between somewhere and somewhere else.

There was, besides, that terrible thing – the sanctity of marriage. Like the Hapsburg jaw, beliefs like that are inbred in families, and equally hard to disguise. "Never been a divorce in the Penrhyn family" my father used to pronounce with his eyes ever more firmly shut against the marital wasteland around him. "Never a divorce in the family," he would address to some teenage niece who'd been screwed by the baker's boy and whose shotgun marriage had six months' mileage in it for all to see. Old Penrhyn clung to his marriage just as – for a hell of a lot better reason, as I liked to think – I had clung to mine. For him it was a point of pride, and of safety. But it was also terror. With beliefs resembling a fakir's bed to lie on all your youth, what horrors arise at the prospect of a Slumberland mattress and a woman lying naked! And what equal horrors at the prospect of being alone!

Sarah was married; as I was. And that was that.

Meanwhile things were good at Penrhyn Productions on the top floor without a lift in Wardour Street. Within three years of leaving the BBC I had virtually paid off my capital loan and was earning more than twice my former salary. I began to notice the glazed look – like sheep snug in a pen – on the faces of fellow-producers who had stayed behind, and how pretentious they now seemed as they strutted around their secure little compound devising films about Kierkegaard or Gothic Revival and attending eternal departmental meetings like the college of cardinals. Earnest men whose passage through life had been from one home of lost causes to another, one shelter to another. OK, I had shit on my boots but I was nearer the soil than they, making my nuts-and-bolts films for the building trade or the Coal Board, with the odd extravaganza which some lunatic president of an American bank wanted on lute-making in

Andorra or the cave-paintings of the Drakensberg Mountains. I loved them all, and I loved the purr of success. It was the sound of my new Jaguar travelling fast uphill into the sun.

It was about this time I got to know Waldron. I had made a short film on the City, financed by one of the more plausible Worshipful Companies of which he was Master. At the Private Viewing of the film Waldron came up to me, red-faced and jangling with worshipful regalia, and confided in me the news which I must have been the only member of that assembly not to know already, that he was to be the next Lord Mayor.

—Penrhyn, he said. Penrhyn, I would like to tell you how concerned I am to encourage patronage of the arts during my year of office.

—Indeed, sir, what a good idea, I replied, wondering what I had to do with such a noble notion.

—You're a talented fellow, and I don't mind saying that I like you.

—Thank you, sir.

—And I know that you like pictures, Penrhyn. You've been most appreciative about my own modest collection.

—It's a very fine collection, sir.

—Now, what about the National Gallery?

—Also a very fine collection, sir.

—You find it so? Well, so do I, I don't mind telling you. Very fine collection. Should be better known.

—I would have thought it was reasonably well known, sir.

—It so happens that a young nephew of mine – my sister's boy, a bright fellow – he's just taken over there. The Director. Not a bad job for a youngster. And I'd like to help him get on. Put the place on the map.

—What did you have in mind? A film?

—Many films. I've been talking to young Kenneth and he thinks it's a top-hole idea. He'll give you all the co-operation you need. All his staff at your service. I want eleven films. It seems to be the number the networks like. We'll sell 'em everywhere, and with this new video-cassette market coming along we've got a double market – television and educational. Think of it, plug in Botticelli in your own lounge. It'll change ordinary people's lives. You know, the man-in-the-street. Go and see Kenneth, and don't worry about the cash. It's all here.

Waldron tapped his breast-pocket, and I went to see young

Kenneth. He was timid and eager. Of course there was all the co-operation I wanted. One film on each of the periods of art represented in the collection – I suggested – plus one which he, the Director, would present himself: his own personal selection. This would make it clear that pictures are about enjoyment, not just stamps in an album.

The Director's crumpled suiting twisted into paroxysms of embarrassed excitement, and frail white fingers tapped the air.

—Of course, he said. Of course! If you really think so. But I'm not very good at cameras, you know.

—Don't you worry, we'll operate those. You just be yourself. Talk enthusiastically just as you are to me now.

—I feel I have to say that some of my colleagues might be shocked at their director professing to *like* pictures: that's to say, have feelings about them, you know what I mean. And I must warn you, my own favourites are not very popular. I'm a *seicento* man, you know.

He was already populating the space between us across the mahogany desk with baroque martyrdoms and powdered portraits, and a smile of pure joy was spreading across his face. I warmed to "young Kenneth", and over *osso buco* in Soho we discovered a cheerful common ground envisaging Waldron's social revolution in Tower Hamlets which the introduction of the Wilton Diptych to every working-class home was shortly to bring about. And so I made a good friend, as well as eleven films for Waldron which brought me considerable prestige in the trade and a gold medal in Llubliana; but which were never – as far as I know – sold to a single television network outside Tonga. We joyfully created the cultural white elephant of the decade. Waldron blamed the trades unions world-wide, and was as happy to lose half-a-million for the love of beauty as any Renaissance prince. He paid wondrously little tax for that year, and became a Life Peer in the New Year's Honours List.

It was for these National Gallery films that Stephen Halliday composed special music. I had met him at the BBC years before, and knew him to be a brilliant wasted man, with a chip-on-the-shoulder modesty which made him reject the label "composer": he preferred to call himself a "music maker". I had found a card he must have given me printed "Stephen Halliday, Music Maker", and it prompted me to go and see him.

Halliday could play just about every musical instrument, badly, except the flugelhorn at which he was supreme: in fact he had been brought in to play this instrument for the world première of Vaughan Williams's 9th Symphony at the Royal Festival Hall some ten years earlier, and I think that a chat-piece about him in the then *Manchester Guardian* must have been the first time I had heard of him.

It was typical of Halliday that he was incapable of musical originality but possessed a genius for impromptu pastiches of any composer you might care to mention. He could "do" you an original Haydn, or Berlioz or Stockhausen with scarcely a moment's thought: it was disturbing in this tender little man that nothing he wrote was ever a send-up. It sounded like the real thing, often better, and he played it – though badly – with passion. He was the guy for me; and, as I hoped, he "did" me (timed to the second) immaculate pieces of Plainsong, Gregorian Chant, Vivaldi, Pergolesi and so on down to Debussy and Manuel de Falla, to such brilliant effect that my fellow film producers, whose special skill is robbing record libraries for musical backgrounds, seriously believed I had discovered an amazing cache of unpublished scores, and please could I tell them where!

One lunchtime my car was out of commission and I was making my way from Stephen's house to Chiswick tube station. A white Mini drew up beside me and a woman leaned over to open the passenger door. It was Sarah. I hadn't seen her for months; it was the summer after I had first met her in Stephen's garden.

—D'you want a lift into town? she said.

I climbed in. We drove off towards Hammersmith. She wore large dark-glasses and a blue shirt belted at the waist. She drove fast and well. She didn't say much. Neither did I. I felt happy, excited. There was something I noticed again about her: it was an air of waiting – for what I wasn't sure. Not expectancy, she was too serene for that. It was as if she knew something about me, about us; and whatever it was filled the silences between us, it played about her lips, it smoothed the small movements of her body as she swept her hair back across her shoulders, fingered the gear-lever, moved her legs in a scissor motion when she applied the brake and clutch. I didn't try to take my eyes off her, and when she removed her glasses I glanced at her black eyes in the mirror. They caught mine. Once when she fumbled for a packet of cigarettes in the handbag by her side I caught a glimpse of the undercurve of her breast, naked.

It was several seconds before I realised the car had stopped and we were in Soho. She was waiting for me to get out. I wanted more than anything to touch her. It would be ridiculous to shake hands. She was smiling now. What was making her happy? Now she was glancing out of the windscreen. A policeman was approaching. We were on a double yellow line. I had to do something. But I didn't know where she lived. I didn't even know her name. Scarcely any time remained. In ten seconds it would be left to chance again, and I wouldn't be working with Stephen much longer.

—Please give me your phone-number.

She did, and I scrawled it on a newspaper, already half out of the car and backing into the policeman. She was still smiling. Those radiant eyes. What were they saying? I knew what they were saying.

—When are you in?

—Most mornings.

—What's your name?

She laughed.

—Sarah Kinley.

Waving to the policeman she was off. I climbed up the stairs to the office. I felt seventeen, elated just as I used to feel with Shirley on my motor-cycle pillion racing out of Criccieth towards Maentwrog and a walk hand-in-hand by the harbour at old man Parry-Jones's place as the sun went down.

Back in the big house on the river there was Jennifer with the children, as though nothing had happened. But nothing had happened. Nothing would happen; at least nothing to disturb all this. Why should it?

I knew why.

I was painting a rose on an empty pane, petal by petal.

But I didn't ring her, and the following week we took Deirdre and Seth to the Casa Bella as usual. It was late July. Above the mountains three eagles were measuring the wind, occasionally folding their wings and dropping down out of sight into the valley. Michele brought us rabbits. The shop-keepers greeted us in Bordighera. We picnicked among the butterflies along the crumbled terraces in the summer wind, and walked among the warm pine-needles in the shadows. It was all as before, and a great peace settled upon us as it always did here in the mountains. Our mountains. Where we had repaired our lives. It would last. It would last. How I loved Jennifer. Nothing, no one would take this from her again. There she sat in the small garden by the sun-room we had added to the old house, and in the evening a breeze caught her hair and she looked up and smiled at me. It was a smile of contentment. We had made it, Jennifer and I. Last night you woke me, opened to me, sweet love, after so long a winter. Nourish my heart. So many white stars have come out of the dark.

* * *

Rain bucketing down this morning. It's Tuesday. The day after St Valentine's Day. A sense of having achieved something after yesterday: Jennifer actually meeting me halfway over the children, with a ray of a chance that we might after all arrange it peacefully. Is the worst over? Will our marriage at last slip quietly out of our lives like an old pirate-ship replete with plunder? And we two left exhausted and bloody, with not much left to steal, but at least able to shake hands and part in poverty?

It doesn't feel like that. When she smiles at me I love her all over again and never want her to leave. But what do I want her for? Comfort? Friendship? A cook-housekeeper? Stimulus? Habit? Or because I need the abrasion of her presence? Oh, why rationalise, tie labels on our pain? I have got used to her, and the prospect of living without her for ever and ever is appalling. No succulent blonde bouncing on my prick each midnight and dawn will ever fuck that loneliness away.

So I have earned my mistresses all tits and giggles and she her lover-boy all earnestness and doing-good, and neither will do us any good. The children will flit between us with sorrowful cognisance of what we are, and then flit away having learned, they hope, never to repeat the same mistakes; and we shall die in separate beds alone.

There are tears in my eyes. Why don't I go and take her before it's too late?

I cannot go through that again.

I cannot go through this either.

There is only that or this: Oh, God! I shall pull the bedclothes over my head and go back into the dark. At least I don't have to witness the hell I live in.

I could take a heap of valium and drug the demons away. But only for a while. Or drink: I could get stoned at seven in the morning. And then what? Fuck the stupid world, I'll get up and savage it with work. In less than three weeks I'll be in the Middle East with Barry O'Rourke and a profitable film series to plan. Let's think about money, then; fame and money. Lots of it. After the Arab films my début as a feature-film director. *Succès fou.* Then so many offers I'll have to hire marshals to keep the queue orderly, and the whole world will audition for me. Sorry, Pope John-Paul, you're not up to the part, nor you Giscard, Brezhnev, lend me the Kremlin for a couple of months, will you? Naturally I'll pay the usual facility fee.

Shit! That reminds me, I've got lunch with the British Travel Association. That'll be another moneymaker, that series "The Sound of Britain". Better get up; a suit this morning. Wah wah talk and a fat contract initialled over the Armagnac. That's what it's all about; that's what I'm here for; that's where I stand in the world. Gareth Penrhyn of Penrhyn Productions is at it again. None better. Never knowingly undersold. I'd like a fuck before I go. Can't have a fuck. Just time for a cup of coffee and off. Let's get on with the day.

I'll look after myself somehow.

Jennifer, don't go!

Day Sixteen

I did ring her.

Two months had passed since the day she drove me to Soho, and I hadn't seen her since. Now my work with Stephen Halliday was over, the music for the National Gallery films was recorded, and I had no reason any longer to go to Chiswick. I would never see Sarah again if I didn't ring her, and this was how I intended it to be.

The summer with Jennifer and the children at the Casa Bella was rich and relaxed. It was as if the jagged edges of my life were smoothed away by the warm insistence of family life. I closed my eyes in the sun and enjoyed it. Deirdre would bring us wildflowers from the hillside: Seth tottered outside in his pyjamas after dark to make fireflies settle and wink on his fat brown arm. Jennifer read Thomas Mann under the ilex-tree. I went for perspiring walks in the afternoon through the pine-woods up to the bare mountain-side where the path zigzagged across the shale. It was heaven, and I only returned to England before the others at the end of August because a week's filming had to be done before the summer was out.

Alone, Sarah began to haunt me. Directing a camera-crew on one of the Frisian islands off the coast of Holland I continually imagined her to be by my side – barefoot in the sand-dunes, salt in her hair, legs burnished in the sun. She was close, she wanted to be involved, her presence supported me in the hundred-and-one problems of daily filming about which Jennifer knew nothing and which I had never been able or wanted to share with her. Sarah was there, beautiful and understanding and desirable. She joined her own life and her own thoughts to mine so naturally I was bewildered with delight, and in my guts there was a longing for her to stay near and never go away.

In the night I woke with my hand between her thighs and kissed her closed eyes until she moved under me, pulling me on to her with her fingers smoothed across my back. In the morning she was bending over the bed with a tray of breakfast carried below her bare breasts. Raised on one elbow I took the tray from her and drew her down towards me until her nipples brushed my chest. In the evening she lay stretched along the wooden balcony against the sea, head buried within her arms, bare back concave between her hair and buttocks. I massaged her shoulders and kissed the hollow of her spine. Under the moon we made love in the black water as the tide rolled us like driftwood across the cool sand.

These were flights of fantasy more real than my own present happiness, bringing messages of urgency that seemed to carry across the span of my life like a birth-cry long stifled. It is not too late; it is not. The last compromise is the compromise of the heart. What is happiness, anyway, if bought at such a price?

It was September. I was back from Holland. I came to the office early to shift a pile of chores that had built up over the summer. A warm late-summer morning. By nine thirty the pile was clear enough. Soho was the last place I wanted to be. No one else had arrived. I phoned her. A soft, cautious voice answered. No note of surprise.

—Have you got a garden? Can I come and sit in it?

She was laughing. I felt exultantly happy.

—Yes, if you like. Where are you?

—Soho!

—But that's a hundred miles.

—It won't take me long. I've got a car this time.

—All right!

She gave me the address.

I left a quick note on the desk and hurried downstairs, relieved that I didn't meet anyone coming up. I was playing truant. And why not? Perks of office. I was the boss. In Old Compton Street I bought a bag of Algerian coffee and a bottle of Frascati. Hang on! Supposing her husband's at home. He might be a little surprised. Or she might be going out at ten thirty. I might even find her five months pregnant. Oh Jesus! And who was she anyway? I knew nothing about her whatever. Nothing at all.

In the parking-lot the Jaguar lurched through the potholes filled with overnight rain. Someone coming to work gratefully slipped into my place. He was welcome to it, poor bugger: he hadn't got a lovely lady to see in a garden. I crossed Oxford Street and cut up towards Marylebone Road and the motorway. Maybe it was the long way round but I wanted to drive fast. The needle touched seventy before the Shepherds Bush turning. I made for Goldhawk Road, not a place that had ever filled me with much joy before. But today there was a street market. Even the sign "Acton 2¼ miles" read like a welcome. Then down towards the river. Here was her road, dark with lime-trees, the sun on the upper leaves just beginning to turn. Number Twenty-six. I parked not quite outside: rang the bell. It was ten fifteen.

I saw her silhouette through the glass door.

—Goodness, that was quick!

—Hello!

She had been washing her hair. She was squeezing long dark strands of it with a towel, her head on one side.

—Come in.

She was alone. In a black tee-shirt and white shorts. Bare feet. The house was cool and dark. She flicked her wet hair back and led the way down the narrow hall to the kitchen where a washing-machine juddered and a splash of sunshine painted the wall through open french windows.

—You asked for a garden: there's the garden.

And she turned with a laugh, extending a bare arm towards the open door with a slight bow.

—Thank you, ma'am.

—You're welcome. You'd like some coffee, I expect.

—You'd be right.

She put the Frascati in the fridge and placed a pot of coffee already made on a tray already prepared. I watched her carry it out into the garden and place it on a low table where I was standing, then lower herself gracefully on to a rug on the lawn. I sat rather more awkwardly beside her as she poured out the coffee. I noticed a book, dark glasses and a packet of cigarettes by the cushion where she must have been leaning drying her hair.

—You're working, unlike me.

—Yes, I'm taking a degree next summer. You must have been working too if you phoned from Soho. Do you always get in that early?

—Only sometimes. A degree in what?

—Philosophy.

I'm not too hot at talking about philosophy, and said so.

—Neither am I, so let's not.

—I like your garden. That must be an Albertina rose.

—It is. We put it in when we first moved in.

—How long ago was that?

—About two and a half years ago.

—What does your husband do?

—Nothing at the moment.

And then after a pause,

—We're not together any more.

My stomach curled up. We neither of us said anything for a few moments. I sipped my coffee. She poured me another cup. Her breasts pressed against the wooden table. A stretch of naked back, slender and bronzed, widened below the tee-shirt. She looked up at me as she passed the cup.

—You're married, aren't you?

—Yes, I've got two children.

I imagined she knew that already. She drank her coffee and lit a cigarette.

—Angus had a sort of breakdown.

—Since you split up?

—Oh, it was coming on a long time.

She folded her arms round her knees, the cigarette smoke filtering upwards through her hair. I could see she half-wanted to talk about it and that it irritated her to do so. Suddenly she sighed and looked up at me again. Her look was a question.

—Married man in a garden with beautiful separated lady. Where does that put me, I said?

I felt pompous.

—At a disadvantage, maybe.

—You think so?

—I'm free. I can do what I like. I've been through it all.

I thought of all the other men she was free to have coffee with in the garden, drink Frascati with, take to bed. I felt jealous.

—You have children, you're not all that free, I said.

—That's true. My mother takes them a lot, so I can get to college. I go in at lunchtime, if you remember.

Her saying that reminded me that it was two months since she'd given me a lift. Why two months, she must be thinking? And whom had she met in that time, I was thinking?

—I thought I wouldn't ring you, and I knew I would.

—I hoped you would.

She was looking down now, pulling at tiny blades of grass. There was a small mole low on her back.

—Are you going into town today?

—No, today's a free day.

My face must have told her anyway, but all the same, I said:

—I'm glad. She was gazing at me. It was as though we had drawn a line under that conversation and set it on one side. We talked of other things. We talked all morning. She told me about her marriage. How she'd been eighteen and pregnant in her first year at Cambridge. She had dithered over an abortion until it was too late: besides, Angus wanted to marry her desperately and wanted the child. She knew then it wouldn't work, but with the child coming it became easy to pretend it would. Angus adored the child and adored her. She got used to carrying both of them;

even enjoyed the role. He needed her support so helplessly: even making love she seemed to be cradling him.

It was not until he got a teaching job in Germany that she knew for sure things would never get better. He was demanding more and more now; would drink obsessively, burst into tears, throw a dozen accusations at her, then roar off alone along the *Autobahn* and return at three in the morning sullen and strange. She used to wonder whether she would get a call from the police first; whether he really wanted to kill himself; and her guilt at realising she half-wanted him to do just that would bring her up sharp. She redoubled her efforts to help him, concentrating all her energies to making him feel safe. Even close friends she began to feel guilty about seeing: if they were women, then weren't they picking him to pieces, he'd ask, with that aggressive, pleading look in his eye? And if they were men, then she was in love, wasn't she? Sleeping with them every afternoon. He began slipping home from school early to make sure, though there was always a different excuse. Even the greengrocer over the road, who was sweaty and sixty, she hardly dared talk to since he'd once given her a peck on the cheek in the shop, and Angus who'd been there was almost out of his mind for two days, refusing to go to work or let her out of his sight.

This was when she agreed to have another child. Of course she shouldn't have done, though sometimes it made things easier being a trio of sane people in the house instead of just two. It was when Angus refused to believe he was Natasha's father that she decided they had to come home. Her mother had this house she'd bought as an investment. She was that sort of woman. Here at least Angus could get free medical care. It took her more than a year to persuade him there was something wrong. He was schizophrenic, the hospital said; he must have regular treatment, come in twice a week. Angus went three times, then swore the doctor was trying to kill him. Six months later she got him to go to another hospital. This time he seemed to go regularly, until after two months she discovered he'd just been walking round London. There was nothing more she could do. They had no money; the children were having nightmares; she was terrified he'd just disappear with them one day. And she couldn't take it any more. She rang up his mother in Bognor and pleaded with her to help him. In her tone of voice Sarah knew the old lady blamed her, but she agreed. To her surprise Angus went without a murmur.

That was a year ago. Now he seemed better, more relaxed when he came up sometimes for the weekend, but she knew she could never have him back. Never. It had been a terrible year.

So this had been the year – almost a year – since I had first met her, radiant, in her father's garden last November. To think how I had envied the lucky confident man who came back to her each evening from his successful job with prospects. I felt moved, disturbed and excited. It was one o'clock. We were eating salami and tomato salad in the sun. She was holding a glass of chilled Frascati, looking composed and beautiful. Her hair, dry now, fell over her arm and touched her bare thigh as she drained the glass and replaced it on the garden table.

—Haven't I told you a lot? I'm all right, though, you see. Now.

She poured herself another glass of wine, drank half of it and lay back in the sun, one hand behind her head. I leant over and placed my hand on her stomach. Her other hand closed over mine. Her skin was warm from the sun.

—I want to make love to you, I said. Very much!

—I know you do. And I don't want you to.

* * *

David is over the moon today. All signed and sealed over lunch yesterday with the British Travel Association, and he starts next week doing a recce for the six "Sound of Britain" films. I've handed him all my notes and suggested treatments, and now he's working late putting the finishing touches to the VD horror-comic. The United Nations information rep is viewing it on Friday. I suppose I'll have to be there. I've seen it so often I'm almost as immune as David, but this UN tenderfoot is in for a few shocks. We'd better have some vomit-bags discreetly available in the Viewing Theatre.

—I won't have to be there, will I, Janet inquires?

—Not really.

She is angling for the Middle Eastern trip with O'Rourke, Archie Hill and me next month. The budget can stand it, thanks to Waldron, but I'm not sure I want her along. True, she'd break up the stag party, but shall I welcome her around in my first weeks after Jennifer leaves? Male company might be a better idea. I'd thought of borrowing Eric's new secretary, the one with tits as spectacular as Janet's, but the silly bugger went and sacked her yesterday. Said she was lazy and useless. He's probably right: he's not one for sexy aspidistras. Perhaps I should get a secretary of my own instead of always using Eric's. I could take her on the trip; but that would infuriate Janet and I don't want to do that. No, I won't take anyone.

—Do you think my hormones are going to be any use after all those months of VD, David grumbles?

He'll do the Britain films beautifully, much better than I could. Ten years ago I'd have found them a challenge. Today they'd be mechanical, full of tricks to fill the gaps where my mind should be. I know too much and care too little. It scares me sometimes how far I've moved away from all that. It's like a guilty secret. Why don't I come out with it? Am I simply putting off telling everybody I'm going to close the office because I'm moving into feature-films? Is it a sense of security, wanting to keep the successful part of me going to bridge the gulf Jennifer will create in my life when she leaves? I think it's probably both of those things. Or am I not at all sure I shall move into feature-films?

Yes, I am sure. Quite sure. I've posed that question so often before, and the uncertainty of my own response has disturbed me. Today for the first time the echo inside me is strong and positive. Yes! No question about it. And it's because at last the seed of an idea is there. I hope it will grow. The mime troupe at the theatre last night is what planted the seed. There were three of them – two men and a girl; and they mimed a story about rival love. A bloody stupid story it was, which was why I stopped trying to follow it and followed my own thoughts instead. The girl was extraordinary. Her movements. Her face. She didn't need to speak: it was better that she didn't. The emotion she radiated swept the theatre in shock-waves. She looked like the young Ingrid Bergman. Jane Young her name was when I looked at the programme. Plain Jane Young, of the Garnett Mime Theatre. Who was Garnett? Who cares? Jane Young. Why didn't I make a film about a beautiful deaf-and-dumb girl? It sounded a bit romantic said like that. But it needn't be, wouldn't be. Do I know why I want to? Yes, I do. Not just because I fancy Jane Young and want to play the big director to lure her into bed? No, it's more than that. Much more.

—I wrote a story about a deaf-and-dumb girl once.

O'Rourke and I are having a drink in the lounge of Martinez

in Swallow Street. He rang this afternoon and wanted to talk about the Arab films.

—Did you ever publish it?

He is sitting opposite me across a little tiled table drinking Scotch. His hair is still light brown, parted like an old-fashioned schoolboy's, in spite of the battered face with its blob of a drinker's nose. I like him more and more: the warmth and the wit he gives out. He likes protégés, I can see that, and already he thinks of me as a protégé. He loves to spin a web of old wisdom round me. From the casual way he has told me about his story of the deaf-and-dumb girl I know how delighted he is to have anticipated my needs, so to speak. It's as if he'd known long ago I'd need such a story, and kept it specially for me.

—No, I never published it. I never found a place for it. I'm a novelist, not a short-story writer, and it was too short to publish on its own. It's not my length of cloth. It's just been hanging around in my old kit-bag.

The voice of the tired old pro.

—Can I read it?

—Of course you can, dear boy. I'll put it in a taxi for you tomorrow, if you like. Tell me about your beautiful Jane Young.

—Is it part of the bargain?

—Naturally. And he bellowed a great laugh from his guts, then gazed wistfully at his empty glass. I beckoned the waiter.

—I'll leave a note for her at the theatre tomorrow. To meet me first, you old rogue.

—Naturally. You're the one who needs comfort, God knows. How are things at home?

—Nothing changed. The month is drawing on.

—You're too bloody nice.

—I'm not, you know.

–No, I know you're not. Selfish pig, like we all are. How else do we ever get anything done? Do you think she really will leave? D'you want her to? It can be terrible living alone; even worse than being married.

—Goodnight, David! Goodnight, Janet!

I have a letter to Jane Young in my pocket, c/o the Garnett Mime Theatre. If I posted it the letter would reach her tomorrow, but delivering it to the theatre feels more appropriate. I'll walk. More appropriate to what? I want her to have it tonight. I've half a mind to stay at the theatre this evening and take a second look at her. But I remember my octogenarian uncle who went thirty-four times to *Hair* (though he didn't have any). That won't do. Besides I have O'Rourke's manuscript with me: he sent it round this morning in a taxi as he said he would, and I want to read it this evening. The letter is on my tasteful headed note-paper, Penrhyn Productions Ltd, signed with a creative flourish. Ring; come and have lunch. Next week. Soon, anyway. (Who are you, Jane Young?)

I don't want to go home. I buy an evening paper outside the theatre. Yes, the doorman would see the letter got to her. Jane Young. Yes! What do I want an evening paper for? Can't even read the bloody thing in the dark street. I walk back towards Soho and the car-park. I don't want to go home. Shall I go to a strip-club? For a fortnight I've been adjusting to Jennifer leaving. Alternate euphoria and despair; lots of adrenalin. Now I'm not at all sure she wants to go. That black girl under the neon glare with the leopard-skin crotch, shall I have her now? Ten pounds worth of poke and pox? An eerie truce has settled on the house. Should I be kind and attentive like the family solicitor smoothing the arrangements of our lives? The pavements shimmer after the rain: smears of cerise and violet from the love-shop. Executives with bland faces in front of day-glo dildoes. A Rolls on a double yellow line. I want to live in peace with my family, not alone: but my rogue elephant has to be free, and how can that be so if the home fires are to burn? Oh, fuck it! Fuck Soho! All this indigestible fodder for my loneliness. This masturbators' supermarket. The Jaguar encloses me. Clunk! I'll have a drink by the river then sit by the fire and read O'Rourke's story.

Do you think she really will leave? Barry asked. *D'you want her to?* What a question.

I want to be with Jennifer, with Deirdre, Seth, Ennis, all my life.

And I want to create something which is more than the day-to-day man I am.

Does that mean I must be two people who greet each other with a wink?

Day Seventeen

Nobody in the office yet this morning. Time to think. Time to calm down. Surveying my orderly little kingdom is a good tranquiliser. Eric's plush office with photographs of two prep-school sons on his desk and an incongruous bullfight poster on the wall; and the alcove where his two secretaries type and quiver and grow pale out of the sun. Now he's lost the one with big tits they've reverted to the customary androgynous mice in tandem. I suppose he does need two of them: he's so essential to me I must take his word for it. Eric's on holiday this week and so are they. The room has the look of Classroom 5b after school has broken up.

The receptionist has gone skiing with some jolly group who rang up and chattered all last week. So the boss is holding the fort till next Monday, guardian of the in-tray, the coffee percolator, and the trophies on the wall – Eric's crown jewels which will have to gather dust till he returns – and of our room: David's, Janet's and mine. It's out of Eric's parish and a perennial blot on his horizon, like an allotment sited next to Kew Gardens. It's where the real work is done, I tell him in order to shut him up whenever he starts housemaiding around. David just tells him to piss off. Janet ignores him altogether: he doesn't exist for her sexually, therefore he doesn't exist.

Do I? I am beginning to think I may. Maybe David has grown too rude of late, or he's laid her enough – I don't know – or just that she's still angling to join the recce in the Middle East next month.

This morning I'm alone here in this friendly place with its racks of film in reels, scotch-taped and labelled, its metal cupboards and stained Formica work-tops and yesterday's coffee-mugs. David won't be in today either: he'll be in the dubbing theatre up the road getting the VD film ready to show the UN information officer tomorrow, Friday. It turns out he's a Turk, Janet discovered.

—He should know all about VD, she muttered. He's probably got it.

A police car wails down below in Wardour Street. Voices shouting. Sounds like an accident. In the distance a burglar alarm which alarms nobody and which nobody is bothering to turn off.

I feel better. The coffee is percolating. Eric's even remembered to leave some brown sugar. His comforts of the flesh. Good! I must get some new mugs or we shall have an outbreak of foot-and-mouth disease in the office and we'll all be exterminated by order. I'll use Eric's mug with the gold rim and the vintage car motif.

Yes, I feel better. Every time I have a row with Jennifer like last night I am miserable and reassured at the same time. A little voice is telling me – "You see, she *is* impossible to live with." She is.

Until then I really believed I'd got it sorted out. It all seemed so clear on my way home yesterday evening. The depression had lifted. There were wisps of light on the river as I left the pub. A couple of whiskies had helped. If she didn't want to go after all then I must make it as easy as possible for her to stay. Pride was involved too, was it not? Absolutely no comments about lover-boy's shortcomings (maybe that was it: shut up, Gareth!). It was a matter of leaving the right door open inconspicuously. But what was the right door? I might have known that if she felt trapped Jennifer was capable of seeing any door as a trap-door.

I was shoo-ing the children upstairs.

—What d'you mean you don't need a bath, Seth? You've got half the football pitch on you. Go on! Good night!

—Oh, Daddy!

—Yes, Daddy! Go on, hop it!

Ennis was already asleep; Deirdre doing some homework in her room. Now Jennifer and I were alone in the kitchen. I took a drying-up cloth off the wall, then replaced it, anticipating a put-down from Jennifer ("I'll do it") and trying not to get my finger stuck in the little rubber gadget. A second drying-up cloth fell on the floor as I withdrew my finger. That always seems to happen. I bent down to pick them both up. My arse was in Jennifer's way getting to the fridge.

—Do leave it to me!

I stuffed both drying-up cloths back into the wall-gadget. Now I didn't know what to do. I hung around. Jennifer seemed to grow more frenetically busy.

Silence.

I poured myself a vodka. This meant getting ice from the fridge, and running the gauntlet with Jennifer a second time. I timed it better on this occasion, and strolled to the other end of the kitchen with my glass in my hand.

—Could you *not* walk up and down? It's awfully irritating.

I sat down at the table and scanned the newspaper. After a couple of minutes Jennifer began to swish the table with a damp dish-cloth.

—Do you think you could take the paper somewhere else?

I folded the paper and placed it on the sideboard.

—Oh, not there. Can't you see I'm trying to clear up? Why don't you go out? You don't have to stay around here.

—I wanted to be in this evening.

—That makes a change.

I let that one brush past.

—Well, I'm busy tonight.

—OK. I just thought we might have a bit of a talk.

—What about?

Jennifer was unfolding the ironing-board and rather pointedly setting the transistor on the table beside her.

—The children, I said.

It wasn't them I wanted to talk about. I didn't particularly want to talk at all. I wanted to try to share an evening with Jennifer.

—We've agreed about them, haven't we? What more is there to say?

So we were back to square one. She did intend to leave after all. Or did she? Or was she just damned if she was going to admit to me that she didn't? I was leaning against the door; began to cross the room thinking what to say next; realised this annoyed her; stopped; leaned against the sideboard; rattled the ice in my vodka. I was finding this increasingly intolerable. I had to ask her straight.

—D'you really want to go?

Jennifer slammed the iron down on its pad.

—Isn't that my business?

I could feel my own anger.

—It's also mine, isn't it? For Christ's sake, you're the one who's walking out.

—And won't you enjoy saying that to everyone! Poor Gareth, what a dreadful wife he's got. It's a wonder he put up with her for so long.

—That's quite untrue.

Jennifer went on ironing. What was the point of trying to talk? Hadn't we been here a hundred times before? I knew the battle positions by heart. We had spent all our resources on armaments and had grown too weary to use them. They lay heavy and rusting in our minds. And they would outlast us like the landscape of Ypres and the Somme. Our children and our grandchildren might revisit the place in sad fascination like picnickers, depart and forget. In Flanders field the poppies grow. Not here they don't. Thistles.

Jennifer had turned on the transistor. Haydn. If music be the food of hate, play on. No, she didn't hate me, nor I her. That was just it. We simply hated ourselves and blamed each other for it. There seemed no way out of that, except to part. Only by leaving could Jennifer learn to cherish herself. The same for me, perhaps. She neutered me, and I strangled her. There was nothing more to be said. Oh, God!

—Then there's nothing more to be said, is there?

—No!

—And you're sure that's what you want?

—What I want has got nothing to do with it, Gareth. What's the use of this? I want to live before it's too late. I'm getting old. I'm nearly forty-five, and what have I got to show for it? Nothing. Absolutely nothing.

She had turned off the transistor. Suddenly she was crying.

—Stop torturing me. Just let me go.

—I can't stop you.

—You are! You are!

—How?

—Just by being here you are. No, that's not fair, I know. You have a right to be here. It's your house. But leave me alone. Stop trying to probe.

And she sank on to the chair, her hands over her face, sobs of despair convulsing her. I wanted so much to comfort her, tell her it was all right really, that it was a bad dream and it would pass.

Just have faith. We'd been happy before, we'd be happy again. I placed my arm across her shoulders. She screamed,

—Don't touch me!

My anger burst. I struck her twice across the hands clasped over her face.

—Bitch, I yelled at her, Bitch! Bitch! I loathe you! And I slammed the kitchen door behind me. I walked along the river, barely noticing the lights snaking across the high tide. I could not, could not, go on with this. Already I felt sick at having struck her, hated myself for it. Would it have been all right if she had hit me back? I doubled up over the river wall and wept, my stomach heaving great sobs of despair and frustration. The anger had ebbed away. I stood up. I pee'd over the wall into the water, an arch of spray in the dark. Such a childlike thing to do that I felt ridiculously young again. Free. There would be no more anguished hoping. I would not try again. Not that again.

The pain embers were still warm this morning. My mind was like ashes. I came here early so as not to see Jennifer before I left. I wrote her a note saying sorry for having hit her. Nothing more. Everything else was numb. I wanted an hour here alone, having forgotten everyone would be out anyway, except Janet. She has arrived and is bustling about clearing up now that the UN film is finished. She is scooping up armfuls of off-cuts and carrying them to the rubbish-bin. I was hardly aware she had arrived. Now as I drink my coffee and watch her I have a strange feeling of life flowing back into my veins. I am laughing. She stops and says;

—What are you laughing about?

—Nothing. I just felt cheerful.

—When are you going to take a holiday, Gareth?

—What do I need a holiday for?

She is picking up the last scraps of black spaghetti here and there around the floor. Grey blouse and jeans tight over a hefty arse. Energetic, lumbering movements. A couple of stone overweight suits her. I am glad she is here.

—If you can take time off when you like, then I suppose you don't.

—It's a bit like that.

Now if I say anything about my going away next month I'll have to explain again why she can't come; and she can't come because she'd take up too much of my time. My own time is feeling distinctly sacred. If she's with me, she's with me for an entire month which will be about three and a half weeks too long – however much I'd like to screw her right now.

She has finished clearing up, brushing the dust off her. There's a button undone between her breasts. She notices it just after I do; pauses as she is about to do it up, not wanting to appear prudish. She's left her bra off again: casual or provocative, I'm not sure. I've been regarding her more and more lecherously of late. This morning we're alone; nothing much to do. She must have known that, the lovely bitch.

—Leave it. Even better, let me undo the others.

There is a rush of hunger in me. I want her – now, here, at ten in the morning. I haven't had a girl since before Jennifer decided to leave. Desire is smothering the pain of that, and the pain of last night. Janet stands in the middle of the room as I unbutton her blouse and cup the weight of her breasts in my hands. I circle her nipples with my tongue, one then the other, holding each breast to my face with both hands, feeling the softness on my cheek. She is breathing hard, her hands under my shirt. Clothes shed around us on the floor. She is stroking me with her fingers; utters a gasp as she comes down on me on the wooden chair. Grabbing her like a sack we collapse on the floor, on the pile rug beside my desk. We fuck with an urgency that blinds me. I am only my prick deep in her. I am biting her, kissing her mouth, her nose, ears, neck, clasping her buttocks under my hands, her breasts cushioning my chest, rushing, tumbling, falling, falling together, weightless. A still pool. Only our hearts thumping alternately. Deep gulps of breath. My face is buried in her shoulder.

—My God, you were hungry!

We are lying on the rug, the sweat cooling on us, my hands stroking her back, lips parted softly over hers, breathing into her, my tongue playing with hers. My heart still sounds like a steam-hammer.

Janet shivers. My knees and elbows feel painfully raw.

—Are you bruised too?

—No, just cold, and rather happy. I like you fucking me like that.

—It was good for you, wasn't it?

—Mmmm!

I disentangle my arms from her and clamber to my feet. She reaches for my hands and I pull her up.

—Come, you'll get frozen.

She snuggles against my chest and belly, shivering, her arms pressed in front of her, shoulders rounded, her face against my neck. Chill air cuts my back. Very lightly my hands move over her body: her buttocks, up the curve of her back, her shoulders, neck. She raises her face, saying nothing, and as I kiss her she slides her arms around my back, fingers spread. Dear Janet, there is no tenderness in the world like this kiss after love-making.

The electric fire has begun to warm the room.

—Would you like some more coffee?

—I'll make it: I usually do about this time.

And she laughs at the thought, switching on the electric kettle, washing out the coffee-pot and the two cups, tipping in fresh coffee from the tin. There is a deep fold below her buttocks. Her nipples harden against my fingers as she leans over with the sugar-bowl in one hand.

—One spoon?

She laughs again, trying not to spill the sugar.

—D'you want coffee or don't you?

She has placed two cups steaming on the desk: my hands are on the nape of her neck and she turns to me. I am rising to her again. She is looking at my face. Solemn now. I am smiling and my eyes are moist. Such closeness and trust with someone I scarcely know; a shared journey in suspended time. Hunger half-sated, we have stepped back to survey. I am gazing across at her, desiring her, but desire not hotly focused any longer but diffused across her entire body: hair pushed back behind small ears; thin curving mouth; parallel creases across the neck, shiny with sweat; deep sloping shoulders; a long shadow between breasts mottled and veined blue, low and full over the ribs; a fold of fat curving like a hammock between her hips above a mat of black hair; heavy thighs ending in dimples above the knees; slim calves; small broad feet. The confidence of appetites shared, and will share again. Little else I want to share. Janet, you could be a thousand others: exchangeable batteries supplying the same charge.

Janet lowers her eyes, embarrassed by my gaze.

—I feel weak when you look at me like that.

—I want you.

Second love-making is slower, more deliberate, gluttonous. We are enjoying our own performance, watching it. She is kneeling over me, guiding me slowly into her as if measuring my prick. I am laughing aloud, uncontrollably. I have a picture in my head, and the deeper Janet plunges me into her the clearer the picture grows. It's in a newspaper I saw last summer of a weedy little man in baggy trousers and a solemn visage posing with his prize-winning sunflower soaring above him against the wall of his cottage in Penge. Twenty feet six inches it was, and he was gripping it stoutly in one hand while his lady gazed at her amazing spouse through paraboloid spectacles. Oh, dear God, Janet, I am fucking you like a sunflower: come with me, come laughing with me to Penge and we'll take the local produce show by storm with my prize flower banging the roof like this and your incredible gourds hanging over me as if they would burst and spill the juices of the desert. Janet, Janet, in my desert how you slake my thirst.

She is lying on me.

—You do have a lovely prick.

—It likes your cunt.

—Lecherous sod!

—Why not?

—It's not true.

—Why not?

—You're so gentle.

—Thank you!

Thank you. Last night I hit Jennifer.

—Why don't you come and live with me?

—Because I'm living with someone else.

—What will he think?

—I don't care what he thinks.

—Then leave him and come and live with me.

—Don't be ridiculous. You don't care a damn.

—I might. I like being with you.

—You're just lonely.

And then the phone went. Janet, being on top, took it, reaching upwards with one hand.

—It's for you. Someone called Jane Young.

O'Rourke's story is brilliant and then collapses in exhaustion some while before the finish. It's obvious why he never got round to publishing it. Somehow the old pro in him got the creature to its feet again and whipped it to the finish. Then he must have dismounted with a sigh of relief and forgotten all about it.

All the same it's just what I'd hoped for when he talked about the theme the other evening at Martinez. It does fit beautifully the idea that came to me at the mime theatre when I saw Jane Young. And now I have something real to work on. What a marvellous feeling, to know I may have got it right at last. At last! No longer is this film of mine a ghost which haunts my corridors of self-doubt. Now it is flesh and blood; an embryo, but it will grow. I shall nourish it. It will be my child, offspring of all those wasted years. No, not wasted: years of training, rather. What better moment than now: all the skills are in my hands, and I am still awake. Ten years earlier and I would have made an expensive mess of it. Ten years to come and it would be a peak I should no longer have the will to climb.

Yes, now is the time. Gareth Penrhyn will be a new man. So what if I struck Jennifer yesterday? So what if I spent all morning screwing Janet on the rug? So what? Over, both of them. They no longer matter. I'll lay out no hyperboles of guilt and lust on their account. A new star is in the ascendant, ah ha! Before the year is out they'll be rushing into the streets in Portmadoc with their telescopes, you'll see. Oh, Gareth bach, Gareth, you always were a clever lad, didn't I say so? How your poor dead father would have been proud of you. No he wouldn't, the silly old bugger. Hello down there, Old Penrhyn, I've made a film, see; a real film, like you used to see in the Gaumont in the one-and-sixpennies! Ah, you whisper in your dust, Gareth boy, does your mother know you'll be late for tea?

* * *

I began to make money, which after ten years in the BBC was like leaving the Catholic church to get married: unforeseen bliss but enjoyed with a preliminary sense of sin. After doubling my BBC salary in no time, now I was earning about four times. They had always treated me like one of the junior gardeners when I worked at the BBC: now heads of departments I met at previews took to referring, with obsequious nostalgia, to my decade with them as the golden years of documentary television. Would I not like to come back – with suitable remuneration of course – they suggested? Dickie's retiring soon, you know; what about it? Of course the post is "boarded" but, between you and me, your application would be most favourably received. Fuck them! My own freedom was the most important territory I'd won, more important even than the salary.

Did Jennifer enjoy my success as much? Yes and no. It meant the end of rationing, so to speak: we could live as we liked. There were plentiful perks to ease her life: *au pair* girls instead of lodgers; a laundry service which delivered hygienic packages on Thursdays instead of a washing-machine which juddered and leaked all Sunday morning; spring holidays in Greece with the children rather than borrowed cottages in Essex; and all the rest of it. Life was more comfortable, and softer. And this she found less easy to take. It is hard on a woman who has given up her career and independence for family survival to accept in middle years that she is no longer needed this way. Jennifer had grown expert at budgeting; now she didn't have to. She had made all the children's clothes and her own; now she didn't need to. Her small nuggets from the occasional editing work for publishers had been welcome; now they seemed scarcely worth the trouble. She was an old hand at the wet weekend during the Easter holidays when Arabella, Imogen, Jake and all the other rich kids along the river had been away parked with mother-in-law in Sevenoaks; now we could hop over to Brittany where the sun was shining.

More than anything I began to sense her fear of losing me. It was as if Jennifer had convinced herself that she was in reality no more to me than the sum of all those thrifty skills which, no longer needed, would shortly render her redundant. Was it true? I had to ask myself this very hard. Had I married a woman or a nanny/housekeeper? The old question. I decided with some indignation that Jennifer would be wrong if she felt that, without being altogether convinced that she *was* wrong. I couldn't imagine anyone else I should ever wish to live with. And if freeing her from chores meant enjoying more of her company, then that was all to the good.

What I failed to see was that her real fear was of loneliness. Her friends were few and far-flung. She and casual acquaintances had tended to keep each other at a certain distance. True, they would meet to organise the school jumble sale or to rally support for a local petition, but outside the umbrella of such happenings they scarcely ever met. Neighbours did not drop in for coffee or a drink, swap gossip, exchange geraniums. A glass wall kept Jennifer to herself. She passed her day as if enclosed within an inner chamber of thought. Day by day there was only me, and I was often away filming or else too deeply preoccupied with Penrhyn Productions to be the reliable company she needed. And if I had been more available my suspicion is that she might have been irked by it. There was a complexity of character in her which I couldn't, or wouldn't, sort out. As a result Jennifer was, increasingly, alone. And gloomy with it. I loved her, and I was ill at ease. I was becoming starved of roses and of sunshine. Home was a kind of Eeyore's Place.

Without realising it I was now looking to Sarah to offer much of the flowers and the sun. The excitement I obtained from my work asked for someone who would share and echo that excitement, not dampen it with gloom. Sarah was radiance, she was serenity and optimism, and she was sex. For more than a year after my impulsive phone-call to her, followed by that long sunny morning in her garden, Sarah and I had kept each other at a distance. Something in both of us kept us from being lovers. To me it was the sentimental equation of true love with true celibacy (thank you, Old Penrhyn, for that foolish doctrine). For years I had pulled every dollybird within reach, discarding them or being discarded like so many cherry-stones. I did not want this to happen with Sarah. I valued her too highly. I kept her on ice. She in her turn was proud of an independence hard-won. She did not want to be a mistress.

And so it drifted on for a year. It was a year in which I grew to know her, I felt, more deeply than I knew Jennifer, who would always remain a mystery to me. It was a year warmed by a tremendous glow of promise, an unfocused promise since she knew that my devotion to Jennifer was unassailable, but none the less real for that. Somewhere in the blur of tomorrow we both sensed there would be a place for us in the sun. Time would provide: God knows how, but it surely would.

The overture had to end some time. Without realising it we began to overreach the checks we'd imposed on ourselves: began treating one another as lovers even though we weren't. It was Sarah's thirtieth birthday: she was looking younger than ever. Her straight hair, the colour of polished mahogany, fell forwards over her shoulders as she laid supper for the children. It was late August. An aunt had lent her a cottage in the Quantocks for the summer holidays. The cottage was tiny and isolated with a friendly jungle of a garden and a small swimming-pool among rhododendrons where I could hear Tamara and Natasha splashing with the occasional peal of laughter. I had driven over from Bristol where I was making a film on Harvey's the wine dealers, and for Sarah's birthday I had brought some revered vintage from their cellars, and a fresh salmon which Sarah was now trying to cram into her aunt's doll-sized oven.

There was a sadness about her which made me fold my arms round her. She was crying gently on my chest and I was stroking her hair. Waves of tenderness and longing rolled through me.

—I'm thirty! Think of that!

She looked up and laughed with tears smudged across her face.

—You still look eighteen.

—An eighteen-year-old with a daughter of twelve?

She was happy now, her eyes bright with tears. She was laughing in little starts, holding my hands tightly.

—Well, so you married young. You did after all.

—Yes, at eighteen in fact. Christ, what a child I was. A child and six months pregnant.

—You've pulled through.

She was looking sad again. Silent for a moment.

—I did love Angus, you know.

—I know you did.

—It just became impossible. He'd have destroyed us all.

—You don't need to justify it.

—I know. It's just . . . it's awful what's become of him. He's just a tramp. Sleeps under bridges. He turns up and I have to turn him away. I can't let him come back.

She curled her arms round me and pressed close. I stroked the skin of her back.

It was ludicrous not to be lovers. I loved her. I loved her at this moment. Peace lay within and around us. Here on a still evening in the summer we held each other in a bubble that floated out of time, out of reason. There were only our feelings and, if we felt as we did now, then that itself was good, wherever it might lead, whatever might come.

Tamara ate nearly half the salmon and announced:

—I like that. She was in her swimsuit, a slim miniature of Sarah, long hair wet over her shoulders. Black eyes. Natasha was grinning at me through the gap in her teeth. It was dark when they went to bed. Sarah and I swam in the night. The bats stitched and stitched (O'Rourke's image – I remembered it from one of his novels) across the water.

—You make me so happy. I'm frightened.

Sarah was standing by the edge of the pool, a towel round her shoulders.

—Why frightened?

I knew why.

—Because you make me so happy.

She stood there pulling the towel tightly round her.

—I can't help being jealous of Jennifer. She has all of you.

—It can all change.

What was that I said? I could hear the sound of betrayal in my voice. Whom was I betraying? Jennifer? Sarah? Myself? All three? Was this where the game began?

She was looking at me. I unwrapped the towel from her. I unhooked her bikini top, kissed her small girl's breasts. We tugged off our swimming things and lay and made love in the long grass beside the pool. We lay silent together in the night. I could see the bats brushing past the moon.

—Will the children mind in the morning?

—Mind? They'll be pleased, darling. They're tired of bringing tea to me in bed alone. Tamara's begun to think there's something wrong with me.

Sarah was standing by me, a slim pale form against the pool and the black trees.

—You're sure?

—Yes! You mean a lot to them. They think of you as a father.

Day Eighteen

—Daddy! Daddy! Look!

Ennis is stumbling flat-footed towards the bed, holding out a piece of paper. I take it. He is bright-eyed with pleasure.

—What is it, darling? What have you drawn?

—That's Mummy. She's in bed. You're there too. And those are my soldiers. They're guarding you.

—And that?

—A dinosaur.

Has he really not noticed that Mummy and Daddy don't sleep in the same bed any longer? Oh, my little dark-haired boy! Soon you won't be drawing pictures like that any more. What will you think of it all? Will you adjust in that instant healing way of children?

—Daddy, why are you crying?

—Just that I love you.

—I cried yesterday. Seth pushed me over.

—Why did he do that, I wonder.

—I bit him. He was horrid.

—Come on, we must all get dressed.

—Don't want to go to school.

He hangs his head, drops the drawing on the carpet.

—Not even if I take you?

—No!

In half an hour he'll keep me to that offer. Oh well, so I'll be late to work. Ennis's nursery school begins at the genteel hour of nine-thirty, which is appropriate for all those debby mums. They either look as if they had a touch of the vapours or they're attired to accompany the Queen to the paddock. Ennis says Emmy farts in her leotard during dancing. Observant child. Should go far.

Then at eleven I have to be at the viewing theatre to show VD to our friendly Turk from the World Health Organisation. I suppose I had better be there. Janet says the film will put him off at least three of his wives. David feels it ought to be compulsory viewing for the mackintosh brigade at the Compton Cinema: it would kill porn at a stroke, he says. Induce a stroke, more likely. Who needs porn anyway, Janet, he goes on, with you busting out of your shirt all round the office?

David and Janet are going to take VD out to lunch. I'm having lunch with Jane Young. I can hardly remember what she looks like; I only remember that when she appeared on the stage earlier this week suddenly I knew the film I wanted to make. Since then the film has taken over. This lunch may be an irrelevant post-script, a wistful chat over shrimp cocktails with a blonde who will know within five minutes that all I have to offer her is my lechery. Maybe not! At the moment I hardly care.

O'Rourke is excited at my reaction to his story. He'll write the screenplay: he's an old hand at that, thank goodness. The ending has to be completely rewrought; he knows that. Being with him for a whole month in Africa and the Middle East should flush a swarm of fresh ideas. I like working partnerships: two ball-games in adjoining courts with breaks to compare scores. I must make sure O'Rourke takes the Arab films seriously, all the same. Me too, for that matter. I have to remember that the oil mafia and the British Travel Association together will be paying for my pleasures – and for my divorce I suppose – over the next year. Waldron at least will foot the bill for the feature-film, if he's as good as his word. He'd bloody well better be after all this. I shall have to tell him very soon I want to take up his offer before he's forgotten it.

This weekend I'm taking up O'Rourke's offer: his cottage in Norfolk. I need to get an outline sketch of the feature-film down on paper, for myself mainly; also to show Waldron next week, and to take with me the week after that to the Middle East so that I have a basic agenda to put to O'Rourke in the evenings as the Alexandrian wine flows.

Thank God my head is full at this moment. Keep busy, Gareth: keep your eye on the landscape beyond, and the rapids ahead won't capsize you. Won't they? Oh, don't think of it. Keep going! Keep going! Two days in Norfolk will do you good: those miserable freezing salt-marshes in February with a lost goose a mile distant for company, and a log-fire alone. I'll work and walk and think. Lover-boy's crossing the Thames for his pound of flesh this weekend. Jennifer announced this item of news with a set face yesterday evening. She doesn't bloody want him. I refrained from saying so, took the hint and rang O'Rourke. Of course you can have it, dear boy. Sorry I can't be there to show you round. But you wouldn't want that, would you? Take your lady; what's her name, Jane Smith? Brown? Higgins? Young! Yes, Young! You haven't actually met her? No, of course you haven't. Of course. Don't see that matters, though, unless she's got a husband. Invite him too! Why not? Triangles are a girl's best friend. The square on the hypotenuse is equal to a good fuck, or something like that. The keys are with Mrs Parfitt at the pub. See you next week!

This weekend, and then only one weekend to go before I am a bachelor and live with my sons. Seth and Ennis, and Deirdre, help me keep calm! We'll have cocoa by the fire and a book at bedtime. Sleep tight! I love you, love you all.

* * *

Even if it was sometimes Eeyore's Place, I was happy at home and happy with Jennifer. So long had passed since my separation from her in our salad days, so many things we had done and fought for to set our marriage on a fresh foundation, that I was proud of it and proud of us all. I could not now, in my late thirties, imagine any further catastrophes, none at least which we should not be able to cope with and cope with together.

And yet! And yet!

As soon as I met Sarah – even on that wintry evening in her father's garden when I first set eyes on her – I had guarded within me a hidden fear (or was it a hope?) that there would always be some rare person who by long odds might step into my marriage and break it apart. It was a fatalistic sense of destiny in which fulfilment and self-destruction were one. Perhaps Jennifer had known this better than I, and it lay at the roots of her unease. She never felt able to trust me, however indignantly I protested she was unjust.

In the two years I gradually, intermittently, got to know Sarah what tiny seed of hope or fear began to germinate? "You set your women on a pedestal; I am not a piece of china," Sarah accused me later. Maybe with her this was so; maybe it was because in my experience *terra* was not all that *firma* and the alternative to the pedestal had a habit of being the gutter. It was not so much Sarah I set on a pedestal as my relationship with Sarah. Here was a rare and protected plant, a perfumed flower of the night, guarded under glass and untouched by human hand. We had cultivated all the clichés of a lover relationship except that we had not been lovers, which made our sentiments of pleasure and adoration even more exquisite, even more immune to the levelling of day-to-day existence. If we conversed among classical pillars in the stately Alexandrines of Corneille we could not more closely have aped the amorous conceits of the court of the Sun-King. Le Cid might have found Chiswick lacking in a certain nobility and his Chimène overencumbered with children and washing-up, but I feel he would have warmed to the poetry of our exchanges.

Then the relationship changed. We became lovers. Now, instead of conducting a fantasy at the court of Versailles, we went to bed. When I was away filming, Sarah would often park the children and come too. She was radiant and lovely and I loved her; and when I returned home I forgot her. She went back to Chiswick alone and waited. Waited for the next trip, for the next afternoon visit, for the next phone-call. Waited for me to pack my bags and come to her.

—It can all change, I had said.

And her caution had fallen away. I had peeled her of her sense of danger, peeled her of her clothes and laid her on the grass by the swimming-pool in the night. And in the morning I was by her side, the first man to wake her in the morning in her bed since she had yelled at Angus:

—I can't take any more.

—It can all change.

Did I know what an insidious message of hope I had handed her? Did I believe it myself? Or did she seize on that fragment of wistfulness to complete a self-deception which by then needed only the blessing of an excuse? Or was this the first sweet move in a manoeuvre designed to bring me to her door: I was to be hers?

So Gareth's girl became part of the baggage-train. Eric's secretaries would book me a double room without bothering to ask. What was the point of being boss if you couldn't lead a double life, after all?

At the same time life with Jennifer grew rosier, the more so now that a surfeit of Sarah dampened off the dangerous hope that she might actually wreck my marriage. She wouldn't. There was no need of it. I could have my cake and eat it. I was a happy man.

—You bring so much happiness into the house, said Jennifer on a fine spring evening. We were sitting on the garden wall overlooking the river. She was relaxed. A cool hand rested on mine. At forty Jennifer's face was finely sculpted, not a fleck of grey in her hair which she wore short now.

—I'm sorry I haven't always been easy to live with, she said.

I was swelling with happiness for her, with her. There was no one, no one in the world, I would rather have been with. The silver light on the low tide had never looked more serene, nor life so rich and good. And Jennifer was pregnant. We would have a third child.

If I had not been happy with Sarah I could not have brought happiness to Jennifer. If I had not been happy with Sarah, Jennifer would not have been pregnant. It was was a crude theorem.

—Don't you see why I always felt Ennis was my child, said Sarah much later? I don't believe you ever understood what pain it was.

Did I really inflict such pain? She had turned face downwards on the pillow in silence, her arms around her head, fists clenched in her hair. We had made love in the first light. Her slim back felt taut beneath my fingers lightly stroking the skin. What could I do, say, more? Out of the open window the roofs of an old town sparkled after the night rain; diagonal planes hoisting a thousand aerials; washing strung between chimneys; a white cat prowling the gutter; swifts screaming; sounds of a street market out of view. Her shoulder sockets were marked by deep dimples.

She lay there without crying. I had a feeling of uselessness, irritation even, boredom. What more could I do, say? I had said enough; could not unsay it.

—Jennifer's pregnant!

The muscles of Sarah's face had locked. She had stared at me, and then past me as though brushing me aside.

—What?

She spoke in the softest whisper.

—Jennifer is pregnant!

I had in all honesty believed, allowed myself to believe, that Sarah would take it easily, even happily. What, after all, did it have to do with us, with what we possessed? Had she not come to terms by now with our separate lives? We were twin units. Not perhaps what we should have chosen in an ideal world, nevertheless an accomplished fact. My life with Jennifer I had fought for and won; hers with Angus Sarah had fought for and lost. If mental illness had not intervened, could she truly say she would have left him for me, caused Tamara and Natasha to suffer for me? Might we not have been in identical situations now but for the hand of fate, and might it not now be she who was bearing Angus's child? Relationships, even love, should not be exclusive. Why not, then, accept what had happened, and go on keeping untouched what we had.

Another theorem.

Sarah raised her head from the pillow, her face drawn and wet with tears. She spoke more to herself than to me.

—Why, why should my deepest instincts betray me?

She was sitting upright now, her hands covering her breasts. For the first time she was speaking to me.

—I've wanted your child so much, for so long. More than anything in the world. Perhaps I shouldn't have. I know it's not reasonable. I don't blame you. But oh! . . . Oh, Gareth!

She leaned over on to me, her hands clutching my back.

—Oh, Gareth!

Through her hair over my face I saw the happy face of Jennifer, her eyes caught in the sun by the river at low tide, and I was numb to the pain being fought in my arms.

Back in Chiswick I dropped her at the house while I went to pick up Tamara and Natasha from a friend's. Natasha bounced down the stairs and threw herself in my arms. Tamara looked up from the table where she was cutting out puppet figures from coloured cardboard.

—Hello! You're back! These are for my model theatre. See!

With delicate fingers she moved the strings of two puppets so that they bowed to one another and embraced. Tamara looked up at me again and laughed.

—Mum just rang to say you were on your way. She says we can stay till tomorrow if we really want to. Joan and Peter don't mind.

—All right! Does Natasha want to stay too?

—Yes!

I drove back alone. As I pulled up under the trees across the road the figure of a man was closing the door of Sarah's house. It was raining lightly and he wore no hat, only a stained raincoat turned up at the collar. He was unshaven and bowed, with rumpled hair. He did not notice me but shuffled slowly up the street carrying a paper shopping-bag. I watched him turn the corner without looking back. It was Angus.

Day Nineteen

—I'm pleased for you, she would say sometimes.

There was neither pain nor enthusiasm in Sarah's voice. She seldom mentioned Jennifer any longer. Jealousy had extinguished her: she had become in Sarah's mind something inanimate which was bearing my child, Gareth's child. It was as if there were no mother at all, only a surrogate one, herself, Sarah. And when Ennis was born he was so dark-haired and slim it troubled me: had Sarah by some witchcraft replaced Jennifer's womb with her own, secretly nurturing my seed within her and ripening it into a likeness of herself?

—What does he look like, Sarah asked?

I lied, said he was round and fair. She nodded.

—I'm pleased for you, she said once more. The matter was closed.

—Isn't he ugly, said Deirdre? Ugh!

—Why is he so wrinkled, Daddy, Seth asked?

—You both looked like that at first.

—No I didn't; don't be silly. Seth laughed, and then very tenderly cradled the sleeping baby with an air of protective superiority. He was relieved to find his new rival so helplessly minute and comatose.

—It's only boys who are so horrible as babies, Dierdre concluded with satisfaction. Why has he got such a big penis?

—All baby boys have big penises, said Jennifer, lying propped on blue pillows.

—Disgusting!

Deirdre turned to inspect the empty cot, fingering the threaded beads. Seth giggled. And wriggled. Jennifer reached out and took the baby to her.

—We mustn't let him get cold.

I laid the scrap of a creature on the baby-mattress and started to fix a nappy round him. It seemed to envelop him from his chest to his ankles. I was all thumbs after five years. Intent not to skewer him on the pin I drove it into my finger, and swore. With the other hand I kept trying to straighten the baby's pink knees so that I could grip the nappy round its stomach. The children watched the whole performance in silence.

Jennifer put her arms round me as I laid Ennis in his cot next to the bed.

—Thank you, darling! I do love you!

We were walking by the low tide on a winter evening. Tamara was beachcombing ahead of us, her jeans a streak of bright red in the fading light. Her black hair curtained her face as she bent to pick something gracefully from the edge of the water. She was twelve. The serenity of the girl, her air of accomplishment and of knowing, never ceased to amaze me. She had always been like this.

—I have a stray daddy, she had said the first time I had spoken to her three years earlier.

That was all. I have a stray daddy.

—I'm frightened for her sometimes, Sarah had said. She's seen so much; she's coped with it almost too well. There are times when I believe she's older than me.

Natasha was skipping between us, each hand holding one of ours, laughing. Then she dropped my hand. I could have walked round the other side of Sarah and put my arm round her. But I didn't. I was happy to have Natasha separating us. She measured the distance which I felt and wanted to keep. Sarah would have liked me to be next to her, reassure her: I could sense that. As it was, my presence was a condescension, something careless. It hurt her. I had hurt her so often like this since the birth of Ennis I hardly noticed her reaction any longer. We walked back to her house. I left her without even crossing the road: I waved goodnight thinking of supper, of the Test Match in the West Indies, or nothing at all.

—Goodnight, darling. I'll ring you tomorrow.

I drove back across the river to my family; worked late in the evening hearing the rain dripping from the bare trees.

Why did I go on seeing Sarah? Did I choose to be cruel? Was it an idle vanity, a pastime, to keep at a certain distance a beautiful mistress who loved me?

—No, she said, you give me so much. I want it always to be like this. You mustn't think I want you like . . . like a husband. I need my freedom too. So, you see, it's all for the best.

And she would run her hands under my shirt and kiss me until I stood hard against her. Then she'd pull away with a smile.

—I love being able to make you want me.

And we'd tumble on to the sofa and make love until we fell asleep; mid-morning, or midnight, or with lunch half-eaten. It came over us in a few seconds and immersed us in the swell of a tide.

This was why I went on seeing Sarah: not only the love-making, but the closeness and the tenderness which were always there for us to touch. For Sarah it seemed always to be there: for me it was more infrequent, and between times I felt careless, far away, bored even.

—Goodnight, darling. I'll ring you tomorrow.

And in the morning I did, feeling chirpy. Sarah and I had a special intonation we used for one another on the telephone. It was not the way we spoke when we met: then we could see and touch one another, so it was not necessary. But talking on the phone was like talking to outer space, and so we had evolved this device to make both of us feel we were in bed together, whispering to one another. At least that was how it began: by now I turned it on automatically and it meant very little except sometimes that I felt sexy and would like to run my hands over her. There were times when this was better than the real thing.

For once her voice did not respond. It was like being pushed away making love. What was wrong? What was it?

—Oh, nothing, she said in the same guarded voice, keeping me at an uneasy distance. I think she had hoped I wouldn't phone.

—Nothing! Really nothing!

—There is. I can hear it in your voice.

—Darling, please. I don't want to talk now.

I was suddenly so far away. I wanted to be there, be with her, hold her, see the look in her eyes.

—You must!

Why must she! No reason at all. I could hear the pain in my own voice: the appeal willed down the telephone to a house a hundred miles away. My rib-cage felt as if it were collapsing under the pressure of panic. I had to be there. I had to know.

—Please!

I was sickened by my own abject tone.

—Please, darling. Let me come and see you. Now!

There was the briefest silence. I could hear her mind taking stock. Sarah was incapable of secrets. She reminded me of Seth hiding something and then dancing around pointing to it behind his back exclaiming "It's there, it's there" in a stage whisper. Even her silences had a way of telling me everything. I couldn't wait half an hour to see her. Knowing the worst now, straightaway, would be more bearable.

—Who did you go out with last night?

It was obvious it must be that. She had said something, I remembered now, about going out with a girl-friend after I left her the evening before.

—Please can't it wait?

Her voice was resigned, sulky.

—Sarah, just tell me please!

—You know!

She was defensive and challenging now.

—Helen and her boy-friend. And a friend of his.

—And you got back late?

—Yes!

—And you slept with him?

—Yes!

That little "Yes!" I replaced the telephone, cold as ash, hand still on the receiver, staring across the room with blind eyes. It felt as if my dearest memories were being cut out of me with a knife. I was trembling. Sarah, my Sarah! I sat back and let jealousy paint lurid images before my eyes: Sarah writhing, panting on the bed, tearing his back with her nails, her lips and breasts crushed; he withdrawing from her with a smirk, holding his prick before her like a triumphant sword. Oh, God, no more! I was in the car, vaguely aware I was crossing Wandsworth Bridge, jumping the lights on the North End Road, turning westwards against the morning traffic. Closer.

This would have been the moment to turn back if I had possessed the will. If my mind had been capable of detachment I should have seen it all and said, Stop, Gareth, it is Jennifer you love; you have fought for her and fought wisely. She has suffered for you, with you, is learning in her own time and her own way to trust you. Cherish what you have. Regard this as an aberration, a vainglorious fantasy. See it for what it is before you are smashed by it. Gareth, put away childish things before it is too late to grow up: you have spent your life weeping over toys taken from you because you did not want them.

Instead I heard again your soft and sad voice by the river, and I feared that what had ebbed that evening on the tide at twilight might never never return. And with all my heart I longed for it.

—I really didn't think you cared, you see.

She was sobbing through her tears, speaking in little gulps, her arms pressed round me.

—But you do care, don't you? Oh, darling, I never want to hurt you like this again.

It was as if the agony had never been.

* * *

Saturday morning in Norfolk. O'Rourke's cottage rests on a spur of gorse and bracken jutting into the marshes. He claims it used to be closer to the sea when he bought it but the east wind has driven it inland. It could be that the sea has receded. ("Ah, that must be it, dear boy.") But there is no wind this morning. From the tiny attic window where I shall work today and tomorrow I have been gazing at the stunted oak-trees around the cottage, half-expecting them to ease themselves upright on such a soft morning. The old woman in the cottage nearby is bent at the same angle as the oaks. She constantly reappears carrying a bucket, followed by a three-legged dog dragging its chain.

Down there the river winds, scythe-shaped, over mudflats towards the sea. It is held in check for maybe half a mile by a long hump of shingle until, abruptly, it breaks through. I can see the tide fanning gently inwards. Over on the right stands the old windmill, its sails long fallen. A bird observatory now, O'Rourke says. There are avocets nesting down there in the spring. In February it has a desolate look, salt-marsh lying like a dead thing, a raised dyke its backbone. I like wildernesses: I understand why O'Rourke chose this place. Which wife was it who went mad here and killed herself? In spring it must all change. I can picture a line of silhouettes, rump-view, of knitted ladies with elbows raised peering at our feathered friends through binoculars, wholewheat sandwiches in their shoulder-bags. The bearded tits, O'Rourke calls them. ("They nest here too, you know.")

I am alone here. Only one more weekend before Jennifer leaves for ever. I feel sure she will now. Am I? Oh who knows? Does it really matter any more? I am learning to be alone. The film is the real thing, and within the reality of that all the rest can be encompassed. It will be the extra dimension I have always lacked, the integration of gut and head I have always kept so firmly apart. Decapitated I have run like a child where the wind blows. Degutted I have manufactured my life with a robot's hands. Such a sense of hope fills me: to be whole, to be open, to be armed, to be constant. To pull out of the wreckage of forty-two years such hand-baggage as I can take with me: a few children, a few friends, a few battered experiences that may serve me well.

The film. It is here in my head. Tomorrow night it will be sketched on paper. Waldron will have it for his files. Out of that blueprint will grow, well ... at least something that is wholly mine, by which I stand, and which will stand by me when I ask myself, grey and finished: What have I done? I have made three children. I made a marriage for a while. And I made this.

And what about Jane Young? Shall I make her too? Star of my film and star of my bed? Of my life? I don't think I even care so very much. That's new, by God it is. Gareth doesn't care about a new woman! The male menopause must have struck early. Or doesn't she interest me? Yes, she does.

A pot of coffee. A heavy sweater. A wooden table. A typewriter. A view of the marshes. February. Alone. Thankfully alone.

Yes, she does! She was smaller than I remembered her on the stage. And softer. I was puzzled that someone so matter-of-fact, prosaic almost, should have flashed such signals across the theatre.

—Just a technique, she said.

How modestly English. She had looked round the restaurant for a few seconds, wondering I suppose what sort of lecher had invited her to lunch this time on the pretext of discussing a film part.

—I've never made a feature-film so I'm as green as you are.

—Ah, but I have!

—What sort?

—Blue!

And she laughed.

—Well, not very blue. I was still at drama school and very broke. I went for this audition, you see, and this guy asked me to strip. It was terribly unsexy, I can tell you. But I got the part.

—And what did you have to do?

—Not what you think. At least not quite.

We were laughing.

—What was the film called?

—You won't believe it. *Finnish Girls Come Easy.* Must be the worst title ever. They thought I looked Scandinavian, you see. Blonde and all that. Oh, it was the wank of the dirty-mac brigade for all of a month.

—Perhaps I ought to see it, for professional reasons?

—Oh, God, I haven't seen it around for five years. More. Hey, I must tell you. It was awful, my stepfather made me take him. I nearly died. He's sweet actually, but I think he fancied me rather. And there we were sitting among all the raincoats. That terrible silence they have. And he right next to me gazing at my tits on this huge screen.

—So you left home!

—So I left home. Well, pretty soon anyway.

—And what about the mime thing? Because you're brilliant.

—I went to study at Marceau's mime school. He was fabulous. Three years.

—So you've only just started.

—Six months.

—And what about the Garnett Mime Troupe?

—Just a few friends started it last year. And they asked me to join them.

—You're better than they are. You know that!

She didn't reply.

—Would you like to have another go at films?

—I don't know. Could you tell me more?

—I'll try.

I realised it was the first time I'd really talked about the film. To O'Rourke, yes, a bit; but mostly in jokes and puns as usual. I told her about O'Rourke, about the Arab films, about meeting him here for a drink the evening after I'd seen her at the theatre and got this idea for the film; about the story he'd written. But mainly I just talked, about why I wanted to make it, what it meant to me. About the idea of the dumb girl. And as she listened her face took on those same expressions I'd noticed at the theatre. I stopped and told her so. She looked confused for a moment and lowered her eyes, fingered with her napkin. I ordered some more coffee. She could be very beautiful.

—I'll let you have a copy of whatever I write this weekend.

—I'd like that.

—Where can I get hold of you? I can't keep leaving notes at the theatre like roses.

—I'll give you my phone-number.

—No, better. Come and have dinner with me on Monday. After the show's over.

—There's no show. It finishes tomorrow.

—Then instead of the show. I'll call for you at eight.

—I'd like that. I'd better go. We've got a matinee today.

—OK. And if any other film director sends you roses tonight tell him to piss off.

—I promise.

Get down to it, Gareth. You've exhausted the possibilities of the salt-marsh, and the old lady with the bucket has done a day's work by now. Pull up the typewriter and begin.

Day Twenty

Twenty pages. That's enough. It's finished. Any longer and it'll have to be two hundred. I don't know if it's any good, but I know it's worked out the way I wanted. Yesterday I felt like O'Rourke's mad wife and contemplated an anguished death among the avocets. At ten in the evening I gave it up and walked to the pub where Mrs Parfitt asked after O'Rourke and talked about his wife until I decided not to join her corpse in the mud. It was more agreeable talking to Mr Parfitt and playing darts. This morning I woke at five, wrapped myself in a heavy dressing-gown and a grim expression, and ideas flowed. At nine I was ravenously hungry, made coffee and eggs, then walked out to the edge of the marsh and watched the sun paint weak colours on the water. By twelve it was finished. I'd better type it myself this afternoon. I don't, as yet, want the office to know about the film. Mean of me, perhaps, since they will suffer for it, but better to play safe at least until Waldron nods.

And what will O'Rourke think about the way I've carved up his story? Jolly good, old boy, he'll say in any case, and I won't know what he really thinks until he's had a large drink and decides whether or not to change the subject. He's lazy and he's run out of steam, I have to remember that. He may be flattered to see one of his addled eggs hatch after all, even if he despises the chick. I believe he'll like it. He'd bloody well better like it.

And Jane: where does she come in? Am I making it for her, and if so am I making it for her as an actress or for her to be mine? Unanswerable. Who ever made such a distinction? I know that her face was there as the film unfolded in my mind this morning, and there were moments when my camera's eye roved after her as she moved. And there was another moment when the director called "It's a wrap" and led his leading lady off the set never to be seen again till morning. Thoughts in the margin, that's all. Jesus Christ, maybe she's a lousy actress away from her sub-Marceau mime troupe. I'll have to audition her, I suppose. I have a sneaky urge to track down *Finnish Girls Come Easy* and run it for myself.

Power over Jane, is that what I want? Is that what every film director wants: the power of the manipulator, actresses as the extended family of his ego? I feel naïve and green in such a world: all those years making nuts-and-bolts films with people, just people doing for me what they did normally in their lives anyway. No, it's not power. Oh, no more power over women, dear God, no! Just people. If I do my part well then they'll be people who step as naturally into the role I make for them as Jane stepped over to my table in the restaurant on Friday. She was wearing blue, and her eyes were blue. I found that strange. I cannot now remember what she looks like. Till tomorrow evening: and then? I don't know. I don't know. Wouldn't it be wonderful . . . Don't! Yesterday I didn't care about her. Today I have been creating a new life for her, and what I shall make will be a new life for me. Christ, I sound like those children's shoes advertisements: Children's feet have far to go. Startrite and they'll . . . whatever it is.

Penrhyn. Penrhyn. You must go back to London this evening. Lover-boy will have departed by now, scattering his little thoughts of Chairman Mao like cigarette ash. And in a week, just over, Jennifer will have departed too. The end. It will all have vanished on the tide. Washed away.

* * *

Sarah was wearing a large Mexican sun-hat; nothing else. A light breeze stirred the leaves of the apple-tree, filtering the sunlight into dappled patterns moving across her body, falling on a breast, a hip, a knee. Only her face remained in total shadow. One hand rested on the morning paper she had laid on the ground by the garden chair. Her eyes were closed. The work I had brought with me lay in a semicircle across the rug I was lying on. Beyond the apple-trees the screen of rhododendrons was still in flower, the grass below it smeared with purple blossom. From time to time a blackbird, agitated by the cat, dislodged more petals. I could see the cat now, stalking through the long grass to try its luck elsewhere. It was midday: a freak Sunday in May. Sarah's aunt was abroad again, bless her.

—Sarah, are you asleep?

—Yes!

—Come and make love to me.

I combed my fingers through her hair above me against the sun.

—Darling, you're so good. How do you make love to me like that, she said.

—You make me very happy.

Her head rested across my shoulder. I lay looking up into the apple-tree watching the shapes of the branches moving slightly.

—Gareth, I do love you. So much more.

She had sat up next to me, looking at me, her hair brushing my chest, her weight on one arm.

—Darling, I must go and get lunch or the children will be back.

I stood up. She hesitated.

—I do love your prick.

And she reached up and held it in her hand. She raised herself on to her knees, took it in her mouth until it stood hard again, then brushed it across her breasts.

—I want to keep it.

—Shall I tie a ribbon on it for you?

—With a label that says "I Love You."

—If this prick should chance to roam, box its ears and send it home.

She laughed and got up.

—It won't do; just won't do.

She turned away to pick up her clothes on the far side of the chair. I picked up mine and walked towards the cottage. Someone was standing by the rhododendron screen. She started away as I saw her. It was Tamara.

I told Sarah later. She shrugged her shoulders.

—Oh well! It had to happen I suppose. So she sees how people love each other. She knows anyway.

It was better than ever with Sarah now. The business of the lover a few months ago was forgotten: at least only a scar on the skin. More than that, the shock of it had changed the way we treated one another; had swept away the remnants of that sentimental puritanism we had both nourished, that precious holier-than-sex reverence for our relationship which – for me at least – had gone musty long before the night Sarah had spent with the anonymous lover. I still didn't know his name. She had never seen him again and didn't want to, she said, and I believed her: it was so obviously the truth. Sarah and I were more open now, more direct towards one another; we no longer tried to turn what we had into some kind of love-ad. We were what we were.

At least that was the way it seemed. But the lover we never mentioned had done something else, and the day I drove in panic across the river that morning I had crossed a bridge over which I could never return. I could never again share Sarah. She was sharing me, but that was different, so I rationalised. Jennifer and I were married long before I had met Sarah. We had children and I loved them. I loved Jennifer, but I loved them in quite a different way. Nothing impinged on my love for Sarah. It was a pity there was only the one word to use. Did she not understand?

—Yes, she said in a resigned voice. Yes, I do understand. I suppose.

I was already trapped. I pretended not to be, but I was. While our affair had been such a beautiful spiritual thing it was not vulnerable to reality, and the hopeless one-sidedness of the relationship did not have to be experienced or explained. Now it did. While we made love in the sun and walked down country lanes hand in hand all was well; but what about the evenings, weeks, nights when I was with my other loves by the fireside and Sarah was looking out at the rain?

She was not of course alone and palely pining. She had friends. Men-friends. She went out a lot, now Tamara was old enough to mind the house and grandparents were not far away if little Natasha felt like picking up the phone. Sarah went out a great deal in fact. I knew most of her friends; they knew about us and all was understood.

—You see, I've got a very good life, she said. And I do love you.

It changed so little as to be imperceptible. But it did change. In the summer Jennifer and I took the three children to the Casa Bella. It was the hottest summer in all the years we had been going there. The grass was bleached yellow and the fireflies played about the house in the dusk. We had built a swimming-pool in the garden and lay around it much of the day, reading or writing in the shade, while Deirdre and Seth ducked in and out of the water with beach-balls and flippers and diving-masks, and baby Ennis kicked and splashed in his inflatable rubber-duck. There was Campari at midday and dark lazy wine over the barbecue in the evenings. Friends came and went on their way to Florence or Venice. I phoned the office and fussed with Eric every few days. The occasional client flew out and we lunched him in the garden. I drafted treatments for films I would make in the autumn, did rough costings for Eric to embellish. Swallowtail butterflies flexed their wings on the buddleia in the sun, and at night weird insects with vast antennae beat against the windows. Jennifer and I lay happily in bed listening to the warm breathing of the night. What more could a man want?

Indeed.

I wanted Sarah as well. When it suited me.

She was always distant for a while after I'd been away with my family. The embers of jealousy glowed again. She had every right to be distant, God knows, I told myself. She placed her arms round me in a tired way, let me undress her, kiss her breasts, her ears, her clitoris, let me enter her, plunge into her, wrapped her legs round my back, came in a deep sigh with me in that well-orchestrated unison we had perfected.

—I've missed you, I said. It sounded gratuitous.

She didn't say anything. We dressed and made tea. The children were playing somewhere down the road. We talked. I looked at my watch. She said she was going out this evening too. With Paul. Paul Bassett. He was such a faithful I called him the basset-hound. Bassett had red hair. Does he have red pubic-hair too? I teased her with horrible self-confidence.

—You know it's not like that.

I could always get a rise out of Sarah. I also needed quietly to be reassured. The basset-hound was safe. He had a wife, didn't he?

—Yes, he's not very happy though. She's a bit of a bitch.

—Does he weep on your shoulder?

—He talks about her, yes! She has other men. They have pretty separate lives.

—I must be off, darling.

—All right!

I was aware of a change. Not then but afterwards. So the basset-hound might not be a dark lover in the night, but he was there. And if he led a separate life he was both there and available. Sarah lived alone and was also available. I was available only by special leave of absence.

I began to think about the evenings they spent together seated across the table in the Hammersmith Pizza-house or wherever: he telling her how dreadful his wife was, how she sneered at him, flaunted her lovers at him, how he ached for his children, how lonely he was. Did she not feel lonely too sometimes, loving a man who was not there when the demons raged?

I asked more questions about him. I noticed I was taking him for granted. It was as if he were lurking meekly in the rain waiting for me to depart. Waiting for more comforts and more confidential chats. I took time off from the office for three days to take her away at a time when I was urgently busy, to reassure myself that she was mine. No sooner had we arrived at the hotel-room than I laid kisses all over her and guided her hand to my prick. There! That's what you are to me. Feel how urgent it is. Let's make love, Sarah, let's make love. Now!

I began to ask myself when it was Sarah last said she loved me.

I was very nice about Bassett. Poor Bassett! What a nice chap! Hope he finds someone right for him. Maybe he's not much good at it.

I was troubled when she said nothing, letting me talk, letting me try and talk my fears away.

Fears? What had I to be frightened of? Did I not know by now what Sarah and I had between us? Who was this puppy to trouble me? I extended my hand across the table and let her stroke it. She said nothing and her eyes were looking down at the table.

One morning I rang her.

—Darling, I can't talk. An awful thing has happened. Angus died yesterday. They think he may have killed himself. I've got to go now. God, I so wanted to see you last night, and I couldn't.

She was weeping into the telephone.

—Sarah, darling!

—I must go. Must go. I've got to sort it all out. Oh, God, it's so awful.

She was choking on her words. I had a meeting with a client in an hour. And Seth was ill with scarlet fever.

—I'll ring you – in a day or two, she said.

There was the click of the receiver. Then silence.

Sarah, where was I when you needed me?

* * *

And lover-boy, where is he, I wonder? Gone purring back across the river having delivered his perorations about life to Jennifer over the weekend. I must get the Airwick out as soon as I get back. So he'll be preparing his little nest for Jennifer right now, will he? The Victorian artist William Henry Hunt floats into my mind; not something he normally does on the North Circular Road but now his images give me pleasure because to my knowledge he painted nothing else in a profitable life but small pictures of birds' nests made of moss and breast-feathers, with the compulsory violet or primrose in attendance. "Birds'-nest" Hunt, he was called. What do you suppose were his thoughts on Rembrandt, and did he make cheep-cheep sounds when he noticed the thing between his legs rising in salute to his lady?

Rain on the windscreen. Mahler on Radio 3. Blast, I forgot to return O'Rourke's keys to Mrs Parfitt. I'll have to return them to him with the film synopsis tomorrow. I'm having a drink with him in his flat before collecting Jane Young for dinner. "You just use the place as a hotel," Jennifer has said so many times: well, she can scarcely say it now, since she's checking out herself at the end of the month.

Hanger Lane. The Ealing Road. I shall skirt Chiswick. Yesterday's territory. How long ago already it seems.

I am going home. I want to see my children. Soon they won't be there. Home will be an echo of them only. What shall I fill the place with? Blondes? Old photograph albums? Booze? Madness? I could sell it: sell seventeen years. Keep a flat nearer work with room enough for the children to come and stay; buy a cottage in the country like O'Rourke's place. No, I'll not do that: I'd go mad like O'Rourke's wife. Maybe I'll go mad anyway.

The M4. Hammersmith Flyover. The North End Road. Wandsworth Bridge. I am going home.

Day Twenty-one

Another Monday morning. No David this week. On my own with Janet. But Eric's back, and the rest of them, so no more dalliance on the pile-rug. Good word, dalliance! Nice 18th-century ring about it. Suits Janet too. My Fragonard lady, she would flaunt her flesh becomingly within the velvet drapes of a four-poster, with some weasel spying on her at the doorway. She behaves as though nothing had ever happened; still clumps around the office being brusque with her breasts a-lollop. But then what's it to her? She's probably been humped twenty times since then.

Eric says the UN will pay up in full next month. The Swiss Tourist Board has also paid, and we get an advance on the Arab films before the end of this week. Bless you, Eric: you haven't been back from your golf trip to Portugal two hours and the business is solvent again. And one of your mice has dusted the trophies already, I see. All's well with the world, then.

—Have a good holiday, Eric?

—Very quiet, you know.

—What you needed, probably.

—Well, I kept my handicap in trim.

—That's the stuff.

Janet is sniggering quietly.

—Various things here I think you'd better sign, Gareth. I'll leave them with you.

—You do that. Thanks.

I am seeing Waldron at twelve. I told him what it was about, and he sounded delighted to my relief. If he likes the synopsis the next hurdle is going to be to find a producer. I don't want to produce as well as direct. I'll need an Eric, but an Eric who knows about the feature-film business. There are one or two I could suggest. All I hope is that Waldron's scheming mind hasn't already come up with some impossible thug to foist on me as the condition of receiving his backing. No more financial independence for you, Gareth, That's going to be a hard sacrifice after years of being my own boss. But I've no choice. I'm lucky I suppose. Wardour Street is bulging with directors politicking around, endeavouring to break into features, and I'm the one they must have assumed by now never would. Happy to be king of my small castle. Could have done it, they say; could have done it a few years ago. Would have made it too: plenty of talent. Ambition. Ruthlessness. But he's left it too late now. Your sense of risk goes after forty in this game. It's nuts and bolts for Gareth now till he drops. I'll show them.

—It's that Jane Young again for you.

Janet's voice. She is holding the receiver, hand over the mouthpiece, looking disapproving.

—Jane!

—Gareth, I'm sorry to ring you. I just wanted to say . . .

Pause. Was she going to call off this evening? It was all a big mistake. A gulf is opening inside me.

—Go on.

—Just that I *am* very interested.

—That's good.

Oh, God, that does feel good.

—I felt I sounded offhand when you asked me about, you know, about films. I think I was a bit dumbfounded, that's all.

—That's quite OK.

—You were terribly nice and I just felt like telling you that.

Oh, you lovely girl.

—And I would like to, very much. I know it's a small chance, but, Yes Please.

—It's not exactly picking a star out of the chorus line. You are one.

—I'm not, you know that. But thank you for saying it.

—See you at eight then. I've got a synopsis for you. I've got to see the moneybags first.

—Good luck.

—Bless you.

Janet has been looking quizzical.

—Huh! What are you doing picking leading ladies?

—Someone who might be useful for a film.

—With a date attached? Sounds like a leading lay you want.

—I thought I'd got one.

—That was last week.

Janet could be right of course. All I know is that the only sign of spring in my desert is a film I shall make about a deaf and dumb girl who may or may not be Jane Young. And, yes, she is a flower of the spring.

Does she become my time of the day? Or will she too fade like the rest?

* * *

I didn't wait for Sarah to ring. I couldn't. I couldn't sleep. I couldn't work. I phoned her from the office and got her mother: Sarah was away. She'd had some bad news. She might be back tomorrow.

I rang the next day and there was no answer. And in the evening her mother answered again. Are you the person who phoned yesterday? Yes, that's right. No, don't bother to leave a name.

The next day I didn't ring. I couldn't face mother again. In the evening I drove round to see if her car was there. It was. I came back and phoned. I got mother. This time I gave my name. Sarah would be back tomorrow. No, she'd gone by train.

I phoned again in the evening. Sarah answered. A soft, cautious voice. Hello!

—It's Gareth.

There was just enough silence to make me feel a not much-wanted friend.

—Hello!

I didn't want to say anything on the telephone.

—Can I come round?

Another pause.

—Well . . . Yes, all right.

I drove to Chiswick. She was tense, edgy. Hardly surprising. I didn't want her to talk about it if she didn't want to. She'd spent three days, ghastly days, clearing up. Seeing the hospital, the neighbour who'd found Angus. He'd been living in a small attic room. Almost no furniture. He'd been on drugs – legally. Impossible to say if he had taken too many deliberately or not. The verdict was "accidental death". She'd stayed with mother-in-law who was in a state of collapse. Mother had stayed here with the children. Oh, I knew that, did I?

—I need some rest. I'm very tired.

—All right, I'll leave you. Shall I see you tomorrow?

—I don't know, Gareth.

—Whenever you like, then.

Then the phone went. I could hear her voice in the kitchen. She was aware I was listening. She was trying to be unspecific, but there was pleasure in her voice. I heard her say, "When did you get back?" and then, "Yes, all right!" There was a long pause while she listened. Then, "Yes!" And again, "Yes!" I heard the receiver go down and tried to pretend I was reading a book.

—I'll go then. I'm sorry. But I do need to see you.

—OK.

There was no expression on her face and she closed the door rather quickly behind me. Usually she waited in the front garden for me to look back as I drove away. I closed the car-door and turned on the windscreen wipers to remove the damp leaves. I felt numb.

I couldn't talk all evening. I could scarcely register whether Jennifer and the children were in the room or not. By eleven o'clock I wanted to scream.

—I feel restless: I'm going out for a walk.

I felt sure Sarah had not gone to bed early as she had said. I had to know. Paul Bassett's house was in Fulham: she'd said that once. She also said that his wife was never there half the time. She had a lover in Hampstead. Paul often looked after the kids by himself, the stalwart lad. I stopped at a phone-box and opened the A to D directory: Bassett; Bassett M; Bassett P; Bassett, Paul, 24 Huntley Gardens, S.W.6. That must be him.

I drove over Wandsworth Bridge. Huntley Gardens was just across the King's Road near Eel Brook Common. There it was. One of those quiet streets of Edwardian semi-detached brick houses. I parked the car at the entrance to the road and locked it. Some drunks were swaying outside a pub. They said something to me. I walked past them. No 4. No 6. Must be this side then. A hundred yards further, not more. A cat on a gate-post staring. Leaves sodden in the gutter. Sodium street-lights. My own breath thick in the damp air. Her car had to be outside: that is where the house would be.

The car was parked a bit obliquely as if Sarah had been in a hurry. The front room was in darkness but the door into the corridor was open and a faint light shone on the wall from the far end of the house. I looked at the window of the upstairs room. There were curtains drawn. There was no light showing between them. I crossed the street, lit a cigarette, and wondered for a moment what I would do if she came out right now. The house was totally quiet. She would not come out. A drip of water fell on to my face from the trees. A breeze was stirring a few leaves on the pavement. The whole street was quiet. I walked back across the road and stood by her car. I recognised everything inside it, the rug, the squeegee on the glove-shelf, even the toffee-papers on the floor. Maps on the rear shelf. One of them was of the West Country.

—Darling, you're so good. How do you make love to me like that? Gareth, I do love you. So much more.

She'd gone!

I leant over the bonnet and drew a Valentine in the space between the marks of the wipers with my finger. G loves S. Making her angry felt better than being ignored. That done, I looked at it, at the house, and walked slowly back to my car at the end of the street. The drunks had gone.

—I really didn't think you cared. But you do do care, don't you? Oh darling, I never want to hurt you like this again.

She'd gone! There was a pit of sickness in my belly.

I was listening to her, grateful at least that she was with me. Sarah's hair was the same, the clothes I knew, the eyes, the voice, even the smile. I was listening to her. I had brought a bottle of wine as a gesture of pretence that nothing had changed. She sipped unenthusiastically.

Now that I knew for sure, the worst seemed to be over. So I had lost her. Someone more available than I, more in need than I, had slipped between us. When Angus died the basset had been there to listen and to comfort. And when his own wife flaunted her lovers and returned smelling of their semen he could call and she'd be there to hold his hand. They grew together out of deprivation. Here were buttresses that would not be removed with a cheerful "Sorry, needed elsewhere: you can have them back in the morning". I understood all that and rationally I accepted it. But what the hell did reason have to do with it? I did not accept it.

—Are you in love with him?

—Yes!

—How do you know?

How could she be? So quickly; so soon. Didn't it betray everything we had done and felt over the past three years. Betrayed.

—Is he a good lover?

I felt the twist of the knife as I said this. I had no right to ask; of course I hadn't. But why the hell not? Perhaps it was vicarious lust. At any rate I felt angry. I wanted to be cruel. The basset-hound, I couldn't see her dying over him, lying over him with her hair in the sun, tying ribbons on his prick.

—Does he fuck you as well as I did?

—Gareth, please!

I wanted to lecture her, bully her.

—I don't believe in your beautiful lover, Sarah. So Angus has died and you needed someone to lean on and I wasn't there. So his wife fucks around and he leans on your shoulder. You've married one cripple; are you going to marry another?

—How do you know I want to marry him?

—Because you always do. That's what you wanted with me, whatever you said.

—That's not true!

—And what happens when you both run out of pity? What are you going to do; make tea for each other?

—Gareth, when you love someone you live with him. It's not just a matter of . . . you know!

—Fucking! No, but you don't love him. You just want someone to live with you, keep you company. Fine; and I can't. I understand that. But if you don't love him where's all that hunger and longing going to go? Are you going to watch television and make love on Saturday nights when you've had enough to drink.

—You don't understand, do you? You never will.

—Perhaps I do understand. I'm being crude about it and a bit cruel because I'm hurt. I'm miserable. I can't believe it. But I think I do understand. You need a man to own.

—That's not true either.

I was making her angry at last and it pleased me. I was bullying her.

—What we've had is a million times better than anything your bloody basset-hound can ever give you. What will you do, put a collar and lead on him and watch him piss against the lamp-post? Come along, doggie! Into your basket!

—Go away! Just go away!

Why didn't I go away? Quite simply. Leave her alone; try to forget it, or if I couldn't do that then tell myself sternly, Give her a month or two, she'll return, she's not that proud. The memories and longings will come flooding back, and tears will wash all this away. That would have been the cool and philosophical thing to do. Cool and philosophical: what an amazing creature to be!

The following weeks were the kind of nightmare I did not believe could have sustained itself so long. I worked in a mechanical fashion which I suppose said something for the resilience of my mind. I even shot a film on the London Docks. Company around all day helped, though there was one evening in the pub when everything rolled across me in a fog and I set my face in my hands on the table among the tankards and wept.

—Just a nervous reaction, I said. I'm exhausted, that's all. Been working too hard. It's my way of getting rid of the strain.

The crew felt awkward, said nothing, offered nothing. Tears break the protocol of living: you can moan and bitch and lose your temper but you mustn't cry. It made me feel specially lonely. I could expect no help, no support; none at all.

In my head Sarah would never leave me alone. Around London everywhere I looked I saw her eyes. Everywhere I listened I heard her voice. Everywhere I turned she ran towards me. But she wasn't there and I wanted to cry out.

Perhaps the best thing would have been to talk to Jennifer. Why didn't I? A mixed hand of different motives. For one thing secrecy, once begun, is hard to break. For another, home was the untroubled base in my life and I needed that sanctuary, even if it choked me to be there. Jennifer sensed something was wrong: a severe bout of depression, I said. Depression she understood full well, and she was attentive and quiet. I often wished she could have squeezed the real reason out of me. Then again, I had no wish to hurt Jennifer. Perhaps it was a misguided sense of kindness; but lodged at the back of my pain was the conviction that if I stuck this out the pain would weaken like a schoolboy's love-pang.

But the pain did not weaken.

I pestered old girl-friends who might, maybe, understand and offer advice. They were patient and allowed me to ramble on, laying before them my indigestible banquet of evidence: what she had said, what I had said; argument, counter-argument; over and over and over again with different subtleties of emphasis, like a saloon-bar golfer agonising upon why he missed a putt. They plied me with coffee which cancelled the anti-depressants the doctors prescribed. Put it all into a film, one doctor advised cheerfully, holding open the door for me to leave. Read a good book – War and Peace – another offered. Take a holiday, said another; take the wife and kids. Weston-super-Mare: somewhere there's plenty going on. Think what you like doing best. (Screwing Sarah, you silly bugger!) A psychiatrist said it was all my fault and I'd better learn to live with it: so long as you can cope, that's the important thing. And he gave me a complicated prescription for prohibitively expensive drugs which gave me hallucinations and which another psychiatrist said ought never to have been prescribed without proper medical supervision. It's all a matter of regularising the system, he explained, and gave me another list of drugs which cost even more.

Once I began to feel a little regularised, my doped state induced a tide of sentimentality and warmth towards Sarah. I inundated her with letters of amazing wisdom and understanding. "Of course", I wrote, "I have known all along this was something you would have to do if you were to find the partnership you seek; and if that turns out to be really what you want" (I left a loophole here) "then I stretch out my arms in happiness to you. Very sweet is the valley in which we said Goodbye." (Jesus Christ!) "You will always remain my lover in my thoughts, Yours ever, Gareth."

I took to waylaying her in order to be wonderfully nice: outside Natasha's school or at the college where Sarah now taught.

—Hello there, darling! Isn't it a gorgeous day. Did you get my letter, by the way?

Of course she bloody well had.

There were no signs that she was pleased or amused by these appearances. It was clear that I no longer existed for her at all, and that she didn't give a fig whether I was there or not. If this was the way I chose to waste my time, so be it. For me, the regular sight of her bathed my wounds and I could go away with the sound of her voice in my ears, to prepare another long sweet letter explaining for the twentieth time how I really didn't mind any more and felt no jealousy towards Paul Bassett whatever. Good luck to you both!

Then one morning there was a change in her manner. She seemed troubled. I'd been away filming again and had not seen her for a week. I went to her house and sat in her kitchen drinking coffee. Even before she said anything I felt a tension in me, an eagerness.

—What is it, Sarah?

She sat at the table, looking down, not moving.

—What is it, darling?

I put an arm across her shoulder. She slumped forward and I held her tight. She was crying. I held her shoulders and said nothing. Kissed her hair. Then I raised her head and kissed her lips very tenderly.

It all came out, slowly at first. She had been alone all week. Paul had said he was leaving for her and bringing the children. He hadn't come. She had rung. Paul's wife had answered; slammed the phone down. Paul had rung back saying there was trouble at home. He'd ring again soon. He didn't. He wrote instead to say he still had a lot to sort out; it might take some time. That was a week ago. Nothing since.

I undressed her slowly as I kissed her, began to caress her with my hands, my lips, brushing my body over hers, whispering to her, hugging her close. I came after her and we lay still, numb. I remember her hands running through my hair, and she was speaking to me against my cheek.

—Forgive me, darling; forgive me! I've been such a fool; such a fool. Please!

—Of course! Of course!

—Gareth, I do love you. How could I have been so stupid?

—Darling, you were unhappy; you were lonely. I know all that.

She pressed her head down against my chest, her fingers digging into my side, her hair loose across my belly.

—It was so awful when Angus died. You've no idea, the guilt! And you weren't here. I wanted you and you weren't here. I couldn't even ring you.

She broke out sobbing again. I held her head in my hands so that she would look up at me.

—It'll never be like that again.

—Oh, God, I hope not.

—It won't, Sarah. I want to come and live with you, for ever. I'm going to leave Jennifer.

A tremendous wave of freedom rushed through me. I was going to do it. I was going to be free. At last.

I told Jennifer that evening.

For a long while she said nothing, just put down her book and stared into the fire. Then she looked at me and her lips moved without speaking. I stood with my hands in my pockets by the window, looking defiant. I was going to do it. I was going to be free.

Eventually she stood up and spoke, so coolly.

—Gareth, you're a fool. A big fool! It's going to be worse for you than me. I'm sorry for you, and I'm terribly sorry for the children.

She put her head in her hands and cried. I was rigid. I couldn't move to her. I remained absolutely still. She was quiet after a while, and looked up at me.

—When are you going?

—As soon as possible.

—Will you tell the children?

—Yes! Tomorrow!

And she left the room. I was free. I felt free. The children would understand that I still loved them, would always love them, wouldn't they? I would show them that as never before. It would be easier now I was going to be happy. Happy: what was that? Had I ever been happy? Now it would all begin.

I phoned Sarah from a call-box. Yes, I had done it. I'd be with her inside a week. I would put most of my stuff in store first. Could we go away for a few days to breathe and get to know one another again? Oh, darling, why has it taken me so long? I do love you. I do love you.

—Daddy's got something to tell you, Jennifer said at breakfast.

—Yes! It's just that I'm not going to live here any more.

Deirdre didn't say anything. Ennis went on gurgling in his high-chair. Seth's face screwed up and tears came into his eyes, but he didn't say anything either. It was like a cold knife in my throat.

This was the worst and it was over. If I could survive this I could survive anything, and I was surviving, wasn't I? I could hear my own voice reassuring Seth that I loved him just the same. Always would. Deirdre too. And my arms were round little Ennis. Soon they'd all understand, and we'd be all right. We'd be all right. Everything will be all right. Believe me.

The momentum carried me through. I packed; crated books, gramophone records. I wouldn't take more than I needed. The house was Jennifer's. I'd pay her monthly: how would she like it? And the children after a while could come to me at weekends: that would be good for them, wouldn't it? They'd soon get the rhythm of it. And we'd be free of one another. Free to live. Free to start again. It had never been any good. No more pretence. No more tension. Wasn't that a good thing?

If I'd gone on like that I might have brought out a bottle of champagne and asked Jennifer to split it with me.

She quietly walked out of the room.

Three days later she took the children away.

Next morning I walked out of an empty house. I stopped for a moment and looked up. All this was over. I drove away. It was over.

Day Twenty-two

—So Waldron will pick up the bill, will he? That's good. Excellent!

This was yesterday evening. O'Rourke leant forward to pour out another Scotch.

—A small one, Barry!

—What's the matter? Got a head?

—No, a date.

—Ahhh! Yes, so you have!

He got up and replaced the bottle on the sideboard, pouring himself half a tumbler on the way as though it were an afterthought.

—The beautiful Jane Young! Young and blonde and beautiful. And deaf and dumb, in a manner of speaking. I think it's outrageous you should be taking out a girl I invented and I haven't even met her.

—So you invented her! But I found her! My star.

—In the ascendant. How lucky you are. Good luck, dear boy!

—You're happy about the synopsis, then, are you?

O'Rourke reached over and picked it up off his desk. Let it drop again.

—Gareth, you're being serious, my God! Yes! Yes! Yes! Much better than I could have done, but then I'm only a writer. Can't expect to have ideas as well. My dear Gareth, it's very good. Now don't ask me again. I don't lie to you – not often at least. Now go ahead and make the damned thing.

—When could you start, Barry?

—As soon as your Moslem Brothers have paid me a stinking lot for these films you're distracting me from right now. Or rather, as soon as they're finished. You should know when that might be.

—For you, six months I'd guess. For me, a year. Maybe longer.

—So I'll have time to think before you climb on my back again, will I? One day I may even have time for my own work. By that time I'll be dead and they'll all be screaming your praises: for he's a jolly good fellatio, for he's a jolly good fellatio!

—If you're going to get pissed I'll have that other drink.

—Good boy! Gareth, I like you. My turn to be serious. Forgive me. It doesn't become an old crab.

O'Rourke was treating me as though I were twenty-five, wishing he were. He was looking beady, reddened by the whisky; that British India appearance of his heightened by a tweed suit and gold watch-chain.

—Yes, I think I've got one more book in me. Then I'll have to start on the memoirs. How many octaves would you like? I have instant recall, you know; and since my whole life's an invention that's very easy. The trouble is, porn gets harder, so to speak, as erections get softer. A sad maxim for you. Wish I was your age. Ah, well! When am I going to meet the lady I invented?

—Thought I'd give her a screen-test first.

—Screw her first, you mean. Go on, you'll be late.

And the boy Gareth was shown affectionately by Uncle Barry to the door of his flat. I wondered if he was going to get very drunk. Washed up alone, an ageing writer sipping whisky. I remembered how his last novel had pilloried everyone who might be expected to review it. What a desperate conceit, and how sad.

I looked at the back of my diary where Jane had written her address. Camden Town. Neat upright handwriting. Better than mine. 17 Albert Crescent. She had written the seven crossed. Three years in Paris, that must be. It was ten to eight. Only a little late. Jane had said she shared a flat with a friend, making it clear it was a girl-friend. Did I care? Yes, I did care. Second carbon of the synopsis in my briefcase. A half-moon over Regents Park. A still night. I was excited, a bit nervous. I couldn't remember what she looked like. Turn right before the Zoo. I liked this part of London. Three door-bells. One of them had Young/Murphy by it. The door-speaker crackled: Hello, come up! The door buzzed and I pushed it quickly. A naked 40 watt bulb and no staircarpet. Top floor, she had said. The door at the top was ajar. A bright light through it and the sound of music: Bartok. Then a voice from a warm room.

She turned from the mirror, hands behind her neck beneath

her hair fixing an aquamarine pendant. She looked so light, youthful, so infinitely subtle in the lines and movements of her face. I talked, not knowing really what I was talking about. She moved easily round the room, leaving trace-images before my eyes, and the scent of her resting where the images lingered.

—How did the weekend go, she said? And the film, did you work something out?

—Yes, I said, holding out a folder of typescript. There you are. Inspired by the Norfolk marshes.

—You did all this at the weekend?

—There wasn't much competition.

—I can't wait to read it.

—Yes you can. I'm going to take you out to dinner.

—All right, I shall read it romorrow.

We drove to Charlotte Street. Being Monday evening the restaurant was three-quarters empty. I looked at her across the table. Her fair hair fell very straight down one side of her face. Her eyes, pale-blue, were the colour of her aquamarine pendant. She wore a soft Laura Ashley dress which fitted loosely over her body and left her elbows and forearms bare. She was wearing a gold bangle at her wrist and a heavy hand-made ring on the middle finger of her left hand.

—Don't you think you'd better tell me who you are, she said with mock seriousness. I know nothing about you at all.

And she steered a lock of hair back over her shoulder and began to talk about herself. I smiled and listened. She told me a lot, sipping wine and holding the glass up to look at me over the top of it. She was younger than I thought: twenty-three. Her father was a baker in Taunton.

—Now we only need a candlestick-maker.

—Why?

—Because mine was a butcher.

She laughed. She had gone to the Central School of Drama at just seventeen and had lived with her mother and stepfather in Finchley.

—The one who belonged to the dirty-mac brigade?

—He didn't really. He just rather fancied me, that's all.

—Anyway, that was the time of your famous strip?

—Right!

Then she had won a scholarship to Paris, which I knew, and studied with Marceau, which I knew. There she met an American and lived with him for two years. When that broke up she came back to London and tried to get theatre work here; which was where she joined the Garnett Mime Troupe.

—Why am I telling you all this?

—Because you asked me to tell you who *I* was.

She laughed again.

—Oh! So I did!

—Anyway you haven't told me much. Why mime? I want to know.

She stopped chattering and looked embarrassed. Those same expressions of deep feeling caught her face, as if she were a series of heads being modelled at speed by a sculptor.

—I think it's just something about words I don't like. They . . . they somehow drown things, things that matter. They shouldn't but they do. Oh, not great literature and all that, but you know what I mean. You see, I can't even say it.

—It's funny: here we are talking our heads off, and yet you don't like words and my world is . . . images. Maybe that was it.

—That was what?

—Why I was drawn to you, at the theatre.

She didn't say anything. Looked at me. There was a knot in my stomach. Her face was soft again. I wanted to kiss her then. I ran my fingers across her hand.

—You had a sort of private world and then you gave the audience the key to it.

—There weren't very many of them, were there?

She looked thoughtful.

—I suppose that's it. A private world. The thing is, I don't know if I really want to share it.

—Don't you?

We looked at each other without saying anything.

—Words don't always drown things.

—No, she said after a while, very softly.

I walked with Jane along the edge of Regents Park by the Zoo, my arm round her. I talked a little. I stopped by the railings with tears on my face. From the ghost of the giant aviary came a few squawks and a stirring of heavy wings. As I turned she was looking up at me. She raised her fingers to wipe my face very slowly. Her eyes shone in a ray of street-light.

—Gareth!

—I am falling in love with you.

I leant over and kissed her. Her hand was in my hair, her neck soft against my hand, her body pressed against mine.

I drove back across the river. An hour later I was lying listening to the rain and wondering why I had come back at all.

Now it is the hour before dawn. Grey. A streak of rain on the window. I'm alone in this room. Why did I come back last night? I could have stayed with Jane Young. Was it that I couldn't face the bed-sit romance on the narrow couch among the Sarah Bernhardt posters, with two flights down to the loo in a borrowed wrap and the unshaven departure after Nescafé along with the tenderfoot lover from the next-door room? All that again.

O heart, we are old;
The living beauty is for younger men;
We cannot pay its tribute of wild tears.

Perhaps. I suppose I did not wish it to be like that. Why is Yeats in my mind?

Though I am old with wandering
Through hollow lands and hilly lands,
I will find out where she has gone,
And kiss her lips and take her hands;
And walk among long dappled grass,
And pluck till time and times are done
The silver apples of the moon,
The golden apples of the sun.

So I came back on a starry night before the rain, with a flame of hunger within me that I had believed might be gone for ever.

This is not the time. Not yet. I do not want to know it all, not now.

The hour before dawn: the devil's hour vivid with images the day will tear down in rags. Hopes fresh from sleep, weightless, soaring in the mind. Memories projected on the night. Radiant skeletons, they will shriek and disappear at cock-crow.

Memories of my lost Wales. The valley to Croesor veined with streams to dam and gasp in. Ink-blue water patrolled by gnats under a vault of alders. "Tea-time! Tea-time, Gareth": my sister's voice from the stone cottage on the slope we took for holidays. Scones laid out on the slate slab we used as a makeshift table. Slugs underfoot at night. The great bed below the rafters. Buzzards mewing over the dank trees. Curlews on the moor. Bacon smells. Walls fit for a castle. The munching of sheep outside the window in the mornings, then thundering away down the hill. Foxgloves in the bracken. Sloes in the hedgerow. Lichens shaggy on the oak-trees.

Caernarvon in November under the hulk of the castle at night, the black water smudged orange and yellow. Fishing-boats askew on the mud. Drunks on the quayside. "I like you, Monica." "I like you too, Gareth." Dew on her collar. Breasts warm under layers of woollies. "See you next Friday, Monica, shall I?" "Expect so!"

Shirley clinging to my waist on the pillion past the Criccieth town clock after school. "She's a bitch, Shirley," said Owen. "She only fancies you because you're going to a posh university." "Gareth goes out with old Parry-Jones's granddaughter, you know." "Yes, only fifteen but a lovely girl. A boy couldn't go wrong with a girl like that, now could he?" Shirley reading Keats by the harbour at Maentwrog, our feet dangling in the water. "Gareth, do you love me?" "I love the mole by your collarbone." "Do you think they made love in Keats?" "He never says so." "Grandfather must have made love a lot." "Probably still does."

Grandfather Parry-Jones sitting out on the terrace in the summer evenings with his women in his eyes, and Maentwrog built around him out of his dreams. "Each dream for a different lady," he'd say with a chuckle. "Shirley will be good for you, you know, Gareth. She's a fine girl." "I know."

Where did she go? Where did I go?

A letter was waiting for me last night from Grandfather Parry-Jones. I'd forgotten I'd written to him when he got his knighthood in the New Year. Not many men over ninety get knighted, he said. They think I'm harmless now, I suppose. It would be good to see you again, he wrote. Come down and stay while I'm still *compos mentis.* I'd like to see you. Make it soon.

I should like to. Yes, I would. It's years now since I've been up to Maentwrog. At one time I would drive over there from mother's house at Portmadoc. A pair of old people gazing into the estuary watching their lives drift away. Mother's dead now – two years – and I've never been back. I love that place; why have

I never been back? Is it all the balding shopkeepers I was once at school with?

Do the cows still stand in the flooded water-meadows? I want to go. I'll write to Grandfather Parry-Jones today (it's almost as if he were my own grandfather) and say I'm coming down straightaway this Friday. No, I'll send a telegram. A long weekend. The last weekend of my marriage. I'll be away. Why do I feel so strongly about old Parry-Jones? Because of Shirley? The first girl I loved. And forgot. Yes, I'll go!

It is almost light now. The first train is already crossing the river towards Earls Court. The children are stirring along the corridor. Another school day. Another office day. All is normal. Next week Jennifer will be gone. The children will be gone. And I will be four or five thousand miles away; or getting ready to be. Jane, where will she be? A spurt of panic. Was she really in my arms only six or seven hours ago? Will the day tear her image down in rags too, leaving only the barbed-wire on which my marriage hung like a shrike's larder? Jane, I want you. I feel so alone. Frightened. How do I know this too won't cool in my hands? Vanish like a cry of love in the night? Nothing left? Oh, no!

Get on with it, Gareth. Nobel-prizewinning film-director found crying into his porridge. Two minutes silence! Shit!

Out into the damp winter morning. Key in the office door. Good morning! Good morning! An hour's paper-work.

—Make some more coffee, Janet, will you?

—If I came on your recce I'd have something useful to do.

—Yes, I could screw you from Casablanca to Kuwait.

—Well, the budget could stand it.

—Could I?

—Probably not. Past it.

—Then I think I won't risk it.

—Bastard!

* * *

We walked down to the river most evenings when Natasha was in bed. Tamara would be doing her homework. The cat would watch us leave, coiled on the window-sill, and be there when we came back.

—From now on my life is going to be all one, I said one evening.

Sarah and I were standing watching the riverboats at anchor under the moon. I was still and peaceful, and I felt light at heart. Happy with Sarah pressed against me. Happy to leave the office each day knowing I would take her in my arms as I stepped through the front-door that evening, happy knowing that she would be waiting to welcome me. Happy to be with her children: Natasha would wake us each morning bouncing on the big bed with a drawing or story from her comic. Happy at night to feel Sarah naked beside me pressing her body close: tired, I would run my hands down her back and over her buttocks, her face against my neck.

—All one, I said again. What a long time it's taken.

Sarah didn't say anything. Was there a troubled expression on her face? It was dark. I couldn't be sure.

—What is it, darling?

—Nothing! I love you.

We stopped at the pub for a beer. Didn't say very much. My eyes were looking past her.

—Come back: I want you, Gareth. I do love you. Sometimes it frightens me I love you so much.

Her dark eyes were warm and wide, her hair shining almost black, a few strands of it falling on to her bare neck. She shivered as my eyes continued down her body and she placed a small hand in mine.

—It takes my breath away.

—You don't want the basset-hound any more?

—Oh, darling!

She frowned and leaned forward to kiss me.

—I never did want him. Not like this. You know that. It was . . . I was just so terribly unhappy. I couldn't bear to be alone any more. I had no more strength left.

—I know. Let's go back and make love.

My life was all one at last. The lonely hunter had gone away. I no longer dreamed after women I passed in the street and would never see again but longed for in the early hours when I lay awake. I kissed Sarah's breasts in the dark and felt her body stir under me, and we fell asleep by one another, breathing slow and deep. How jagged and withdrawn my old life seemed: I could scarcely believe how easy the days could be. She would come over to me as I sat reading in the evening and rest her head on me while I stroked her hair. We would listen to music saying nothing as the winter settled in. We lived in a cocoon of contentment and I closed my eyes. Sarah, my lovely Sarah. It had been so long.

Day Twenty-three

I had not seen the children for more than a month. Jennifer wrote icy and accusing letters. She had every right to.

—What's the point, Sarah said angrily? Why does she have to make it worse?

—She's hurt. Of course she's hurt. And she's alone.

—She never loved you.

Didn't she? I think she did. I was still numb to any feelings for Jennifer. I had put her out of my mind. But her letters hurt. Especially when she swore she would never let the children come to Chiswick. Let that woman have my children? Never! I had to arrange with friends to use their flat in Notting Hill as a reception centre. They had no children of their own. I went out to buy books, toys, sweets: what else do children need on a wet Saturday afternoon? Jennifer would leave them with neighbours. "I don't want you to come to the house."

I took them in the car to Holland Park. We walked to the summer restaurant on a mid-winter day in the rain. Ennis had stayed behind. Jennifer had considered him too young. He couldn't even walk yet. I was miserable he wasn't there. I'd brought a red push-chair for him. It was in the back of the car. Deirdre and Seth fought each other in the puddles. She tore his jacket. He spat at her. We ate a revolting lunch. Was this the caterers' conspiracy against my efforts? Why did we have to come here, Deirdre asked? Cauliflower – Ughhh! The hamburgers took half an hour to arrive. By then Seth had tripped over a potted plant. You shouldn't leave it in such a bloody stupid place, I snapped at the waiter. He was Spanish and didn't understand. Shrugged and cleared up the mess. Everyone was an alien. The food was alien. The flat in Notting Hill was spick and span. The children played soldiers with the netsuke. Wouldn't they like some orange-juice, the hostess said? Wouldn't they like some chloroform, she meant? We've got this book at school, Seth announced. I had bought it specially. What do you do here, Daddy, said Deirdre? What a funny place. Can we watch television? They watched television most of the afternoon while it rained.

I rang Sarah to say I'd be back around six. She sounded cool. I felt guilty. When I put down the phone Seth was wearing a garland of pink loo-paper, and jumping up and down on the Danish sofa. The owners of the flat were sipping brandy silently in the kitchen. You're very kind, I said. Not at all, they said, sipping more brandy. We know how it must be. It won't be long, I reassured them.

Around five I restored some neatness to the flat and ushered the children into the car. It was still raining. Leave them on the corner, Jennifer had asked. I pulled the car up by the familiar post-box. Two small figures in red macs walked off into the rain, holding hands. I wanted to yell in misery. I smiled out of the window.

—Bye-bye! See you soon!

—Bye, Daddy!

—Bye!

They held hands and skipped away through the puddles. Two figures in the rain. My children – on loan and now handed back. I put the car into gear.

Was this something Jennifer was doing to me, or something I was doing to the children; or to myself? I drove back to Chiswick. Natasha opened the door as she saw me get out of the car. I've got a new nurse's uniform: look!, she announced. She was dressed prettily, and beamed. She took my hand and looked up into my face.

—Mummy, Gareth's back.

Sarah was making a dress for Tamara. She looked up. I didn't go over and kiss her.

—Hello, you're early, darling!

What could I say? I wanted to say nothing over a large drink.

—It was wet.

—Have you had some tea?

—Not exactly.

—I'll make you some. I was just going to collect Tamara.

—Where is she?

—At Joan and Peter's.

—Can't she walk?

Sarah looked hurt. I was slumped on the sofa.

—It is raining. And it's dark.

—Well, I'll do it then.

I jumped up and twiddled my car keys officiously.

—You don't have to.

—Of course I will.

—Darling! What is it?

And Sarah got up and put her arms round me.

—Was it awful?

—Ghastly!

—Oh, darling, it's going to be like that for a while, isn't it?

—I suppose so.

I closed the front-door behind me and got back into the car; drove the quarter of a mile to Joan and Peter's house. Joan was a cheerful dumpy woman in an Arran sweater. The children had been dressing up, she said. Tamara was Cleopatra; or rather Elizabeth Taylor as Cleopatra, Joan reckoned. She wanted to show her mother. Joan would lend her a long shawl to keep warm. Tamara appeared in a white chiffon shift with one shoulder bare. Her black hair was caught at the back with a brooch. She wore massive eye make-up and a gold chain round her waist. Peter approached in paint-stained corduroys and muttered through his pipe that he could understand why Sarah didn't want her to walk back alone. I hung the shawl round Tamara's shoulders. Madam's car is at the door. Nothing less than a Jaguar for Cleopatra. Joan said wasn't she perfectly lovely?, she looks twenty, not fourteen. Tamara tucked the long skirt round her legs and I closed the car door and walked round the other side. I thought of Seth and Deirdre walking away through the rain in their red macs.

Sarah was angry that Jennifer would never let me bring the children to the house. So was I, all the same I felt I understood. In a bloody-minded way I was proud of Jennifer for it, and I supported her when Sarah blew her top.

—How long is this going to go on for? You are their father and this is your home.

—Give her time, was all I could say. I felt I should have been indignant but I wasn't. Of course it was painful only to see the children on neutral ground. My mother had died earlier in the year; her house in Portmadoc was sold; besides North Wales would have been too far to take them for a weekend. Was it moral blackmail on Jennifer's part? Sarah felt so.

—She's using them as a weapon to get you back. I think it's disgusting.

Sarah was stoking her anger as she realized how passive a line I was taking. She turned on me and accused me of cowardice, and I flared up at her.

—What do you know about it? You've never been parted from your children. Jennifer's their mother. D'you really expect her to share them with you. And d'you expect me to take her to court for it? Or what?

Sarah shut up after this.

I began to feel a divided man. Before leaving Jennifer I had nearly always been a divided man, so it came naturally. Now I felt, again, that I was holding myself in precarious balance between the two of them. Was this my most comfortable role: the uncommitted lover? Sarah sensed it.

—Do you remember when you said your life was going to be all one from now on, she said?

As soon as Sarah reminded me I knew how far I had already drifted from those early evenings when we walked by the river in love. I felt perplexed, sad, hopeless even.

—I knew at the time it wouldn't be like that, she went on. I was frightened for you. I knew it would be hard.

—Yes, it is.

It was all I could say. I was thinking of my children. What had they done for Christmas? Did they have a tree with lights, and presents hung on it? Were mine hung on it too? What had they said when they opened them? Did they miss me as much as I missed them?

—Darling!

It was an effort to say that. Sarah was standing in a nightdress by the door of our room. Why did she have to wear a nightdress? Why couldn't she be naked?

She was looking at me, and she read my mood. Slowly she pulled at the bows on her bare shoulders and let the garment slip on to the floor.

—Sarah, you're wonderful! You're beautiful! Let me touch you.

And I stepped towards her and ran my hands down over her body. So slim, as when I first knew her. Her muscles tautened as I pressed my hand over her belly and between her thighs.

—I do love you, Sarah. And I desire you.

—And when I'm old and wrinkled?

—Then I'll be old and wrinkled too.

—But you'll still be a horny old roué. I know you. And thank God you will!

We made love and slept. It was like it always used to be.

* * *

Eric is doing his nut. His two little mice are scuttling between telephones bearing scraps of paper with flight times and embassy phone-numbers scrawled on them. There is a neat pile of passports in front of him – mine, O'Rourke's, Archie Hill's – and round them this confetti of information settles. It intrigues me how a man with so cool a head for accounts and tax affairs can be so bothered by a mere logistical problem of obtaining nine visas in ten days ("Each embassy insists on keeping the passports for a week, Gareth, that's the trouble". "I'm sure you'll manage it," I say carelessly. Janet is sulking because her passport is not on the pile), and how to fly to Sana'a via Kairouan and Istanbul.

—How's it going, Eric?

It's now midday. He's been at it since ten. I fear I may have undone the benefits of his holiday and sent his golf handicap tumbling.

—We'll be lucky to get you across the Channel at this rate.

—It might come as a surprise to our oil sheikhs to learn that Abraham built the greatest Ka'ba of them all in the Town Hall at Calais. Keep going.

I've agreed with O'Rourke that we start the recce in Cairo. Geographically it's more or less the centre of Islam, and from there we can make two broad loops; one to the east taking in Arabia, the Persian Gulf, Iran, Iraq, Turkey etc; the other westwards along North Africa to Fez and Marrakesh, an excursion up into Spain, then back through Northern Nigeria, the Sahara and Tuareg country across to the Sudan.

Besides, I love Cairo. In an old-maidish way I look forward to beginning the whole project over a cup of marvellous coffee at Groppi's surrounded by feudal matrons and their obese children guzzling pastries, and then drifting with the crowd up the Kasr-el-Nil back to the hotel with its naked lift like an exhibit from some early mining disaster. The Cosmopolitan Hotel, at the hub of Cairo's concrete decay, its battered French-colonial splendours set amid a rooftop world of crowing cockerels and shuffling figures in striped pyjamas. Eric once went on a package holiday to Egypt and can't understand why I won't put up at the Sheraton. "Because everything is triple-booked in Cairo, Eric, and at the Cosmopolitan at least they know me and the bribe will be cheaper"; which is untrue on both counts but it's the kind of answer Eric wants to hear. I look forward to being back in that human farmyard. I want to peck around in the dust.

Waldron is doing his City-slicker act and arranging for money to be on tap at the central bank of every city we visit: I only have to give him the list. Airline tickets "on the house". Business friends waiting in dark glasses at the barrier, our personal *Tontons Macoute.*

—We may need them, dear boy, said O'Rourke. Otherwise in Saudi Arabia we shan't get a drink. Hateful country. They threatened jail on me last time for having a quarter-bottle of Scotch in my luggage. I only wish I could be around when the oil runs out.

—So long as it's not before they've footed our bill, Barry.

—No fear, no fear!

The problem of the visas is solved, Eric says. Waldron's office has just rung back to assure him they'll take care of all that. Surprise, surprise! Eric looks mightily relieved. Now it's back to the flight timetable. Oh, for Christ's sake, Eric, make out an open ticket the longest possible way round, and get the agency to invoice Waldron. What's the use of trying to book a flight from Riyadh to Suleiman-el-Pong on Disaster Airways for Thursday, March 14 at 1642 hours – check-in time a week before the flight which probably doesn't exist anyway?

Janet smells this morning. I have a hunch she's going to give in her notice. Now she knows she's not coming to the Middle East she won't have much to do until David's got some film to edit on "The Sound of Britain". It'll be cheaper to let her go, and employ a new assistant editor when David's ready. He may not even need one. Perhaps I should sack her first. Having screwed her last week, sack her this. No, that would sit on my conscience. Lightly, but it would. But I do wish she'd stop sulking – and niffing. This is a clean, happy office; it says so on my smile.

Soon there won't be an office at all.

I must go. I'm meeting Jane Young round the corner for a drink, and then Waldron for lunch to talk about a producer for the feature-film. Will he go all heavy on me, or am I sufficiently his bright-eyed boy to have my own way? God, I must be costing him millions.

—Nonsense, you're about to make him millions, said O'Rourke when he phoned this morning. Don't have a single twinge of conscience, dear boy, or you're lost.

Maybe he's right. The old pro again.

—Do you think he really will let you make the film you want to make?

Jane was dressed in a pink cashmere sweater and jeans. We were perched on bar-stools squeezed among lunch-time executives. Her hand was small and cool.

—Yes, I do! Waldron's one of these people it's taken me years to believe in, because he's basically so unbelievable, unless you understand the psychology of money.

—Do you?

—In one way, yes! Waldron's never got close to anyone in his life, and money has supported his loneliness. Perpetuated it and made it bearable. He's bought houses, pictures, merchant banks, me, I suppose! They're none of them ever enough. He has to go on: more possessions, more money, more avenues. He can't say "my wife", "my boy-friend", "my children", but he can say "my film", "my pictures". Sounds better than "my bank". He's starved of outlets for his feelings, and he's prepared to pay someone else to spread the passions around for him. He weeps in front of his pictures. He couldn't do that in front of a human being. It's a tragedy, isn't it? Yet without people like that where would I be? No one to pay for my films, and no one to watch them either.

—I hate to think of it like that.

—I don't. I revel in it.

She gave me a stern look. She didn't believe me. I hadn't really thought this one out; all the same I wanted to say it. I was in a mood for speeches.

—I don't want a sweet soft world of the arts. That's rubbish. If it wasn't for a lousy world there wouldn't be any arts. People like us just orchestrate the mess. That's why we're needed.

—Don't include me. I'm just an out-of-work actress you've picked up.

—Well, you're part of the orchestra even if you're not playing.

—You make it sound more like an opium-den.

—I think it can be. But only bad art is opium. If I'd tried to make a feature-film ten years ago it would have been opium.

—And now it won't?

—And now I hope it won't. I just feel I'm ready for it. I know enough about reality to be able to invent it. And that's tremendously exciting.

The conversation surprised me. Here was a girl I fancied like crazy and I was lecturing her about art and life. Keeping her at a distance. It was a strange experience not to be melting into sentiments in front of a girl I was falling in love with. I wasn't sure how Jane took it. Did it chill her? Well, the sooner she knows my opinionated, hectoring self the better. She was going off to spend the night with her mother, and I dropped her in a taxi at the station, not before arranging to take her out tomorrow evening, Thursday.

—Do you ever stop talking for a minute, she asked?

—It was my turn.

She laughed and placed a hand on mine. I caught her eyes, those intense pale-blue eyes, and as she was about to climb out of the taxi I drew her towards me and kissed her.

—If I don't talk my head off I want to make love to you.

—Goodbye, Gareth. And good luck! I'll cross my fingers for you.

I took the taxi on into the City to meet Waldron. I was late. He was cheerful. He had bought a new Graham Sutherland. Another emotional cop-out. Then we discussed producers. I believe with any luck there may be no problems.

Later in the day. The street is dark. A sheen of frost on pavements in the moonlight. A few smears of light between curtains.

Once Jennifer used to turn the front-door light on for me in the evenings. Years ago. I had forgotten. This could well be my last evening at home with the family – ever! – if, that is, I go to

Wales on Friday for the long weekend I've planned. I shall tell Jennifer. Will she be relieved, angry or indifferent? How absurd that I don't have the faintest idea after all these years. That's it, isn't it!

Suddenly it really is about to end. My God! I hesitate outside the front-door. My final entry. All these weeks of phoney war; now the armies are on the move. It's too final to be sad any longer. Let's just get it over with. There's the film: that helps. There's Jane: that helps. I wish I were with her now. And yet I want to be here tonight. My last evening. I haven't even thought how it's all going to be done. How do you break up seventeen years? With an axe? Are we going to divide up the furniture in the approved fashion? Or is Jennifer intending to depart with only her personal possessions? It's the little things that will be the hardest: who's going to keep the photograph albums, the children's presents to us both? Don't: that hurts! Oh, Christ! I wonder if Jennifer feels the same. The front-door is open. It's cold. Bloody February! Would it be any easier to smash a marriage in the sun? Or just sweatier?

Deirdre and Seth are watching television. Ennis is hopping downstairs holding a witch's hat. (Who gave you that, your mother? No, I must not say that.) Darling Ennis. He jumps into my arms.

—Daddy, why did you cry the other morning?

—Because I was unhappy.

—Oh! Throw me in the air.

—No!

—Why?

—You're too heavy.

—Then give me a train-ride.

—All right!

—All the way to Italy! Go on, Daddy!

—Are we going to Italy at Easter, Daddy? Deirdre's voice from the next room. Marvellous how children accept change and cannot conceive that it will make the slightest difference. Why not Italy for the Easter holidays as usual? There's the Casa Bella, so why not use it? What difference does it make if you and Mummy don't live together: you can be friends, can't you, for the holidays?

I had scarcely thought about the Casa Bella. Shall I ever use it again? The place where most of all Jennifer and I have been happy. I feel like keeping it as a memento. I can't imagine ever taking anyone else there.

Liar! Even while I tell myself that, I can see a girl with long hair and long legs stretched out beside the pool. I wonder who you are. Nobody! You always were nobody!

—Is there anything you want to settle?

—Why should there be?

Jesus Christ, I should have thought there were a hundred reasons why. But Jennifer does not wish to talk about it. She is preparing supper for the kids and does not wish to talk about it. So back to the familiar gavotte in the kitchen with me trying to avoid standing exactly where Jennifer needs to be. This time I shall leave the drying-up cloth where it is. I have told her about my weekend in Wales, assuming I hear from old Parry-Jones. She knows I may not be back till Monday, and Monday is the 28th. The last day of the month. The last day of the month she asked for.

—Oh! she said. I see! And that was all. She did not wish to talk about it.

All right then. Let it be. Jennifer does not want to divulge. We'll leave it at that, and I shall return on Monday in time to watch the pantechnicon pull away bearing seventeen years of married life, with the children waving cheerily like Romanies out of the back. Goodbye! Goodbye to everything!

"You shall have my chairs and candle,
And my jug without a handle!
Gaze upon the rolling deep
(Fish is plentiful and cheap);
As the sea, my love is deep!"
Said the Yonghy-Bonghy-Bò,
Said the Yonghy-Bonghy-Bò.

Goodbye!

Day Twenty-four

A year, a whole year, before I can start on the feature-film. Robert Altman will have made three in that time. And yet maybe it's not such a bad thing. A year in which I shall have to find my feet as a lone male. Lone male! Rogue male! Who knows? Gareth is cum with luv to toune, lewde sing cuccu!

Already I am piecing the film together like pictures for an exhibition. It may not be the approved method, but within a year the entire film should be shot in my head. O'Rourke is disgusted.

—Images! Images! he says. Just pretty pictures. Ideas, dear boy, and people; that's what you should be working with, not the shroud of Turin.

—You wait, Barry, is all I can reply. Feeble, but how can I explain the way a film-maker works? Or at least the way this film-maker works? Impossible to put over to Barry how colour, grain, angle, lens, camera movement, light – how these things are as deeply my affair of the heart as words are his: how I need to unwind a thread without words.

—Oh, it's going to be a box-office stampede, Gareth, I can see that! A love-story without words. Do you permit deep breathing in your silent order?

Barry is occupying his favourite speakers' corner of his flat, one arm on the mantelpiece with a glass of whisky in his fingers, the other arm propped paternally against a tall mahogany book-case, at least two shelves of which contain the collected works of B. O'Rourke in various languages and including his more dilettante offerings such as *An Encyclopaedia of Revolution.* O'Rourke the old Tory anarchist: the "40s" man!

—At least it should make my job as script-writer comparatively straightforward. Have another Scotch.

In this mood anything I say will be a hostage to his mirth. It would have been better if I hadn't tried to explain. Writers are all visually illiterate anyway; any denial of the supremacy of words threatens their job and sends them mumbling to the Society of Authors for support. I did try to explain: that words will cocoon the story, hold it in place, not be the fabric of it.

—You'd have done well in the silent-film era. Born after your time, dear boy.

So many films are made with the rotten conceit of a camera hidden in the soul. It's an old literary device, and it works for books because words on the page can speak thoughts. In films words can't be silent; so on the screen they merely sound like a man talking obsessively to himself. I don't want to bug someone's mind. I want to know the signals, the semaphore people make. These, after all, are all the witnesses we have. To claim access to more information than that is a cheat.

—One thing for sure; you'd never have made a writer! Did you ever want to be a painter?

No!

Is it possible to recreate the images life throws at you? The way two people meet unexpectedly in the street? The child I saw one day who called out "Daddy!" from across the the road and ran straight under a car: I thought for a moment the cry was for me. The girl on the beach with a dog at low-tide, seen only from my balcony and I recognised her five years later serving beer in a Wandsworth pub? Are these things a man can only write about? As images would they ever work a second time, and with a different cast? But then supposing the cast were to remain the same? The idea for this film came from watching Jane Young; and the images I am collecting are her images, images of her. I know I am watching us both fall in love. Is this a sore case of narcissism or is it art? Is this the nature of art? To be at once face and reflection, voice and echo, matador and *aficionado*?

—Of course it is, dear boy! No writer after the age of thirty ever does anything without thinking how it will look in a book. The same for a film-director, I imagine. You're just waking up to it a bit late, Gareth.

Barry's face is more benign now. Maybe it's the whisky, or maybe he's remembered that he likes me; has forgotten that he envies me.

—But still, now I've been allowed to see your Jane Young I'm inclined to believe it may have been worth waiting for. She's lovely, dear boy, lovely. A naiad. Thea was a bit like that. A sea-goddess.

—Thea was a virgin.

—Jane merely looks like one. That's the best kind. Virginity's nothing to do with fucking or not fucking. It's all in the mind. You know that.

I had brought Jane round to Barry's flat after leaving the office. We were not expected. Barry was a bit drunk. Then she had to go off for an hour to do some evening shopping.

—Are you in love with her? Yes, of course you are. Or you know you will be. That's the best moment – all too short. Like the suicide jumping from the hundredth floor: at the fiftieth he shouts "So far so good!"

Barry's pale eyes had been wandering over her while he talked: his famous-author-on-show act. He was reloving all the women he had mythologised in those novels of the desert, so unlike any women I have ever encountered in such parts. I thought of the wife who had gone mad and drowned herself in the Norfolk marshes. Another myth? No, she really had: they had said so in the pub.

—But for God's sake don't let her make your film for you, that's all. Films by a director in love are even worse than novels by an author in love. Stand aside, at least by day.

His laugh was false and sad. I saw Barry drinking himself into old age alone. Had he run out of naiads waiting to be discovered in remote Levantine places, or maybe Barry's body and spirit revived with the first breath of a scirocco on his face, and here he merely withdrew? An old crab, he called himself. I would soon know.

There's the doorbell. I have a feeling of limbo, of vertigo almost. Are you in love with her?

My last evening at home is over. My old life is over. What next?

* * *

I had never thought of Sarah as moody. Stubborn, yes. Storm-clouds followed by a deluge of tears. But moods, no! Her serenity either rode such petulant things or it was simply that moods were no part of her nature. She was what she was. God knows, she had been through enough: marriage to Angus when still a child almost, his illness, separation, death, earning for three as well as being mother and housekeeper. And to have been so much alone. Always it seemed composed, contained, on the tracks, radiant. She was the living answer to those disgruntled letters in the *Guardian* from women expected to be cook, nanny, companion and mistress all at once – women I always suspected were inadequate in each role – and here was Sarah who was all those things and rather more besides, and serene with it. She had taken me into her life like a harbour receiving a new ship from the storm. Darling, so long as you go on loving me, that's all I want, she would say in my arms.

But then . . . perhaps my view of her was too simple, and I should have noticed that no contentment was ever that rounded. Mine wasn't, so why should hers be? There began to be days, weeks, when she withdrew. Her face became set. She would suffer from migraines. She woke early before dawn, and I would grow aware of her sitting up in bed quite still, duvet drawn up round her bare shoulders, staring into the grey light. When I asked her what was wrong she would start and say, "Oh nothing", too dismissively. And then she'd smile as though she had to.

I became flippant, took to deflecting her moods playfully as a way of not having to acknowledge them. Deeper, they irritated and disturbed me. I knew what they were about, and I began to make unfavourable comparisons with Jennifer. Jennifer would not have behaved like this, I would say to myself. How unfair! Whatever Sarah's commitment was, it was visceral; it was pinned in her guts; and I had left Jennifer because hers was all in the head, or seemed to be. It was precisely this gut reaction of Sarah's that had magnetised me. I could trust her blood and flesh and heart: we would always share the same hunger and the same joy. Now I was telling myself Jennifer would not have allowed herself to feel this way. Of course not. It was why I had left her: that particular kind of chemical starvation had become unbearable, and Sarah's love was a lifeline I could not bear to cut. An umbilical lifeline: I have a basic Freudian image of a supertanker refuelling me. Now I knew that this was changing, and I knew why.

Sarah wanted a child.

She wanted a child who would ease the pain of the child she

felt ought to have been hers: Ennis. She needed a child of mine, and the need was an ache so deep she was made ill by it. She would wake at night and feel the infant moving inside her; and she would lie with her hand resting on her belly to feel the vibrations of its heart. She would rearrange the room so that there would be a place for the cot. She even wrote to the National Childbirth Trust for literature about breathing exercises which she did not have the chance to conceal from me in the morning post. And when we made love she arched her pelvis to admit me as deeply as she could and to speed those two million spermatozoa into her womb as if one wasted might render her barren.

Why didn't she just leave off the pill for a month or two without telling me? It wouldn't have been Sarah's way. She was not that imperious. She was waiting for me to say "Darling, I want a child"; in the meanwhile choking on the pain and the longing, lying there in the night sobbing, eyes fixed on the ceiling and saying nothing. Every morning she took the pill and I knew she wanted to spit it down the loo, but she didn't and she wouldn't say so; and I didn't say anything either. When I kissed her breasts she would close her eyes and wish it was my child's lips.

I knew then that I never wanted her to have my child, and it disturbed me. Why could I not bear the idea? After all, I had chosen to live with Sarah. One day soon I would presumably marry her. I loved her, didn't I? I had left Jennifer for her. Why should we not have children? She was only thirty-three. She had a job she could return to. It wasn't a question of money. I even loved children; had I not said so often, shown it to her own children? So why then? I lay awake at night turning it over in my mind.

I knew perfectly well why. Sarah pregnant, and mother of my child, would destroy a myth.

As the weeks passed it grew worse. I played for time.

—I need to think about it.

—Of course you do, darling.

She was so sweetly reasonable. At least we were now able to talk about it; except that sooner or later I would have to say Yes or No. Our present life now had a time limit. I tried to persuade myself that my objections were chimeras and nothing more. I thought how beautiful the child would be, and how loved. How happy it would make Sarah. How Tamara and Natasha would cradle it, adore it. How it would bind us all closer together. How without such a child I might never feel I had made the final break from Jennifer: part of me would always belong in the big house on the river.

But it was not the child that worried me; it was Sarah. The thought of her swollen with a child, my child; giving birth, giving suck. The strength of my revulsion horrified me. Why? Why did it? Was I the child, was this the meaning of that gut relationship I felt, and of that Freudian image of the lifeline from ship to ship? I Sarah's child? Surely people didn't really have quite such obvious Oedipus complexes, at least not with surrogate mothers eight years younger than themselves. This was altogether too contorted. And yet I could not dispel my horror at the prospect of that swollen belly cradling another life. Neither could I release the image of the Sarah I had desired so strongly. What was Sarah to me, then, that this threat of change cast such a shadow?

It was dark. No moon. She was asleep. I saw her in the moments I had needed her most. I saw her girl's breasts in the moonlight by the summer pool. I heard her laughter as she ran towards me with wet hair streaming along an avenue of rhododendrons. I saw her naked on the ribbed sand with the tide tugging at her. Real images or dreamed: I no longer knew. But, oh God, what ghosts, and how they reached for my stomach and made me gasp. And in the blackness I reached out and lightly with my fingers touched Sarah's closed eyes, one then the other, then her lips – slightly open – her ears, her neck, her breasts, her belly then gently between her legs until involuntarily they parted and I stroked her clitoris between my thumb and forefinger. Sarah! Sarah! Deep in her I knew that nothing in my longing for her had ever healed the rift that had lain within me all my life. Nothing had changed after all. She was not, and never would be, the creation who would make my life all one, who would combine in one person the woman I wanted and the woman I needed, who could fulfil me and secure me – lady of the dawn and lady of the day. I wanted to be Sarah's lover, not her husband, not the father of her children. I wanted her to be fresh to my eyes, to my touch. I wanted her voltage, her signals. I wanted everything with her to end in bed. And after four months bed was becoming a place where we slept, dreaming of other things.

I missed Jennifer. If I was going to be two people then I knew which one had a home. And what the hell is home? A place to feel safe in: a place to be free of the harpies.

* * *

And a place to leave. There is nowhere I belong to now.

I feel like a thief in the night. The family is sleeping. If I were really leaving it would be easier. I am here as a ghost until Jennifer and the children are no longer here, then I must return and come to life again, find myself again, begin again. Here. I have no idea what that is going to feel like. Is a sudden great peace about to settle on my life, all troubles fled; and I shall establish a quite new contact with these surroundings which at this moment feel as numb as I do? Or will the real pain only then flow back, a sense of irretrievable loss which will quietly and unobtrusively unpin the fabric of my life?

A suitcase is open on the bed. I shall fill it with a few things for the weekend. The alarm-clock is set for six. I want to slip away unheard. No more goodbyes: I could not bear it. Better to have got it over already, and to be going away for the end. To Wales, my Wales. Perhaps it's the best thing to be starting again where I started before. Gareth's going to a posh university: won't be speaking to us any more. Bet his father's proud. Maybe it'll be free meat this weekend. A fine boy, Gareth! There he goes, look, on his motor-bike, with that girl again! Quite a little minx: look at the way she's holding to him. And those bare legs, skirt pulled up like that. What they get up to these days. My father would've given me a good hiding. Old Parry-Jones's granddaughter, they tell me: which of his wives, I wonder? They'll be off down to Maentwrog, then, if they don't kill themselves on the way. Plenty of money there, I shouldn't wonder. Oh, young Gareth knows where he's going all right. Shan't see him round here much longer. He'll be off into the wide world. With that little minx clinging to him, most likely, soon as she's left school. You'll see!

It's a still night. Low tide under a waning moon. Looks like a dead planet. I shall be off in the morning. With Jane.

—Will you come?

She just nodded. I kissed her.

—You don't think he'll mind?

—He'll love it. I'll ring him in the morning.

—Goodnight then!

—Goodnight, darling!

Her eyes were bright under the street-lamps. Oh, let this one not fade too. Or everything will be dark.

—Till tomorrow!

Day Twenty-five

Pub lunch in Camden Town – cottage-pie, Cheddar cheese, glass of wine, cona coffee. How formal we are, like fond cousins no longer close. I might be driving her to some mutual relative for tea. Give my love to Maud and the children, won't you? It's been good to see you, Jane, after so long. We must do it again.

Her blonde hair is pressed against the headrest next to me, ruffled across her face by a breeze from the quarter-light window. She is in jeans, cross-legged; one hand on the arm-rest; eyes vacantly following the road-signs. Luton. Leighton Buzzard. Woburn. Bedford. The M1: To the North. We are going to Wales to become lovers and to fall in love. Falling out of life. Free fall. Fallen angels. Bare trees in flat winter fields. Motorways Divide. M6: To the North-West. Traffic on conveyor lines moving silently among the tower-blocks, like Metropolis. Now decelerating and leaving the motorway westwards towards Shrewsbury. A few humps. Then a shadow of hills. Home lies over there. We have hardly spoken all the way. An ashen February evening, dusk sliding into the valleys. Croeso i Gymru – Welcome to Wales. Llangollen. They used to have a handpump at this petrol station not so long ago; cursed you if it was raining – damned Londoners in their Jaguars, coming here to buy up all the hill-farms. I don't want a bloody hill-farm, I want some petrol to get me home.

—You still think of it as home, don't you?

—Yes!

It surprises me how quickly I said that.

—Yes, I suppose I do!

The hills march on either side. Black beasts in the dusk. No, less malign: great black pillows I move across softly. I turn off the engine at the top of the pass by the new reservoir to hear the wind in the night. Stinging rain on my face. I don't know how long I have been standing here. Jane is by my side. She has undone her coat to part-wrap it round me. I can feel her warmth, her breasts, her pelvic bone. I kiss her deep in the rain.

She draws back her face just an inch or two, shouting through her laughter against the gale:

—This is quite the most godforsaken place anyone ever brought me.

—And you hate it?

—It makes me want to make love.

The clouds are torn and sliding past the moon. In the headlights is the first signpost to Portmadoc: 6 miles. The estuary lies like old pewter in the moonlight. In the blackness on the edge of the water must be Maentwrog.

—It's down there.

—That black splodge? Is it another godforsaken place?

—If it makes you want to make love, yes, it is!

—It might be something to do with you, of course. Gareth, why do you make me so happy? Tell me. And tell me why you talk your head off and then you're silent for hours.

—I want you.

—I want you too. Or I wouldn't have come. I want you very much. I didn't think I'd tell you that. But I want you to tell me about Maentwrog. Kiss me first, I'm scared. It sounds horribly grand.

Her hair has dried, soft through my fingers. Her ears are still cold, and the tip of her nose.

—Do you always warm up in bits?

—How unromantic you are. No, not true, you're terribly romantic, aren't you. The hard film-man soft as cheese, isn't that it? I do love being in Wales with you. You're supposed to be telling me about Maentwrog.

—If I ever get a chance to.

—Kiss me.

—No! I shall tell you. What shall I tell you? Parry-Jones bought the place donkey's years ago. He's over ninety now. He's a kind of great-uncle to me. I used to take his granddaughter out when we were schoolkids.

—I know, I know; and she was blonde and she looked like me. You told me. Now tell me about the place.

—He was an architect. Very successful. Made a lot of money in America running up Art Nouveau palaces for real-estate tycoons with wives who wanted to keep up with Paris. Round about the time of the First World War – pre-Slump, anyway. Then he got fed up and retired early, and he's spent the last fifty years – or nearly – adding bits to Maentwrog. It's his life fantasy. He always wanted to live in Italy but he loathed the idea of the Noël Coward life so he built a kind of Portofino in Wales. Then he became a sort of one-man Welsh conservation society: when he heard something odd or interesting was being pulled down he marched in and bought it; re-erected it at Maentwrog. So now it's a mad jackdaw village with everything you could think of – a Norman keep, a tithe-barn, a street of timbered shops, a clock-tower, a gazebo. You name it. Even a gallows.

—Christ! And he lives there all alone?

—No, he still lives in the original house, down on the water. He's got retainers, tons of friends. He used to have tons of wives too. I think he's finally widowed now. He's a lovely man. The perfect decadent. Arrogant as hell, incredibly generous.

—And he loves you?

—In a way, yes!

—I think I do, too. I must be mad. Why did you want to bring me here? Was it because of that girl? I want to know.

—Shirley? No! That was a million years ago. You know, it's mad to be sitting in a lay-by in the freezing winter underneath Snowdon talking about why we're here.

—So it's crazy. I want you to warm my hands and I want to know why you brought me here.

—I wanted to bring you somewhere that meant a lot to me, I suppose. There's nowhere else. You know something, I want to spit out the last twenty years; can you understand that? My father was a shop-keeper; I told you. He sold meat. And he's dead. And now old Parry-Jones has bought up a row of shops and they don't sell anything. I love the place. Perhaps I shouldn't but I do. The guy who's got my father's shop's in the National Front. I hate the bloody shop. I always did. I hated my father, too, in a way.

—God, you've got a lot of guilts, haven't you?

—I've always loved old Parry-Jones.

—And you feel you oughtn't to because he's decadent? And that makes you decadent?

—In a way, yes, but it's more than that. He's free and he's done what he really wanted. That's what I love in him. To hell with decadence. I think I just resent that my father never did anything he wanted to do – ever! Never once in his bloody life did he enjoy himself and come clean about it. It would have undone him. Buttons would have flown off in all directions. Imagine it! It would have been like locusts. A button storm! Millions of them!

—You are ludicrous and I do want you.

—I want to share things with you, so much. Just you, that's all.

—You frighten me.

—Do I?

—No! Kiss me! And don't let go!

I can feel the tears on her face against my cheek. It's gone, all those years. Those endless years. It is not too late. Jane, don't let go. Don't!

* * *

Once she had talked about wanting a child Sarah grew relaxed again, and open. I no longer woke at night to find her sitting bolt-upright in bed, duvet up to her shoulders, unable to sleep; and she no longer drifted round the house by day in a dazed state of inexpressible pain, a thin smile on her lips. Now it was out in the open and our life could proceed serenely in the knowledge that I was seriously thinking about the matter.

I wasn't thinking about it: I was playing for time. How much time? Ten years; until she was too old to bear a child? Unthinkable! Time, then, until I could bring myself to confront her with the answer "No!" That was it, really, wasn't it? No, I did not want a child; I did not want Sarah's child; I did not want Sarah. This was the irrefutable chain of reasoning I was avoiding. But it was more convoluted than that, because in a way I did want Sarah, just so long as she remained a creature several degrees removed from an earthly human being, remained an allegorical figure who inhabited my life and shared my bed and stoked my dreams, and who allowed me to return from the nuts-and-bolts day of a commercial film-maker into my bower of beautiful ladies who wore beautiful clothes, had beautiful thoughts. said beautiful things, had beautiful desires and were beautifully content with this narcissistic Eden which I somehow imagined to be flourishing among the suburban bricks and mortar of Chiswick.

And now this gorgeous allegorical nymph was threatening to step out of her pastoral negligée and pat her belly announcing "I'm pregnant!" It was not what was meant to be. Not at all!

What I had imagined to be the perfect homogeneous life had become instead more divided than ever. The more I was aware of my midsummer night's dream coming to an end, the more I longed for an awakening, not here, but with Jennifer who had never been a dream and whose acerbic reality at least offered a known and secure base. More than that, she was a base I had struggled for, cherished, needed – still needed of course – and had methodically betrayed. Jennifer had been someone who had never, never aroused the burning fickleness of my fancy and so alone had secured a hold upon the reality of what I was. This was her strength, and it was the strength of the marriage we had. I had smashed that marriage because I was obsessed by a perception of its limitations, and it was an obsession which allowed me only to look outwards and upwards towards the stars and never inwards and downwards towards the chasm. Now I was experiencing the sickening, black vertigo of falling, and I was totally unprepared for it. It was only a matter of time before I hit the rocks.

It was early summer. A whole winter and spring had passed since I'd left Jennifer and my children. At least I now saw the children regularly, and they appeared so utterly resigned to the present state of affairs that I used to cry out after they had left: – Wait! It won't always be like this: it can't be. And I would go back into the house and hate Sarah for being there, for being nice, for seeming to understand, for believing it would all work out in the end; and I would resent the demanding presence of Natasha, resent being free to read to her, resent that it was she or Tamara who brought us cups of tea in bed in the mornings and not Deirdre or Seth or Ennis. There were knots of pain inside me which tightened week by week and gradually strangled the surrogate pride and warmth I had always felt towards them. Sarah sensed the change and it hurt her deeply, though she never raised it, merely took quiet steps to keep them off my back while I brooded. It was another of those acceptable conditions of life which, she seemed to feel sure, would work out for the best in the end.

She had other remedies.

—Darling, why don't we think of moving? If we had a larger house it would be so much easier for your children to come and stay. They could come for whole holidays and things, couldn't they?

Of course she was right. I could have made a down-payment on a house any time; and now that Sarah's mother – in a fit of generosity she much regretted – had handed her the deeds to this house, there was no financial reason whatever why we shouldn't live somewhere spacious and even fairly grand if we wanted to.

I didn't want to. The more impermanent the better.

—Yes, I said damply. Why not? in a tone of voice which said Why bother?

And then I diverted the conversation.

—Why don't we all go away for a few weeks? I reckon we could do with it. Sweep the cobwebs away.

As I said it suddenly I half-believed it. A great weight lifted, and I smiled at Sarah as I had hardly smiled at her for months. She warmed under my change of humour, threw her arms round me and straightaway began to plan how it might be done. By eleven that evening it was all decided; we had got through a bottle of wine, said to hell with the washing up, shut out the cat, made love, and I was now standing dressed in a towel phoning Paris to see if a friend's house in Provence might be free in a couple of weeks' time.

It was. We were going. Everything was fixed. The children's half-term was in a fortnight. They had a week, and Sarah, as a teacher within the state system, had the same week off. With the extra weekend at the beginning that made ten days. Ten days in Provence at the end of May! The world seemed a whole lot brighter. Then Sarah came up with a further idea. Tamara was away from school with tonsillitis and wouldn't be going back yet awhile in any case, so why didn't Tamara and I leave a week earlier, take the car, and then she and Natasha would fly out (if we had the money: did we? Yes, I said, we probably did!) which would be much quicker and give everyone even longer there. Marvellous! We told the children at breakfast. They were over the moon. Natasha wanted to get off school like Tamara and leave early with us, until Sarah pointed out she'd then miss the air flight and she'd never been on an aeroplane before, had she? So we were all set. I took a fortnight off work. David and Eric between them could hold the fort perfectly well. God, I wanted to get away; to meander down through France in the burgeoning summer, stopping for coffee and calvados and gothic cathedrals and *pintadeau aux morilles à la crème.* Already I could feel the sun and a smile on my face. Gareth reborn.

Perhaps I had been asking too much after all. The thickening depression of the past months might have been due, quite simply, to false expectations weighed down by perfectly natural withdrawal symptoms. I had left a long marriage: so what did I expect? To walk straight into a new one without a twinge of regret? Clearly Sarah, who'd been through this herself, understood my state of mind very well, and this was comforting. Maybe the worst was already over and the sun would come out at last. I had made the right decision: yes, I had. As for a child, well maybe that would be a good idea, too; meanwhile, just think of the pain Sarah had been compelled to cope with, surviving her own longings as well as my filthy humour and evident doubts about the whole business. A holiday in the south would finally slam the door on a wretched episode of readjustment, and here it was. A few days of relaxed driving across France, a day or so to get the cottage fixed up, and we'd be all together again with no immediate worries on our minds.

I wondered why I hadn't suggested the Casa Bella. There it was, empty and waiting. But no, I knew why. It was the repository of too many rich memories, and they would have to be relived in anguish. We needed somewhere that was fresh to us all, with no associations, no labels, no need for skin-grafts.

The cottage was a Provençal *mas* owned by a sculptor I knew who used it for the summer. The place itself was like a stone-carving set in an open quarry of a landscape near Les Baux. Three rooms on a hillside without water or electricity, and a rough terrace shaded by rattan lashed against the Mistral. A chunk of log-table rested in the centre of the terrace, with olive-stumps planed down for chairs where you could sit and look out over the grey-blue hills and dusty fields Van Gogh painted. The inside walls of the *mas* were whitewashed over rough stone, reddened with smears of slaughtered mosquitoes from last summer. Now it was summer again, too early for invasions of biting things from the swamps of the Camargue, and the evenings were long, burnished and soft. I sat out on the terrace in shorts and sandals reading Yeats which Tamara had been reciting in the car earlier in the day – Christ, no one in Portmadoc ever heard of Yeats when I was fourteen, rising fifteen – and listening to the little waterfall I had located concealed among rocks and a curtain of bamboo down at the bottom of the hill. Our source of water. Tamara had come into view, strands of black hair wet over a white beach-robe. She was picking her way barefoot with a bucket of water in one hand and her clothes clasped to her, jeans dangling.

—It's freezing, that pool. But quite deep. You can dive.

—I think I'll drink it with pastis.

—All of it?

She was grinning, dripping water from hair on to the rough flags. She put down the pail.

—Just pour a little on top. You see, it turns yellow.

—Ughh! Horrible stuff.

—There's some wine inside, if you like. Then we'll go and find some supper.

—Did you know there's a well round the back of the cottage? Looks murky. There's a frog in it. Making a hell of a noise.

—That reminds me of a saying, God knows who said it, terribly wise, the frog in the well may not know the great ocean but he does know heaven.

—Ooh, I like that! It's terrific here!

—It's OK, isn't it?

—I love bathing just like that, naked. And those fantastic rocks.

—Like the second day of creation!

—What happened on the first?

—Don't remember.

—Thought you knew about those things.

—I do. I'm just not letting on.

She laughed again, steering hair from her eyes.

—I like wine. Where are we going this evening? It'll be dark soon.

—I don't know. We'll go and look for somewhere. Arles perhaps; it's only twenty minutes away. Or the sea. A bit further. You've never seen the Mediterranean, have you? You'd better dig out your bathing things.

—Could we really?
—Why not? It'll be dark though.
—What's the point of being at school when I can be here?
—You'd get bloody bored.
—I wouldn't.
—Go and get dressed, anyway.
—Yes, sir! Gareth . . .
—Put something on. Go on!
—All right, all right! What about you, then?
—It'll only take me a minute. Look, the sun's going, Tamara.

There were two and a half days before the others arrived. It was Wednesday, the first time I had really noticed Tamara. Driving down I had wanted to be by myself in France. She had sat gazing out of the window mostly saying nothing. She was still the abrasive, self-reliant girl I'd been with a good deal too much. The mysterious, beautiful, Hardy-like girl who had always been too old for her years, no longer a miniature of her mother, but bigger than Sarah already; slim, long-legged, black-haired. A girl who'd be off our hands in three years. A girl of whom you never knew where her affections lay, they were buried deep somewhere within her silent curiosity; they'd emerge one day, I wondered where. At times I thought about that moment with concern for her, and envy for the recipient of them. She moved her hands as if her fingers carried high voltage.

From this Wednesday evening I was no longer alone. I saw Provence fresh because she was there. I drove her around: the Pont du Gard, Arles, Aix-en-Provence, the Camargue where we went riding across the dry salt-marshes, Palavas where Courbet had once hailed the sea like proud Cortez, Aigues Mortes where we watched the sun go down from the battlements. She took my hand as we walked back to the car, and she sat opposite me in the little restaurant by the creek drinking *vin de sable* in a glass held in long fingers before her face, black eyes wide. With what? No more the sulky petulant face, the indifference, the schoolgirl flick of the chin; she was within herself something new, as if an invisible flower had bloomed there and opened her like petals. I no longer knew who she was, and I wanted to be with her.

And what was I to her? I did not know. Nor maybe did she, and didn't need to know. The next day we walked in the hills above the cottage and she took my hand as if it belonged to her, and I remember knowing that if a child feels this then one should try to think as a child, for an adult's process of thought is no guide in this. But where would it lead, how could it survive? Perhaps it needn't. This is enough. It passes into our orbit of being and is part of ourselves without special identity. It *is*, like the experience of music, like magic, like . . . love?

It was not until I thought about Sarah that there were spectres across the sun.

She was due to arrive tomorrow, with Natasha. I did not want her to arrive. I did not want her to break this. Tamara was looking at me puzzled as if waiting for me to say something, or was there something she needed to say? We were walking down the hill towards the cottage slowly, her hand clasped in mine. It was growing dark. A streak of orange sky had already lost its fire. A stone rattled down the slope ahead of us. She stopped and turned to me. The wind was ruffling her tee-shirt across her breasts, and her hair across her mouth. She still held one hand, not grasping it any longer. Just looking. For how many minutes? Not long. The hills were screaming around my head. At length I said We'd better get back, muttering the words and looking away. We'd better get back. And freeing my hand from Tamara's I turned and scrambled down the slope. She followed a few yards behind; went inside the cottage and began to light the lamps, saying nothing. I stood on the terrace for a moment, churning with confusion and staring at the dying sky; then without looking back I ran. I ran down the rough bank beyond the cottage in the dusk, sliding among boulders through the vineyard, a terrible wild misery piling around me as I ran; until the curtain of tall bamboos rose ahead of me and I swept them apart and slumped on to the rock beside the waterfall, my body retching with inexhaustible tears.

Day Twenty-six

Why? Why such panic among the boulders and the dusk of so sweet a day? Why did I not press her lips gently and guide her without pain to an acceptance of the reality of our lives, of our roles?

Ah! The reality of our lives, of our roles: what more precisely could describe the opposite of where my strongest inclinations lay? Reality! Whatever was that? According to the script at hand Reality at that moment consisted of, as follows: Himself (proto-divorcee) co-habiting with and shortly to marry Herself (widow and present lover of above as well as proprietor of common domestic residence), two stepdaughters (one of primary school age, the other adolescent) and a cat (neutered); the family [*sic*] at present vacationing in France after a demanding winter, Himself and elder stepdaughter already abroad with car (his, Jaguar, black), Herself and younger offspring shortly to follow by air; all to drive back to England together and thence resume family [*sic*] life until such times as natural changes or acts of God may alter balance of same. NB for the satisfactory pursuance of the above it is to be noted that affections appropriate to a remoulded family pertain throughout, though it is also noted that elder stepdaughter, at a vulnerable age in her development, has formed an attachment to Himself of the kind colloquially described as a "crush", this to be regarded as normal and, so long as satisfactorily handled, beneficial to stepdaughter.

Who wrote that? Somebody who holds society together. Someone whose values are to be respected. Someone I respect. Somebody I hate.

Maybe we all display moral kiss-curls to the world in order to survive. Maybe in the end our responses to a work of art are the only truly honest ones because we do not have to live with the consequences of them. Hence the true yearning is to turn life into a work of art, not the other way round. Pygmalion got it quite wrong and we have been misled by his example ever since. We are all art-collectors when we fall in love.

At last I understand those days with Tamara, and the species of invisible flower that opened her like petals; and why I had to rush away in order to survive.

And I understand old Parry-Jones, his life spent creating an open-air theatre of follies which his loves and his dreams might inhabit freely, their exits and entrances answering only a call of the senses.

And I begin to understand why I am here, this Saturday, in Wales where I was born and grew; with Jane Young who in my film-to-be will play a deaf-and-dumb girl, and with whom I am in love.

So here I am: Gareth Penrhyn, film-maker, back in the place where I first struck out beyond the ripples of my home in order to discover that valued thing, a life of the mind; all those products and legacies of living, those books and paintings, places and passers-by, all that fearful and gorgeous kaleidoscope of impressions which makes up the world of the eye. It was those discoveries and enrichments which set up in the brain the prospect of an attainable wonderland. The Art of Life: wasn't that what it was all about? I had cultivated it, studied it, filmed it, believed in it. Yes, believed, too (because it seemed the natural thing to assume), that people organised their living as far as possible in respect of such an Art, however miserable the conditions and unjust the distribution of comforts. Wasn't that what everyone really wanted? There existed, surely, some kind of Grand Plan conceived by some interfering deity but grown within us, a natural social order of things to which we all contributed without necessarily even knowing it, and from which we drew our strength and our moral imperatives. That, as I understood it, was Reality.

And I was wrong. Reality is something imposed. We do not function out of respect for any such order, but against it, though in paradox if we should win the fight we would destroy ourselves or become outcasts. In order to survive we lose.

And then we steal.

In the last six miles to Maentwrog clouds slid over the moon and it began to snow: a few spots at first blotted by the wipers, becoming a flurry of white strokes in the headlights breaking black against the windscreen, then as the wind dropped only the snow was visible – flakes fat, heavy, claustrophobic. How could one breathe, move in this?

—You never said it was going to be winter sports.

Jane was leaning forward to peer into the white curtain ahead.

—What happens if we get stuck?

—We get stuck! They'll dig us out in a frozen embrace in a week's time.

—If the rivers freeze over we can go skating like those Dutch pictures, miles and miles.

—Now who's being romantic?

—It is rather romantic, this: are we nearly there?

The last stretch to Maentwrog wound through a narrow tunnel of trees, etched white already, the road twisting a double hairpin to the harbour and along the shore. Under the porch of the house a light was blazing, and snow-flakes were picked out against it like moths. A round woman in an apron, hair in pins, smiled broadly and set our bags to one side of the hall. She hailed upstairs in Welsh that we'd arrived.

—D'you understand all that, Jane whispered in some surprise?

—Of course! she was saying, Your guests have arrived, Sir. Would you like them to wait by the fire? Parry-Jones loves talking Welsh.

—How's his English?

—English? He doesn't speak any English!

—Great! Snowed in for two months with a hundred-year-old bard who can only talk in click-language.

—Good training for your deaf-and-dumb part. Anyway, why should you worry, you're a mime actress? He's coming!

—I do love you. I shall be terribly polite.

Slow footsteps on the stairs grew louder and an old man came into view at the end of the hall. A hand like a knot grasped a carved stick which seemed to grow out of the end of it. He was dressed in a ginger tweed suit with a bright-green necktie and brown brogue shoes brightly-polished. His face thrust out its bones like Jurassic outcrops, silver hair curled over his ears and collar, and a yellowed Kitchener moustache thatched an enormous crinkled smile. I loved that face.

—Gareth, welcome!

I introduced Jane and Parry-Jones led us through a door, one hand on my shoulder, the other on Jane's. The stick dangled from his arm.

We stood by the log-fire, the three of us, in that drawing-room I had known since a child, unchanged; the grand-piano down the far end of the room by the french windows which tomorrow would look out over the estuary; the Corots along the wall lit from each frame by a warm protruding lamp; the deep leather sofas and chairs, dark-brown and polished, with arm-bands holding a brass ashtray on the side of each; the Shiraz carpets; the massive log-box; the portrait of himself by Augustus John over the fire, also lit; and Parry-Jones himself only a little thinner and older than I first remembered him twenty-five years ago, resting one arm along the mantelpiece as ever, a deep glass of whisky in the other hand. He was wearing the same flamboyant waistcoat of embroidered silk he once said Pola Negri had given him on some dashing occasion. Jane was warming her hands held out to the fire, her hair burnished by the flames. An inexpressible fullness of contentment overcame me, as if nothing beyond this great warm room possessed any substance of meaning or any power to trouble the mind.

—So I am not altogether so ancient, Gareth, that my old friends no longer come and visit me, and bring with them ladies as attractive as this one. You did warn me, I admit, but not enough! Jane, you are like Karen Brandt: incredibly like her. Uncanny! Except perhaps her figure was not as good as yours.

Jane drew her hands back from the fire and turned to look at the old man with a surprised smile.

—Who was she?

—Of course you wouldn't know. She was a great star in silent films. Lovely! The same expression as you. Oh, we had a wonderful time. I believe I may have married her, come to think of it. Can't remember. Of course she's dead now. You're an actress too, isn't that right?

—Yes, I am.

—Not the same profession any more. Difficult to be a star now. Either a face or a superstar. Young thing here the other day; what was her name? Glenda Jackson. Now she's got it. She's a star. One of the few. Would have married her in my day. Not as pretty as you, though, my dear.

I caught Jane's eye. Parry-Jones was enjoying himself hugely.

He took her glass, refilled it; poured himself another Scotch from the decanter with the chain and disc round its neck. His hands seemed all veins and knuckles.

—Gareth can help himself: he's always been good at that.

I did. Parry-Jones appeared about to launch himself after these preliminary skirmishes, just as I always remember him. He would die expostulating, a Scotch in his hand. He took a long swig.

—And now you must tell me what you're doing with yourself. It's years. You've kept away. What have you been doing; getting rich? Getting divorced? Making trouble? Living?

He lingered over the last word as if testing its bouquet, washing it around his mouth and thrusting out his lips.

—But I know, he went on. You've been making films. I've even seen them, some of them. When you going to make a *proper* film, Gareth? You know!

And he gesticulated into the air as if there, somewhere in the invisible proximity, lay the true and gorgeous material of art.

—But you are; that's right! You said so! And Jane . . .? Ah, I see; I see! Your star too! Let me kiss you. Lovely she is: amazingly like Karen Brandt. Quite extraordinary! You could be a star: no question. Gareth, you must tell me about it. Tell me everything. Over dinner. We'll open some Margaux. You must be tired. I am from talking to you, and looking at you both. Take your bags up. Myfanwy will show you where. The Blue Room. Remember? Go and change. We'll dine at eight. In – what is it? – an hour. I'll rest here. I'm old, horribly old! You know, Karen Brandt climbed Cader Idris with me, d'you know that, Jane? Right to the top. Wearing long skirts. Some girl! Legs like yours. Pity she's dead. Take another drink with you.

Upstairs we were alone. My first weekend with Jane. The end of my marriage. I hadn't thought about it all day. Jennifer would be packing the children's things this weekend. Don't think about it: not now! The whisky was in my hand. A small coal-fire glowed in the bedroom grate. Deep floral curtains hung on brass rings. The double-bed turned down already. Chocolates on the bedside table. A tasselled table-light. The huge old bath I remember which filled like Niagara. The smell of old linen, and towels on hot pipes. Jane outlined against the fire.

This morning Jane is still asleep, an arm across me, deadweight.

The skin of her back is soft to my fingers, and her hair to my cheek. It is the hour before dawn again, the hour when the imagination runs naked before the pain begins; only today there is no pain. I am with Jane. The fantasies have flown. I can hear the wind rattling the windows. There is a faint glow of the fire against the wall. My whole body feels aware of her. I do not want to move a muscle. She is with me. It must be Saturday outside. I wonder if the snow has settled. Shall we take a *droshky* across the white land? Jane is asleep in my arms. This is how it will be.

* * *

It would always be like this. The panic which engulfed me as I ran from the stone *mas* on the Provençal hillside was a storm-warning. It would always be like this. Sarah was now dead to me as an old album of photographs: smiles of happiness fixed in quite another life – can it really once have been mine? Yes, the panic was a species of premature guilt, a hideous deformity of terror at being so close to smashing social taboos; spectres of ostracism, of lifelong dereliction, of jail, of a kind of life in death.

And it was something else. It was the panic of knowing I could no longer bolt the door and keep the demons out. They were within. I could no longer begin again with Sarah and do it better: it would be worse. Tamara would be there, and her presence would always expose and mock the pretences of my newborn life. Without her I might learn to live and love a gentle way, out of gratitude, out of tiredness, out of simple appreciation of daily pleasures: we might have grown old in some tenderness at least and mutual respect, Sarah and I. Not now. That was exploded. The barricades were in ruins. It was not even Tamara who mattered: that was an impossible longing that would pass, so long as satisfactorily handled. as the script said. But what she had destroyed in my life with Sarah could not be remade. That too had passed. I should have to go or be destroyed also. Go where?

After the storm-warning there fell a calm that was vivid and uncanny. We were figures sharply-drawn in a landscape brittle with menace. Splashes from the waterfall caught the last gimlets of light. It may have been half an hour I sat there. I could see a light on the hillside, and occasionally a silhouette or a shadow. As

I began to retrace my steps through the vineyard, placing my feet quietly, I could see Tamara standing on the terrace as though she knew I was coming. Closer, I could see she had placed a bottle of wine on the outside table with two glasses, empty.

—Where have you been?

—By the pool.

—I brought us some wine.

—Good!

—When does Mummy come tomorrow?

—Around midday. At Nîmes.

—Is it far?

—No!

I poured out the wine. Moths banged against the oil-lamp, in and out of the night. The wind had dropped. There were clusters of lights here and there down towards the sea. A nightjar skimmed the edge of the terrace. The drilling sound of frogs by the stream. We said nothing.

The storm, when it came, developed a precise rhythm. For half an hour after waking I felt almost at peace; then the state of calm would evaporate like morning mist until I was compelled to get up because if I had not I would have yelled.

Thereafter all day, every few minutes of the day, the panic rose and fell a little, rose again, fell a little, hour after hour after hour.

There were better moments when I could find a place alone and collapse, but the tears never came from deep enough. Further, much further down lay a well of pain which yielded no tears.

Now I understood the meaning of madness. I had always held a benevolent view of the state of madness, imagining it to be a condition of almost pleasurable remoteness from the grammar of living. I had not thought of it as a living hell, and now I was in the madness of hell. The world screamed at me from within and I did not know how to scream back. I was being devoured by beasts of a malice beyond imagining.

The spirit tried to fight back. I developed a technique for blunting the most severe pangs when they came, which was to pant fast as the crisis struck, then as it began to subside to emit deep breaths with a sort of growl or moan. This was rather like the technique taught to mothers in the final stages of pregnancy.

It was, I suppose, a kind of labour, except that it went on for months without anything to show for it.

Then there were the pills: innocuous-looking little pink jobs with a name reminiscent of a South American mountain, of which I was allowed three a day – no more! These had the effect of administering a muffled explosion inside, like an abdominal depth-charge, upon which the demons inside me would float stunned like fish to the surface. So that when I vomited, which the little pink pills frequently made me do, I had the sensation of ridding myself of hellish things like some lost soul in an altar-piece of Hieronymus Bosch. But I was only permitted three pink explosions a day, and the demons ran riot at least ten times a day more than that, so that it became a decision of great matter when I should decide to take one, and how long I might get through the day without.

It was comforting to remember how some survivors of German POW camps said they had pulled through by making themselves recall all the stations on the London Underground, or the bowling analysis of each England cricketer in every Ashes series since the death of Queen Victoria. Such games I indulged in to stay alive. It was like playing chess with the Devil: so long as I could keep the game alive he could not win.

But neither could I. Perhaps the worst of it was that it did not feel like an illness which would one day pass. I began to believe it would never, never go away. It was what I had become. It was myself: it was what everything in my past life had been preparing me for, and therefore the only liberation would be to kill myself. That seemed the only thing left to do. To kill myself.

Yet only suicides did that. Killed themselves. Was I a suicide? One of that lonely band of whom the rest of the world shook their heads and said, "Too bad, too bad!" There must surely, if I tried harder, be some other way out than that. I thought about the Church. I thought about massive enterprises of doing good. If I worked with people palpably worse off than I was, would that not wash away the pain in an ocean of pity and fear? What about a course in transcendental meditation or some other mental ju-jitsu of an oriental kind that would release my pure spirit and set it floating above?

And then one day I knew.

It was autumn. Last autumn. A mere five months ago. The only occasion in my life when I had suffered anything like this torture before had been the previous year, and I had resolved it almost in an instant by deciding to leave everything and go and live with Sarah. But it had not been a resolution; it had been a betrayal, a drug. And now the drug had worn off. What I was experiencing now was the very same torture, just several degrees worse. The only way I would ever be free of these demons would be to withdraw utterly from their reach, to return to where and what I was before this nightmare occurred.

I would have to go back to Jennifer, to my family, to my home, to all those things I had betrayed – if I could. If I could. Or was it already too late?

Day Twenty-seven

Wales in winter. Jane, this place is again home after so long because I have brought you here.

Drawing back the curtains everything lay white. I revived the bedroom fire and brought you breakfast which Myfanwy, smiling, arranged on a tray for me to carry upstairs. Do you enjoy being spoiled? My hands felt cold against your thighs. You lay long-limbed in the bath with hair streaming, soap drying on your breasts above the water. On the quay with the sun out you were standing in a fur-hat and a long white scarf wound about your neck and shoulders, and when you turned to face me the impact of your presence was as though you had impaled me in the stomach and lifted me weightless. Those pale eyes of yours were laughing, your chin tucked out of the wind. A pale Welsh winter sun. Love is a growing, or full constant light.

So much to do. So much that seems possible suddenly now that you are with me. The film together. A life together. Everything else is numb and far away. There will be time for all that.

I showed you Maentwrog. You walked fur-wrapped among the winter gardens, gazing incredulously at the mosque, the campanile, the Greek temple, the grotto. I hope our life is not this unreal, you said: I feel like Alice in Disneyland. What happens if we wake up?

And in the evening you walked in the frost under the hulk of Caernarvon castle, our breath mingling in the night air which stung our faces. A fox froze in the headlights round a bend in the mountains. I braked and skidded on the icy road .You gasped and put your hand up in front of you, and even as you did so the moment was over. We drove quietly down to Portmadoc, small houses huddled round dim street-lights, and called in at the pub where I used to play darts as a schoolboy while my headmaster held forth on small matters in the Private Bar. *Ee's there, Gareth, watch it!* Tom would say, leaning conspiratorially over the bar. *Ssh! Ee's there!* The old bugger had caught me leaving the pub the night before I heard about my Oxford scholarship, and had called me in after prayers next morning all set for a show-down. Then he'd had to shake my hand. Proud, he was. Nothing in the bar had changed, except for a juke-box. The dart-board moulting with use. The shove-ha'penny board with Clem still lovingly polishing the coins on the slate.

—Evenin' Gareth, not seen you a long time!

Here was another kind of home. I felt warmed, and you stood smiling on the fringe of my nostalgia. I led you back to the car with my arm round your heavy coat. Back at Maentwrog Parry-Jones was still resting. We sat with glasses of whisky by the newly-made fire in the bedroom and you straightened out one knee to lock a leg between mine, leaning back with your head against the chair, eyes closed. We lay there not saying anything, your body stretched against mine.

—Supposing it just dies, you said suddenly.

—Why should it?

—I don't know. Maybe it's no more real than Maentwrog.

—D'you feel that?

You didn't say anything. I wished you had. You looked thoughtful; defensive.

—I look at you sometimes and I find myself saying He wants to have you, devour you, and discard you like a pip.

I felt hurt, a bit disturbed.

—Darling! I said pleadingly.

—Maybe Jennifer hasn't gone after all.

Why was she probing?

—What will you do then?

—She will. I know. It's been a wrecking game. It's finished. You have to believe me.

—Do I?

—Really!

—Kiss me!

* * *

All that summer of madness I made an effort to remind myself of one thing, that I had considered myself once to be a happy man. Sooner or later each nightmare, however shattering, had passed. It had always been like that, no matter what shit was flung at me or in what oceans of desolation I floundered. If I had possessed something that could be called strength, this was where it lay: in a certainty that, given the smallest chance, I would survive. At first I would offer myself these reminders in a spirit of superior knowledge: it was like reassuring some primitive soul that an eclipse of the sun would pass. But in time, when it did not pass, when the demons did not go away, these reminders took on a darker role. Instead of bringing reassurance they brought judgment: clearly the platform of survival had now gone, cracked and broken up. It was no longer to be relied upon, or by now I would have found it. I concluded that something essential in me must therefore have snapped – the mainspring or whatever it was – and it was only a matter of time before I ceased to function altogether. There could only be oblivion to look forward to, and I hoped it would come soon. Self-pity offered the last demeaning comfort.

And then it all changed. From the instant I knew I wanted to return to Jennifer the furies departed as if the cock had crowed. I walked a freeman in a new dawn, scarcely able to believe it.

Suddenly I was filled with optimism and strength. Of course it would be hard; of course Jennifer would be unwilling to accept me back; of course I would have to change. But with courage and persistence and honesty all these things could be achieved: I was quite certain. It was inconceivable that it should be otherwise. It was as though I were now clad in spiritual armour against which all opposition would prove futile. Paradise would be regained, and that was that. I set about marshalling my forces of light.

And Sarah? What did I feel about Sarah? Self-justification would have been the most arrogant hypocrisy. My treatment of her was indefensible. I had played for her, played with her, used her, lied to her, and now I was abandoning her. So who was Gareth Penrhyn, who set such store by human kindness, was capable of love, devotion even, a man of sensibilities, quick in anger against injustices, observer of social decencies, a man with a ready handshake, but a man who had managed in the course of a normal life to betray first his own wife and children and now Sarah and hers? What did it feel like to be such a creature, walking confidently along Wardour Street in the evenings after what was called an honest day's work, to climb into his swish car and drive back to the embrace of a family he was scheming at that very moment to ditch?

It felt like nothing. What should a man do: slit his throat, cry into his beer, put on rags and climb a mountain on his knees? So these things had happened for which I was largely to blame; and I was aware of it, aware that they ought not to have happened. But guilt I could not feel. The one area of responsibility in which I did feel deeply troubled was – money. I had been able to do these things because I was in a position to pay for them: I could, literally, pay for the consequences. Sign them away with a cheque. Sarah, like Jennifer, could not do that; might have been able to, but with children round their necks it was out of the question. This was part of the fraudulent ethic of bread-earning upon which lady journalists expounded in the *Guardian* so rightfully and so self-righteously. Of course it was so. I had slogged to earn money to gain myself the freedom to exploit what was clearly an unethical privilege, and to exploit those not in a position to share that privilege. But would a woman liberated from such financial dependency merely acquire an equal privilege to exploit, to abandon, to say to hell with whatever interfered with the drive to personal and primal fulfilment? In which case either Jennifer or Sarah might justifiably have got their knife in first; I'd be in the gutter and five children would be just as badly off as they are now. At least there would be equality of exploitation.

Such rabbitings of the mind got me nowhere. Did I really expect them to? I could not pretend that my full attention was focused on explaining myself to myself. It was a sideshow I put on between traffic-lights to divert a bad conscience, and a bad conscience was something I could afford now there was no doubt in my mind what I intended to do. It was only a question of how and when to do it. Now I lived for the weekends when the children came to stay. I longed to say to them Daddy will be home soon: everything will be all right again. And I wondered if they would care. How I wanted them to care! Deirdre, Seth, Ennis, Daddy will be home soon. And I dreamed of what we would do together in the evenings, where we would go together. Christmas. Their birthdays. Bonfire night. And in the holidays we would go back to the Casa Bella: the eagles would be circling over the mountains as always, and in the summer the fireflies would flash among the shadows of the ilex-trees. It would be as it used to be. Daddy had been ill and was all right again. I wrote to Jennifer.

And the next day I told Sarah. She didn't turn her head.

—You've been gone for so long I feel I've said goodbye to you already . . . Oh, Gareth!

And she dropped her head and cried. I was about to place my hands on her shoulders, and I couldn't. I wanted to, and it would have been too unkind. I was dealing out so much cruelty, why did I stop there?

—It might be best for all of us if I left now, tomorrow.

She turned quickly, her hands resting on the table. There was a look of terror in her eyes. Then she raised her hands to her face and shook her head from side to side. I couldn't move. She was wearing a red dress I remembered I had bought for her the first time we had gone shopping together, the day I had walked with her by the river and had said, *My life will be all one from now on.*

It all flowed back, what I had felt for her, our hopes, what could have been: the truth, the quiet, the closeness, the confidence that we would manage, that it was right and would always be so. Oh God, how did it happen? Why did it all go? Why?

That last, sweet, terrible remorse!

If she had run into my arms I would have held her and held her.

Jennifer's reply was quite brief. I'd been gearing myself to expect more. She wrote: "I'm glad to know what you are feeling; and I don't want to stop you coming back to your own house. I've had time to do a lot of thinking, and I'll tell you about it. The children have missed you a great deal."

That was all.

The last remark hurt like acid.

I could not tell what it all meant. At least she was not going to bar the door; and that was enough to lay in store a thousand hopes. Everything would work out, given time. I was sure of it. And there'd be no turning back any more. Not any more.

November, then December. These were charade days. It was hard then – even harder now – to perceive where any reality might lie. I had risen vertically out of the depths of summer; now the exhilaration of new sunlight and sudden horizons were like thermals on which I rose circling over a toy planet. Icarus on inflammable wings.

The Icarus of Wardour Street! The office had hardly seen me for several months. Suddenly I was blowing in with cosmic confidence trailing contracts plucked from dazed industrialists and grateful corporations. New staff! Yes, come and join us, there's room for all! Take a secretary or two! New equipment! Book a table! Book a flight! Here we go! You look gorgeous this morning, whatever-your-name is.

—What the hell's come over you?

David was looking disbelieving.

—You ride in here like John Wayne, fire ten rounds in all directions and ride off again. What's it all about, for God's sake?

—I'm just happy!

—I'll say! That makes a change. Don't you ever sleep?

—Not much!

I got up at five, often earlier. Streets like empty waiting-rooms. Soho turning in its sleep spilling rubbish and cats. Three hours tycoonery on paper before Eric said Good Morning and hung his umbrella on a personal hook, then David with a grunt and Janet with a yank at her bra-strap. Later, doner-kebab brought up by one of Eric's mice, or I'd lunch somewhere with Waldron plus side-kick to discuss the proposed Arab films – talks about talks; or with a smooth-cheeked signatory of the Swiss Tourist Board or the Coal Board or the Gas Board or the BBC. Games I enjoyed winning. The condescending sneer of power.

I returned spinning to Chiswick in the evenings. I had found a flat not far away, intending to live in it for the interim period, still not knowing how long that would be. A week? Two months? The sooner I moved out of Sarah's life the better. Then, the day before I was going, she came into the spare-room where I now slept. I thought she was going to cry, but she was laughing. We had hardly spoken in the weeks since I broke it to her that I was leaving. Now she was laughing. She had washed her hair like the first time I had visited her, in the garden. She put her hand on my arm as I was sitting at the table. It was ten o'clock in the evening. Don't say anything, let me talk, she said. I've been thinking it over.

And she talked. Yes, she knew what a bastard I'd been, how she'd been used, and deceived, all that. It was like everyone had always used her – parents, Angus, others – if that was the way you chose to look at it. But now, at the point when she felt she had taken so much pain there could be no possible room for any more, the pain had lifted. She didn't see it like that any longer. She had witnessed my pain, too, and that too had gone. Affection and warmth had returned – in me and in her, no matter what we had felt and what we had done. She had been wrong, as I had been wrong; we should neither of us have pretended we could live together in peace. She had known all along I still loved Jennifer: she had allowed herself to be persuaded it would change, heal over. It had been a devouring kind of love; yet before we had made such demands on one another there had always been an understanding and a respect between us, and a love which was not possessive. Why, then, should relationships be exclusive – had I not once said that? – they need not be, if only the sense of ownership could be resisted. She understood that now; she felt I understood that now. She saw that old look in my eyes.

There were tears in my eyes. She came over to me and we slept together.

I cancelled the flat.

Sarah seemed happier than I had known her since we first lived together. At weekends Natasha brought us tea in bed in the mornings as she always used to. A small grinning face at the end of the bed. And Tamara? I had hardly spoken to her, noticed her, all summer and autumn. The weight of my guilt and despair had banished her. Now that too had fallen away, and I saw her again moving silently through the house, belonging intimately to herself as she always had. I no longer knew what lay in her mind, and I was glad. A boy-friend with a frizz of sandy hair walked silently in and out of the house, and there were sounds of Elton John through the wall. They're so sweet, those two, said Sarah: I don't believe they even kiss each other.

—I don't understand, Gareth; you're leaving and it's like a new honeymoon. I feel we're closer than we ever were.

We were lovers again and that was why. We were the point of focus of each other's senses, and that was all, and that was all it should ever have been. It was free play. Where our eyes met was a burning-glass and the moment our eyes turned away the glass was dimmed.

—What will you do when I go?

—I shan't want you any more.

—Never?

—No! Maybe after a very long time, but probably not. I'll never go through all that again.

—It's like a marriage in reverse, isn't it? After the honeymoon, the parting?

—Don't make it sound so sad. It has to be like that, doesn't it. What we've had is too good to spin out, and too painful to relive. We can't go in for reunions, Gareth.

—I suppose not.

—Come to bed!

—I shall miss you.

—D'you think I won't?

* * *

The light is going: the estuary is the texture of lead. Sunday evening. Shoes wet by the fire. We have been trudging through the slush. Jane is lying on the bed in a dressing-gown, sleeping. If we make love again it will be to cheat the sensation of a weekend running out. Our last evening. Tomorrow London again. It has made us silent, withdrawn. Parry-Jones has announced champagne for tonight. Jane will wear her white low-cut dress which will rouse him to talk about Karen Brandt, long dead. I want to be away from here. Too many yesterdays. Even today has become a yesterday. I wish it were. Last night he told me Shirley was a grandmother: his great-niece who was a convent-girl with her arms round me on the pillion. Husband is First Secretary somewhere or other. Divorced now. She's in Australia. I feel morose. A few smears of snow across the flower-beds. Someone has turned the lights on in the sitting-room, suddenly blacking out the garden. I'll draw the curtains; take a bath before going in search of another Scotch. A bad moment of the day, this. Today especially. Everything in the mind feels like an agenda I don't want to read.

Tomorrow is the last day of February. I can hardly remember the beginning of the month, only how long it has taken to pass. Jennifer moves out tomorrow, my children with her. Lover-boy takes over. I should have had them immunised. I'll wreck his credibility, at least in their eyes. Smug little Trot. Surrogate Daddy-O! Jesus, she can't stand him any more than I can! Maybe a bit more than she can stand me! Oh, Jennifer, for God's sake!

I feel better. Better for a whisky and anger.

—The roads'll be clear for your drive back tomorrow, Mr Penrhyn, said Myfanwy who was building up the fire while I poured out a couple of glasses. Sir David'll be sad you're going.

I never thought of Parry-Jones as Sir David. It made him seem more ordinary. Sir David Parry-Jones, knighted for services to longevity.

The bath is full already; the mirror and the tiled walls are blurred with steam, and an ice-cube in the whisky glass balanced on the rim of the bath splits with a crack. When I look again all the ice has gone, but the Scotch chill enough to tear a cold path down my throat. I bury myself a little deeper in the water, feet just resting on the end of the bath. I play a game of sticking my big toes up into the nozzle of each tap to see whether I am forced to plunge my freezing right toe back into the bath-water before or after the scorching left toe. The right toe wins because it cheats by warming up the tap: I wonder whether the left toe has got blistered. Feeling a lot more cheerful I hoist the plug with my undamaged toe and heave myself out, seizing a massive bath-towel from the hot rail and wrapping it round myself.

The bedroom feels chill, cooling the perspiration on my face. I stir the fire to life with a couple of logs. Jane is still sleeping. Her Scotch is untouched. One bare leg is stretched out over the edge of the bed. I unfasten the cord of her dressing-gown and draw it gently from her body. Her belly is warm to my touch. I kiss her breasts and her nipples sharpen under my lips. Her legs close round me as I lie on her, and an arm slides across my back, her fingers pressing against my neck.

—You! she says when I roll away from her and sit on the edge of the bed. She runs a hand across my thigh.

—I brought you a whisky. It's probably warm by now.

—Not all you brought.

—I want to kiss you. And look at you.

My beautiful lover. I am so happy to be with you, and to see you happy.

—You have a way of making people happy, don't you? You said this afternoon.

—And yet I've had the most miserable marriage on God's earth.

—I wonder if you really have.

I remember you saying yesterday Maybe this is not more real than Maentwrog.

Or maybe this is the reality I seek. And everything else is the price I pay.

You are standing naked by the fire drying your hair. Shall we really live together? Make a film together? Jane, who are you when I'm not dreaming about you?

Tomorrow Jennifer leaves; with Deirdre, Seth, little Ennis. Their faces tear through the décor, and each of them is waving goodbye. No! Deirdre, Seth, Ennis, don't go! Jennifer, don't go!

—What is it, Gareth? You look awful.

—It's only that I've got so much to do tomorrow.

—I know you have.

I cannot believe they will have gone. I cannot believe they will go.

Day Twenty-eight

My last night in Chiswick; the end of a year. I was back in the spare-room: my suggestion, and I wished I hadn't made it. The room felt like a decontamination chamber. I waited by my half-packed suitcases hoping Sarah might come in; instead it was Tamara.

—I'm glad you're going; you've hurt all of us too much, she said straight out, standing by the open door in her nightdress.

And then she'd gone.

When I realised I was alone I could feel a pain in my stomach. That judgment would lie within me a long time. I pulled my clothes off slowly, pausing now and again to take the impact of Tamara's words. Then I turned out the light and pulled the duvet round my neck. Forget it! Forget it all! Tomorrow I'd be back in the big house by the river: Jennifer's and my house. Where we'd always been. Where my children had been born. Where I belonged. Where I wanted to be always. Always. Tomorrow would be Christmas Eve. I'd be home for Christmas. I'd packed the presents away, carefully wrapped in blue paper with gaudy Santa Claus labels attached with silver tape. We'd arranged everything, Jennifer and I. A week off work and I'd seen her almost every day. She had been calm, detached, matter-of-fact almost. It felt like sitting and talking to a business agent of long acquaintance. Well, it was better like this than renewing the marital bloodsports. At least it was the closed season.

I woke and lay awake for a while, then looked at my watch. It was five, the hour I'd been getting up for the past month and more. Today I was going home. I dressed in jeans and a heavy sweater and quietly opened the door. Through there Sarah lay asleep, and through there Tamara. Natasha downstairs. Let them sleep ("I'm glad you're going; you've hurt all of us too much"). I wondered if I shouldn't just slip away now, be gone from their lives into the night. Another stolen freedom. No! I left Sarah a note outside her door saying I'd gone out for a walk. Then I walked towards the river, my eyes stinging with the frost. In the underpass under the dual-carriageway the walls bore black graffiti sprayed on to the tiles like angry tablets of the law: Cannabis Lives; Elizabeth II rains OK; Man United Rules; Paks Britannica. A light had been wrenched from the ceiling leaving naked wires, and underfoot smashed glass glinted on sodden newspapers, letting off a pungent whiff of urine. A cloth cap lay in a puddle, and a brown shoe, paint-spattered, heavily worn at the heel.

A wind cut across the towpath and ruffled the water. It was almost high tide. Frost salted the river wall. Here was where I used to walk in the spring evenings with Sarah, and the pub where we used to sit outside planning our lives with our eyes matched. Now plastic chairs stood stacked behind raw netting. I walked downriver towards Hammersmith Bridge. This was mugging country, but there was nobody to mug me at six in the morning on the day before Christmas. Tonight I would be at home by the fire. A milk-float crossed the bridge slowly, and then a lorry with figures bunched in the back, the bridge-lights picking out a cluster of stern faces as it passed. I climbed the steps and gazed down at the black water stained with weak light. There was no one else on the bridge, no one else in sight.

I felt totally alone, on one side of me the river melting into the night westwards, the other way it curled out of sight under the silhouette of warehouses against a sky faintly yellowed by sodium street-lamps. I was alone between two lives, belonging to neither. The end of a year; the end of half a life. An interval borrowed from the night.

Sarah never said goodbye; she just nodded without raising her eyes and went on wrapping Christmas presents. Natasha was playing with a friend. The door of Tamara's room was closed. I shut the front-door behind me.

* * *

Jane is dressing, the skin of her back taut as she bends over to smooth her tights against her calves. Her hair falls forward across her face. Her breasts are bare.

I know that our silence is created by the things we have not said: we have not talked about the film, we have not talked about our life. I cannot fill that silence now. Soon we shall be leaving for London, and tonight we shall not sleep together. Knowing that, we have already grown apart.

—Darling, I'm going down to find some breakfast.

The smell of fried bacon is more urgent than her bare breasts.

Parry-Jones is sitting by an empty coffee-cup reading *The Times*. He looks up and rustles the paper with long bony thumbs.

—There's food on the hot-plate if you're hungry: not been there long. Very good sausages.

I wonder if the sausages come from my father's old shop in Portmadoc. He used to make good sausages.

—Hope you slept well, Gareth. Sorry you have to go today.

—So am I.

—Quite a girl, that Jane of yours. You living with her?

—No!

—You should! Here, take *The Times*; I've read enough. I'll be in my study. You're not going just this minute, are you?

The coffee-pot is Liberty's pewter, looking as if it had grown sleezily in the night from the tray it stands on.

Myfanwy is inquiring what the lady would like for breakfast. I say she'll be down in a minute and I am sure what is here will be fine.

I don't seem to have missed much in the news these last few days. The firemen's strike goes on, with both sides sulking noisily from entrenched positions. Bernard Levin thundering heavily again about fun-revolutionaries: for once Vanessa Redgrave is not in the chorus line. New Australian wonder-bowler routs England: he has an extra finger on his bowling hand, is this fair play, *The Times* inquires? Apparently there is nothing in the rules about it. How middle-aged of me to be reading the test match report first. In a few years it'll be the obituaries.

God, this is the last day of February.

I wonder if Jane has put on a bra today.

I wonder who has died while I've been away.

I have known many kinds of fear, but never this one until today; and only now after two hours driving through Wales in a numb silence have I begun to master it, to grip its meaning as I grip the steering-wheel in my hands.

Waldron is dead.

I am out of a job. There will be no Arab films, and no feature-film. Jane will not be my star. There may never be a new start for me. I shall need all my energies to keep my old life going – my old despised life. Suddenly I am trapped: a staff to pay, a future to look to, a family to pay for. And no one to rescue me any longer. I have always felt myself to be immune from helpless panic of this sort. No longer. Tycoons can shoot themselves: I can only feel sick. I must move: whatever I do I must move or fear will overtake me. Oh, God, why do people I need die? Waldron, you bastard, why did you die?

The news stared at me until I understood it. A six-inch obituary: Lord Waldron of Beaconsfield. Former Lord Mayor . . . City financier . . . international banker . . . Master of the Worshipful Company of Cutlers . . . aged 67 . . . unmarried . . . noted art collector . . . also took an active interest in the British film industry.

I half-expected it to add . . . believed in Gareth Penrhyn. A fleeting thought entered my mind that perhaps he knew death was coming and had made provision for those enterprises on which he was currently engaged: might not his will underwrite the dreams of Penrhyn Productions? Unlikely! In any case wills take years to unravel and take effect. In the meanwhile . . . There was no point in considering it. I was alone.

I phoned O'Rourke. No answer. Then I remembered he was at the cottage, with no telephone. It was the only way he could write. He was probably working on the Arab scripts right now.

Impatiently I waited until half past nine and phoned the office. It was a relief to speak to Eric. Yes, he had heard the news: it had been on the radio yesterday. Yes, he would cancel all travel arrangements, ring Archie Hill, send O'Rourke a telegram, contact Waldron's office, be free to discuss everything with me first thing tomorrow morning. I put the phone down with a sense of enormous gratitude to Eric for being there and being entirely predictable. Bless you, Eric!

So I am on my feet at the count of nine: frightened but getting my strength back. Three hours ago I would have said that the feature-film was my lifeline, and without it I might as well give up. Now I know I shall simply give *it* up, at least shelve it until a more propitious time. How effortlessly priorities alter focus under stress. The luxury of art will have to wait until the fight is over. There's graft-work to be done. Craft-work. Ring-craft! Perhaps the fight is what it's really about in the end. I wonder.

—Gareth, are you very worried? I suppose that's a silly question.

—It's not at all a silly question. Yes, I am worried, but less than I thought. And I know one thing.

—What's that?

—I'll survive. And I'll never lean on anybody again.

* * *

—Oh Daddy, it's lovely you're here for Christmas. Will you always be here now?

—Yes!

—Promise?

—I promise!

Ennis was looking at me over the shoulder of a large teddy-bear he had unwrapped from the base of the Christmas tree. Across the room Seth was piecing together some Lego weapon of mass-death whose powers he had already itemised with an angelic sweetness in his voice – Seth who winces if I crush an ant. Sounds of Deirdre, my walking discothèque, drifted from an upstairs room. Jennifer sat curled by the fire, sipping vodka and smiling over a sketchbook of Ennis's drawings which he had presented to us at five that morning mummified with sellotape. The silence of the telephone all day had wrapped a curtain of privacy round Christmas.

Seth turned his attention to the gramophone. New records made him want to play his old ones. It was his long-ago favourite, the Butterfly Ball: side three, the most favourite of all, scratched and etched by a dozen cushion-fights and "let's have that bit again" until the needle now behaved like a train rattling over the points at Clapham Junction heading God-knows-where. "Soon we'll be all right again . . . right again . . . right again . . . right again." It would stick there, wouldn't it?

I raised my eyes towards Jennifer. She did not look up. Soon we'll be all right again – at last?

* * *

The first suburban outcrops sprawl on either side of the motorway. We have hardly spoken since leaving Wales.

—How far?

—About ten miles, that's all.

In the end all we can find to talk about is mileage. Two lines of Donne are in my mind:

Love is a growing, or full constant light:
And his first minute, after noon, is night.

She is so beautiful sitting next to me, and I cannot even be bothered to take her hand. Jane has become another interchangeable blonde. She might be a Meissen figure in bone-china and enamel. I am driving fast to drop her at her flat: and I am driving fast to reach home. It is the last day of the month, the end of my sentence. Jennifer will not have gone. I know that. It was all a game; a painful psychological game. She needed to get her own back, I understand that now; not simply to punish me – although that too – but to relieve her bitterness. As for lover-boy, that's just a joke, we both know that. Puny little Trot!

Highgate, 1½ miles. Then Camden Town. In twenty minutes I shall have said goodbye to Jane. She knows. She has always known. Mine was the only fantasy. Yet fantasy is the voltage which has powered me through this month, this dreadful month. Now it's as if I am watching the generator being wheeled away; it is no longer needed. It's the day of the end of the fair. Armies of brawny lads are arriving to dismantle and crate up four weeks of my life:

One blonde I made.

One film I didn't make.

One millionaire dead of a coronary.

One soft memory of eyes in the lamplight in the rain. Pack them up and move on. The show is over. Goodbye, Jane! I'm going home. Tomorrow life will pick up its old slow routine. Nuts and bolts; that's what it's about. Soon we'll be all right again . . . right again . . . right again . . . right again.

* * *

Christmas. New Year. January. Our life acquired a stillness and a calm as if it had been sprayed with a local anaesthetic. We moved, Jennifer and I, through the chambers of each day bandaged and quiet. When we spoke it was muffled, and produced no reaction. Hands rested on the doorknobs before turning them. Faces looked out over the dark garden without explanation. Mouths opened as if to speak, and did not. It was like living within a humming shell, attuned only to small unidentifiable sounds which might have echoed some distant reality or they might not.

Then slowly, as though working their way through heavy bandages, blades of pain began to cut our silence. Hands became taut, a grip menacing, expressions of the face lined with tension, then anger, grief, before setting again into hopelessness. It happened gradually and inexorably. At first I believed it would pass; then I hoped it would pass. Finally I just held on. Every worst component of our life together seemed to be joining before my eyes into some monstrous robot that was growing and destroying all around it – us! The children would play at its feet, not noticing. We came and went, worked and shopped, and each time we returned the monster was larger and more hideous, and there were fewer and fewer areas of our life beyond its reach. There was no longer space in which to recoil. We were being pulled into an arena walled by a scream for blood rising in crescendo, and there was no way out. Was this to be the grand *finale?*

One evening a young man was in the kitchen.

—He's my lover, she said after he'd left. Why should you mind?

I did!

I took the children away for a weekend to break the tension, hoping when I returned that it might all have blown away. But it was like stepping back into the torture-chamber with my tormenters refreshed and ready to go.

—This can't go on, can it? I said.

—No, it can't!

It was the first time we had agreed on anything in a fortnight.

The next morning she announced she was going to leave for good. She asked for a month longer before going.

And that was it. A month.

A month ago. The month which finishes today. It has taken me all this time to perceive what that ultimatum meant. She needed to get equal with me – as simple as that.

The evening sun is on the river. I feel euphoric now. Jane has gone. That's finished, like the film. Dream-work done. The fair is over. In fifteen minutes I shall be home. Now at last we can properly build, begin to live again, live truly, truthfully, this time. Only those who have already given up insist it is futile to go on. Blake got it right: "those who restrain desire do so because theirs is weak enough to be restrained."

Here is where I live with those I love.

The red front-gate bleached grey under the street-lamp.

The brick pathway I remember laying while Jennifer was nursing Deirdre.

The door with its bronze claw-knocker I found in Italy the summer we moved into the house.

The entrance-hall dark, as ever. How many times have I believed the house to be empty until the children's rooms burst open and voices cried out, "Daddy's back – what have you brought us, Daddy?"

I throw my coat over the banisters; drop my bag on the floor beside it. The first door is Seth's room: let's see what the little devil's been getting up to. There's the poster he painted in lurid colours – Dr Who sleeps here!

The room is dark.

The room is bare.

They're gone!

A figure is standing within an empty room. His eyes take in the space around him. Walls bear the imprint of invisible pictures. One tap drips on to a brown stain in the wash-basin. Snoopy stickers on the mirror. A seagull's feather in a plastic mug. A rag slung over a pipe-bend. Scratches on the radiator. A burn-mark on the wooden floor. A disc of light thrown on to the ceiling, unsteady in the breeze from the open door.

Maybe the real farewells are the ones without tears, because they are a kind of loving.

Gareth Penrhyn, forty-two, nuts-and-bolts film-maker, married seventeen years, three children. Alone.